# The Less You Know The Sounder You Sleep

Juliet Butler

4th ESTATE • *London*

4th Estate
An imprint of HarperCollins*Publishers*
1 London Bridge Street
London SE1 9GF

www.4thEstate.co.uk

First published in Great Britain in 2017 by 4th Estate

1



Photograph on page 422 courtesy of the author



A catalogue record for this book is available from the British Library

ISBN 978-0-00-820375-7 (hardback)
ISBN 978-0-00-820376-4 (trade paperback)

This book is based on the author's experiences. Some names, identifying characteristics, dialogue and details have been changed, reconstructed or fictionalised.



Printed and bound in Great Britain by
Clays Ltd, St Ives plc

To David Llewelyn – literary consultant – without whose persistence Dasha's story would never have been told.

'A happy life consists not in the absence, but in the mastery of hardships.'

Helen Keller

# THE END

## 12 April 2003, 12:05

I know I'm dying. I just don't know how.

The ceiling rushes past me in the First City Hospital as we're pushed down the corridor in a white-coated swirl of medics. First City; we've been here before. Masha, my Mashinka, you're here with me. But this time it's different. This time I'm alone.

Two nurses are running along with us, one on each side. They're talking, their voices muffled through their surgical masks.

*How long has she got?*

*God knows!*

*Where are we taking them?*

*Emergency unit.*

*Do the doctors know? Can they separate them?*

*No, no, of course not, they'd need a team of twenty surgeons.*

Everyone's always thought we're fools. That we can't understand, because we're Together.

*What do we tell her?*

*Nothing, of course. Tell her nothing.*

The nurse bends over me and speaks loudly and slowly.

*Masha's fine, she's just sleeping, that's all.*

I start crying.

*Hush, hush now, everything's going to be fine …*

# PAEDIATRIC INSTITUTE, MOSCOW

## 1956

> 'One cannot hold on to power through terror alone. Lies are just as important.'
>
> Josef Stalin, General Secretary of the Communist Party, 1922–53

## Age 6
## January 1956

### Mummy

'I'm bored,' says Masha.

Mummy's sitting by our cot, and she doesn't look up from all her writing.

'I'm really, really booored.'

'You're always bored, Masha. Play with Dasha.'

'She's booooring.'

'No, I'm not,' I say. '*You're* boring.'

Masha sticks her tongue out at me. 'You stink.'

'Girls!' Mummy puts down her pencil and stares at us over the bars, all cross.

We don't say anything for a bit, while she goes back to writing. *Skritch. Skritch.*

'Sing us the lullaby, Mummy – *bye-oo bye-ooshki* – sing that again,' says Masha.

'Not now.'

*Skritch. Skritch.*

'What you writing, Mummy?'

'None of your business, Masha.'

'Yes, but what you writing?'

No answer.

Masha squashes her face through the bars of the cot. 'When can we have those all-colours bricks back to play with? The all-colours ones?'

'What's the point of that, when Dasha builds them and you just knock them down?' Mummy doesn't even look up.

'That's because she likes building, and I like knocking.'

'Exactly.'

'Can I draw, then?'

'You mean scribble.'

'I can draw our Box, I can, and I can draw you with your stethoscope too.'

A bell rings from outside the door to our room, and Mummy closes her book. A bit of grey hair falls down so she pushes it behind her ear with her pencil.

'Well, it's five o'clock. Time for me to go home.'

'Can we come home with you, Mummy?' I say. 'Can we? Now it's five clock?'

'No, Dashinka. How many times do I have to tell you that this hospital is your home.'

'Is *your* home a hospital too? Another one?'

'No. I live in a flat. Outside. You live in this cot, in a glass box, all safe and sound.'

'But all children go home with their mummies, the nannies told us so.'

'The nannies should talk less.' She stands up. 'You know exactly how lucky you are to be cared for and fed in here. Don't you?' We both nod. 'Right, then.' She gets up to kiss us on top of our heads. One kiss, two kisses. 'Be good.' I push my hand through the cot to hold on to her white coat, but she pulls it away all sharp, so I bang my wrist. I suck on where the bang is.

The door to the room opens. *Boom.*

'Ah, here's the cleaner,' says Mummy, 'she'll be company for you. Tomorrow's the weekend, so I'll see you on Monday.'

She opens the glass door to our Box with a *klyak*, and then goes out of the door to our room, making another *boom*. We can hear the cleaner outside our Box, banging her bucket about, but we can't see her through all the white swirls painted over the glass. When she comes into the Box to clean, we see it's Nasty Nastya.

'What are you looking so glum about?' she says, splishing her mop in the water. She's flipped her mask up because Nastya doesn't care if we get her germs and die.

'Mummy's gone home all weekend, is what,' says Masha, all low.

'She's not your *yobinny* mummy. Your mummy probably went mad as soon as she saw you two freaks. Or died giving birth to you. That there, who's just left, is one of the staff. And you're one of the sick. She works here, you morons. Mummy indeed ...'

I put my hands over my ears.

'She *is* our *yobinny* mummy!' shouts Masha.

'Don't you swear at me, you little mutant, or I'll knock you senseless with the sharp end of this mop!' We go all crunched into the corner of the cot then, and don't say anything else because she did really hit Masha once, and she cried for hours. And Nastya said she'd do something much much worse, if we told on her.

When she's gone, we come out of the corner of the cot into the middle.

'She *is* our mummy anyway,' says Masha. 'Nastya's lying like mad, she is, because she's mean.'

I sniff. 'Of course she's our mummy,' I say.

## Supper time and bedtime in the Box

Then one of our nannies comes into our room with our bucket of food. She puts it down with a clang on the floor outside the Box, and we both reach up with our noses, and smell to see what she's brought. It's our Guess-the-Food-and-Nanny game. We can't see her, but the smell comes bouncing over the glass wall and into our noses, and it's whoever guesses first.

'Fish soup!' Masha laughs. 'And Aunty Dusya!'

I love it when Masha laughs; it comes bubbling up inside me and then I can't stop laughing.

'Fish soup it is, you little bed bugs,' calls Aunty Dusya from outside the Box. Then she clicks open the glass door and comes in with our bowl, all smiling in her eyes.

'Open up.' We both put our heads between the bars with our mouths wide open, to get all the soup one by one spoonful each.

'*Nyet!!* – she's getting the fish eyes, I saw, I saw!'

'Now hush, Masha – as if I pick out the nice bits for her.'

'You do, you do – I can see, I can!'

'Don't be ridiculous.' It's hard to hear Aunty Dusya because she's got her mask on, like everyone. Except Mummy, who's got the same bugs as us. And Nastya, when she's being mean. 'And stop gobbling it down, Masha, like a starving orphan, or you'll be sick again. *Yolki palki!* I don't know any child at all for being sick as often as you. You're as thin as a rat.'

'I'm thinner than a rat,' says Masha. 'And Dasha's fat as a fat fly, so I should get the popping eyes!'

I don't know what a rat is. We don't have them in our Box.

'What's a rat?' I ask.

'Oooh, it's a little animal with a twitching nose and bright eyes, that always asks questions. Here's your bread.'

'I want white bread, not black bread,' says Masha, taking it anyway.

'You'll be asking for caviar next. Be grateful for what you get.' We're always being told to be grateful. Every single day. Grateful is being thankful for being looked after all the time. 'I'll come back in half an hour to clean you up, and then lights out.'

Masha stuffs her bread into her mouth all in one, so her cheeks blow out, and looks up at the ceiling as she chews. We know all our nannies' names off by heart. And all our cleaners' too. And all our doctors'. Aunty Dusya says only special people can see us as we're a Big Secret. She says it has it in black writing on the door. I don't know why we're a Big Secret. Maybe all children are Big Secrets? Masha doesn't know either.

I love black bread because it's soft and juicy, and fills me all up in my tummy. I have to stuff it all in my mouth, though, because if I didn't, Masha would take it.

Aunty Dusya comes back to wash us after we've done a poo and a pee in our nappy, and gives us a nice new one.

'I'm scared of the cockroaches, Aunty Dusya.'

'Nonsense, Dashinka, there aren't any cockroaches.'

'Yes, there is!' Masha shouts and points up. 'See that crackle up there?'

'Well, there is a small crack in the ceiling …'

'That's where they come out when it's dark, and they go skittle-scuttle across the ceiling, then drop down with a plop on top of Dasha, and then they skittle-scuttle across her too, and she screams until I squish them and they go crunch.'

Aunty Dusya looks up at the crackle then, and picks up the stinky bag with our nappy in.

'Well, we used to have cockroaches, once upon a time, when you were babies, but not now. There are no cockroaches in the Paediatric Institute. *Nyet.*'

She looks over at us, all cross and black, so I nod and nod like mad, and Masha pushes out her lip, like she does when she's being told off, and twists the knot on our nappy with her fingers.

Then Aunty Dusya goes and leaves us alone, and the lights go off with a snap, and the door bangs shut with a *boom*.

I lie and listen hard, because when it's dark is when they all come out.

'I'll squish them,' says Masha in a hushy way. 'You wake me and I'll squish and squash and squelch them. I know all their names, I do … they're scared of me … Yosha and Tosha and … Lyosha …'

After a bit I can feel she's gone to sleep, but I can hear them all coming out and skittle-scuttling, so I reach out and hold her hand, which is all warm. Masha's hand is always warm.

## Having our heads shaved and dreaming on clouds

*Skriip skriip.* Aunty Dusya is doing Masha's head with a long razor, and slapping her playfully when she wriggles. 'Stop squirming, or I'll slice your head right off!'

'It hurts!'

'It'll hurt even more with no head, won't it? Stop being so naughty! Dasha sits still for all her procedures, why can't you?'

'I'll sit still,' I say, quick as quick. 'Do me. I like having my head razored. If we had hair, we'd get Eaten Alive by the tiny, white, jumpy cockroaches.'

'Lice. That's exactly right, Dashinka.'

'But can you cut the top bit of my hair off too, and not leave this?' I pull at the tuft they leave at the front.

'You know we leave that to show you're little girls, not little boys. You wouldn't want anyone to think you were boys, now, would you?'

'But everyone knows we're little girls anyway. And Masha pulls mine when she's cross.'

'Like this,' says Masha, and goes to pull it, but Aunty Dusya gives her another little slap and her mask goes all sucked into her mouth with breathing hard.

Dusya's got a yellow something on today. I can see it peeking under the buttons of her white coat.

'Why don't *we* wear clothes like grown-ups? Do no children wear clothes?' I ask.

'Why would you need clothes, lying in a cot all day? Either that or in the laboratory … doctors need to see your bodies, don't they? Besides, we need to keep changing your nappy because you leak; we can't be undoing buckles and bows every five minutes.' She pushes Masha flat on the plastic sheet of our cot, and starts on me. *Skriip skriip.* It tickles and I reach up to touch a bit of her yellow sleeve. It's more like butter than egg yolk.

'There. All done. Off you hop.' We wiggle our bottom off the plastic sheet in our cot and she folds it up and then leaves us, wagging her head so her white cap bobbles.

'*Foo! Foo!*' Masha's huffing and puffing because she's got bits of cut hair in her nose, so I lean over and blow in her face, as close as I can get.

'Get off!' She slaps my nose.

'*You* get off!'

'No, *you*!' We start slapping at each other, and kicking our legs until she gets hers caught between the bars and howls. Then we stop.

Saturdays are good, because we don't have to shut off like we do when Doctor Alexeyeva comes in to take us into the Laboratory. But Saturdays are bad, too, because Mummy isn't here and there's nothing to do.

I hold my hand up and look through all my fingers. That makes the room seem broken and different, it's the only way to make it change. I look at the whirly swirls of white paint on the glass walls of the box, then I look up at the cockroach crackle in the ceiling, and it breaks up into lots of crackles, then I look up at the strip light, and my fingers turn pink, then I look at the window to see what colour it is on the Outside now. Sometimes it's black or grey or has loud drops or a rattly wind trying to get in and take us away. It's blue today and I smile out at it, and wait to see if there'll be a little puffy cloud. Mummy says there are lots of other buildings like ours on the Outside, but we can't see anything ever. Just sky.

'A bird!' Masha's been lying back, looking up at the window all the time. 'Saw a bird! *You* didn't!'

I didn't, she's right, but we both stare at the window and stare and stare, as they sometimes come in lots of them. But not this time. I stare until my eyes prickle. Then I see a cloud instead, which is even better – we imagine being inside clouds and on them and making them into shapes by patting them. And they move and change, like nothing in our Box ever does.

'I'd sit on that one up there, see? *That* one, and I'd ride all the way round the world and back,' I say.

'I'd shake and shake mine,' says Masha, 'until it rained on everyone in the world.'

'I'd jump right into it, and bounce and bounce, and then slide off the end, down into the sea with the fishes.'

When we do imaginings of being on the Outside we're not stuck together like we are in the Box. In imaginings you can be anything you want.

## Learning about being drowned and dead

'Well, *urodi*. Here I am, like it or not.' On Sundays, our cleaner is always Nastya. She's got a nose like a potato, and hands so thick they look like feet. We must have done something very bad to make her so mean to us, but I can't remember what, and Masha can't as well.

'Urgh. You should have been drowned at birth.' She's got the mop and is splishing the water over the floor again, banging the washy mop head into the corners. *Shlup, shlup*. I put my hands over my ears and nose, because I can't shut off with her, like I can with Doctor Alexeyeva. Masha sucks all her fingers in her mouth.

'Shouldn't have been left for decent people to have to look at day in, day out …' I can still hear Nastya through my hands '… and when the scientists have finished with you here, they'll drown you, like kittens, and put you in a bag and bury you in a black hole, where you'll never get fed or cleaned again.' She makes a big cross on her chest with her fingers, which is what lots of the nannies do with us.

I won't think of the black hole, I'll think of the blue sky and bouncing on the clouds. I keep my hands over my ears and nose, so I don't hear or smell anything, and close my eyes tight, so I don't see anything as well. Except clouds in my imaginings.

When she's gone, Masha starts pulling me round and round the cot, and I count the bars to see if they're still the same as all the ones on my fingers and our two feet (not counting the foot on our leg at the back because the toes are all squished on that one). We only know up to the number five because Aunty Dusya told us years and years ago that we were five years old, just like there are five fingers on my open hand. Now we're six, but I don't know when that happened. Maybe it was when Mummy brought us the wind-up Jellyfish to play with? Mummy says we don't need to learn how to count or read or write anything, because she'll do it for us.

'What's drowned?' says Masha, stopping going round and round for a bit.

'I don't know,' I say. 'But I think it makes you dead.'

'What's being made dead like?'

'It's like being in a black hole with nothing to eat.'

'Let's play Gastrics.'

'*Nyetooshki.* I never get to put the tube down you.'

'That's because I'm always the Staff and you're always the Sick. Here.' She gets a pretend tube out. 'Open up. Down we go.' I open my mouth but I'm starting to bubble laugh, because she always puts her finger in my mouth pretending it's the tube and wiggles it, and I bubble laugh before she even does it.

'*Molchee!* Do as you're told, young lady!' she shouts, just like a nurse.

Then we both jump, as the door bangs open again.

'Morning, my dollies! Now – what have I got for you today then?'

'Aunty Shura!' shouts Masha. Aunty Shura's nice, too, so we can't have done anything bad to her either. 'It's ground rice!' says Masha pushing her nose in the air to catch the smell coming over the Box.

'With butter!' I shout, but I can't smell it. I only hope it.

'Yes, Dashinka, with butter,' says Shura, and clicks open the door to the Box, carrying our bowl in her two hands.

She sits on a stool, and spoons a spoon of it into Masha's open mouth, and a spoon into mine.

'*Foo!* It stinks of bleach in here,' she says, wrinkling her nose. 'Nastya overdoing it again. Enough to drown a sailor.'

'What's drown?' I ask, keeping the ground rice stuck in the top of my mouth, so I don't lose the taste when it goes down in me.

'Hmm, it means when you're in water and can't breathe air.'

'Do you get dead when you can't breathe air?'

'Sometimes.'

'What's getting dead like?'

'Goodness! What silly questions.'

'Is it like being in a hole and hungry all the time?' I ask.

Her eyes crinkle up so I think she's smiling, but I can't see for sure under the mask. 'Now, now. That's quite enough. *Mensha znaesh – krepcha speesh*: the less you know, the sounder you sleep.' It sounds like a lullaby, all shushy and soothing. And when she's scraped the last little bit out of the bowl, she goes too. So we go back to crawling round the cot while I count off the bars on my fingers and toes.

## Fighting to get single and then learning not to

'Why have you got two legs all to yourself and we've got only one each, and an extra sticky-out one?' I ask Aunty Shura, next time she comes in. But she pushes my hand away, because I've lifted up her skirt through the cot bars to see what's there, and I can see, plain as plain, she's got two legs all to herself.

'Well I never!'

'Why though?' I ask. 'Why?'

'Because … well … because all children are born like you, with … one leg each …' She pulls her mask up higher, then she loosens the laces on her cap and does them up again tighter.

'So all children are born stuck together, like us?'

'Yes, yes, Dashinka. They're all born together …'

'And then what happens?'

'Then … they … ahh … become single. Like grown-ups …'

'So, do we grow another leg each, when we get single?'

'When *do* we get single?' asks Masha, trying to pull herself up on the top cot bar. 'When? When? When *do* we get single?'

'Now then, you two Miss Clever Clogs, you know you're not allowed to ask questions …'

'But when? When do we get single?' Masha asks again. 'Tomorrow?'

Aunty Dusya looks all round the Box for something she must have lost, and doesn't look anywhere at us. Then she goes out with a *klyak* of the glass door, without saying anything at all.

'I want to get single now,' says Masha crossly, and grabs with both her hands on to the bars. I can see the black in her eyes that gets there when she's angry. She snatches my hand, and twists my fingers all back, and starts shouting: 'I want to get single now! Go away! *Urod!* Get off me! Get off!'

I get scared as anything when Masha is angry. She kicks and scratches and punches and pinches, and I kick and scratch too, to keep her away. But I know it won't make us get single.

'Girls! Girls!' After we've been fighting for hours and hours, Aunty Shura runs back in the Box, but she screams when she sees us, and I look, and see all red blood on us, but I keep kicking and punching to keep Masha away, and Shura runs out again.

She comes back with Mummy, who pulls at us both, and tells the nurse to tie us up to one and the other end of the cot with bandages. Masha hates being tied up all the time, so she starts shouting with bad, Nastya swear words, and so Mummy stuffs a bandage in her mouth too.

'You two will kill yourselves if you carry on fighting like this,' she says, leaning over us with her eyes all screwed up small and angry. 'Do you understand? You're black and blue from fighting all the time, but one day, one of you could die.'

She leans right into me then. 'Do you want to die, Dasha?'

I shake my head. I really, really don't want to die. I hate being hungry. And I hate the dark. So I decide then and there that I'll do something which will make sure we never die.

I won't ever, *ever* fight back again.

## Looking out of the window to the real Outside

The next day Mummy comes back into the Box.

'What you are, is bored,' she says. She puts her notebook down on her chair. She's with a nurse. 'You need some fun.'

'Oooh, can we have Jellyfish back?' asks Masha, sitting up on one arm, with her mouth open. Jellyfish has gold and yellow and black and blue patches on his hard back, and lots of dangly legs, which rattle and shake when he's wound up with the key. He makes a buzz, and trembles and we only had him for once. For one day. He's loads and loads of fun.

'No. You know you're not allowed toys. That's only for the filming. But I'll tell you what: as a treat, I'll let you look right down out of the window at Moscow. Now that you're not in the Laboratory so much, you have nothing to do, day in, day out.'

And then she does this wonderful, wonderful thing.

She gets the nurse to push our cot right over to the side of the Box, which is by the wall. Right under the Window.

'Now then. Hold on to the top bar of your cot and pull yourselves up.' Our legs don't stand by themselves, but our arms do, so we keep pulling and pushing until our chins and arms are on the bottom of the Window.

And then we look out and round and down and up, and we can see *all* of the Outside at once. I can't think at all for looking and laughing.

'Well?' she asks. But we're so bursting to happy bits with looking and laughing, we can't talk. It's full as full can be of new things, moving and happening.

'Those grey blocks across there and all down the street are like our hospital block,' says Mummy. 'We're six floors up here, which means six windows up from the street. The black holes are windows, like this one. The little black things moving down there on all the white snow are people. And the bigger black things, going faster, are cars carrying people inside them ...'

I'm still so bursting inside with happy bits I can't hardly hear her talking.

'Those orange sparks come from the trams on the tramlines – they're the black lines in the snow. The trams carry lots of people. And all the red banners up there on the buildings have slogans, which help people to work harder and be happier.' I don't know a lot of the words she's saying, but I have no breath to ask.

One side of a block is all covered from top to bottom with the face of a giant man with kind eyes and a big moustache, which turns up at the ends, and makes him look like he's smiling a big smile to go with his gold skin and gold sparkly buttons.

I point at him and look up at Mummy, but I still can't talk.

She looks at the giant for a bit and then says, 'That's Stalin. Father Stalin. A great man. He's dead now, but he will always live in our hearts. Just like Uncle Lenin.'

## Questions we're not allowed to ask about life on the Outside

'Look! Look! That one's fallen flat! Look! Haha!'

'Where? Where?'

Masha's pointing, and I'm looking and laughing too, but I can't see it yet. There's so much on the Outside, I need a hundred eyes or a hundred heads to even start seeing it all. 'There! See the people trying to get him up. There!' I follow her finger.

'I can see! Haha! It's the ice, Masha, they're slipping on the ice because the snow's melting, isn't it, Mummy?'

I turn to her. She's sitting behind us, writing in her notebook on her stool. She nods. We stay by the window all the time now, and it's the best thing in the world. My head and eyes are all whizzing and whirring like Jellyfish legs, with all the things down there. Like fat green lorries full of soldiers who keep us all safe, but whose faces look like boiled eggs, looking out of the back, or children being pulled along by their mummies on trays, or packs of dogs, or lines of people waiting to get food from shops, or the clouds going on and on forever, getting smaller like beans, and the blocks going on and on forever, getting smaller too. And all watched by giant Father Stalin.

'Why are some people allowed on the Outside and some aren't?' I ask after a long bit. 'Like us?'

'Because on the Out— I mean, out there, everyone is ordinary and you're Special.'

'When we get Single, will we be ordinary too?' asks Masha.

'What do you mean, "get single"?' She stops writing and her eyes go small.

'Aunty Shura said, when we grow up, we'll get single and grow an extra leg each.'

'Hmm. Aunty Shura should chatter less and work more,' says Mummy, and makes a sniff as she rubs her nose. 'Aunty Shura will get a talking to.'

'Aunty Shura said *all* children are like us, but they're not, see.' She points at the street. 'Not on the Outside, anyway, not even the baby ones.'

'That's quite enough of that. How many times have I told you not to listen to the nonsense your nannies talk, what with their prayers and their fantasies.'

We look back out again. I still don't know why we're Special. I hope it's not nonsense that we'll get single. I hope it's true. I'll go Outside then.

'Can we see all the whole wide world from here?' I ask.

'No, Dasha,' says Mummy. 'I've told you before. This is only a small part of Moscow, which is the city where you live. I do wish you'd listen.'

'Are there lots of cities? What happens when the city stops?'

'Yes, there are lots of cities. And when it stops there's grass and trees and a road, until you get to the next one.'

'What's grass and trees? Can you draw them for me?' asks Masha. Mummy makes a whooshing with her mouth like when she's tired or cross.

'I really can't draw everything, Masha. In fact, I can't draw at all. I'm here to write. Why don't you both try and stay quiet for five minutes?'

'How long's five minutes for?' I ask.

'Just please be *quiet*, and I'll tell you when five minutes is up.'

I take a deep breath, to see if I can hold it for five minutes, and look straight at giant Father Stalin to help me. I hold my breath forever, but then it starts to snow and Masha laughs, so I do too, with a big sssshhhh as my breath blows out, and we pretend to reach our hands out and snap the fat flakes up as they bobble past our window. I'm getting lots of breaths in now, to make up for not having one for hours, and Masha looks round at Mummy.

'Why can't we go on the Outside too? Why are we in the Box all the time?'

'Five minutes isn't up,' she says.

We wait again for more hours, and I hold my breath again, and count to five Jellyfish over and over, and then forget, because I keep seeing things, like how the snowflakes make the black clothes all white when they land on them.

I start breathing again, but I keep my mouth tight closed to stop all the questions spilling out. I don't want Mummy to be cross with me, so I stuff them all in my head for later. Like, what sort of noise does snow make? How do the trams and cars move? Why can children smaller than us walk? I look up. And what does the sky smell like?

'AAAKH!' Masha screams all excited in my ear, so I scream too, and Mummy shouts crossly, and I start shouting, 'What? What?' until Masha points at a man who's fallen under a tram. Everyone's stopped in the snow to look and the tram's stopped too, but then it goes on forward a bit, and the man is left squished in two pieces with all his red blood out on the snow.

'He's dead! He's dead!' shouts Masha, all excited as anything and laughing, and she jumps so much, we fall back into the cot.

'And now you can stay there!' says Mummy, and pulls the thick curtains closed, shutting the Outside all out.

'Is he really dead, Mummy?' I ask, panting.

'No, no. He's not. He's just … ill.' She peeks through the curtains.

'Will the doctors mend him?'

'Yes, Dasha. They'll take him to hospital to be sewn together and made all better.'

'But he's in two bits. Can they sew two bits together?'

'Yes.' She doesn't look up.

'Will they take him to a hospital like ours?'

'Well ... a hospital for grown-ups, not children, but yes.'

'Are we sewed together? Are we ill too? Is that why we're in hospital?' I ask.

'*Do* stop asking questions, Dasha!' Mummy stands up, picks up her pencil and notebook. She looks all tired and old. 'You know it's *nyelzya*. Not allowed.'

'*Nyelzya, nyelzya*,' mutters Masha. 'Everything's *nyelzya*.'

The door to our room opens then, and Mummy looks round to see who it is. She's tall enough to see over the glass walls of our Box, but we can't.

'I don't *want* to be ill!' shouts Masha. 'I'm *not* ill! I want to go on the Outside!'

'*Molchee!*' hisses Mummy.

'I won't be quiet! I *yobinny* won't! I'll run away I will, I want to be single like all the other people there on the Outside, I want—' Mummy reaches down then, quick as quick, and slaps her hand over Masha's mouth to stop all the shouting coming out, but it's too late because the glass door opens and Doctor Alexeyeva walks in with the porter, the one who carries us in to the Laboratory.

We both get all crunched into the corner of the cot to hide when we see it's Doctor Alexeyeva come in, and we start crying, because it means it's time for our Procedures. Masha covers her face with her hands and I squeeze my fists tight and my eyes tight too, waiting, until I make everything go black and empty in my head.

# February 1956

## Leaving the Box

It's sunny today and our cot is back in the middle of the Box, not over by the window any more.

Serves us right, said Mummy, for being so naughty. But it was Masha who was naughty ... not me.

It's worse, being back in the middle, than it was when we were always in the middle, because now I know the world's happening through the window and I can't get over there and see it happening. I can only do lots of imaginings about it in my head. But it's not the same.

And I ache and ache, thinking that Mummy is cross with me, which is even worse than missing the world. I know it must have been Doctor Alexeyeva who got us back in the middle of the Box. I heard her shouting at Mummy, just before I switched myself off, saying me and Masha were being spoilt and treated like *real* children.

There's a white patch of sunlight on the floor, which is moving. I can't see it moving but when I close my eyes and count to five Jellyfish over and over again, for hours and hours, it's hopped a tiny bit over when I open them again.

Masha's asleep, but after a bit she wakes up and yawns.

She looks up at the ceiling and then at the window and then she asks me, 'What did she mean when she said *real* children? Why aren't we real?'

'I don't know, Mashinka. I asked Mummy, didn't I? I asked why we're not real, and she wouldn't say.'

'Why doesn't anyone ever *say* anything? Why not?' And then she starts hitting me and punching me and telling me to go away so she can be real like everyone else. But I don't fight back any more. I just curl up small as a snowflake, until she gets too bored to keep hitting me. And then we both cry.

After a bit Masha goes back to sleep.

After a bit more, the door to our room opens.

'Girls!'

It's Mummy. Her voice is all high, instead of low like it normally is. 'I have a wonderful surprise.'

Masha wakes up again, and does another big yawn as Mummy opens the glass door, *klyak*. She doesn't have her notebook and pencil in her hands, she has clothes instead.

'*Nooka* – I have these beautiful white blouses for you, see?' She holds them up in front of us. 'And a pair of trousers, specially tailored, just for you.' She holds them up too.

Masha starts bobbing around all excited and smiley, and reaches out her hand to grab one.

'That's right, good, good, let's get you all dressed up,' says Mummy in the same high voice, like she's not her, but someone else. I'm not as excited as Masha, because she really *does* sound like she's someone else. 'Look at the frills on the front, and the buttons. How many buttons, Dashinka?' She holds out the blouse, so I take it.

It's all soft, not like our nappy or our night sheet, which scrapes my skin.

'Can I have a yellow blouse, not a white one?' asks Masha, still bobbing around as she tries to get it on, but can't, because she needs one arm to keep sitting up.

'Of course not. Goodness, what a spoilt little princess you are.' She turns away then, and has her back to us.

'I'll help then, Masha,' I say. But I don't know how to tie buttons up, so I pull through the bars to catch Mummy's coat and get her to help. She turns round, but her nose is all red and her eyes are shining. It's almost like she's crying, like some of the nannies do when they see us for the first ever time. Sometimes they cry and cry and cross themselves and don't stop forever. And Masha and me just watch them and don't talk, but we sit there thinking it's funny how some grown-ups cry even more than we do. Then she puts my blouse on too, and ties the buttons up. She tells us to lie flat and puts our legs in all the sleeves of the trousers, and ties them up at the front with two big buttons.

'Well, well, *yolki palki*, you'll look as pretty as two bridesmaids in this when you go to your new home. Yes, as pretty as two little—'

'New home?' I stare at her. '*What* new home?'

Masha stops playing with the frills and stares at her too. Then we both push ourselves away into the corner of our cot.

'Don't be silly. Nothing to be afraid of. Now then, are we all ready? The porter's waiting to take you away.'

'Porter?'

'Away?'

'*Nyet!!*'

'We want to stay here!'

'This is our home!'

'*You're* here.'

'I'll be good, Mummy!'

'We won't ask any more questions.'

'Don't let us go!'

'When?'

'Are you coming with us?'

'MUMMEEEE!'

Masha and me are talking all over each other, but Mummy has her eyes closed and is shaking her head from side to side, and holding tight on to the top of our cot as if it's going to roll away.

'Stop this at once!' She opens her eyes all of a snap, lets go of the cot and goes out of the Box to open the door to our room. 'You may take them away now,' she says. 'They're ready.'

A porter walks in, but not Doctor Alexeyeva's one. He's different. He smells different and has no mask but has a moustache like Father Stalin. But it's not Father Stalin. This man doesn't have kind, smiley eyes. He looks at us for a bit, then goes all yukky like he's going to be sick. I feel like I'm going to be sick too.

'Go away!' shouts Masha as he bends to pick us up, and she starts hitting him with her fists.

'Stop that at once, young lady, and do as you're told!' shouts Mummy. 'Just do as you're told! Do as you're …' she chokes, like she's swallowed a fish bone, so Masha stops hitting him.

He smells like old mops as he lifts us out of the cot, but we have to hold him tight round the neck to stay on. We're both scared as anything and crying.

Mummy kisses us both on the tops of our heads, like she does always, every night after she's sung to us, and then she opens the door to the Box. *Klyak*. He pushes out through it sideways.

'*Nyyyyyyet!*' I'm holding his neck with one hand and leaning to Mummy with the other, I'm screaming for her to take me back. Masha's doing the same.

The porter staggers a bit. 'Hold still, you little fuckers, or I'll drop you on your heads, and then you'll be going nowhere!'

Then Mummy opens the door to our room as well, to let us out for the first time ever. She's swallowing and coughing and her face is all blurry and wet. 'I'll visit you, girls. I'll come and visit. I promise.'

'Mummeeeee!' I scream. 'Mummeeee!'

She's holding on to the door handle now, tight as tight, not saying anything. As he takes us away from her, I look at her over his shoulder, getting smaller as she stands in the door to our room, not moving to run and take us back. Until I can't see her at all because of all the tears in my eyes.

Then I hear her voice. 'You've got each other!' she calls as we go through another door. 'Always remember – you've got each other …'

# SCIENTIFIC NATIONAL INSTITUTE OF PROSTHETICS (SNIP), MOSCOW

## 1956–64

> 'Stalin often chose the path of repression and physical annihilation, not only against actual enemies, but also against individuals who had not committed any crimes against the Party and the Soviet Government.'
>
> Nikita Khrushchev – General Secretary of the Communist Party 1955–64, in his Secret Speech denouncing Stalin; 25 February 1956

## Age 6
## February 1956

### Being brought to our new hospital and told we can walk

I'm still holding on to the porter, taking us away from Mummy, and I can feel Masha's fingers round the back of his neck, holding on too, but I can't see her. He takes us down a long thin room that goes on and on, to some gates, which pull open with a crashing, banging, into a small box room with a woman sitting in it who says, 'What floor?' The gates crash again, and I'm just thinking we're taken to be drowned because the scientists are all finished with us, like Nastya said, but then the little room shakes and my tummy whooshes up and out of my head.

We land with a crunch and come out of the room into a big space with green walls. The porter carrying us keeps banging through more and more doors until we're on the real Outside. I look up and try to breathe, but my mouth gets filled with icy air that rushes down inside me like a freezy tube, and I feel like my cheeks are being slapped.

'Quick, get this thing into the car,' gruffs the porter, talking to a nurse. 'Dressed in frills as it is.'

The door of a black car opens and he pushes us into it, pulling my fingers off his neck. The nurse gets in too, but we're all tumbled as it's not flat like a cot so our other leg is all in the way.

'*Gospodi!* It's like trying to get ten cats in a bag,' hisses the nurse, and she pushes us on to our tummies so we have our faces in the seat. I think of kittens being drowned, and want to cry, but can't find the air to breathe.

The car makes a roar and starts shaking. I turn my head a bit and can see a man dressed in black holding a round bar in the front seat. He has a little white tube in his mouth, which makes smoke and smells prickly and hard.

'God, what a stink,' he says and sucks so hard his cheeks pop in.

'What do you expect?' says the nurse. 'They can't hold it in. And they're shit scared.' She says *nooka* to us then, like the nice nannies do, and starts picking us up and plonking us the right way round.

'You'll suffocate, you two will,' she says, 'before we get you there – and then I'll be for it.'

Get us where though? A bucket? A hole? I wish Masha would ask, but I can feel her tummy turning right over and bumping into mine turning over too. I'm yelling inside, yelling for help. I can hear me, loud as anything, but it's not coming out. Help, Masha! Don't let them drown us! But she won't even look at me, she just takes my hand and holds it tight as tight can be, while all the buildings rush past through the windows, like they're running away as fast as they can, turning the world in a spin.

'Here it is, thank God. I need some fresh air,' says the man, and stops and makes the window go down so that another man in a hat can stick his head in and look at us.

'You got the *urod*?'

'Yeah. I wouldn't look at it, mate, it'll give you nightmares for weeks,' says the man in the front. I sit right up then and I can see eyes with no head, staring at me out of a shiny bit of glass in the front. I shut my eyes tight, because it's a monster, and hold Masha's hand even tighter.

'OK, take it round the back. They don't want anyone to see it.'

'Not fucking surprised.'

The car goes off and we go through hundreds of blobs of snow. I can see a building with a long red strip on the top telling people what to do, but there's no picture of our Father Stalin here.

We stop. The door opens, and a porter pulls us out into the cold and carries us up a curly, dark staircase, round and round, then through doors and into a big room with shiny green walls and long windows, as tall as the wall. There's a cot with no bars, pushed against the wall and there's no Box. It's got a dry white sheet on it, not a sticky one, but he puts us down on it anyway and leaves, booming the door closed. My heart's banging like it's jumped into my head and so's Masha's. We try and breathe and listen. Really hard.

*Boom.* The door opens and two nannies come in with a trolley. No masks.

'Well, well,' says one, 'you'll need a bit of cleaning up.'

I see then that Masha's been sick on her blouse, and it's over her mouth, too, and hair. The nanny goes to wipe Masha's face with a cloth but Masha hits her.

'Fuck off!' yells Masha. She's scared we're going to be drowned. The nannies gasp. 'Fuck off, *urodi!*' Masha yells again. She's so scared, I can feel her trembling coming all through to me.

'*Yolki palki!* These two are like rabid dogs! *Nooka* … we're here to feed you and care for you. Look, look, see? Here's some nice soup for you both.' She takes two bowls with spoons off the trolley and gives it to us and I can smell it's yummy cabbage soup, but I'm holding my breath because they don't have masks and I'll get their germs. Masha always, *always*, eats so she takes the bowl and pours the soup in her mouth. Then she takes mine and pours that in her mouth too. Then she sicks it all up over the bed. The two nannies don't shout, they just make lots of tuts, and clean up, then go out.

We don't say anything for a bit.

'Where's Mummy, Masha?' I say after we've been sitting, looking at the door for hours and hours.

'Don't know.'

'Is this our new home?' I ask.

'Don't know.'

'There's no glass Box here. I want a glass Box to be in.'

We look over at another door, like the one in our own room, which goes into the Laboratory. It's white too. I go cold and look at the window instead, and the snowflakes.

'Big window,' I say.

We both think that's maybe good, but I want Mummy here anyway. I want her here so much that the wanting is bursting inside me, pushing everything else out and making me cry again.

BANG! The door opens and a woman comes in with a white coat and cap, like all the staff at the Pediatriya. She's not wearing a mask though, and she has big red floppy lips like sponges. She walks up near to us. Not too close to hurt us, but I still hold my breath against the germs.

'I'm Nadezhda Fyodorovna. You can call me Aunty Nadya, if you like.' She crosses her arms and puts her head on one side. '*Tak tak*, you needn't look so frightened. We're going to look after you now. You're here to learn to walk.'

I swallow lots of air in surprise. Walk! Like the children on the Outside? Will they wait 'til we get single first? Or maybe they'll *make* us single? I want to ask her everything, but my voice is all buried inside still and won't work. I nod.

BANG! The door opens again and another woman in a white coat and white cap comes in, and walks right up to us. She sticks her head in Masha's face and then mine. I put my hands over my eyes because she's got thick eyebrows like Nastya, and grey skin, and looks cross. I start hiccupping so I put one hand over my mouth and keep the other over my eyes.

'*Tak*,' says this other woman in a big voice. 'What do we have here, hmm?' She takes my hands off my eyes and my mouth, and looks at me. I try to say I'm Dasha, but my voice is still all swallowed up, so I just nod. She looks at Masha then, but Masha's got her fingers in her mouth and is all frowny.

'You do understand plain Russian, don't you?' says the grey woman, and I nod again, to be polite. 'You certainly speak plain Russian, so I've heard. Very plain. Hmm.'

She touches the other woman's arm. 'Come along with me, Nadya, into the nurses' room. Let them settle in for a bit, while we wait for Boris Markovich.'

They walk across our big room and open the other door, but it's not bright white with lots of lights like inside the Laboratory. It's a small dark place with a desk and two chairs. My heart stops being all tight at that. We're still up in the corner of our cot with no bars, as we're afraid we might fall right off the edge. I like bars better. I can see Aunty Nadya through the crack in the half-closed door. I can see her put her head in her hands and start shaking and crying all over the place.

'She's crying, Masha,' I whisper. But Masha just sniffs.

'Stop this at once, Nadya!' says the other woman in a crunchy, bad voice. 'One would think you'd never seen Defective children before. Pull yourself together!'

People think we can't hear. I don't know why. Maybe other children can't hear so well as us? But if we couldn't hear really, really well, we wouldn't know anything at all, because we don't get told anything. I can see Masha's listening to them too.

'*Ai, ai, ai!* It's the state of them, Lydia Mikhailovna. It's not that they're together, it's not that at all, it's the state of them. They're like two frightened wild animals – that's what they are. What did they do to them in there?'

I make a humming noise. I don't know why she thinks we're like wild animals when we've never been on the Outside before. I've seen wild dogs on the street from the Window; they're thin and mean.

'I'm told by Comrade Anokhin that his scientists merely observed their behaviour, Nadya. I have no reason to disbelieve a member of the Academy of Medical Sciences, and neither should you.'

'But just look at them,' she's sobbing and sniffing now, 'they flinch as soon as you look at them, they can't feed themselves, and if they *do* speak, it's in the worst common language of the cleaners.' I squish up my nose. That's not fair. I don't swear like Masha does. Mummy told us not to. It's Masha that swears. I try and stop listening and think of Mummy instead, coming to take us back home. But all I can see of Mummy in my head is her holding on to our cot hard as if she's going to be blown over, and that makes me want to cry again. Masha feels my crying bubbling up, and pinches me hard so she can keep hearing them.

'Oh, do stop snivelling, Nadya. You're a physiotherapist whose job is to treat them, not a simple peasant woman to sit and weep over them. You'll be praying next! Your task is to rehabilitate them.'

'But, Lydia Mikhailovna, how am I to do that? Did you see their legs? Completely withered. And their arms, too – the muscles are non-existent. It's a terrible thing, just skin and bone

… *ai, ai ai*, how am I to work on that, Lydia Mikhailovna? How am I ever to get those little stick legs …'

'None of that talk. You *will* get them to walk. You are the best physiotherapist in this hospital. And this is the best Prosthetics Hospital in the USSR. And that means the best in the world. As for Comrade Anokhin, *his* job was to observe them, in whatever way he desired. As a student of Dr Pavlov, he is pushing back the boundaries of Soviet scientific achievements and that is why his observations will continue while they are in our care. At least for as long as they survive.'

Survive? I look at Masha, just at the same moment she looks at me. Her eyes are open wide. Survive means not being dead. Yet.

She pinches me again to stop me crying, but then the door goes *Boom* again and a thin old man comes into the room. His face is nearly all nose and big glasses. He's smiling and his teeth are yellow as old garlic cloves.

When they hear the door, Aunty Nadya and the other woman come quickly out of their room. He nods at them and walks over to us.

'*Nooka!* Well now! What's all this then? So they had enough of you two bedbugs in the Paediatric Institute, did they?'

He lifts his eyebrows and pushes his glasses up his nose with a finger so his eyes grow big and they gawp at us through them. After a bit I stop thinking of crying, and look at his gawpy eyes instead, like great big popping fish eyes.

'That's better,' he says. 'Right, so we're going to get you two on your feet, are we?'

Aunty Nadya shakes her head. 'It'll take an eternity, Boris Markovich, to get those bony little legs to support them – completely atrophied, they are. I've seen a lot of children in my time, but this, this … *Aaakh nyet*, an eternity …'

'We don't have an eternity, Nadya, as you know. We have Plans. Five-Year Plans, new Targets, new Thoughts. So there'll be no going back for them, thank God, only forwards. And I'll wager, if anyone can get those two trotting along these corridors of ours, it's you. We both know that …'

Aunty Nadya sucks her spongy lips in. The gawpy-eyed man leans towards us. 'I'm the Director of this …' he waves round the room '… um, hospital. SNIP. That's easy, isn't it? It stands for the Scientific National Institute of Prosthetics – Snip for short. This is your home now.'

'Snip!' says Masha. 'Snip!'

It's the first thing we've said to them and everyone laughs as if it's a big joke, so she says it again, louder. Masha likes making people laugh.

'Snip!!'

'That's right!' The man's smiling even more, crinkling his face into lots of lines, and Masha's smiling too. 'Easy, isn't it? So, is there anything we can get you now? A jigsaw, perhaps? Picture books? Mmm?'

We don't know what they are, so we don't say anything.

He lifts his eyebrows up again. 'Well, would you like to meet some of the other children then? Eh? Don't suppose you've met many children before, have you? Come along, what would you like? I can tell by those bright little eyes of yours, you can understand me.'

I know what I'd like more than anything in the world.

'I'd like to go back home,' I say. 'To Mummy.'

His eyebrows go right up, and he looks back at the two women, but their eyebrows go right up too, so they're all standing there with their eyebrows right up as if they're not hearing me, and I remember to tell them what everyone else calls Mummy in the Ped.

'I want to go back to Anna Petrovna. We want to go home to her.'

He laughs and pats my head. 'No, no, no. Snip is your home now, not the Paediatric Institute, and you have Aunty Nadya to look after you instead of Anna Petrovna. Anna Petrovna must stay in her own hospital.' I start crying again in silly sobs that won't stop, so he pats my head again. 'Now don't you worry, you'll have lots of fun with us – Aunty Nadya will show you how to do a jigsaw.' He smiles again, then bangs the palm of his hand on the bedstead as if he's angry about something, and makes the bed jump. 'Come along, comrades.' He turns to go. But when they're all at the door, he stops.

'Nadya?' She looks at him. 'Clean them up properly and then let the other children in to play with them, will you?'

## The stupid children are let in to play with us

They're all talking at the same time and bouncing and tumbling and saying stuff I can't hear because it's all being said at the same time. 'Dima ... your name ... stand on my head ... three months here ... upside downs ... Mummy ...' and jumping and laughing, 'til my head's buzzing like nasty shiny equipment that won't turn off.

'Go away!' shouts Masha. We're in the corner of our bed, but they're on that too, all different sizes and colours and making such a shouting they can't even hear us.

'Here!' It's a boy who's tall as a proper grown-up. 'Piggyback!'

He moves to pick us up and put us on his back.

'Hold on to me!' he shouts. I hold on like mad because I'm scared he'll drop us with a bang on the floor. The other children run round after us, whooping. Masha's holding on too, and we're thumping up and down on his back. She's grabbing his hair, which isn't razored, and he yells in pain and dumps us back on the bed, but it's covered with children and we squish some of them so they yell too. We've never seen real children before and we never, ever get touched normally, except to have our Procedures, so Masha hates other people's skin on hers. She starts hitting and scratching and yelling at them to go away and the children start squealing, and one howls with a big open mouth, like a hole, making so much noise, like there's a monster coming out of it or something, that I put my hands over my ears and squeeze my eyes closed.

'*Tak!* All right, you lot, all right, that's enough!' It's Aunty Nadya who's come into the room. She claps her hands and they all go quiet as quiet. 'Shoo, off you go, back to your ward. That will do for one day.' Then the door goes *Boom* as Aunty Nadya closes it after them. We lie on the bed breathing in and out loudly and I can feel Masha's heart banging. Aunty Nadya goes out too then, tut-tutting, leaving us alone.

'Stupid children,' Masha says after a bit.

'Stupid children,' I say.

## April 1956

### We get leech therapy and a fairy tale for being sick

I hurt all over, like I do when Masha's been kicking me, but it's not just the bits she kicks this time. It's everywhere. And I'm so hot I tremble all the time. Masha's the same but worse. She's gone all floppy and hardly talks at all.

'Well, well and how's the fever today?' Aunty Nadya comes in with her trolley. She's been looking after us since we got sick from the children's germs. That was weeks and weeks ago. I knew we'd get germs, but I can't always be holding my breath. Mummy told us about how germs are our enemies, but I wish she'd told them here in SNIP too. No one listens to us.

'Well, you're over the worst. Nearly lost you, we did!'

'Where?' I say. 'Where did you nearly lost us?'

She just laughs and says, 'You'll be glad to hear we'll have no mustard plasters today.'

'*Ooraaa!*' I clap my hands. Mustard plasters are hot as hot.

Masha lifts her head up. We get a pillow here, which is for your head to rest on. We didn't back home. One each.

'No *banki?*' she asks.

'No *banki*,' says Aunty Nadya. I look at the trolley, just to make sure, because grown-ups trick you like mad. *Banki* are little glass cups, which she lights a fire in, so it can suck up our skin in lots of round, pink lumps. It doesn't really hurt, not like proper hurting, but when she plips them off they leave these bumps all over, like soft jellyfish. I can count to ten now, because she's taught us all the way up to ten, and I always count the ten red lumps on our backs. It's easy-peasy. I bet I could count to a hundred, but there's only ten cups.

'No cupping. We've got the little leeches today.'

'*Fooo!*' Masha hates leeches more than anything. I look hard at the trolley and I can see them now, all squelchy and squishy and black, in a nasty big jar of muddy water.

'Won't!' says Masha. But she's too floppy to be too cross. I see them sticking on the glass and want to cry. Every time they take that first bite I feel sick, and won't look at them or think of them, slimy-slithery on my tummy.

'*Teesha, teesha* ... hush now. You know they suck out all the fever and badness. They're good little worms with magic healing juice for you. You're two funny little fish, you are – you don't so much as blink at the sight of our biggest needles, but show you a leech and you're all over the place. You're squeamish, that's all. I'll put them on your backs today so you won't have to see them.'

'*Nyet* ...' moans Masha and wriggles and wiggles. '*Nyet* ...'

'*Da*. Just lie still.'

'Tell us the fairy story then,' I say and pull at her sleeve. 'About Lyuba. Loud as loud can be, so we can't hear them eating our blood.'

'Well, what nonsense, you can't hear leeches ... But very well. Once upon a time ...' I hear her pop open the jar and splash inside for a leech. I can smell them. They smell like the porter who took us away. Like dirty mops. I grit my teeth together and listen as hard as I can to get everything else out of my head. '... in a faraway land, there lived an old couple, who thought they could never have children. But one fine morning they found a baby girl who'd been left on their doorstep, and brought her up as their own.' I go all tight and put my fist in my mouth, waiting for the leech, but she puts it on Masha first.

'*Aiiii!*' she squeals, but I know it's not the hurt, it's the thought of its slimmery slimy body. That's the worst thing.

'She grew up to be perfectly beautiful. Lips like rosebuds, eyes as blue as the summer sky and hair like spun gold. They adored her and gave her everything she wanted and called her Lyuba – which means Love.'

I think hard as anything of Perfect Lyuba as Aunty Nadya puts the leech on me and holds it 'til its teeth dig inside me. 'By the time she was sixteen, her parents had been forced to sell their house and their land to buy dresses for her perfect figure and rings for her perfect fingers and fine food for her perfect little mouth. But she still wanted more.'

'*Ai, ai, ai, ai!*' cries Masha.

'*Teekha*, Masha! Listen! And then they said: "Lyuba, my love, we must find a husband for you who will love you as much as we do and give you everything you desire." So word went out over the land that Lyuba was looking to be wed. Handsome princes came from far and wide, and to every one, she gave a task. The first had to bring her pink river-pearls, the second golden sea-pearls and the third a necklace of black diamonds.'

She only puts three each on us, so I've got two to go. If I was Lyuba, I'd want to stay with my mummy forever, not marry a prince and get pearls and things.

'Then a young peasant boy came to her, and said he would give her the greatest gift of all, his True Love.'

Masha groans. She thinks love's stupid. She likes the next bit best.

'Lyuba laughed scornfully and struck him over the head with her gem-encrusted cane, intending to kill him, but instead she was at once turned into an ugly leech squirming in the mud. "There!" said the peasant boy. "You have what you deserve. You are a spoilt, blood-sucking leech. But now you have the power to do good, and heal the sick. When you have healed a hundred thousand humans, you will be returned to your original form."'

'What's a hundred thousand?' I ask through my pillow.

'It's more tens than you could ever count. So Lyuba sadly swam through many ponds and rivers and streams until one day she was picked up in the Moscow River and put into a big jar in a city pharmacy. The jar was sent to a big hospital where she was used for her magic juice to save a hundred thousand sick citizens. The hundred thousandth one was the peasant boy who was dying of pneumonia, and she saved his life too.'

'Are these leeches saving our lives?' I always ask this.

'No, you're *zhivoochi*. They're just helping you get better faster.' We get called *zhivoochi* lots. Even back in the Box. It means you're a survivor, which means you keep not being dead even when you should be. 'So do you know what happened then?' Aunty Nadya asks and looks at us. We do, but shake our heads. 'She changed back into a beautiful girl. But now that she wasn't spoilt, she had a beautiful soul too.'

'So the peasant boy fell in love with her ...' I say, quick as quick.

'And she fell in love with him ...' says Masha, quick as quick too.

'And they lived happily ever after!' we say together, and then we all laugh because we always finish the fairy tale like that. Together.

She takes the leeches off with a *shlyop shlyop* and plops them back in the jar. I don't want to look, but I can see they're all fat as her fingers now, and happy. I wonder if one of them is a mean prince who will turn back into him and marry me.

'So, girls,' she says, leaning over us and rubbing stinky spirits on the bites. 'Tomorrow Uncle Vasya will come and visit, and he'll have a present for you to keep.'

'What? What? A jellyfish?!' asks Masha, getting herself up on her elbow.

'It's a secret.'

'One present each?' I ask. Because I know, if it's only one, Masha will keep it.

'You'll see,' says Aunty Nadya.

We like Uncle Vasya more than anything. He was in SNIP too, after he got both his legs blown off in the Great Patriotic War, and she was his physiotherapist, just like she's our physiotherapist. And because she loved him, and he loved her, she took him home when he was all better. And they married and live happily ever after.

'Masha,' I say, when Aunty Nadya has gone and it's all quiet, 'do you think she'll take us home when we're better too?'

'No. She doesn't love us.'

'Yes, but what if she *did* love us?'

'Mummy loved us and she didn't take us back to *her* home.'

'Mummy still might come and get us. She might be just waiting until we get better here.'

Masha looks up at the ceiling for a bit.

'I don't think I love Mummy any more.'

'Why not?' I ask.

'Because she made us go away.'

'But she made us go away to get better.'

'We were better anyway,' Masha says.

'Well … she said she'd visit.'

'And she hasn't. So I don't think Mummy loves us any more. Why should I love her, if she doesn't love me?' She sniffs so much then that her nose goes all sideways.

Well, I don't care what Masha says, I still love Mummy. But I won't tell her that. It's my secret.

## Uncle Vasya gives me a dolly called Marusya

'She's called Marusya,' I tell Masha.

'I know, idiot. You've told me a thousand times.'

I've got a dolly. All of my own. Uncle Vasya gave her to us yesterday. She's all soft and rubbery and when I hug her inside my pyjama top she's just as warm as me, and I can feel her little heart, like I can feel Masha's, but Marusya's goes faster, plip, plop, plip because she's so small.

'Anyway, how do you know she's called Marusya?' asks Masha. 'Uncle Vasya just called her *Kooklinka* – plain Dolly.'

'She told me.'

Masha shrugs.

Uncle Vasya told me she got lost from her last little girl and has been very sad waiting for another one. That's me. She fell out of a car, he said and almost got run over and was very frightened at being alone but she walked and walked and hid in a train until he found her all dirty and tired, hiding in a cardboard box in his street. So he told her he knew just the little girl for her. Marusya's Defective like us, he says, but I can't see why, except that she's got only one ear, which is the one I whisper into, so not even Masha can hear what we say.

'I can't hear her talking. How can *you* hear her talking?' says Masha after I've been whispering a bit to Marusya.

'She only talks to me. Uncle Vasya said she didn't talk to him hardly at all, except to say she was sad at being lost, and that she came from East Germany.'

'Where's East Germany?'

'Outside Moscow. A long long way away.'

'How did she get to Moscow?'

'Wait. I'll ask her.'

'I don't want her to talk to me anyway,' says Masha, sniffing. 'I wanted a tractor. Like in the picture book.' I'm really glad about that. Masha took Marusya for herself to start with, but just bounced her off my head for a bit and then got bored. So I get to keep her to myself now. 'I know!' she says, all laughing suddenly. 'Let's do roll-overs!'

'All right.' I put Marusya under my pillow. I'll ask her later.

'I'm a hedgehog!' shouts Masha and we roll over and over on our bed to one end, and then upside down on our heads, to the other end, laughing like mad as the room goes round and round. And Masha keeps trying to get us to fall off and I keep trying to get us to stay on.

'I'm a hedgehog too!' I shout.

'You can't be one too, I was one first!'

'All right, I'll be a … a … curly caterpillar!'

*Boom!* Aunty Nadya comes in with her white cap and popping eyes.

'*Tak, tak, tak*. What's all this? I told you to do your leg exercises, not break your necks!'

'We was, we was! Look!' says Masha, and kicks her leg in the air, so I do too, laughing like anything. Aunty Nadya does her special frowning, which is a smile really, and slaps our legs.

'Were, not was. We were. Right. Time for another massage to get those muscles working. Sit up straight.'

'Can Marusya have her legs massaged too?'

'Yes, Dasha, you can do her, and I'll do you. Now then, we must work extra hard because I have some very exciting news.' Her eyes pop at us like she's trying to keep them in, but the exciting news is pushing them both out of her head.

'What? What?!' We shout together.

'We are going to be visited in a month's time by a Very Important Guest. He wants to see what progress you've made since you left his care in the Paediatric Institute, so you must make me proud of you. It's the great Doctor Anokhin himself! Pyotr Kuzmich Anokhin!' Her eyes are all bright and sparkly.

We don't know who he is and where his care was, but she's so happy about him coming that we're all happy too. I want to make her proud of us lots. Perhaps she'll love us then. And take us home with her. That's if Mummy doesn't come for us first.

## Age 7
## September 1957

### The great Doctor Anokhin comes to see us with his lesser doctors

'They're here! The cavalcade has arrived. They're here!' Aunty Nadya is standing by the window. She's been standing by the window for hours. 'Now then, just do as you're told and try your very hardest.'

'How Very Important is he again?' asks Masha, bouncing up and down.

'Well, he's the successor to the Great Doctor Pavlov …'

'So more important than a Professor *and* a Hospital Director, like Boris Markovich …' I say.

'Or even a Tsar …' laughs Masha, still bouncing.

'Well, I don't know about a Tsar, I'm sure,' Aunty Nadya laughs back. 'But he's not quite as important as our First Secretary. Nearly, though! He's very famous. And he's bringing people to film you for a documentary for the Soviet Academy of Medical Sciences. That's why we've got flowers and this nice rug in your room, and pink ribbons in your hair.'

I pat my own pink ribbon on top of my head, which must be the same as Masha's, and feel it all puffy like a butterfly. They don't shave our heads any more so we have two little plaits each. Aunty Nadya said Anna Petrovna (Mummy, that is) worked with Doctor Anokhin and that she might come to see us too. That's what I'm more excited about than anything in the world: seeing Mummy again. Because I miss her all the time, every minute and second. And most of all at night. Even after all these months.

Marusya got stolen from me. One of the nannies here said it was the night nurse who took her from my folded arms when I was sleeping because there's a shortage of East German dollies like her, and they can't be bought for love nor money, the nanny said. I cried for days and days, because I hadn't even said good-bye or told her she'd been taken away and that I'd never, ever have given her away. Not ever. And now I don't know where she is, and she's probably crying too and thinking I don't love her. And all I want in the world is for her to know I didn't give her away, but that she was stolen from me.

But I won't think of that now.

*Boom!* My heart jumps like a frog, but it's only Lydia Mikhailovna opening the door, looking cross as she whooshes into the room.

'Take those ridiculous ribbons out of their hair, Nadya. We're expecting scientists, not school boys!'

'I thought … for the filming …'

'Take them *out*.' Masha grabs on to her bow and holds tight, but Aunty Nadya pulls them out anyway, tugging so hard it hurts. 'Right!' says Lydia Mikhailovna. 'They're here. Everything in the entire hospital is scrubbed and clean. The children are all quiet in their wards. Boris Markovich is outside meeting them. They'll be here in a moment.' She pulls down at her lab coat and goes all straight and starched. 'You have the corsets and the pole ready, Nadya?'

'Of course.'

Everything's ready! Everyone's been going crazy all morning, running outside our room, up and down, and bringing stuff in like posters of Young Pioneers blowing trumpets, and lots of flowers and more red rugs and other pretty things. But now it's quiet as a stone everywhere.

We wait. Then we can hear voices and steps in the corridor. Lydia Mikhailovna's still standing up all straight, like she's blowing a trumpet too, and Aunty Nadya keeps tucking her hair back under her cap, and I can hardly breathe for waiting for them to get closer and closer and then *Boom!*

The door opens.

A man in a suit comes in and says: *Nooka?* It must be Him. He's in front and he holds out his arms to us like he's known us forever.

'My little girls!' He's smaller than all the other people crowding into the room behind him and has a smiley, crinkly face that looks kind and not Very Important at all. He's got no moustache or golden uniform or faraway eyes like Father Stalin. His eyes are like apple pips and his suit is all floppy. 'My little girls!' he says again. His girls? Why are we his girls?

'Well now, Comrade Doctor, and here they are indeed.' It's Boris Markovich. I didn't even see him. 'Your little charges. I believe you'll see an improvement. I shall leave you in the capable hands of Doctor Voroboiskaya.' He waves at Lydia Mikhailovna, who's standing by our bed, and then pushes out through everyone, and leaves.

'Yes, yes. So here we are again, my little berries. How time flies,' says the Great Doctor.

I don't remember him a bit. Neither does Masha. I keep trying to look through all the people crowded in our room to find Mummy. 'And here are your old friends Doctors Alexeyeva and Golubeva.' He turns to two women behind him and my heart goes all shrunken like a nut because I do remember them. They're two of the ones we always shut off for in the Laboratory. Doctor Alexeyeva nods at us and we back up on to the corner of the bed and squeeze into the wall. Lydia Mikhailovna tuts with her tongue crossly. Masha puts her fingers in her mouth and sucks so hard that Lydia Mikhailovna tuts again, even louder.

'Now don't you worry!' says the Great Doctor, laughing as if we've done a joke. 'Doctor Alexeyeva won't be working on you today. Haha.' Then he comes and sits on our bed where I'm nearest and brings two green, shiny things out of his pocket in crackly paper. 'Here we are. Two sweeties. Chocolate sweeties. Had any chocolate before?' We both shake our heads. 'Haha! Thought not.' He gives them to us and Masha unwraps hers and pops it in her mouth, then reaches round and takes mine to unwrap and pops it in her mouth too.

'Haha!' He laughs again, and everyone smiles a bit with him but I don't think it's funny. I wanted to taste chocolate too. 'Nothing changes with these two, I see!'

I'm looking and looking at all the faces and men putting up big lights on poles with round, black cameras with glass in them, but I can't see Mummy anywhere in the room at all.

'And what have *you* lost, Dashinka?' he says, looking behind him.

I want to ask if she's come, and I try and say it, but it doesn't come out of my mouth loud. It doesn't really come out at all.

'What's that?' He leans into me with his ear and I can smell something sweet, like he's had lots of chocolates already.

'Has Mummy come?' I say again and this time he hears and looks round at the doctors with a frown.

'Mummy?' he asks.

'Ah, yes, that must be the … late Anna Petrovna,' says Doctor Alexeyeva in a quiet voice and shakes her head all sadly. I nod and nod like mad. That's her! And if she's just late we can wait a bit.

'Hmm. Anna Petrovna, eh?' He looks back at me. 'No. She couldn't come today, I'm afraid. Not today. But she'll be sure to visit before long, eh? In a twinkle. We'll see to that.'

'Tomorrow?'

'Yes, yes, Dasha. Tomorrow. Definitely tomorrow. Right, let's see what you two little berries can do then, shall we? Cameras at the ready? Yes? Off you go!'

Aunty Nadya nods at us and we start undoing our pyjama tops, every button by ourselves, having a race, and all smiling because of Mummy coming tomorrow and because we want to show off too. When we're all naked we lie back on the bed and Aunty Nadya slides the metal pole under us, flat on the bed, so we can hold on to it with our four hands, pulling higher and higher up the pole to squeeze us closer and closer. That's because we have to be close as anything in order to walk. Like scissors cutting. Masha's laughing, all excited at showing off, which makes me laugh too. I bet I get closest to the pole, because I always try the hardest to be good.

'And now show your coordination, girls.' It's Lydia Mikhailovna. Coordination means lifting our two legs together for ten times and then lifting them one at a time for ten times. I could do hundreds of times, but we can't count that far. We'll be able to count when we walk though, because then we'll go to the SNIP schoolroom and get taught writing and reading and counting, like real children. I bet Mummy will be surprised as surprised when she sees us really walking. I can't wait to see her face.

Then Aunty Nadya dresses us in the two corsets and ties the laces tight as anything between the two of us until we're nearly pulled right together. She stops when Masha squeals. It hurts.

'Wonderful, wonderful.' He claps his hands. 'Now then, we've brought your old friend the electroencephalogram to see what's happening in here.' He taps our heads with his two fingers. Doctor Golubeva steps towards us with two metal helmets and all the wires like sizzling, biting snakes coming out of them, plugged into a trolley. We both can't stop from shouting out then and reaching for Aunty Nadya to make her stop it, because of remembering them in the Laboratory. I don't want to even think of them. Aunty Nadya looks all goggle-eyed at us but doesn't move, and Lydia Mikhailovna stamps her foot and goes, '*Tssss!*'

Anokhin gets up then, and holds us down so she can put the helmets on. His eyes are still all kind and twinkly, but his fingers are digging into my shoulder.

'Now, now, girls. There's no need for this, is there? Done it all before many a time. Same old routine. Sit still. That's good.'

Doctor Alexeyeva comes over too, to watch us while they stick the helmets on, and I remember her dead fish eyes and sharp smell and get some sick in my mouth, which I swallow, and I'm trembling with being scared as anything of her. More of her than Doctor Golubeva even, who's pushing buttons now. The helmet starts buzzing like stinging wasps and squeezing my head like it's going to be cracked open like an egg. I try to look at Aunty Nadya to get her to help us, but I can't see because of my shaking eyes and we both can't stop from yelling with the hurting. But Aunty Nadya doesn't stop them.

When it's over, I feel like my head is all buzzed to bits and has come off my neck, and I'm crying and so's Masha, even though Lydia Mikhailovna is stamping at us not to, as she wants to be proud of us, and I want that too, but I just can't stop crying and shaking. I hate myself.

Aunty Nadya has her hands all tied in knots in front of her, twisting them.

'Pyotr Kuzmich,' she says, 'I'm sorry, but was that necessary?' There's a Big Sucked-in Silence in the room except for me and Masha sniffling.

'Now don't you worry about them, Nadya, it doesn't really hurt … simply squeezes a little. All necessary in the name of Soviet Science, I'm sure you'll agree?'

There's another Big Silence as they wait for her to agree.

'It's just …' she starts.

I look up at her because she's still talking but she's all blurred with my tears.

'It's just that we were told you simply observed the girls … in the Paediatric Institute.'

'Yes, yes.' He's rubbing his hands like he's washing them. Like they're sticky. I'm glad I didn't eat his nasty chocolate sweetie now. 'Active Observation is what we choose to call it. Active Observation of the brainwaves in this case. Anything else?' He looks round. 'Thought not. Well, good work, comrades. In six months' time they'll be trotting around like ponies – an achievement to show the whole world.' He gives a little salute. 'Until the next time then.'

After they all go out Aunty Nadya stays to dress us in our nappies and pyjamas and says we did really well not to leak, which just shows we can, if we try.

She then holds my face in her two hands and kisses my nose and does the same to Masha before she leaves because her shift is ending. She closes the door behind her.

'Didn't like him,' says Masha, after a bit.

'Didn't like him too. I'm glad Mummy sent us away from there with him, to here,' I say. 'She's coming tomorrow, Mummy is. To see us.'

'Mmm …'

'Masha. Why's he going to show us to the whole world?' I ask after another bit. 'What's the whole world?'

'Don't know,' she says. 'No one tells me anything.'

She puts her head on her pillow, her end of the bed, and I put my head on my pillow, my end of the bed, and wish I had Marusya.

I'd hold her so tight I could hear her heart and I'd kiss her all over. Not just the tip of her nose.

## 3 November 1957

### We walk to the schoolroom and learn about Laika the space dog

'What's the date today? Dasha?' Galina Petrovna, our teacher, points her stick at me. I have my hand up.

'It's November the third, 1957!'

She asks us this every morning and I always know what the exact right date is. Masha doesn't. She keeps forgetting. I know the months and the four seasons and what's a vegetable and what's a fruit. The only fruit I've seen in real life are apples and oranges. We've had an orange twice. But there are lots of other ones too.

'Yes, yes, Dashinka,' she says. 'And what's the day, Masha?' Masha screws up her eyes and I put my hand up high as high again because I know it's Tuesday. She keeps looking at Masha though, who just puts her pencil up her nose while she's thinking and makes the others laugh.

We sit right at the front of the classroom, which is really the canteen and smells of cabbage and fish. I know almost more than any of the other children, because the most they ever stay in SNIP is three months, but we've been here for more than seven times three months now, so that's seven times longer than anyone else.

'Well, it was Monday yesterday, so today is …'

'Tuesday!' grins Masha.

'Exactly. And I want you to remember this day forever and rejoice because this is the day of a Great Soviet Achievement.' Masha yawns. There are lots of Great Soviet Achievements going on all the time. Like dams and bridges being built and quotas being fulfilled and Five-Year Plans being met. I think me and Masha were a sort of achievement too, when we first walked, but I don't think anyone rejoiced except Aunty Nadya. She fell in a pile on the floor as if getting our legs to work had stopped hers from working. I keep thinking how much I wanted Mummy to see us walking. She'd be so amazed she'd fall off her chair! But she never did come the day after Anokhin visited. We waited all day with our hearts beating so fast I thought mine would burst in two. But she didn't come at all.

I won't think about that. We had to use crutches to start off with and then we learnt to walk by just putting our arms round each other and balancing like that. And then once we'd started we couldn't stop, we could go everywhere all by ourselves. We went running in and out of all the wards and bumping down the stairs to see Lydia Mikhailovna in her office and into the schoolroom-canteen, and even down to the kitchens.

Galina Petrovna looks round now, with her eyebrows up to make sure we're all listening. She looks like a bird with a beak for a nose and big ringed glasses and smooth black hair. She's my favourite (apart from Aunty Nadya) of all the grown-ups we know – that's the doctors and nurses and nannies and cleaners. She's so happy at this Achievement, whatever it is, that she's almost dancing in one place. I'd like to see the People rejoicing in the streets about it, but we're still a Big Secret so we don't go Outside. If I can never, ever, *ever* go Outside I want to do schoolwork hard, as well as I can all the time, so I can be a doctor, and work in here when I grow up. Masha wants to work in the kitchens so she can eat oranges all day.

'Yes, Pasha?' I look back at him with his silly hand high up. He's ten and we're seven so it's not fair when he knows stuff and I don't.

'Our scientists have launched a dog into space, Galina Petrovna.'

'Exactly! We are the only country in the world advanced enough to do this. And what country are we in, children?'

'The Union of Soviet Socialist Republics!' we all chant – even Masha.

'And where is that?'

'In the Best of All Possible Worlds!'

'*Tak tochno!* Any questions? Hands up.'

'How do you launch a dog into space, Galina Petrovna?' asks Masha. 'With a catapult? Does she float? Will she drop back?'

'I said hands up, Masha … How many times …'

She holds up the front page of *Pravda* to show us a photo of a dog inside a metal kennel with cushions. 'She's called Laika and she was sent up in this capsule in a big space rocket. Soon we will send a man into space. The first man in the history of mankind. Then we will put the first man on the moon and perhaps soon, in our lifetime, everyone on earth will be living on a Soviet moon.'

She looks round at us, smiling as proud as can be of this first Space Achievement. I'm proud as can be too, but I don't want to be fired up in a rocket and go whizzing through blackness from star to star forever, or even live on a Soviet moon. I'd always be afraid of falling off it into space. Masha would though.

Then I think of another question and put my hand up, quick as quick, before Pasha can. 'Where did Laika come from?'

'Ah. She was a stray on the streets of Moscow. Scientists take strays for their experiments because they're *zhivoochi*, they're survivors, and don't belong to anyone.'

'Like the dogs kept in cages on the top floor?' asks Masha.

Galina Petrovna nods. We've never seen the dogs up there, but we can hear them sometimes at night, howling. They're used by the scientists in SNIP. Aunty Nadya told us that Academician Anokhin started out working with Doctor Pavlov, who's famous all over the world for working with dogs in laboratories. She says Pavlov built the best laboratory ever, called the Tower of Silence where they experiment on them. I wouldn't like to be one of his dogs in a Tower of Silence. It sounds scary. There's rabbits up on the top floor of SNIP too but we never hear them. I wonder what noise rabbits make?

'Why will a man be next? Can I go up next instead, Galina Petrovna?' asks Masha, and the kids giggle all over again, and I do too.

'Well, I'm not sure Dasha would like that …' She's smiling too.

'She can stay here and watch me go *zoooom!*' She shoots her hand in the air. 'I want to go into space. I'm *zhivoochi* too.'

'Will the dog Laika come back down again?' I ask, with my hand up.

'No, I'm afraid not. The technology to de-orbit hasn't been developed yet so she'll just be flying around looking at the stars out of the window for a few days.'

'Will she die?' That's Pasha again.

'Yes, yes. She'll be painlessly put to sleep, ah … killed, that is … after one week of umm … flying …' she coughs, 'round and round in space.' There are no hands up now because it's a bit sad to think of her being killed up there, all on her own. 'But she doesn't know that now, does she? So she'll be looking out at earth all beautiful and blue, and thinking what a lucky Laika she is.' Galina Petrovna smiles a big smile at us and we all smile a big smile back.

## Age 11
## March 1961

### We have our weekly bath and meet Lucia

The best day ever in the week is Saturday. It's bath day in the *bannya* down in the basement of SNIP. We get a whole tub for just us and one other kid. We're at the front of the line. We're always at the front. We've been here a million times longer than anyone else, so Masha's the boss of everyone, even if they're older than eleven, which is what we are.

'*Yolki palki!* Stop shivering,' says Masha. 'You make me shiver too.'

'It's cold …'

I hug myself to see if I can stop, but it doesn't help. I keep hugging myself anyway.

Tomorrow's Sunday, which is Visiting Day, so we all need to be soapy clean for parents. We don't have any parents, of course, but Aunty Nadya says we need to be soapy clean all the same, in case the other kids' parents see us. But they wouldn't ever do that, because we have to stay stuck away in our room all day on Visiting Day so we don't traumatize the Healthies.

The door to the *bannya*'s open and we can see the rows and rows of free-standing tubs, all being filled up with steaming hot water from jugs. I'm so excited I almost forget to shiver.

'Hey, I'm first in, see?' It's a girl, loads taller than us. Her head is shaved so she's from a State Children's Home, not a family home, and she thinks she can get right to the front where Masha is, because she's new and doesn't know Masha.

'Get lost,' says Masha.

'Get lost yourself, midget.'

'This is my place. Get to the back of the line, shit-face. Don't want you making my bath stinky.'

'Who are you calling shit-face?'

I shrink back, away from them. No one messes with my Masha. Last week we were walking down the stairs from Ward C and there was this gang of boys at the bottom, waiting to beat us up, and Masha got her skewer out, the one she'd stolen from the kitchens when I was talking to the cooks on purpose so they wouldn't notice. She keeps it stuck down our nappy. It's almost longer than anyone's chest and she pushed the point into the skin of the neck of the first boy and said 'Just try it, fucker' and then walked on right through all of them without looking back or anything. I swear I'd die without Masha.

But she's got no skewer now. We're all naked so it's only her.

'How long you been here?' she says to the girl.

'Week.'

'Well, I've been here five years and this is my hospital and my spot and everyone knows it, don't they? So get the fuck to the back of the line.'

'Yeah, you, get lost.' All three of us turn. It's Pasha who's in line behind us. He keeps coming back to have more prosthetic legs that fit as he grows. I haven't seen him for ages and ages though. He's got a deep voice now but it's still him. I can tell easily. I didn't even know he was back.

'She'll come and skewer you to your bed if you don't,' he says and laughs. It comes out all deep again but it's still his Pasha laugh. The girl looks back at Masha and shrugs, but stays where she is.

I didn't know Pasha was right behind us. Right there, behind us, only half a metre away, but I didn't know. I hug myself again and wish we'd get called in right now. There are loads and loads of us here, all standing naked, waiting forever, and Pasha is older than us. I wish he wasn't right there behind us.

'Yeah? Try it and you'll get stuck first,' says the new girl.

'That's a laugh. Whatcha gonna stick me with? Babushka's knitting needle?'

'OK, children. Come along, come along!' It's Aunty Mila the bath attendant calling us in.

'*Oooraaa!*' Masha and me go running in, slipping and sliding on the wet tiles and jump with a swish and a plop into the very first tub. The girl runs in with us and jumps into ours too, squealing like anything.

'Splash!' laughs Masha and kicks her foot to splash the girl. 'What's your name? Besides Shit-Face?'

'Lucia,' she goes. 'What's yours? Besides Midget?'

'Mashdash. I'm Masha and she's Dasha, but we just get called Mashdash.'

'All right then, Mashdash. I can hold my breath underwater longer than you. Ready?' She holds her nose and so does Masha, but I don't. I like floating, not getting all wet in my mouth and eyes and stuff. It makes me scared that I'll never come up and get air again. Lucia goes down and blows loads of bubbles but Masha doesn't, she just waits 'til Lucia starts coming up, then she ducks her head in and comes right back up again.

'I won!' she shouts. I laugh because Lucia doesn't know she cheated. Masha's funny.

Aunty Mila comes to scrub us with a brush and soap and Masha goes *miaow* like a cat and tells her not to bother with me, as she wants double time. But Aunty Mila does me too and then she does Lucia and pulls Masha's ear before she goes to the next bath to scrub them. I'm floating in the water like a fish in the sea or green seaweed, and I'm melting away until I'm nothing at all except water too. It's like being all single in the water, like it's just me floating away. I'll be sucked down the plughole and swooshed right out to sea and then get washed up on a warm shore. And there'll only be Pasha there but that won't matter because there'll be coconuts to live off and we'll learn to climb the coconut trees and swim …

*Ding Ding!* The bell goes to say our ten minutes is up, clanging like the fire alarm, and we have to get out, quick as anything, and run for our sheets to get dried with, while the next three jump into the bath.

'What ward you in, Mashdash?' asks Lucia.

'None of them. We got an Isolated room,' says Masha, because Lucia wasn't talking to me.

'Fuck you. Why? You infectious?'

'Nah. We're special. Not like you.'

'Fuck you. I'm in Ward D. You a State kid or Family kid?'

'State.'

'Good. Family kids suck.'

'Yeah. They suck. *Mummy, Mummy, Mummy, I want marmalade and oranges ...*'

'Yeah, makes you sick. I'll come see you tomorrow then.' She's dried herself in two seconds flat. Quicker even than us.

'OK. Ask for Mashdash.'

'See ya then.'

'See ya.' She hops really fast, back to the changing room, and then I see she's got only one and a half legs.

## We make four wishes because we're bored

'She was all right,' Masha says, stuffing a chunk of black bread into her mouth all at once when we're back in our room. She stole it off the plate of a little kid in the canteen and hid it down our nappy for later. We get all our bread and food weighed out on scales by the gramme. I lie back on my pillow with my leg hanging over the bed and think a bit about what we're going to do all day, now we don't go to school any more. It only goes up to primary school in SNIP, so now we're eleven, it's stopped. Aunty Nadya has other kids to work on because we can walk, and run, and climb, and if we haven't leaked in our nappy for more than an hour, we're allowed to ride our red tricycle round the Physio hall as a treat. It's Masha that leaks anyway, not me. She can't be bothered to try not to. But I do. I squeeze down there like mad. Uncle Vasya bought us the red tricycle. Apart from Marusya, it's the best present in the world.

I try not to look at the chunk of spongy black bread because I'm starving. I know we get Fully Provided For, and I'm grateful, but I still always seem to be starving. There's only a bit left now and Masha's chewing away at it, looking out of the window. She never shares.

I make a steeple with my fingers and press it against my nose. I miss not learning. It's like I've only just started knowing things. It's like opening a bag of all different sweets and trying a few, then having it taken away. It's like when we were taken away from the Window.

Galina Petrovna said I had Amazing Potential, and almost cried sort of, when we had our last day of schooling with her. I think she *did* cry, almost, although Masha said she didn't. It's *nyelzya* to borrow school books, but Aunty Nadya sometimes brings us picture books filled with coloured photos of sharp mountains like in the Altai, and blue lakes in Siberia, which are the deepest in the world, and of snow in Murmansk where it's almost always night time even in the day time. I wish she'd leave the books for us when she's gone, but she can't, or they'd get taken, like Marusya was. You don't get to keep your own things in an Institution.

'D'you think Lucia will come tomorrow?' I ask. I don't usually make any of my own friends because Masha doesn't like the sort of girls I like. I don't care though, because they keep going away, so you have to keep saying goodbye as soon as you *really* get to like them. While we keep on just staying and staying.

'Course she will.'

'Mash …' I lift myself up on my elbow because she's lain down the other end of the bed now and is sucking her fingers. 'We won't get sent away will we? Like the Uneducables. To an orphanage? Now that we can't study any more?'

We've heard all about the orphanages for Uneducables from some of the other kids. You don't even have to be that Defective to be classed as one, just a bit Defective like having a squint in one eye. They say you get tied to a cot all day, and not fed until sometimes you starve to death. I think that can't be true because the grown-ups say Defectives are all cared for. But you never quite know …

'*Nyetooshki*. We're not morons, are we?' She doesn't lift her head from her pillow. I shake my head. There are three classes of Uneducables. There's the Morons, the Cretins and then the Imbeciles, but I can't tell the difference when they're brought here for treatment, I really can't. They all seem nice enough to me.

'And anyway,' says Masha, all muffled, 'Anokhin needs us. You heard Aunty Nadya.'

'Is she telling a lie though? Maybe she's tricking us?'

Grown-ups tell lies to make us feel better. Maybe Uneducables *are* tied up and starved to death …

'He keeps coming back, doesn't he? With his *yobinny* delegations to show us off.' She yawns and then pretends like she's catching bubbles in the air with her hands. *Plyop, plyop plyop.* She swallows them for wishes. I do the same. One wish for being adopted by Aunty Nadya and taken to live with her family. Second wish for getting Marusya back. Third wish for being a beautiful Lyuba non-leech with perfect spun gold hair and perfect cornflower-blue eyes and perfect rose-red lips just like all the strong peasant women in the posters everywhere, standing in fields of wheat. And the fourth wish is to be all on my own in the field of wheat. And for Masha being all on her own too but next to me so she can stay close by if she likes.

## Lucia comes on Visiting Day

The next day – Horrible Visiting Day – is all warm and sunny. It's spring time again and we're looking out of the window at the other kids from SNIP playing in the grounds. Family kids aren't congenital like us, because congenitals get taken away by the State when they're babies and their parents sign rejection forms. We're the *Otkazniks* – Rejects. Most of the family kids in here were born normal and have had an accident, like they've been run over by trains or cars. Tasha got blown up by a German hand grenade in a disused church. Petya climbed a telegraph pole and got electrocuted. They were here about two years ago. Or maybe three. Or even four. The years all get muddled now. I liked Tasha lots. She said she'd write but she didn't. They never do … I don't like it when people call us *Otkazniks* because no one knows for sure we were actually rejected.

'I want to go *out*.' Masha's sticking her nose and her forehead and her flat hands up against the window, like they're glued there. I can see her breath puffing shapes on the window, and I puff some too, then I quickly draw a smiley face in it, winking at me, before it disappears.

I want to go out too, but we're still a Secret so we can't.

'Let's play Kamoo-Kak – *Who's-What?*' I say. We play that all the time. It's when you have to think of a person and the questions are all different sorts:

What sort of flower are they like? What sort of colour are they like? What sort of transport are they like? What sort of fruit are they like? What sort of animal are they like?

I go first, and mine is daisy, yellow, bicycle, strawberry and bird, which Masha guesses as Galina Petrovna first off. I think I've done her before.

We go back to pushing our noses against the window again. I can hear all the laughs and shouts from the corridor as the mummies come in and I stick my fingers in my ears. I hate Sundays. I look out of the window at the block opposite, and imagine that I'm the girl who lives there. I've called her Anya, and she's got curly blonde hair and wears a white pinafore to school. She walks past the five shops called Bread, Vegetables, Meat, Wine and Clothes, with her school bag swinging on her shoulder, every morning, and then jumps on a tram to go to school. But not on Sunday. Aunty Nadya says there are playgrounds in all the back yards with slides and swings, so I imagine I'm Anya now, being given buckwheat porridge by her mummy this Sunday morning and then going out and whizzing down the slide over and over again with Pasha until neither of us can breathe so we sit in the sandpit and eat loads of chocolate instead.

'Hey, Mashdash! Get a life!'

We jump and come unstuck from the window. It's Lucia. She's found us! She's got freckles and green eyes like Pippi Longstocking. She goes over to our bed, drops her crutches and starts bouncing on it.

'The Administrator here's a right bitch. Confiscates everything but your heart. I had a grass-snake skin, all curled up small, and she found it and tore it in half right before my eyes.'

'She'd tear your heart out too and stamp it with *Property of SNIP* like everything else in here if she could,' says Masha, going back over to the bed. 'She'd have a thousand hearts in a five-litre jar in the freezer in the kitchens. And eat one a night.'

We laugh at that. But I think I might, maybe, hold on to my chest at night now, in case she comes in with a knife. Masha says the strangest things, it gives me nightmares sometimes. And our Administrator really is the meanest person in the world. She hates us more than she hates anyone else. Sometimes I think it's her who took Marusya, not the night nurse. Masha thinks so too. She says she'll get revenge for me.

'I reckon she's an American agent,' says Masha. 'I'm watching her so I can denounce her.'

'Yes! And if she *is* one and we denounce her, we might get a medal!' I say excitedly, and they both look at me like I've said something stupid, then look away.

Lucia lies back and does a bicycle with her leg in the air and then tips herself over so it's resting up on the wall, and she's all upside down.

'What're you in here for?' asks Masha.

'New leg. I was in an orphanage. I wasn't a congenital, I was healthy as anything, my stupid mum just didn't like me. But I ran away from there and got my leg all chewed off by a mad dog. So after that I got sent to an orphanage for Defectives. That sucked even more. It's much better here in SNIP. You get fed and the staff treat you like people.'

'Did it chew your leg right off?' I can't stop myself from asking. 'The mad dog?'

'Stupid question,' says Masha. 'She's still got half left.'

'Well, it didn't exactly chew it off. It got hold of me and wouldn't let go. I got found five days later by the militia, all delirious with fever. They sent me back to the orphanage, but by then my leg had got all stinky and had to be cut off.'

Her voice is all squashed upside-downy as she reaches higher and higher with her leg and then falls off the bed sideways and we all laugh.

'How come you've got to stay here for so long?' she asks, picking herself up. 'Most of the kids here have legs and arms missing, but you've still got all yours.'

'We're some sort of Big Secret, so we can't ever leave SNIP,' says Masha.

Lucia sits up and hugs her leg up to her chin looking all interested. 'A Secret? No shit. Why?'

'Because, we're Together.'

'What's so secret about that?'

'Dunno.' Masha shrugs. 'Maybe we're a secret experiment. Maybe the scientists joined us together. I haven't seen anyone else Together, not ever. Have you seen anyone else Together?'

'Nope. But then you haven't seen anyone with a leg bitten off by a dog either, have you? Doesn't make me a Secret. Don't they tell you why?'

'No. They don't tell us anything.'

'S'pose they know best. Better not to know,' she says, and balls one fist into her eye, rubbing it. 'Does your head in, knowing does. Anyway, you're lucky. It's healthy here. You get two hundred grammes of bread a day – and butter and meat. We get shit-all, and they pump us full of injected crap to keep us quiet.'

'Do they tie you to the bed too?' I ask, thinking of the Uneducables.

'Yeah, sometimes. Or tie you up in a sheet so you can't move. It sucks. Wish I was a Secret like you two and could live here.'

She unthreads a shoelace from my boot, which is tucked under the bed, puts the middle bit between her teeth and gives me both ends behind her head. 'I'm a pony. Click click.' I laugh and pull the reins. She throws her head up and down and whinnies and we all laugh some more as she rears up and paws in the air. Then after a bit she looks round the empty room. 'Don't you have any toys or books or stuff? If you really live here, don't you get your own stuff?'

'*Nyetooshki*,' says Masha. 'It'd get nicked. If it's not screwed down or stamped with an SNIP stamp, it gets nicked.'

'Same with us in the orphanage. My mum brings me stupid books, when she should bring lard or cooked potatoes. Books get nicked by the staff as soon as you look at them, to sell on.'

'At least your mummy visits,' I say.

Masha rolls her eyes. 'Ignore my moron here. She's obsessed with mums, right?' I bite my bottom lip. I kept waiting for Mummy after she didn't come that tomorrow time and so in the end, Aunty Nadya told us that she wasn't our real mummy at all. She said she was only one of the staff. She says our real mummy is in Moscow, because we were born here and that she probably couldn't cope with the two of us as she was too busy working. So now I write letters to my real mummy every week telling her what we're doing and how we're getting along. Because everyone wants a mummy, don't they? Whoever she is … Aunty Nadya says she doesn't know if Mummy actually properly rejected us, so she takes them and posts them for me. I always put a return address in big capital letters at the top, but she hasn't written back yet. I've been writing for years and years. Masha says Aunty Nadya just pretends to post them, because she can't tell us anything at all about our mummy, however much I ask. Lydia Mikhailovna says to Banish her from my Mind. One of the nannies says she went mad, and another one says she died having us. But I believe Aunty Nadya when she says that Mummy is just really busy.

'Yeah,' says Lucia, rolling on to her stomach, 'my mum didn't sign the rejection form when she gave me away.' She gives a big yawn and stretches like a starfish. 'Silly bitch. I could've been adopted if she'd like *proper* rejected me. If she'd signed the forms and stuff. Then I wouldn't have had to run away and get my leg bitten off almost. She comes in every month and brings me shit-all, when all I want is black bread because I'm always fucking starving. Just my luck to be born to someone like her. She's retarded.'

'Why did she give you up if you were Healthy?' I ask.

Lucia shrugs. 'She was an *alkasha*, I s'pose. The militia make them send their kids to orphanages.'

That's strange. Alcoholics normally have Uneducable kids, but Lucia's as sharp as a knife. Our real mummy can't have been an *alkasha*, because we're sharp as knives too.

'C'mon! Let's go out into the grounds and knock over some kids who're learning to walk,' says Lucia, jumping off the bed and grabbing her crutches.

'We can't,' says Masha. 'We're a Secret, remember?'

'What? You're too secret to even go into the grounds? *Chort!* That sucks to China and back. Well …' she makes for the door. 'I'm off. It's stuffy as fuck in here. Can't you open the window?'

'*Nyet*. They think we'll fall out.'

'That sucks too. All right. See ya.'

Once she's gone, Masha's eyes start getting black like they do, and she walks fast round the room, up and down and across and back again. I can feel her crossness at being stuck in here with nothing to do, growing up and up inside her. She thumps the wall.

'Let's play *Who's-What?*' I say quickly. 'Or pretend to be a fighter pilot … I'll be the Fascist and you can be the Red.'

'Shut up!!' She keeps pacing up and down, up and down, getting tighter and tighter until I feel like I'm going to burst. 'I want to go OUT! It's because of you I can't go out! Because you're stuck to me. Get off! Get off me! I hate you – go away, I'll kill you and then they'll cut you off!' Then she starts hitting me with her fists and pulling my hair and scratching my face and kicking me in my leg, so I do what I always do and lie back as far as I can with my hands over my face.

Poor Masha. The only time I can ever really go away from her is when I close my eyes and imagine it. But she can't do that as well as I can. I don't think she can even do it at all.

After ages and ages of being beaten up, she gets slower and then stops and turns over and puts her head right deep into her pillow. I'm trying to stop my nosebleed, cos the Administrator will kill me if I get blood on the sheets, so I push my pyjama sleeve right up my nostril. I can wash the sleeve out myself later. After a bit, when Masha's gone to sleep, I decide to think of what I'm going to write in my next letter to Mummy. I'll write: *We hope you're well. We're well thank you. We haven't been punished all week so far for being naughty. We get a bit bored so if you come and visit us that would be nice and you don't have to stay long if you haven't much time, and you don't have to bring anything either. Your daughters, Masha and Dasha.*

## April 1961

### We get the news about Yuri Gagarin and watch him on television

We've been moved into General Ward G now and the little kids are hiding under their beds because Masha's telling them about how her father's a Cannibal King in Africa. She says he's got a bone through his nose, from one of the children he's eaten up, and she's told them he's visiting her today.

'He makes a soup out of them and spits their bones out,' Masha's saying, 'and makes a necklace for each of his wives. When I was little, I burnt his soup and he took an axe and chopped me in two. That's why I'm like this, and he'll do the same to—'

'Children! I have news for you!' It's Lydia Mikhailovna who's just thrown open the doors. She hardly ever visits the wards so the kids all scream when the doors bang open, because they think it's the Cannibal King come to visit with his axe.

'What on earth are you all doing under there? Come out at once.' She looks across at Masha and I think she's going to be angry, but she's not. She's happy. Happier than I think I've ever seen her. '*Tak!* Everyone come along to the Room of Relaxation. I have an important announcement to make. Something wonderful!'

Wonderful? What? Maybe we're all being taken to the Circus? The family kids told us about the Circus, where sparkly ladies fall out of the sky, and clowns are so stupid they make you fall off your seat laughing, and lions that eat their trainers right before your very eyes. We all run outside and find the kids from the other wards there, excited as a buzz of bees. I can hear the word *kosmos* going round and round, and think maybe they're sending us off in a rocket to start the Soviet moon at last.

We race off to the Room of Relaxation, which we're never normally allowed in. It's full, and everyone's crowded around the new television. We've never seen it before, but we heard it was there from the nannies. It's a little black box where you can see everything that's happening on the Outside, zooming right inside to it. But only in black and white, not colour like the real world. It's so healthy!

'Now then. Quiet!' Lydia Mikhailovna's standing with all the staff, even the kitchen staff, by the television. 'This is a wonderful day!' she says again. 'A day of one of the most incredible Soviet Achievements we have ever seen.' She looks around at the staff, who are all smiling fit to burst. 'We have sent a man into space!'

There's a sort of gasp all round. Space? To the moon? Did he die like Laika?

'That man was Comrade Gagarin,' she goes on, 'he orbited once and then returned to earth and the People are rejoicing throughout the Soviet Union.'

Masha's pushing to the front, round the side of the room, by the windows, and I look out and I can see the People celebrating, I really can, hugging each other and throwing caps in the air and running somewhere.

'This proves that our country, the Soviet Union, is the most advanced in the world. In the entire world,' says Lydia Mikhailovna loudly. 'We are now going to watch Comrade Gagarin being congratulated by First Secretary Nikita Sergeyevich, right here in Moscow.'

'Gaaa!' groans Masha. 'It's another *yobinny* Achievement and not the circus.' But she's got us to the front so we have the best view of anyone of the television. There he is! I can see him! Walking down a long rug at the airport, dressed in a uniform like Father Stalin's. He's so … so *handsome*. I just stare and stare. Lydia Mikhailovna's talking about how the Soviet Union has finally proved its superiority, and how Communism will now spread throughout the world, as everyone can see it's the best system possible, but I can't stop staring at him. I've never seen anyone in my life so perfect before. I kind of all swell up like dough with happiness that he's been so brave and that he's Ours. Comrade Khrushchev takes his hat off and hugs him so hard I think they're both going to cry or something, and then there's pictures of the crowd holding big banners of Gagarin's face, and there's schoolgirls with bows in their hair, running up to him with bunches of flowers. We're all laughing now and the staff are hugging each other too. I've never seen anyone so happy, all at the same time. Masha's shouting '*Oorrraaaa!*' at the top of her voice and doesn't even get told off.

When all the huggings are over we all go out of the Room of Relaxation and I think this must really be the best day ever, even if I'm not going to the Circus or to the moon because I'm living here, where Yuri Gagarin is.

In the Best of All Possible Worlds.

## Lydia Mikhailovna tells us off for Masha being naughty

'So. I expect you know why you've been called in this time?' Lydia Mikhailovna's sitting behind her big desk in her office and we're standing in front of it. She's all cross again, like she always is when we've been naughty. But everyone else is still happy. It's like the sun is shining all the time. We cut a photo of Gagarin out of the newspaper, which was stuck up on the news board (that was *nyelzya*, of course) and keep it folded up under a loose tile in the toilets to look at. He's got a dimple and light green or maybe blue eyes. I'm not sure, as it's black and white. I think they're probably blue. He's a hero. It just shows, this does, that we're the best country ever. It just shows.

Masha's twiddling the button on her pyjama bottoms. We both know we're being told off because of Boris this time.

'Boris called me Mashdash-Car-Crash! It's *nyelzya* to call Defectives names,' says Masha quickly. 'We Must Respect Deformity. That's what you always say, Lydia Mikhailovna.'

'True. And breaking his leg in two places is showing respect?'

'It was an accident,' she says sulkily.

'So you accidentally stole a bottle of vegetable oil from the kitchens, while Lucia was pretending to faint, and then accidentally spilt it on the floor, just as Boris was coming out of his ward?'

'I didn't know he'd go over with such a crack—'

'His leg was both fractured and broken. Extremely painful. As if we haven't got enough work to do in here.'

I shiver. It was horrible. I feel sick remembering it. The bone was sticking out all white and knobbly in his only leg.

'*Yolki palki!* It was him who got the other kids to hang us over the banisters by our feet. I thought my last hour had come, Lydia Mikhailovna!'

'I will hear no more excuses. What am I to do with you?'

'Send us into space?' says Masha and does her little kitten look.

'Don't tempt me.' She picks up a piece of paper. 'So. Here is a list of your recent activities. One. Playing hide-and-seek in the top-floor laboratory, which is strictly out of bounds, and being eventually found trapped in a rabbit cage.' I bite my lip and look past her at the paintings of Comrade Khrushchev and Uncle Lenin. That was so scary. I was crying loads. I thought we'd never *ever* be found, but once we got in, we couldn't get out. Masha couldn't get the door back open and the rabbits just sat there with their bulging eyes staring at us for hours and hours and I thought we'd die in there.

There's an empty patch on the wall where they've taken Father Stalin down. Maybe they'll put Yuri Gagarin up now instead.

'Next ... calling up all the emergency services from the guardroom phone while Lucia again feigned a fainting fit. We were treated to the fire service, the militia ... and you even managed to call an ambulance to a hospital. Three. Stealing syringes and scalpels from the Medical Room and skewers and knives from the kitchens to use as threatening weapons on fellow patients, one of whom claims he was stabbed through the hand.'

'I tripped,' says Masha, being sulky again.

'Four. Traumatizing young patients with some ridiculous story of a severed hand that stalks SNIP and then placing surgical gloves filled with water in their beds. And Five, riding a food trolley down the kitchen stairs. Repeatedly. Well. The list goes on, culminating in Boris.'

I'm biting my lip so hard now I can feel blood in my mouth. The worst punishment is having our pyjamas taken away so we're just in our nappy. Last time was for two weeks and we couldn't leave the ward then for anything.

'And you, Masha, you beat your sister black and blue behind closed doors.'

'Don't too. She keeps falling off the bed.'

'And you, miraculously, stay on it?' She's rapping a pen on the table with a *toc toc toc* like a time bomb. I hold my breath and I'm thinking the same thing, over and over, hard in my head. She's going to send us away. Please, please, please don't send us to an orphanage for Uneducables. 'Well,' she says eventually, 'I think it's high time we got you out.'

'*Out?* No, no, no!' I jump up. 'Please, please, Lydia Mikhailovna! We'll never be naughty again.' I lean right over the desk with my arms out to her. 'Don't send us away! Please! Please!'

'*Gospodi!* I don't mean away, Dasha,' she says, putting the pen down. 'I mean out. Outside. To exercise. I'm not sure it's such a good idea, because there's a chance you might be seen by the Healthies in the street …'

Outside? I stop crying. Out into the grounds? Into the fresh air? I can hardly hear her for the swirling in my head. '… but,' she goes on, 'we have planted high bushes around the fence and Boris Markovich believes it will benefit you both to get out of the building.'

'*Oooraaa!*' shouts Masha. 'We're going out to play! When? Now? Right now?'

'No. Tomorrow. The Administrator will sort some clothes out.'

## We go on the Outside for the first time ever

'Mwaah! It's hitting me! It's hitting me!'

We've walked down the steps into the Outside and the wind is all slapping us, trying to knock us over, and Masha's shouting like anything and waving her arm around because we can't balance. My head's spinning like it does when we do loads of somersaults. The grass is mushy, not hard like the floor, and there are no walls anywhere to keep us upright. *Plookh!* We sit down with a bang that makes me hiccup.

'Get up this instant!' shouts Lydia Mikhailovna, turning around. She was walking off down the path, thinking we were behind her. 'I've taken you outside to exercise, and exercise you shall!'

'Caaaaan't,' goes Masha in a high voice, the one she has when she's really scared. 'It's all moving!'

'Don't be so ridiculous. Nothing's moving.'

But she's wrong. It is. All the trees are waving and the grass and the bushes and leaves are jumping about like crazy so we can't stand up in case the ground comes up right in our faces too. We hardly know which way is up with the clouds all moving too.

'It's too big, there's too much space, there's nothing keeping us in! Caaaaan't!' goes Masha again. I can't even breathe because the air's colder than me, not the same as me like it is inside, and it keeps trying to whoosh in my mouth when I don't want it to. Lydia Mikhailovna stands over us for ages, trying to get us up, and stamping her foot, getting crosser and crosser until Stepan Yakovlich, the groundsman, comes over and picks us up, laughing like anything, and carries us back inside.

## We go out with Lucia to play

'I can throw a pine cone so high it never comes back down and gets burnt up by the sun,' claims Lucia.

'Bet I can throw it high enough to kill a dirty old crow,' says Masha. 'Watch!' She picks one up off the grass, and throws it at Lucia. I laugh when it bounces off her head.

We kept trying, every day, for weeks and weeks to stay standing outside, because Aunty Nadya (who was cross she wasn't even told we were going out for the first time) said we could learn easy-peasy to walk on squishy ground in the wind, just like we learnt on firm floors with no wind before.

Now we're so good at balancing that we've been let out to play with Lucia for a bit. Just us. We even get to wear the trousers and red shirts they keep for when the Academy of Sciences come in to film us because they don't want us in the pyjamas we wear all the time. Proper clothes for proper playing, not just for show!

'*Aiii!* That hurt! I'll show you where this one's fucking well going!' Lucia picks the cone up and grabs us, pushing us down into a tumble on the ground, and then stuffs it into Masha's mouth. I'm laughing like anything.

'Stop, stop! Let's play tag,' says Masha, pushing her off and spitting out bits of cone. 'You're it, count to five.'

We go running off across the grass like mad things, zigzagging and then running straight on and on and on because the grounds are so big you can run forever and not even hit anything except a tree. I look round and see Lucia's cutting us off to tag us from the side, so we both stop in our tracks to run back the way we came. She's even faster than us though, and pushes me instead of tagging me, so we all go down in a tumble again, hardly able to breathe for running so much.

'Hide and seek!' shouts Masha, tickling Lucia off her. 'You're it.'

'Get lost! I was it last time.'

'Well, now you're it again. Shut your eyes and count to twenty.' Masha pushes Lucia's face in the grass, and we run off to the bushes because the tree trunks wouldn't hide us both. There's a big bush by the gates with purple berries that Lucia says shrivel your insides up, turn them black and tie them into knots if you eat them, but we run towards that faster than anything. We're not going to eat them. Just hide in them.

Then I hear someone screaming, really screaming, like when Boris broke his leg. We both stop and stare. It's coming from the gate. There's loads of Healthies from the street standing there, holding on to the bars and they're shouting and yelling, *Monster, it's a monster!*

Monster? Where?! We look back, but there's only Lucia, who's got up and is running towards us, but we're so scared we don't move to run and hide from her in the bushes any more, we just keep standing there, thinking we're going to be eaten up by a monster which we can't see but everyone else can.

'Fuck off, you lot! Fuck off!' Lucia's caught up with us and she's waving at the crowd, which is getting bigger all the time as more people run over and start screaming too, saying things like *Help! Help me, God!* One of them's fainted, but for real, not pretend like Lucia does, and all her apples spill out of her bag and run under the gate. I'm shaking all over for fear. I can't see anything, I keep looking all around me.

Lucia's not scared. She's angry, and starts yelling and swearing at the Healthies. Then she grabs a hosepipe and turns it on them full blast. '*You're* the fucking monsters! Have this to wash your fucking mouths out with!'

'Comrades! Comrades!' Stepan Yakovlich the groundsman has run up and starts shouting at them all too. 'For the love of God, comrades!' His dog, Booyan, jumps up at the gate barking and snarling like he wants to eat them and Lucia's still spraying them, then Stepan Yakovlich turns and picks us up because we can't move from being scared stiff of the monster and runs with us both clinging round his neck. I hear a woman wailing, 'How could they let that live?' And then we're back inside.

## We're told not to traumatize the Healthies

It was us.

Us that's the monster.

But why? How? Monsters are ugly and evil and scaly and breathe fire. Monsters are Imperialists, or leeches, they're green and slimy and mean. Monsters aren't us! I can't stop crying, however much Masha swears at me and punches me. She's just angry. Not hurt like me.

'For goodness' sake!' Lydia Mikhailovna has been called in because I'm so upset that the nurse thought I was going to have a fit. She's standing over me with her hands on her hips. 'You're going to run out of tears at this rate!'

'She's using all mine too. I'm getting all dried out. I'll drop off of her like a prune, soon.'

'Do be quiet, Masha. You could show a little sympathy.'

'They were screaming at me too. The pigs—'

'And how many times did I tell you both to stay close to the building? Eh? And not to go traumatizing the Healthies? Not to draw attention to your condition? Now we'll never see the back of them. SNIP is virtually surrounded by baying crowds looking for a two-headed mutant.'

'B-But, but, but, why?' I say through all my snotty tears. 'What's wrong with us? Why are we a m-mutant?' I can hardly get the words out, I'm crying so much.

'Have a handkerchief, for goodness' sake,' she says, getting one out of her pocket and snapping it in front of my face. 'You're not monsters. As such. You're different. Deformed. And healthy people are not used to deformity of *any* kind. It is our duty to protect them from you, but sometimes, especially when orders are disobeyed, this proves impossible. However,' she sniffs and looks out of the window, 'this attention from them is something you must accustom yourself to in life.' I go to hand her back the hanky. 'Keep it,' she says with another sniff, 'as well as that word of advice.' Then she goes out and bangs the door.

After a bit, Masha looks up at the ceiling. 'Stop whimpering,' she says, 'we're only monsters to those pigs. If they don't need us, we don't need them. Not like we're monsters to anyone who matters, is it? Not to anyone in here. You heard what she said, we've just got to get used to it.'

I nod. But how do you get used to someone fainting in terror when they see you? I put a pillow over my head. I don't want to go back Outside ever, ever, *ever*. We turn into monsters when we go Outside.

## We hear about Pasha losing his legs and he kisses Masha

'You're a sheep. A stupid. Silly. Stubborn. Shitty. Sheep!' Masha thumps my arm to emphasize each word.

There are only two kids in Ward G right now, and they're sitting in silence, watching her hitting me. Masha doesn't normally hit me in front of other people. Most of the kids in our ward are doing schooling or physio at the moment, so we're just sitting on our bed by the window. The crowds are still there by the gate.

'No. Won't go out,' I say, holding my bruised arm. 'Won't.'

'They'll take us out the back door through the kitchens, that's what they said. We can play in the yard where the skips are.'

'Won't. Can't make me.' She's tried, but she can't. I won't even start to walk.

'But think what we'll find in the skips. All sorts. It'll be like looking for treasure. We might find dog brains or … or, gold nuggets.'

'Won't.'

'Or scrunched-up newspapers with pictures of Yuri Gagarin.' She looks at me hopefully. 'Loads and loads of photos of him.' I shake my head. It's stupid now to think of going up in space with Yuri Gagarin like I did in my dreams. He's a Healthy.

'Won't.'

She slams her fist down on the bed.

'*Yolki palki!* I'll smash your skull in!'

'Hey, Mashdash!'

It's Pasha. He's poked his head round the door. 'Wanna go play with my dice on the stairs?'

'Yeah, I'll come,' says Masha, hopping down from the bed. 'Better than staying here talking to this Cretin.'

Playing dice with Pasha isn't going Outside so I hop down with her and we run off down the corridor with Pasha scooting in front on his trolley. He hasn't got his new legs yet. Aunty Nadya's husband, Uncle Vasya, has no legs either but he has a proper fat chair like a wooden car to sit in with three big wheels and two paddles which he pulls and pushes himself along with. Everyone else just uses trolleys on the floor until they get given new legs. Uncle Vasya didn't want false legs. He liked his own best. Pasha's fast. Faster than anyone. Bet he'd be faster than Uncle Vasya even.

'Let's play Kiss or Pinch,' Masha says, once we're all sitting on the stone stairs by the half-open back door. Pasha's sitting next to her. I'm glad he's not sitting next to me. Kiss or Pinch is a silly game. She throws the dice.

'Odd number! Pinch!' She can pinch him anywhere and she always pinches really hard.

'*Aiii!* You pinch like a crocodile!' He throws the dice.

'Odd! Kiss!' He kisses her in her ear so loud I can hear and she jumps back.

'You kiss like an exploding bomb!'

I don't get turns. I'm glad. I don't want to get kissed by Pasha. I don't even want to watch him kissing Masha.

They go on playing for a bit and then Masha says, 'Tell us about how you got your legs chopped off.'

'Again?' He rolls his eyes. 'You're strange, you are. OK. I'd gone down with my mates to watch the prisoners working on digging this ditch outside our village. We played this game that whenever the guard wasn't looking, one of us would jump out and tag a prisoner.'

'Why?' I ask.

'Cos you get some of his meanness passed on. See?' He tags Masha then goes to bite me, growling. We all laugh. He's got dimples like Yuri Gagarin. 'I was lookout on the railway track, it was a dead-end track, see, so there was never any trains. Then I hear this noise and turn round and there's a train reversing down the track. Come out of nowhere, it did.' Masha's sucking the dice in her mouth. I think she might swallow it when it comes to this next bad part.

'So I'm wearing my cousins' shoes, which are too big and laced up round the sole and my ankles to keep them on, so when I go to get off the track, one of them's stuck in the rails, see? So I'm sitting there screaming my head off and pulling to get the shoe out and the kids are running up the bank to the train, to get the driver to stop …'

'Why didn't you just untie the laces?' says Masha in a thick voice because the dice is still in her mouth.

'Didn't think of it. All I can think of is this train rolling back towards me with sparks flying, and then ZING!!!' We both jump. We always do at that bit. 'I got electrocuted and next thing I know I wake up in hospital with no legs left.'

'What happened to them?' says Masha. She knows what happened to them, so do I, but she wants to hear again. 'The train rolled over me and cut them clean off. If I hadn't got electrocuted and fallen back, I might've been cut in half myself.'

'But what happened to the legs?' says Masha again.

'My dad went back and got them – he thought they'd be able to sew them back on, but they couldn't because he didn't put them in ice, see. So he buried them in the garden instead. Maybe he thought they'd grow back into a new me. Anyway, Mum goes out and cries over them every day but they'll have rotted away and have all worms in them by now.'

'Healthy!' says Masha, and takes the dice out of her mouth, wipes it on her sleeve and throws it again. 'Kiss!'

'Shhh!' Pasha puts his hand over her mouth. There are voices by the back door and we're not allowed to sit on the stone steps. I can smell stinky papirosa smoke.

'Bloody nightmare, getting in this morning,' says one of the voices. It's probably one of the nannies or cleaners because the nurses don't swear.

'It's spread all round town like wildfire; they're like a pack of slavering dogs out there. It's disgusting.'

'Can't blame them really. They want to see the Two-Headed Girl. Give them something to blab about.'

'Some of the questions though …'

'… like – has it been sewn together by Stalin's scientists as an experiment …'

'… or come down from Outer Space … heard that one?'

'Heard them all. Brought back by Gagarin …'

'Work of the Devil …'

'Poor kids. One thing they're right about: they should never have been left to live.'

'Seem happy enough …'

'For now …'

They go off then.

We don't say anything for a bit. I'm shivering. Or trembling or something. I wish Pasha wasn't here.

'*Yobinny* idiots,' says Pasha. 'Ignorant goats, the lot of them. There's nothing wrong with you two. Except you can't kiss for peanuts. Well, Masha can't. How about you, Dash?' He leans over to me. 'I should get two kisses for the price of one with a Girl with Two Heads, right?' He laughs.

I don't want to. I'm feeling sick, but I kiss him on the cheek anyway, as he's right there, so close I can smell his soapiness, and I feel all tingly when I do. And stop shaking. And then he kisses me back on my cheek. And that feels all tingly too.

Aunty Nadya always comes in to say night-night before she goes off her shift, so I ask her then. It was Masha who told me to. I ask in a whisper so the other kids can't hear.

'Why are we Together? Were w-we sewn together?' We looked, when we got back to the ward, but we can't see any stitches or a scar or anything, not even the smallest little trace. 'Are there other children who are Together like us? Or are we from another p-planet?' I don't remember being on another planet but we'd have been babies when we came down. The only thing I *do* know is that Gagarin didn't bring us back.

She jumps back, all shocked and cross.

'Well! What on earth put all that nonsense into your head? What ridiculous questions! I don't know how you think them up, I really don't.'

I bite my lip. I have to ask the next one, quick. Masha's looking out of the window like she's not listening at all, like she's not interested. 'And what … what would happen if we got c-cut in half?' Masha told me to ask that, after Pasha told us about his legs. We remember that man we saw from the window in the Ped, who got cut in half by the tram and got sewn together, Mummy said. What would have happened if *we* were on the track?

Aunty Nadya looks like someone's slapped her. She stands there with her mouth in a big O.

'Cut in half?!' She says it so loud some of the other kids look round, so she pushes her hair back into her cap and straightens her white coat a bit. '*Gospodi!* That's quite enough of that! It's *nyelzya* to ask questions. Do you understand? *Nyelzya!*' We both nod. She straightens our bed covers and then leaves. Just like that, without even kissing us.

'Told you not to ask,' says Masha, sniffing. 'Go to sleep. And don't wake me up with all your stupid tossing around.'

I can't sleep. Not knowing why we're Together gives me lots of nightmares. And now I'll probably have nightmares about being a slimy monster too. Not Masha though. She sleeps sound as a stone. I wish I'd been born Masha instead of me.

## Age 14
## March 1964

### We go on a day trip to see Uncle Lenin

We're naked down in a well, but it's not a dark well, it's all lit up and the walls are made of slippery glass, so though we can see the opening at the top, we can't climb up to it. There's people's faces, lit up white, staring in at us, all around on every little bit of glass with their mouths open wide like leeches sticking to a jar. I can't hear them but I know they're screaming and their hands are flat against the glass, trying to get in at us. The glass cracks at the bottom and I see the crack run up past me to the top and know it's about to break wide open and let them all in to grab us and tear us to pieces like wild dogs, because we shouldn't be alive … I start screaming too …

'Shut up!' Masha slaps me.

'Arrghh!' I sit up. She slaps me again.

'You and your stupid nightmares! You've woken the whole ward.'

I blink and look around at the beds lined up against the wall in the darkness, but my head's still full of those faces.

'It was that dream, Mash, down in the well … the same one.'

'With me?'

'I'm always with you in my nightmares.'

'Thanks a lot … Well, never mind, you're awake now, and so am I, what with all that screaming. And anyway, Aunty Nadya says, "Bad Dreams – Good Life. Good Dreams – Bad Life." See? And today's the best day ever, because we're going Outside on our Day Trip!'

She jumps out of bed to pull back the curtain. It's starting to get light. 'We're going to be dressed in our new trousers and shirts.'

'I know.' I get up and we go over to the window to look out at the weather. It's icy cold, but there's an orange sunrise making everything glow red. It's going to be sunny. I press my nose against the window, reading the big red slogans as hard as I can, to stop the pictures from the nightmare filling my head. *To Have More we must Produce More. To Produce More we must Know More.* I see it every morning, but I don't ever know more. I hate that all the other children in the world are going to school and learning all about everything, so they can work to build Communism, and me and Masha aren't. We're fourteen now and we should know loads, but we stopped knowing things at eleven. As Lucia would say, it really sucks. (She said she'd write when she left but she never did, just like all the others. Perhaps she ran away again.)

'Real trousers made from Boris Markovich's curtains! *Lya-lya topo-lya!*' laughs Masha. I stop frowning and smile at her. She's funny. There's a shortage of fabric Outside, so they used the curtains from Professor Popov's office to make them with. And we're going in his black Volga, driven by his own chauffeur. '*We're* going to see *Lenin! We're* going to see *Lenin!*' sings Masha, dancing down the ward and sticking her tongue out at the other kids who are slowly waking up.

The 7 a.m. bell clangs and we run down to the washroom to be first in line.

* * *

Two hours later we're in the car on our way.

'What's that? What's that?' shouts Masha, bouncing up and down in the back seat.

'It's the Red October chocolate factory – see, it says Red October across the top,' says Aunty Nadya, who's sitting with us.

'It's *huge!* How come it's so huge when there's no chocolate? Where does all the chocolate go?'

'Well now … there's a shortage because it has to supply the whole of the Soviet Union, you see. That's a lot of chocolate.'

The only time we ever get chocolate is when Anokhin comes to visit us in SNIP. None of the other kids have ever tasted it. Not ever. Not even the Family kids.

'When we build Communism, we'll eat it all the time!' says Masha. 'For breakfast, lunch and dinner! There'll be chocolate factories everywhere instead of just this one!'

Ivan Borisovich, the chauffeur, winds down his window. 'You can smell the chocolate fumes,' he says, smiling into the mirror. We both sniff with our noses in the air and we can, we really can smell nothing but chocolate. Everyone's happy, even Aunty Nadya is bursting with happiness through her frowny face, I can always tell.

'Does all of Moscow smell of chocolate?' asks Masha. 'All of it?'

'No,' he says, smiling. 'Only here.'

'Can we go to the Red October chocolate f-factory instead?' I ask. 'I don't think I want to go to the M-Mausoleum.'

'Now then, Dasha, how many times have I told you that we'll drive right over Red Square, up to the door, and give you a king's chair ride with a rug over your laps, so you'll look like two Healthy girls.'

'Red Square! Red Square!' sings Masha, bouncing again. 'Look! What's that? What's that?'

'That's a ferry boat which takes tourists up and down the Moskva River.'

'Can we go on a f-ferry boat instead?' I ask.

'No, Dashinka. This is an educational trip, before you join the Young Pioneers. The ceremony's on Saturday and all the children in Moscow go to the Mausoleum before they join. You know all that. About time you joined the Pioneers. Better late than never ...'

I look out, pressing my nose to the window, staring at all the flat-faced, grey blocks of flats, all looking the same, with their hundreds of windows where families live. The pavements are full to bursting with people who've just come out of the Metro, walking in black coats and black boots. I've never walked on a street before. I've never been down in the trains that run through tunnels in the ground. Aunty Nadya says the Metro stations are like palaces, with sculptures and chandeliers and sparkling mosaics. Palaces for the People, she says. They're lucky. I'd love to walk on a street and go on a train under the ground and be like everyone else.

'What's that, with the golden hat?'

'Cupola, not hat, Masha. It's a Russian Orthodox church where ignorant people used to pray to their god.' I stare at it as we drive past, it looks all small and scared, squashed between the big grey blocks, but its gold cupola shines brighter than anything I've ever seen before.

'Is it *real* gold?' I ask.

'Yes, yes, it is.' She sniffs. 'Very thin gold leaf.' Then she shakes her head. '*Pozor*.'

I don't know what's disgraceful about it, but I don't say anything. The road's wide but it's empty, like the river, except for some lemon-yellow taxis and some other official black Volgas with chauffeurs like ours.

'What's that? What's that with the spire? It looks like a fairy castle. Is it a fairy castle?'

'No, Masha, of course not. *Gospodi*, you are about to join the Pioneers, do stop dreaming. It's one of Stalin's towers. There are eight of them. They're the tallest buildings in Moscow. See, there's another one over there.' I stare out to where she's pointing and see it for myself, all soaring and beautiful. I love Moscow! There are trees and islands and flowers and chocolate factories and People's underground Palaces. Moscow must be the best city in the whole wide world.

I just don't really want to go to the Mausoleum.

We drive down a cobbled side street near Red Square. There are still no other cars. My heart's beating like a drum and I keep wiping my hands on the rug because they're sweaty. I want to keep driving and driving and looking and looking and never stop.

'*Chort!*' Ivan Borisovich brakes hard and we nearly knock our heads on the back of his seat. There's a militiaman standing with his hand up right in front of us, on the edge of Red Square. We look past him, across all the cobbles going on and on for ages and ages, across to the little black Mausoleum surrounded by crowds where Lenin is. Ivan Borisovich gets out to talk to him, but we can only hear bits, like *only official cars* and *nyelzya*. He gets back in the car and lights up a papirosa.

'Won't let us drive across. Now what?'

'*Nyetnyetnyet!*' I grab at Aunty Nadya. 'I'm not w-walking, there's a long, long queue, they'll all be watching us g-getting c-closer! I'm not, I'm not!'

'Of course not! Outrageous!' says Aunty Nadya, and gets out of the car leaving the door open. 'Now then, Comrade Militiaman, I have two girls here who are Defective, but they are about to join the Young Pioneers. You cannot deny them the right to visit the Mausoleum as part of their propaganda education. This car belongs to the Director of the Central Scientific Prosthetics Institute and as such is official. Everything is arranged. I demand that you let us past.'

'*Nyelzya*,' says the militiaman again. He spits on the ground and taps his baton on the bonnet. 'Turn around.'

'We will NOT turn around!' storms Aunty Nadya. 'These girls are invalids, they cannot walk across Red Square.'

'Let them crawl then. And invalids should be locked away, not paraded across town for Healthies to see.' He spits again.

I want to cry but I can't even breathe. Masha's bobbing all up and down like a rubber ball trying to see him.

'He looks like Gagarin in that uniform,' she says.

He doesn't look like Gagarin to me. Not at all. I hate him. Why should I crawl? Aunty Nadya stamps her foot angrily and gets back into the car, but Masha jumps out of the other door dragging me with her and round to the front where he's standing. I go bright red.

'Please, Uncle Militiaman,' she says in her little kitten voice, making big eyes at him. 'We're sick, see. Really sick.' He staggers right back when he sees us, like he's been punched in the face, and almost falls over. Masha takes a few steps towards him. 'We've not got long to live, Uncle Militiaman, and all we want is to see Lenin's tomb before we die … just like he has … died I mean … please …' He keeps right on staggering back as Masha keeps walking towards him, his eyes popping out of his head and his mouth open. 'And it says in all the slogans that Our Militia Protects Us. That's what it says. I saw one on the way here. I did. I saw it.' He doesn't say anything at all, he just swivels his baton crazily at Ivan Borisovich, meaning drive on.

'Hehe!' laughs Masha, jumping back in. 'That showed him.' Aunty Nadya still looks cross, but Ivan Borisovich is laughing too. Sometimes I think Masha loves being Together.

No one notices us as we get carried down to the tomb, getting darker and colder with each step. It's silent. All I can hear are footsteps. I'm shivering so much my teeth are chattering. I don't want to see a dead body, even if it's Uncle Lenin. I really, really, really don't. I can't look, but I do, out of the corner of my eye. He's lying down, dressed in a dark suit and tie, as if he's just come out of a meeting. He's in his own glass box, all lit up. I can see people's faces all bright and white and ghostly as they shuffle slowly past him. His beard looks like it's still growing and his eyelids are blue with blood and his hands have veins in them. He would hate to be there. He'd hate to be behind that glass, dead, being stared at by all those eyes. I can't be sick here. I can't scream. Can't, can't, can't! Squeeze my eyes shut … hold tight to Aunty Nadya … put my head in her neck … swallow down the sick.

'*Zdorovo! Zdorovo!* Can we go again? Can we?' shouts Masha as we come up the stairs and out of the exit into the sunlight and I can breathe again.

'Certainly not, Masha. Your sister is scarcely alive with terror.'

'Mwaah! She spoils everything, she does,' Masha whines. And pinches me hard under the rug.

## June 1964

### We're saved from death by a new friend, and join the Young Pioneers

'*Aaaaaarghh!*' We're both screaming our heads off because they've got us by the ankles and are dangling us over the windowsill, four floors up, just about to drop us.

'See who's Boss now, you little fuckers?' It's Boris. He's back to have a new leg fitted and he wants revenge. They came up behind us. We didn't see a thing. They'll drop us, I know they will. We got dropped once before, and only survived because of the snow drifts. Now there's only nettles. I can see them down there, I can, miles away. We're going to die! My head's all filling with blood, and I'm scrabbling at the wall, upside down.

'Help! Help!'

'Wrong. *I'm* the Boss. Bring them back up.' I can hear a girl's voice, but can't see anything. Everything stops. 'That's if you don't want your guts spilt on the floor like apple sauce,' the voice goes on. Then slowly, we get pulled back up into the room and fall to a heap on the floor, all scraped and dazed. There's a girl on a trolley with a great big knife. Its sharp point is touching Boris's belly.

'Crazy fucking witch,' says Boris in a shaky voice.

'Get out,' she says in a low, threatening voice. 'And don't come back.' They move away slowly. There's four of them. We didn't hear any of them coming up on us from behind. They grabbed us and threw us over the windowsill before we even knew what was happening. When they've gone, she sticks the knife back under her trolley into some sort of secret sheath. 'So. Want to play draughts then?' she asks.

'All right,' says Masha, getting up and pulling her pyjama top down. I'm just nodding madly and trying to stop my heart jumping out of my chest by pressing on it.

I've seen her around. She's pretty, with the longest, thickest black eyelashes and the biggest brown eyes. Masha always said she looked like a cow, and probably just mooed, which is why she never talked to anyone, and so she hardly noticed her. But I did.

Her name's Olessya. She was lent the draughts board by Galina Petrovna, the teacher.

'You two can be the same turn,' she says, once we're back in the ward. 'First you, then next time Dasha.'

'Dasha doesn't want to play,' Masha says, leaning over the board and not looking up.

'Well, I want her to,' says Olessya simply. 'OK?' Masha glances up in surprise, then shrugs.

*Khaa!* I'm going to play! I've always just watched before. I hope Masha doesn't make a wrong move that I've got to make up for!

'You a Reject then?' asks Masha, moving a black piece without really thinking.

'Yeah. Actually, I'm a twin, like you two.' She moves her orange counter. 'My sister Marina's blonde and blue-eyed. My dad said if we hadn't been twins, he'd have killed the MosGas man, cos him and my mum are both dark-haired!' We laugh.

I look and look at the board, and then take a deep breath and make a move. I hate that Masha's got to make the next one for us.

'We were born Healthy,' says Olessya, looking at the board, 'but Dad gave us his cold when we were five and we got polio. We had fevers for a week, but when we got better our legs had stopped working. Crippled, and that was that.'

She tips her head on one side, thinking, and then moves another counter.

'Polio's a bitch,' says Masha. 'SNIP's filled with Polios.' She looks back at the board. 'You both get rejected then?'

'Yeah. Never saw my parents again. We had a baby brother who was healthy so they had him to raise. I've got one eye that strays, so I got sent to an Uneducable place out of town and Marina stayed in Moscow in an Educable orphanage.'

'Shit,' says Masha. 'Separated. That sucks.'

I carefully move my piece and look up at Olessya.

'Are you g-getting schooling here, though?' I ask.

'Yeah. Been here five weeks and I can read and write and do maths now. Healthy! I'd stay here forever. You're lucky. Good rations and nice staff.'

'I know. We're grateful. But we don't get schooling because we've had our f-four years. They don't do secondary here. It would be n-nice to have more lessons.'

'Shame,' says Olessya. 'I've heard there's a good boarding school for Defectives in the south of Russia somewhere. Galina Petrovna told me. She says I should get myself transferred there. Why don't you go there?'

We both look at her like she's crazy.

'Go to live in a school?' says Masha, lifting a counter from the board. 'Oh yeah, why not? Might as well fly to the moon with Gagarin on his next trip while we're at it!' We both laugh. But Olessya doesn't.

'Everything's possible,' she says. 'Everything. You just need to try.'

Olessya won at draughts because Masha kept making the wrong moves. I knew she would. I was so cross I actually felt like crying, but now we're standing in the Room of Relaxation for the Young Pioneers ceremony, and it's so exciting I've forgotten all about that and I'm nervous as anything. I wish we had the whole uniform and not just the red scarf to wear with our pyjamas. We've been wearing nothing but pyjamas indoors for eight years now and only get dressed if we're being filmed by the Science Academy or go outside. But never mind that now, I'm going to be part of the Young Pioneers, and then the Young Communist organization – and *then* a Party member like Doctor Lydia Mikhailovna, Professor Boris Markovich and Doctor Anokhin … You have to be a member of the Party if you want to be a doctor, like I do. Aunty Nadya's a physiotherapist. I wonder if you have to be a Party member for that? I don't think so.

We're a bit behind with joining up because you normally become a Pioneer when you're ten, but never mind that either. We'll catch up.

'Attention!' We all straighten up as Lydia Mikhailovna walks in to inspect us. She marches up and down the line like we're proper soldiers on parade. There's a great big mural all across the wall at the far end, showing Uncle Lenin patting a Young Pioneer on the shoulder. He's a Healthy Pioneer (there aren't any Defectives in the posters) and there are mountains, and ships in the sea, and peasants in fields of corn, and new factories with chimneys. There's everything you could ever want to see out there in our beautiful Russia, and it's always sunny. Aunty Nadya brought in a conch shell once and held it to my ear so I could hear the waves crashing as if they were right there, caught in the shell. I could really hear them.

'One, two, three, march!' Most of the kids are on trollies and can't march, but we all get ourselves over to the Red Corner to where the big bust of Lenin is, and line up again.

The Komsorg, who's come in from the local Young Communist Youth Organization, is looking sick and yellow. Aunty Nadya says it's frightening for the Healthies from the Outside to see us kids when they're not used to it. The Komsorg keeps looking at her watch as she goes through our oaths. There's this loud patriotic music coming from the State Radio speaker on the wall, which reminds me of the time that engineer came in to mend our speaker on the wall in G Ward. He kept looking round at us from the top of his ladder, and was trembling so much that in the end he ran out, saying he couldn't be expected to work under those conditions. I try to understand people, I really do, but I've never seen us so I can't see what they can. I can only see Masha. And she's pretty.

'... duty to uphold the great morals of Socialism ...' The Komsorg's still talking. Now she starts going on about Equality and Justice and Doing No Wrong. It's a bit awkward, as we're standing next to the little kid Masha tried to stuff down the rubbish chute the other day. He would've gone right down too if he hadn't held on really hard to the frame. And on the other side is the girl she fed with marbles that we found in the skip (they must have been confiscated from one of the Family kids – we were so excited, but we couldn't keep them as all our hiding places have been found out). Masha told her they were magic balls, which could make her invisible. She really tried to swallow them too, but they were too big and she coughed them up, but she almost died choking. Masha had to hold her upside down while I slapped her back to pop them out.

'Young Pioneer!' I jump. It's my turn. 'Are you prepared to fight for the cause of the Communist Party of the Soviet Union?'

'Always P-p-prepared!' *Chort!* I keep stuttering now. It started after I went Outside that time, to play hide and seek, and realized I was a monster. I just can't get words out any more, unless I'm alone with Masha.

'I, D-Daria Krivoshlyapova, joining the r-ranks of the Vladimir Ilyich Lenin All-Union Pioneer Organization, in the presence of my Comrades, do solemnly p-promise to love and cherish my Motherland p-passionately ...' Masha looks up at the ceiling, like she's got nothing to do with me. She hates me stuttering. She says it's pathetic.

There's a big poster of the Young Pioneer, Pavel Morozov, on the wall. Masha said she'd denounce her father in a second, if she had one, like Pavel did, and have him sent off to be shot too, for anti-Soviet activity. Then she'd be famous like he is. She keeps on trying to find ways to denounce the Administrator. In summer, when all the staff went, she got into the Administrator's room and went through all her files to see if she'd forged documents to help bandits, like Pavel's father did, or was an American spy, or is involved in anti-Soviet agitation, but there was nothing. I was scared to death, but it was healthy fun. I felt like a proper Activist.

'And now you have been sworn in, we shall sing the USSR Hymn,' says the Komsorg, and we all go at it, at the top of our voices because we're all so happy and proud. Actually, I'm *so* proud to be in the Best of All Possible Worlds I could really burst or something. Defectives are killed at birth in Amerika. Everyone says so. But we're cared for. Well, maybe the Uneducables aren't so much ... but we are. I almost feel like crying, I'm so proud. Masha's singing louder than anyone. She's shouting out, *We were raised by Stalin to be true to the People, Inspired by him to heroic deeds of labour!*

As we're filing out, Lydia Mikhailovna taps me on the shoulder at the door. 'Don't forget. Delegation tomorrow with Doctor Anokhin.' Masha sniffs so hard her nose goes all sideways. As if we could forget … 'And that's quite enough of that sneer, Masha! You are very lucky to be playing a small part in Soviet Scientific Progress. You should know that, now more than ever. Get a sound sleep.'

A sound sleep is the last thing we'll get …

## July 1964

### We perform for Anokhin's delegation but Popov steps in

'Not going in.'

'We've g-got to, Mashinka.'

'Why? They can't make us.'

'They can. We'll be sent away if we don't, to an orphanage. We must.'

We're sitting on our bed waiting to be called into the Conference Hall at 11 a.m. The black Volgas full of delegates from all over the USSR, and this time from all over the world, have been driving up all morning outside the window. We watched. Loads of them. Like cockroaches swarming up to rotting food.

'What's so bad then?' Olessya's sitting with us. 'About the Delegation?'

Masha's twiddling the button on our pyjamas and both of us are jiggling our legs up and down like mad things. I wish those marbles really could make you invisible. I'd swallow them all, however big they were, and disappear right now.

'Dunno,' says Masha.

'You two get delegations in to see you all the time, don't you?'

'Yeah, but they're usually in a little room, for doctors from our Soviet republics,' says Masha. 'They lay you out naked as a baby on a slab and get all these pip-eyed medical students in from Kazakhstan and Kyrgyzstan and Uzbekistan and Fuckistan to poke at you, and pick at you like a piece of meat, with all their medical jargon. But the ones with Anokhin are different. That's like being up on the *yobinny* Bolshoi Ballet stage.'

'Yes,' I say, 'the small ones aren't f-fun but they're OK. One of the K-Kazakh students asked our doctor, "Can theys tork?" And Masha sits right up and says, "Hey, we can speak Russian better than you'll be able to in five lifetimes, you illiterate camel!" and he looked like he'd been shot through the heart, d-didn't he, Mash? D-didn't he?' But Masha doesn't even smile. She just keeps jiggling her leg, making the floor thump.

Olessya's sitting on my side. Everyone sits on Masha's side normally, except Olessya.

'That's what keeps you in here, isn't it? The delegations … the research …' she says slowly.

'Yeah, well, right now I don't want to be here,' says Masha.

'Girls!' It's Lydia Mikhailovna, come to get us. My tummy turns right over in a somersault. 'Come along. Everyone is gathered in the Conference Hall.'

We get up slowly and follow her. Down the corridor, on and on, round one corner and then another and another.

'Come along, stop dawdling.'

We go round the back of the Conference Hall to where the stage is. It's dark as anything. There are wooden stairs going up to the stage, which is all covered off by a heavy red curtain with a gold sickle and hammer on it so we can't see them all sitting in rows and rows of black suits.

'Right. You know the routine. Get undressed.' Lydia Mikhailovna's standing over us. I can hear them all buzzing in the hall behind the curtain. Like wasps waiting to sting. We undo our buttons, take off our pyjamas and untie our nappy.

Masha's sick then, and Lydia Mikhailovna's all cross, saying she should have asked for a bucket if she felt nauseous, not thrown up on the floor.

'Fucking *kefir* for breakfast,' mutters Masha, wiping her mouth. 'Knew it was off.'

We're naked now and shivering like anything. Waiting. We can hear Academician Anokhin on the stage. *Very rare example of ischiopagus tripus twins ... under our care, quite remarkable that they have survived into their teens ... under our care ... remarkable ... survived ...* There's a circle drawn in chalk on the stage that we have to stand in, behind the curtain. I want to swallow marbles. We walk up slowly and step into it. We wait. I won't fall down, I won't. Soviet Progress. Grateful. Grateful. Grateful. Best of. I squeeze my eyes shut and dig my fingers into Masha's neck where I'm holding her. She digs hers into mine. The curtains slowly open. I can't see anything because the spotlight is on us, bright as anything and blinding me, but I can hear the gasp go up. They always gasp.

Anokhin comes up on to the stage with a pointer. *Two hearts, two brains, two kidneys, two nervous systems, two upper intestines, one blood system, one liver, one lower intestine, one leg each and a shared leg at the back. Turn!*

He taps my forehead with his pointer and we turn. The spotlights come from everywhere.

I'm glad I'm blinded and can't see them. I won't cry. We've been told to keep our eyes open and look straight ahead but the light's so bright my eyes are watering.

'Turn!' He taps the back of my head. I turn to face them again, blinded by the spotlights, I take my hand off Masha's neck to wipe my cheek because my eyes are watering. I hope they don't think I'm crying or anything stupid like that because I'm not crying. I'm not.

*Crash!* There's a noise like a chair falling over and then the door to the hall bangs. I look at Masha. Did we do something wrong?

'Stand on one leg,' says Anokhin. Masha lifts hers up because I'm stronger. 'Run to the edge of the stage and back,' he says. We run to the edge of the stage and back. 'Hop,' he says. We hop.

He talks and talks and talks while we stand in the spotlight, in the chalk circle, doing what he tells us to with his pointer for ever and ever until he runs out of talk and dismisses us. There's a round of applause as we walk off. Lydia Mikhailovna is waiting for us backstage. We get dressed slowly in our nappy and then our pyjamas and go down the wooden stairs. She stops us at the door and we can see Boris Markovich standing in the corridor with his hands in his pockets. Doctor Anokhin walks up to him and holds out his hand.

'Comrade Popov. You left the auditorium?' he says with his eyebrows raised. Boris Markovich takes a step back and doesn't take his hand out of his pocket.

'Yes, I left. I could watch no more. They are not one of your dogs, Pyotr Kuzmich.' He says that all quiet, but somehow really loud. 'We no longer live in Stalin's Soviet Union. We live in the country that Lenin intended. These are normal, intelligent, fourteen-year-old teenagers, not a dumb animal. They should never be forced to witness the spectacle of a room full of men, analysing their naked anatomy.'

Anokhin gives a little smile and tips his head on one side.

'Then next time blindfold them,' he says. And walks off.

## We go to amputate our leg, but I mess it up – as usual

'I got a plane, got a plane!' shouts Masha, pulling a wooden plank out of the skip. She's half in the skip and I'm half out. I won't go all in because it stinks of blood and dead dogs. They incinerate the experimental ones but throw the strays, which hang around the grounds, in here to rot when they die.

'I'm the Soviet fighter pilot and you're the Fascists!' she says, jumping back down, and we start racing around with the plank on our back, bombing the little kids playing with us. They run away screaming like we're really bombing them. Masha whacks one with the plank and he goes flying into a tree trunk and just lies there, so I think he's actually dead. Then he gets up and goes right back to being a Fascist. There's all sorts of stuff in the skips. We go out there every day now, and find bits of metal for swords to play Whites and Reds with, or nails to play surgeons and patients with.

I'd rather be inside, sitting with Olessya, but she's in the schoolroom, learning. They give all kids an elementary education here, whatever their age. She's just taught herself up to now with books the kind nannies in her orphanage gave her.

After a bit, we all sit down to get our breath and sort through what we've got; like, who's got the bloodiest surgical gloves, or sharpest bit of metal. One piece is like a mirror, but I won't look in that.

They don't have mirrors in SNIP to protect us from seeing ourselves, but me and Masha went off one Sunday to the Old Wing where the Party Conferences are held, and went right into the Party Hall where no one has ever been, because it's strictly off limits. It used to be a ballroom for decadent people before the Great October Revolution, and it had a wooden jigsaw puzzle floor and lights like worlds of falling diamonds. And a massive mirror with a golden twirly frame. I didn't understand what it was when I first saw our reflection as we walked up to it. I thought it was just a door leading to somewhere. Then we saw this lumbering, ugly thing with bits sticking out everywhere rocking towards us ... like nothing we'd ever seen before. It was me and Masha. It was how everyone else sees us. I won't even think about it now, it makes me sick. It makes me want to cry every time I think of it. Even Masha was so shocked she couldn't talk for ages. It's like we'd never really seen what other people see, with our great big stupid third leg waving above us like some scorpion or something. But now we've seen we're all mashed up together and not like anything else on earth, I can't forget. We hid in bed under the sheet for days and days after that. Aunty Nadya said, over and over, that we were beautiful, but she's lying. It's another of their Lies. The Healthies outside by the gate are right. That Nastya, the cleaner in the Pediatriya was right. The driver who took us there was right. We're *urodi*. No one in the whole wide world looks as ugly as us. Olessya said some stuff about what matters is what's on the inside, not the outside, but if we look like this on the outside, no one's going to bother about what's on the inside. They'll just run right away screaming.

In the end, Aunty Nadya said if it would make us feel any better we could have our third leg amputated as we don't need it.

So now the amputation's all set for next week.

Masha's drawing a Nazi swastika in the ground with a metal shard. She shouldn't. That's treason or something. She's crazy, Masha is. The others are laughing at one of the kids, who's pulled a surgical glove on his head like a cockerel.

'So, Mashdash,' the kid says, taking it off with a snap, 'you doing the amputation next week?'

'Maybe,' says Masha. Like there's a choice now.

'Well, you can hear them sawing through the bone,' he says. '*Karr, karr …*' and he goes like he's sawing at his good leg with the shard of metal.

'Fuck off, piss-face. They'll give us anaesthetic. Knock us out.'

'No they don't! They don't! Honest they don't! It's only local, right? So you're in there with all the lights and the surgeons and you can see the saw and its sharp teeth and everything. All the time.'

'Yeah, yeah – and the vibrations go all up your body to your head,' says another kid, all excited to be making Masha cross, 'and you can see them mopping up all the blood with towels, there's loads and loads of blood, everything's red. The whole room goes red, they just can't get enough towels in there to mop it all up.'

I put my hands over my ears to stop listening, but I can still hear them all.

'There's a shortage of anaesthetic, you might not even get *any* …'

'… Uncle Styopa in our village got caught up in a crop mower and they just gave him a bottle of vodka. He passed out during the operation, but they didn't know if it was the vodka or the pain!' They're laughing.

'You can smell the blood above even the antiseptic,' says one little kid.

'Fuck off!' shouts Masha, getting up. 'Fuck off, the lot of you!'

We get up to go.

'Aunty Nadya said we'd have anaesthetic,' I say as we go back inside.

'Yeah, but she didn't say it was only local. I'm not doing it if it's only local. Fuck. I like my leg. It's mine. Well … half of it is.'

'I like it too. It balances us when we climb. How are we going to climb without it? Aunty Nadya says it's like our tail.'

Masha shrugs.

'But they gave us general anaesthetic to have our appendix out, Mash, Remember?'

'Yeah … in the end. But they weren't going to give us anything to start off with – just tie us down.'

I shiver. That was awful. I had a terrible pain in my stomach, which kept making Masha throw up. But she didn't want to go to a hospital to be looked at because, whenever we do that, we end up with loads of doctors crawling all over us, poking every bit of us. Like maggots in meat, as Masha says. But we had such a high temperature that our SNIP night-duty doctor diagnosed appendicitis and Lydia Mikhailovna was called back in from her flat to take us to the Botkin Hospital. The pain was so bad it was making everything dizzy and black, but the doctors wouldn't operate as they didn't know how much novocaine to give us and thought they'd kill us by mistake. They wanted a signed form from Professor Popov, or Anokhin, that if we died, it wouldn't be their fault. But Anokhin was in Amerika and Popov was at his country dacha so in the end they said the best thing to do was operate without any novocaine and just tie us down. We screamed and screamed then, at the very thought, like we were being tortured. Well, actually, it would have been torture – and Lydia Mikhailovna was screaming at the doctors that we had a burst appendix and would die anyway from blood sepsis if they didn't operate *with* novocaine, and one of the nurses started screaming when she walked in and saw *us* screaming. So then Lydia Mikhailovna took us to the Usokovski Hospital instead, but no one would operate on us again, so in the end, she sent a driver to get the forms from Professor Popov in the country. It was early in the morning before they finally put us under. And Lydia Mikhailovna was still there, sitting right by our bed when we woke up, looking like death herself.

So now, talking about it, we think she actually likes us.

'Hey, *I* know,' says Masha, 'let's go to Lydia Mikhailovna's office, right now, like right now, and tell her we don't want our leg off after all.'

I nod happily, so we go running off and knock on her door and tell her.

'No, it's all arranged, girls. Next Wednesday. Amputation.' Lydia Mikhailovna has her hand up in front of her.

'P-Please, p-please, it's *our* leg. We want to k-keep it!'

'No, Dasha. And that's final.'

'But it will be general anaesthetic? Won't it?' asks Masha.

Lydia Mikhailovna looks down at her desk and starts arranging papers. 'No. It will be local. Academician Anokhin will be present with his Medical Sciences film crew to observe your reactions, and Doctor Golubeva from the Brain Institute will be measuring your brain activity with her electroencephalogram helmets. They need you conscious.' She doesn't look up. 'Scientists need you conscious to monitor reactions.'

It's the morning of the operation and I'm so scared I can't see straight. Masha keeps thumping me and saying I'll ruin it. Olessya's sitting with us on the bed.

'You won't feel anything. Nothing at all,' she's saying to me in her low, quiet voice, which is like being stroked. 'And the helmets are so painful anyway, you won't even be thinking about your leg, will you? It won't take long. You'll be back here in a minute ... we'll play draughts.'

I'm shaking all over though and sobbing. I think I'd rather die.

'Stupid sheep! Bad enough to go through an operation, without having a fucking shipwreck by your side!' Masha slaps me hard on the cheek.

'Enough of that!' Aunty Nadya's walked in. 'As if she isn't in enough of a state as it is.'

'Just needs some sense knocked into her,' grumbles Masha.

'Well, be that as it may, everything's ready so come along, girls. We'll have that leg off in a jiffy and you'll look like new.'

'Now?!! *Nyetttt!*' I try to crawl back up the bed away from her, but Masha's pulling the other way and Aunty Nadya's pulling my hand and they half drag, half carry me down to the operating floor. I start screaming at the door to the theatre. They're trying to take my hand out of Aunty Nadya's and leave her behind and shut it. I scream and scream and don't even feel Masha's slaps and won't let go of Aunty Nadya's hand until they let her come in too.

There's bright hot lights everywhere and the room's so full with doctors and cameras I hardly see Anokhin until they put us flat on the table, face down, and he looks into my face with his chocolatey eyes. There's no room for Aunty Nadya round the table because of the surgeons, but I won't let go of her hand so she has to crawl down under the operating table, still holding on to mine. Doctor Golubeva fits the helmets and turns them on and everything goes juddery like my brain's being fried. She comes into SNIP every few months with the helmets, but we never get used to it. I scream even more and I can hear Masha yelling at me and then I see the saw that they cut your leg off with, sitting on a tray, right in front of my very own two eyes. It's like the one Stepan Yakovlich uses to cut down branches, maybe it's even the same one. Then a man comes at me with a needle as big as my arm.

'Inject all round the root of the leg,' says another voice I don't recognize above all the noise. 'Let's get on with this. *Gospodi!* … these two were bad enough as babies …' The needle goes in like a hot burning skewer and I try and get off the table then, pulling Masha with me, and hear Anokhin shouting:

'Hold her down! Nurse – hold her down! God in Heaven, this is turning into a circus act!'

I can't stop shaking and as soon as the injections are done Masha pops up and starts punching in me the head.

'You idiot! You stupid weakling, you coward!' she screams, hitting and hitting me. The nurse lets go of me to push her down and I try to crawl off the table again, to get down under the operating table with Aunty Nadya.

'This is absurd!' shouts Anokhin. 'Tie them both to the table and let's just get on and saw this wretched limb off!'

And then everything goes black.

I wake up in bed and as soon as my eyes open Masha starts hitting me again.

'Bitch! Spineless snake! They didn't take it off because of you!'

'Stop that this *instant*, Masha!' shouts Aunty Nadya.

Then everything goes black again.

When I come to properly, Olessya's sitting with Masha, holding her, to stop her hitting me, and Aunty Nadya's telling me what happened.

'You fainted. I could just feel your hand shaking and then it went all limp and wet. I thought you'd died.'

'Wish she had. And left me in peace ...'

'Do be *quiet*, Masha ...' She turns back to me. 'I could hear them all saying: "What's happened? What's wrong?" And Professor Popov shouting, "Dasha! Dashinka! Wake up!" So I couldn't help it, I crawled out from under the table and saw your surgeon, Professor Dolyetsky, and Doctor Anokhin and Professor Popov walking out of the door to smoke. They were standing there, sucking away like their lives depended on it in the corridor. I could hear them talking. Professor Dolyetsky said it could only be a reaction you had to the novocaine and that it was strange because you'd had novocaine before, and I was thinking, What's strange is that they don't realize Dasha just fainted from sheer terror.'

'Yeah, fainted like a fat fucking fly in the sun,' says Masha. 'You've ruined all our chances of looking better now, with your lily-livered—'

'*Teekha!* So, then Professor Dolyetsky turns to Anokhin and asks if they should carry on anyway, since you were still breathing, and Anokhin agrees, but then Popov steps in and says, "No, we will not go on with the operation. These are human beings, not rabbits." So you were taken back here.'

'And now we're left with this bloody tree trunk,' Masha shakes our leg, 'and you're the miserable weak worm who hates looking like a freak. You're a fucking freak with or without the fucking leg!'

'Masha! Stop swearing this instant! Have some pity!' Aunty Nadya's holding one of her arms, and Olessya's holding the other to stop her thumping me. 'Have some pity.'

'I'm s-sorry ...' I put my hands over my face. 'I'm s-so, so s-sorry.'

I wish I was strong like Masha, but however hard I try, all the weakness just comes gushing out like a whole sea that never stops pouring and pouring over me and drowning me.

All my strength went to her.

## August 1964

### We hear from Olessya in Novocherkassk and Anokhin says we're one person split in two

We've got a postcard from Olessya. We're sitting reading it on the back steps by the bath house. It's quiet here.

*We can eat peaches and apricots right off the trees here and it's sunny and hot all the time. They even have white bread and fresh eggs and milk.*

'Lucky cow. Hardly ever even seen white bread, and all we get is pickled eggs and powdered milk now,' says Masha.

*The Director is a kind man and the teachers are kind and we are following the school curriculum for a diploma. The kids are fun too and we have a big courtyard and orchard, inside the walls because it's in a pre-revolutionary, really rich, merchant's house. Good thing we're all equal now! We have a side cupboard by our beds we can keep our own stuff in and no one steals it. Well, write to me too. Olessya.*

She's in the boarding school for Defectives in the South of Russia. She was here in SNIP for six whole months and Galina Petrovna said that she learnt more in that time than most children learnt in four years and she couldn't bear to send her back to the orphanage for Uneducables. So she got her into this school in Novocherkassk. Turns out Lydia Mikhailovna knows the Director.

'Lucky Olessya. She escaped,' says Masha and chews the end of the postcard. I want to hold it, but Masha won't let me. I sort of think I'd get the smell of peaches and milk from it.

'Bloody blue stamps,' goes on Masha miserably. 'Property of SNIP. Sheets, towels, curtains, pyjamas, socks, tin cups, plates, soles of our shoes. Can't believe they don't just stamp it on our foreheads.'

'Are we really Property of SNIP, though? Are we going to stay here forever, Mashinka?'

'No fucking way. Once we denounce the Administrator, we'll be recognized, and then we'll be let out to work for the Communist cause.'

'But we keep trying to denounce her and don't find anything. Are you sure she's an American agent?'

'Course she is, idiot. She looks like all the capitalists in the posters with their mean narrow eyes and low foreheads and long noses. Course she is.'

'But they're all men in top hats. With cigars.'

'She's still a capitalist, clearly, and we'll get her. Then we'll be Heroes of the Soviet Union. You just wait.'

Masha always thinks everything is going to work out for the best if you just try hard enough.

Aunty Nadya told us that when Anokhin went to Amerika he met two boy twins our age, who are just like us except they're being exploited by their imperialist parents and put on show for money in cheap circuses and given no education. Not even any education at all. I don't know why they weren't killed, like all the other Defectives in Amerika. I suppose it's because they were money makers. They can't even read or write, he says, they just have to stand on stages for people who pay a green dollar. Aunty Nadya said Anokhin thought they should be rescued and brought to the Soviet Union and that we ought to marry them and see what sort of children we had together. Masha says she's not marrying freaks, thank you very much.

Just because Anokhin wants more baby freaks to put under his microscope.

'When's our next mission then?' I ask, looking out of the window. 'In denouncing her?'

'Tomorrow, 1400 hours. Lydia Mikhailovna's office. She's meeting with the Administrator. She might give something away, we've got to be alert.'

It's summer, so SNIP is almost empty for three months. A lot of the staff are at their dachas, including Lydia Mikhailovna's secretary, so we sneak in at 13:30 and hide behind her solid desk in the anteroom. We can hear everything from there, even if they close the door to Lydia Mikhailovna's office.

'Got the notepad?'

She knows I have.

'Yes. Got the notepad.'

We're just starting to get cramp when Lydia Mikhailovna walks in, but she's with Aunty Nadya, not the Administrator.

'I confess I have no idea what all this is about, Nadya,' she's saying as they tap past us. I can see their shoes. 'It's all rather unconventional, to say the least. And with Boris Markovich away it seems very odd that he should be addressing us, behind his back as it were.'

'Comrades! Comrades!' I shrink right back into the wall like a snail going into its shell. It's him! Doctor Anokhin. Masha looks at me all pop-eyed and puts her fist in her mouth. They'll kill us if they find us here. But if they shut the door to the office we can sneak out. Please, please shut the door …

'No, no, Pyotr Kuzmich, don't shut the door, there's no air in Moscow in summer,' says Lydia Mikhailovna.

*Fuck!* mouths Masha.

'So, thank you so much, Lydia Mikhailovna, for taking the time to see me,' he says, 'and yes, you too, Nadya.' We can hear scraping chairs but can't see anything.

'Not at all, Pyotr Kuzmich. An honour as always.' That's Mikhailovna.

'So really I just wanted to discuss our girls, our two little berries – very fond of them I am too, as you know. If you're an aunty to them, Nadya, then I feel like their uncle. Yes, indeed, an uncle and aunty. Family.'

Masha looks at me and sticks her finger down her throat. She hates him. I don't like him much either. I get cold every time he comes near us with his chocolatey smell.

'As you know, the girls are a complete mystery to scientists around the world in that they have identical genes and identical upbringings, but frankly speaking have two totally disparate characters.' He coughs but no one says anything. I'm hardly breathing at all. My foot itches but I can't move a centimetre. They'll hear. I don't know what disparate means. Desperate? 'And this is not an, um, conscious decision of theirs as I have observed them from birth and this dissimilarity in character, believe me, was clear from within hours of birth. Hours.'

I frown. He was there at our birth? He's not *actually* our uncle, is he? Or did he really create us? I don't understand a thing. I wish I was back in bed.

'So yes, I'm not sure if you're aware of this new research, fascinating really, into the left and right hemispheres of the brain? It centres on how the dominant hemisphere might actually contribute to differing behavioural patterns. This, ah, theory, is beginning to gain ground in the West and is not, in the strictest Marxist-Leninist sense, acceptable in the Soviet Union since, as we all know, one's character is formed purely by environment and not by genes. Nurture not nature.'

'Of course!' It's Lydia Mikhailovna.

'However, it cannot be denied that here we have two identical sisters, who are biological mirror images of each other, duplicates in every possible way. Except for character. What we believe is, since the egg that produced these twins divided so late, it seems possible that the left and right hemispheres of the one brain split off into two heads contained in the same body. You might be aware of Wolcott-Sperry's experimental split-brain surgery – the severing of the corpus callosum?'

Masha's frowning and I know she's as lost as I am. What on earth's he on about? What egg? We're not chickens. What corpus? And what split head?

'Science fiction, you might say,' he says, 'but this definitive lateralization of the brain function proves that a right-handed person – like Dasha – uses the left-hand side of the brain, which tends to be analytical and logical, making her more serious and thoughtful. Being left-handed, Masha uses the right-hand side of her brain, making her impulsive and emotional. A person who lives for the moment. Left-handers are also historically more prone to violence, and we all know about the beatings she gives Dasha. Now then. We know that the right side of Masha's brain is larger than her left and vice versa in Dasha. We know that Masha's heart has abnormal cardiac rotation to the right, while Dasha's has correct alignment on the left, presenting us with reversal in heart situs. Yes? Yes? When first taught to write, Masha wrote in a back-to-front mirror-image script with her left hand, until forced to use her right. So it almost seems that the two hemispheres of the one brain have actually divided out within a single body – each hemisphere controlling half that body!'

There's a longish pause.

'Are you suggesting that Masha and Dasha are in fact one person? One brain somehow split into two?' says Lydia Mikhailovna.

'Yes, yes! Exactly. Now, just picture the conflict!'

'I don't need to picture it, Pyotr Kuzmich,' she goes on. I can hear a chair scraping and my heart nearly stops. Is she getting up and coming out? I squeeze into the wall. 'I have it staring me in the face every day. I don't know about all these hemisphere theories, all I know is that it's hideous to even think about what it must be like for Dasha to live with Masha. Truly hideous. Masha, who is domineering, selfish, childish, abusive and frankly of far inferior intelligence.'

I bite my lip. I can feel Masha tensing all through me. She still has her fist in her mouth.

'Just imagine,' Lydia Mikhailovna goes on, and I'm thinking: Please stop! Stop! It's not true, you don't know us, Masha's strong and brave. I need her! 'Just imagine … what it would be like to be joined forever, for every minute and second of your life, to someone who cannot and will not empathize with you, or indeed anyone else. Someone who genuinely sees you as a spineless, weak attachment whose only use is to do your bidding night and day. You and I, Pyotr Kuzmich, choose the ones we wish to spend our lives with, and if we are irritated by them, we go into another room to get away. How that poor child stays sane is something I will never fathom. Every moment of her life she must repress her own feelings, suppress her every desire, subjugate herself constantly to an egotistical, self-seeking psychopath!'

I bite my lip so hard I can taste blood. Masha's burning up. If she jumps up and starts yelling, we're done.

'Well now, yes, Lydia Mikhailovna, I can see, from a human point of view, a psychological point of view, Dasha is the one who suffers most. As the logical one she understands their relationship is symbiotic. Certainly, Masha is headstrong and impetuous, so Dasha must be compliant and submissive. But what interests me, as you may have seen from the dissertation, what interests me most, is pain sensitivity.'

'Pain sensitivity?'

'Yes, yes, pain sensitivity. It appears that when an organism suffers constant levels of pain and trauma throughout its early years, then the pain threshold is considerably raised in later years and that organism becomes almost inured to pain. In addition, yes, in addition, the memory of that trauma can in fact be completely wiped out – as we have seen with the twins. Quite remarkable that their recollections of their time in the Paediatric Institute are so very selective – indeed, they seem to have no recall at all of the daily um … procedures.'

'I'm afraid we have no knowledge of your experiments either. Having not been informed of them – which I must say, I view as an omission,' says Lydia Mikhailovna coldly. Masha's still furious. She's taken her fist out of her mouth and now both of them are balled up stiffly at her sides like hand grenades about to go off. 'And we have not had access to the dissertation, as I believe it is kept at Red Level in the Academy of Medical Sciences. I did make enquiries.'

'Ah, of course, of course, our red, secret classification … well, well, never mind. Suffice to say that they both have a remarkably high pain threshold. The appendicitis incident, where Dasha scarcely complained despite the appendix having burst … And the helmets, yes, in fact one of my students tried out the neuro-helmets and almost flew through the roof, yet the girls are very tolerant of them. Very tolerant indeed.'

'I believe it's more the anticipation of pain, Pyotr Kuzmich, which causes Dasha's suffering.' It's Aunty Nadya. 'Rather than the suffering itself.'

'Well yes, Nadya, yes, she's a sensitive soul in that way, our Dashinka. However, let's get down to business. The reason I'm here is because my team would like to conduct a few more, aaah, procedures to test their pain sensitivity now they are young adults.'

I gulp and look at Masha. She's biting her thumb. What procedures? What does he mean?

'It would only take a few weeks, perhaps just a week, a matter of a scratch with a scalpel here and there, electric shocks, burning and freezing – you know, very similar to what we did to them back in the Paediatric Institute – and then we could monitor their … aah … levels of discomfort as teens. Hmm? As compared to early childhood?'

Lydia Mikhailovna puts on her quiet, icy voice.

'Am I to understand that these electric shocks and freezing and … and burning, were the norm for them in the Paediatric Institute?'

There's a slight pause.

'Well, not norm, of course,' he says eventually. 'But that was certainly part of the research that we would like to follow on with now. For comparison, you understand.'

Masha and me look at each other.

'We would have to consult with Professor Popov,' says Lydia Mikhailovna.

'*Aaakh*, Popov! The man is not a true scientist, Lydia Mikhailovna! Forgive me, but we Soviets have just stepped in to prevent a Third World War. Great times demand great feats. We cannot afford to give way to bourgeois sentimentality and fallibility. No, we must not be accused of—'

'But, Pyotr Kuzmich!' Aunty Nadya speaks up, sounding a bit scared, but also upset. 'Could you not conduct these experiments on your dogs?'

'Dogs, Nadya, are rarely born conjoined, and cannot rate pain on a scale of 1 to 5. We require a pain-threshold experiment with human conjoined twins. These are the only living pair in the Soviet Union.'

I frown. Conjoined? What's conjoined mean? I've never heard that word before.

'But these are children, Pyotr Kuzmich … little girls,' goes on Aunty Nadya.

'Not exactly children, are they, Nadya? Not real children? And I fear your love for them is clouding your reason and the aims of Soviet science—'

'You're wrong. I don't love them,' she says, clear as anything. 'They're not my own children, are they? Not my own flesh and blood. I pity them. I just feel pity for them. As I do to all my patients. Even scientists should feel pity, Pyotr Kuzmich.'

We stay sitting there for a bit after they've all gone and after we've heard their feet tapping off down the corridor. We just sit there, not talking.

'See,' says Masha, after a bit. 'Told you she didn't love us. You and your stupid mummies and aunties.'

'Yes, Masha.'

'If she doesn't need us, we don't need her.'

'No, Masha.'

'Psychopath, am I?'

'No, no, Masha. That's just Lydia Mikhailovna being crazy. She doesn't understand.'

'Inferior intelligence, am I?'

'No, Masha, no, no, you're the boss. They don't understand. I need you. Being tough is better than knowing your times-tables, right?'

She gets up then, and puts her arm round my neck for balance. I put mine round hers for balance too. And we walk right out and back to the ward.

## Olessya writes again and Aunty Nadya adopts someone who isn't us

> *It's so healthy here. They're taking us on holiday by a river to stay in a camp in the woods for three months. We fish and cook our own food on fires and play all the time. You should come for the next school year. Can you?*

We're sitting on our bed playing cat's cradle with our shoelaces, looking at Olessya's postcard for the millionth time. All the kids are hiding under their beds again because Masha told them we had magic powers to split their heads in half, like us, and make them all become our together-twin slaves, with right and left parts of their brains. She has a stick, which she says is a wand, and if she strikes them with it, they'll divide into two, with a lightning bolt – like we were. So it's quiet as anything. It's so odd, to think we we're actually one person divided into two parts of our brain, but I'll try not to think of that. I'll think of the postcard instead.

We're still sitting looking at it when Aunty Nadya comes in.

'I have something to tell you, girls,' she says, looking around at the empty ward with all the little feet sticking out from under the beds. She shakes her head wearily and sits down. 'It's about Vasya – you know, Uncle Vasya's little nephew. I've brought him in a few times, to play.'

'Prick,' says Masha, but makes it sound like she's hiccupping and Aunty Nadya doesn't even notice.

'Well, his parents are alcoholics and they've just been deprived of their parental rights by the militia, which is the same, of course, as Rejection. So he could be sent to an orphanage.'

Masha sits up, interested.

'But we can't let that happen, of course, so we've decided …' she gets up then and goes over to the window and looks out, then looks back at us, all red in the face '… we've decided to adopt him. Our little Vasinka.'

When she says that, I go all hot and then all cold and then hot again, I can feel it. I've hoped every day for eight years that she'd take us home, like she took Uncle Vasya home. I'd hoped she'd adopt *us*. All we State kids want, every minute of every day, is to be adopted into a family. But she's not adopting us. She's adopting a Healthy boy. And he's not even her own flesh and blood, either. He's Uncle Vasya's flesh and blood. She's adopting someone else. I feel that stupid hard ball of sadness, which is what makes me cry, pushing up from my chest to my throat. I won't cry.

'Prick,' says Masha again, louder. And this time Aunty Nadya hears, but doesn't say anything.

'I know that you always wanted me to adopt you, girls.' She comes back to the bed, sits down again and goes to pat my hand, all apologetic and still flushed in the face, but I take it away and rub my nose. I take a deep breath to force the ball back down. 'I couldn't, you see. It's difficult to explain, but with all the red tape and bureaucracy and you being so unusual, and Anokhin and his research, you know … You need to be hidden away, not live in a normal flat to go wherever you please …'

'Blood is thicker than water,' says Masha, looking up at the ceiling and sniffing.

'Now that's not true. You know I never had children of my own …'

'We know that, all right.' Masha takes the shoelaces we were playing with and wraps them tight round her fingers like she's strangling them.

'It's just … Little Vasya would be helpless without us … he hasn't got a patron like Doctor Anokhin. So I'll bring him in to visit then, shall I? You'll be like his sisters now.'

Masha pulls the laces even tighter, and knots them viciously.

'Yes,' she hisses. 'Bring him in. You just bring him on in to his big sisters.'

So that's that.

When she's gone and I've finished crying, we go outside to sit on the tail end of a lorry in the back yard.

'Right. Fuck it. We're out of here,' says Masha.

'How do you mean?'

'We'll go and ask Professor Popov to let us go to Olessya's school in Novocherkassk.'

'He'll never let us.'

'How do you know? You can't eat honey 'til you've smoked out the bees.'

'But we've already tried asking people, haven't we? We've tried. Galina Petrovna just cried. And Aunty Nadya said over her dead body, and Lydia Mikhailovna told us never to speak of it again. We can't go to Professor Popov … can we, Masha?'

'Course we can. Haven't smoked the last of the little buggers out yet, have we?'

'Lydia Mikhailovna will kill us. So will Aunty Nadya.'

'Fuck them. Let's think about us. I'm not sitting around waiting for our *yobinny* pain-threshold week, even if you are. And how many more years of cabbage soup on Monday, fish soup on Tuesday and living life in pyjamas can we stick?'

'Yes.' I swing my leg, thinking about it, and she does too. So we sit there swinging our legs. 'And if we don't get a diploma,' I say, after a bit, 'I can't be a doctor.'

The lorry driver walks up.

'Want a lift to the meat factory, Mashdash?'

'*Nyetooshki!* You'd bring us back as sausages, Ivan Ivanovich!' laughs Masha.

'Don't worry, no one would eat them – too tough!' He laughs too and climbs into the cab.

We hop off and start weaving round the skips to the back door. 'And if we don't go to school, I can't be a lorry driver going all over Siberia,' says Masha. 'We'll make an appointment when he gets back. You can do the talking.'

## Professor Popov gives us a talk

Professor Popov sits down on the edge of his horse-hair sofa with us and gives us each a boiled sweet. I pop mine in straight away before Masha can take it. I suck on it slowly, wondering if his bulging eyes would come off with his glasses? I've never seen him without them.

'Well, girls. This is an unexpected audience. To what do I owe the honour?'

I think he's asking us why we're here so I just start talking quickly.

'We want to go to a p-proper school, B-Boris Markovich, so we can get a d-diploma and learn a profession and work to build C-Communism like everyone else.'

'Well, well, well!' He looks from me to Masha and then back again. 'A noble desire, indeed. And whose idea was this, pray? Hmm?' He looks at Masha, but she's twiddling with the button on our pyjamas and looking up at the ceiling. 'The problem with you two is that one can never take you aside, Dasha, to get to the truth … One never knows if young Masha here is the instigator and you simply the reluctant mouthpiece?'

I don't know what he's saying. He talks all complicated.

'Umm … the truth?' I say.

'Yes. The truth. Do you really want to leave us, Dasha? Listen to me. Is that what you want?' He leans right forward and looks straight into my eyes.

'Oh yes! Yes! I want to get an education m-more than anything in the whole wide world! I want to g-go to school and be t-taught.'

'Hmm … Well, in that case I shall call Konstantin Semyonovich, the Director, a good kind man whose own son is an invalid. I know him, as does Lydia Mikhailovna, personally.'

'*Ooraaah!*' Masha jumps up and down on the sofa, making Professor Popov bounce, and we all laugh like mad.

'Well, let's not count our piglets 'til they're in the pot, but I think this is as good a time as any. As you know, we have another new General Secretary now and times might perhaps be changing after our little … ah … post-Stalin thaw.' He looks out of the window across the room for ages and ages, and we're just wondering if he's forgotten us or has gone to sleep with his eyes open when he says: 'As it happens, I was thinking of moving on myself now. I shall be stepping down. And the new Director here … well, suffice to say that he knows Soldatyenko, the

Deputy Minister of Social Protection, in person and it seems that word is getting out around town about you two little bed-bugs. Yes. Word is getting out and the rumours are growing. The crowds around the perimeter fence here are as thick as ever, and yes, Comrade Soldatyenko is not a happy man and would be quite content to have you both disappear like a piece of fluff.' He holds the palm of his hand out and blows on it. 'Yes, and a Deputy Minister is more important, I'm afraid, than a Professor. Or even … someone with an international reputation like our friend Anokhin. Hmm.'

He gets up with a massive sigh and pours himself a small glass of cognac before flopping down in his own armchair. 'Yes, girls, yes, I shall be going too. I've planted enough bushes in our grounds here, and now I shall plant them at my dacha instead. We're beginning a new, and I hope, exciting, era of Socialism. An era of communal leadership, hope and change. We old guard can take our leave and hand over the banner to the new …'

Masha rolls her eyes. He always goes rambling on when he starts on the cognac. We half listen, but we're so happy to be going to school with Olessya where there's peaches and white bread and sunshine that we're both bursting with laughter inside and keep catching each other's eye and trying to stop giggling. Then Masha lets out a massive *pookh* of wind and we laugh out loud, all three of us together.

We're leaving SNIP!

# SCHOOL FOR INVALIDS, NOVOCHERKASSK

# 1964–68

'Khrushchev denounced the cult of Stalin after his death and we have denounced the cult of Khrushchev in his own lifetime.'

Leonid Ilyich Brezhnev, General Secretary of the Communist Party, 1964–82

## Age 14
## August 1964

### Taking the train to our school in Novocherkassk

We're on the train, a great big, steaming green locomotive!

'No you don't, my beauty! You sit right here and don't budge a centimetre,' says Aunty Nadya, grabbing Masha's shirt to stop her climbing up to the top bunk. She's taking us to the school in Novocherkassk to settle us in. 'I'll go and get our bags from the corridor.'

'C'mon, you, quick,' says Masha, as soon as Aunty Nadya's squeezed out of the door, and she starts climbing the ladder to the top bunk. But the train starts off with a massive jolt, throwing me backwards, and when Aunty Nadya comes back in she finds Masha holding on to the top rung and me swinging around upside down, trying to catch on to something.

'Well, this is a fine start! Almost killed yourselves before we leave the station.' She grabs me and shoves us crossly into the bottom bunk.

'I didn't wave goodbye to Stepan Yakovlich!' shouts Masha, pressing her nose to the window. 'Where is he? I want to wave goodbye!'

'He's long gone. You should have thanked him for giving you that piggyback along the station.'

'That was so healthy! No one noticed us at all,' I say, pressing my nose to the window too. 'I want a piggyback all my life through, then we can see the whole world.'

'Let's just get to Novocherkassk in one piece first, shall we …' She looks like she's grumpy as she packs our bags away. But she's not. She's excited too, I can tell.

We wave at everyone on the platform, but no one waves back. They're all too busy. Then we're out of the Yaroslavsky Station and going past rows and rows of housing blocks with wildflowers springing up everywhere, and then, a bit further along, there's factories with red banners shouting *Forward to More Feats of Labour!* Or: *Unity and Strength of Labour Towards Communism!* I can't even read them all, there's so many and they're going past so quickly. Then we're outside Moscow for the first time ever, and there are all these little log cabins painted in different colours with cows in the yard, real live cows, and hens and ducks and wood piles and …

'Look!' shouts Masha. 'A horse and cart! I'm going to drive a horse and cart and work on a collective farm when I graduate.'

'You said ten minutes ago you were going to be a locomotive driver,' sniffs Aunty Nadya, unpacking pickled cucumbers and dried fish from some newspaper. I don't say anything, but I still want to be a doctor.

'I am!' shouts Masha. 'I'm going to be both. I'm going to keep changing jobs all over the place.'

I look back out at Russia. I thought it would be more like the mural in the Room of Relaxation with fields of corn and mountains and lakes and combine harvesters and peasants in headscarves in the fields, but it's all flat as anything and it's just grass.

And most of the time, there's trees along the tracks, so you can't see behind them anyway. Every time we stop at a little station we wave like mad out of the window at the fat women selling boiled potatoes or apples or salted lard from metal buckets, but they don't wave back either. They're only interested in trying to sell stuff. Me and Masha play a game to see who can see the bust of Lenin at the station first. Ten points for Lenin and one hundred for Stalin and five points for a painting or mosaic of Brezhnev.

When it gets to night time, Aunty Nadya puts us to bed. Masha gets to have her head at the window end and I'm at the foot of the bed. Aunty Nadya snores in the bunk above, even louder than the train going *klyak-brr-klyak* along the tracks, rocking us like babies. I love trains. I could stay on one forever.

Next morning we're coming up to our station. It's August so it's hot and sunny and we're both sweating buckets. Aunty Nadya told us that Anokhin was Categorically Against us being taken away from Moscow because he said we'd die in two minutes in the sub-tropical climate. But Soldatyenko, the Deputy Minister, is more important even than him. And Soldatyenko didn't want us in Moscow any more. I don't think he cares if we die or not. Masha was pleased as anything that we're so important that a Deputy Minister knows about us, but I'm not sure I was …

'Here we are then, this is our stop. All ready?' Aunty Nadya's got everything packed neatly by the sliding door to our cabin. 'Hair combed? Faces washed? Yes, yes, well let's wait 'til everyone's off and then we'll hop off last. We're being met by a driver from the school.'

The station's packed solid with people. So solid you can't even see the platform. The platform looks like it's alive with people or something, not like any of the other ones we passed. There's even children up in all the trees and standing on the walls.

'*Chort!*' Aunty Nadya's looking all black. 'That's really too bad. It really is.'

And then I realize with a bump, which comes just the same time as the train stops, that they've all come to see us. I try to get down under the little table but Masha won't let me, although she realizes too. Aunty Nadya's got all our bags in her hands now and is red in the face and her eyes are bulging; she's saying over and over 'Who can have told them? It really is too bad …' She goes out with the bags into the corridor. In a moment she's back.

'The platform's not long enough, we'll have to jump out on to the rails.'

'N-no, no, no!' I hold on to the table leg.

'You must, Dasha, you must!' She pulls us so hard my slippery hand lets go of the table leg and then she pulls us along the corridor to the open door. The crowds are down on the rails as well as the platform, and everyone's shouting at the passengers: *Where's the Girl with Two Heads?* Aunty Nadya pushes us out of the doorway, but we're both clinging on to either side of it. 'Look! Here's the railway guard,' she says. 'Quick! Jump down and he'll catch you.' I look down. He's in a green uniform with red stripes, shoving everyone aside and holding his arms up.

'Jump!' he says. 'Jump!'

It's miles down and they've seen us now, so there's all this shouting and mad pushing. I can't do it, I can't.

'You *must* jump!' It's Aunty Nadya behind us, trying to pull our fingers off the door. 'If you don't we'll end up in Rostov – you must!'

I close my eyes and we both let go at the same time and jump. His cap's knocked off as he staggers back but he grips us hard, and starts pushing through everyone on the platform. I've got my head in his collar and my eyes squeezed tight shut still, and everyone's battering against me, and I can hear Aunty Nadya shouting: 'Comrades! Comrades! Please! Please! Let them through!' And the crowd shouting: 'There it is! Look! Look!' Then we're out of the station and a car door opens and we're thrown in the back. Aunty Nadya puts her coat over us, slams the door on everyone and we drive away.

## The kids in school hate us, but Mashinka wins them around

'Well, I do apologize, Nadezhda Fyodorovna, I do regret it, we did swear the staff to secrecy, but you know how gossip flies in these small provincial towns … News like that, well, it's like trying to draw water in a sieve.'

We're sitting in the corner on a narrow, metal-framed bed in our dorm. It's empty because the kids are all out somewhere, but I can't hear them and we didn't see them when we came through the big double gates into the courtyard. The head teacher, Vera Stepanovna, told us they were out singing in the choir or something, when she brought us up the wooden staircase. She's standing with Aunty Nadya, who's still shaking her head.

'Was it really necessary to inform the staff? Surely they're used to deformity?' They're speaking in low voices, but we can hear everything. Aunty Nadya knows we've got hearing like a bat.

'I'm afraid it was Konstantin Semyonovich, the Director, who decided to hold a meeting for all the pupils and staff to explain …'

'Pupils as well?! *Aaakh!*'

'Yes, yes, pupils too, he just wanted to tell them that though the girls may be ah … together … they should be given the same respect and—'

'Of course they should!' interrupts Aunty Nadya crossly. 'Does that really need explaining in a school like this?'

Vera Stepanovna undoes a button on her collar. She's wearing a shiny, grey suit that looks like the pearly buttons are going to pop off.

'Yes, yes, perhaps it was a mistake, I think it must have been the kitchen staff ...' Masha rolls her eyes. (Telling kitchen staff a secret is like handing them a megaphone and a platform.) 'The worst thing,' she goes on 'is that the children, who are already upset that our school is nicknamed the Cripple Can, in town, now think that with ...' she starts whispering, 'so-called *freaks* coming here, the school will be turned into a circus. There are dozens of townspeople outside the gates as we speak.'

'What exactly are you saying?'

'Um ... the children might not be too ... welcoming ... just to start with. Although Olessya has, of course, told them all about them ... Poor Olessya. She's in the Sanatorium at the moment with pneumonia, but we hope for the best ... Well,' she raises her voice then, looks over to us, beaming, and shouts as if we're deaf or something, 'I'll be off, girls. You make yourselves comfortable!'

Aunty Nadya comes over to say the car's waiting to take her to her lodgings in town. She's going to stay here in Novocherkassk for a few weeks to make sure we have everything we need. She kisses us goodbye quickly, then stomps out.

Masha thumps the pillow. 'Olessya's sick? That's all we fucking need.'

'What did she mean, she "hopes for the best"? Will she be all right? Do you think we can contact her?'

'In the San? No chance, she'll be in quarantine a month.'

There are footsteps on the stairs and we look up as the other girls come in. They don't even look at us.

'Screw them,' says Masha. 'If they don't need us, we don't need them.' She pulls our blanket over her head and lies down on the pillow. I don't have a pillow at the foot of the bed, so I fold my hands under my head and close my eyes tight to stop the tears squeezing out. I'm worried about Olessya, that's all. I don't care about the girls. I don't care at all. I've got Masha, I have. I've always got Masha.

* * *

Next morning the kids get washed and dressed and go off to their lessons, still not looking at us, and we're taken down to a little classroom for a test to see which class we should go in.

I'm feeling a bit dizzy. Everything smells different. Everything looks different. We went to breakfast in the food hall, but everyone sat away from us like we stink or something. I hoped we'd get a boiled egg at least, like Olessya said, a real fresh egg instead of powdered eggs, but it was just buckwheat porridge with water and salt.

'Right, girls. I've made this board, you see, to put between you, so we can have no copying.'

'*Chort!*' says Masha under her breath. She always copies from me.

'Here's the test. Nothing too daunting. I do understand you've only had a primary education. Off you go.'

I get writing. It's not too hard; basic maths and Russian grammar. Our elbows clash as we write. Seems odd if we really did split in two from one person, like Anokhin said, that we use our inside arms not our outside ones. Masha keeps sucking her pencil and looking up in the air. She finishes way before me.

Next morning we get black bread (not white) and lard (not butter) and are taken to the 8th form classroom of fourteen- to fifteen-year-olds like us. None of them even look up. They're just ignoring us. Vera Stepanovna's at the front by the blackboard. We slip into a desk right at the back, and Masha starts dipping her fingers in the inkwell and flicking ink at me, which makes me really cross as I'll never get it off my blouse.

'This is Masha and Dasha, girls and boys, I'm sure you're all acquainted …' No one says anything or looks round. 'Yes, well now, I have just had the results of your test back, girls,' she flaps our test papers at us, 'and I'm afraid we have a problem. You, Dasha, attained good marks, so in theory should go in the 7th form; but you, Masha, need a lot more catching up on the four years you've both missed, and should really go down into the 5th form.'

There's some titters round the class.

'That's no problem, Vera Stepanovna,' says Masha, sticking her inky hand up. You can put us both in the 7th form and knock a hole between the two classes. Then I'll just poke my head through into the other one!' The kids turn round to look at her then and start laughing a bit, in a nice way, not a nasty way.

Vera Stepanovna raps her ruler on the desk, but she sort of smiles too.

'I think we can find a better compromise than that, Masha. You shall both go into the 6th form. I might as well take you there now. You children sit quietly and read your text.' Some of them sneak looks at us as we walk out, but they're not unkind. Just interested.

The 6th form looks the same as the 8th form, but the kids are younger. The only free desk is at the front, so we have to walk right through the classroom and sit down. It's dark in here. I'm glad. There's no electricity or hot water in the school in summer. There's this bright red slogan above the blackboard saying *Indoctrinate the Next Generation into the Collective Way of Life!* But everything else is kind of dim and brown.

'So, yes, where were we …' says our history teacher, Irina Konstantinovna, once Vera Stepanovna has gone. She's all jittery and jumpy, and looking everywhere except at us as Masha clatters around looking for pencils in the desk. The teacher's fat and has got purple hair. She's scared stiff of us. We can always tell when new people are scared stiff. Some aren't, like the head teacher and the kids, of course, but some are. She turns to write on the blackboard, but keeps dropping the chalk because her hands are trembling.

'So, yes, yes,' she says, turning back to us. 'Ninochka, my little sunbeam.' She points at a pretty girl with blonde curls. 'If you could just recap for the er … newcomers … yes, what have we learnt in the last ten minutes, my little sunbeam …'

'Oooh, if she's your little sunbeam, I'll be your little raincloud, Irina Konstantinovna?' Masha's waving her hand in the air and the teacher looks at us for the first time. 'You're going to need a raincloud in today's sunshine, not a sunbeam.' Masha always knows how to make people who first meet us see we're just two ordinary kids. The others laugh and I look round at them a bit, for the first time, to see what they're like, and there's this boy with dark eyes looking right at me. He's not even looking at Masha at all. And he's not laughing like the others.

Then the blonde sunbeam starts talking about how they've been taking notes on the Splendid Surgery of the Great October Revolution. I'm not big into surgery at the moment, whatever sort, but I suppose they're talking about amputating the Tsar's family and bourgeois elements and all that. She's going on about Bubnov, Bukharin and Berzin, and I'm taking notes, like I know who they are, but I don't. Not yet.

When the bell goes for the end of the lesson, we get up to go out, and the boy with the dark eyes looks right at me and winks, and I blush. Masha feels me flush and looks back at me, frowning.

'Hey? What's wrong with *you*?'

'Nothing's wrong, Mash. Nothing's wrong at all.'

## September 1964

### We make some friends in school

I screw my eyes up tight and listen. It's morning and Masha's still asleep. I do it every morning because I'm afraid, if I open them, I'll be back in SNIP and not here, in the school. Everyone's nice to us now they've got to know us. We've been here for six weeks, but I still can't believe my luck. When Aunty Nadya realized we were happy and settled in, she went back to Moscow. Back to her little Vasinka, as Masha said. But actually, she seemed even more upset to be leaving us than we were. She said she'd write and come on visits.

The bell goes then. It's the loudest clanging in the world and everyone wakes at once. I open my eyes and sit up. Masha puts her pillow over her head.

'Dashinkaaaa.'

It's Little Lyuda from the bed next to ours. We've pushed them together, so we can tuck our legs under her blanket, otherwise they just hang over the side of our narrow bed and our feet freeze. She hops up next to me. She's pale as a flea and jumps like one too.

'Dashinkaaaa … it's your turn on the rota for the bathchair today, isn't it? Can I sit on your lap, can I? I get bashed to pieces on the Crocodiles.' The Crocodiles are these green wheelbarrows that the nannies take kids who can't walk in, from lesson to lesson. There's only one proper bathchair; it's so healthy – just like Uncle Vasya's. Masha's the fastest in school at going down the ramps.

'Yes. Yes, you c-can!' I say and glance quickly at Masha. I don't think she'll mind.

I hug myself. It's our bathchair day and Olessya's coming out of San too. This is the best day ever.

'Mwaaah,' says Masha, throwing the pillow off and shivering because it gets so cold at nights, even though the days are warm. 'I'm not getting up.'

She always says this, every morning, so I just pull her out of bed then, and we run down to the washroom as fast as we can.

'How are we supposed to wash our fucking nappy in icy-cold water,' she says, balancing us by leaning against the wall, while I scrub the nappy out like mad in the sink. 'It makes our hands raw red.'

'*My* hands, you mean.'

She yawns.

'Same thing. And that soap's black as coal.'

'It's still soap.'

'And this one's still damp from last night,' she says, poking the day-nappy I washed last night. (It's just a big brown rag really that we knot round us.) 'What's the use of hanging them out to dry on the pipes when the pipes aren't hot? You should wring them out more.'

'I'm wringing as hard as I can, Mash,' I say, squeezing the last drops out.

'C'mon, c'mon,' she says crossly. 'Or we'll be late for breakfast.'

We hang it up, get dressed, and run up the stairs to jump into the bathchair, with its three wheels and paddles to push us along. Little Lyuda hops into our lap and we scoot across the courtyard so fast the townspeople by the gates don't even see us.

'*Oooraah!* White bread and cheese!' shouts Masha as we sit down at the long table.

'Cheeeese!' go all the kids like little monkeys. Everyone loves Masha now.

'Learnt the poem then?' Slava, the boy who winked at me on our first day, is sitting opposite us. We're the two top kids in the class, him and me, I'm learning really quickly. He gets better marks, but I'm catching up. He's looking at me when he asks, but Masha replies, 'We only have to learn one between us, thank God, so she was up all night reciting it like a sheep bleating in a field.'

I've got all my bread in my mouth so that Masha doesn't take it from me. I can't talk, so she slaps me on the back, trying to get me to spit it all out in front of him. She knows I like him. She likes him too, he's funny, but she doesn't like him the way I do. He has this nice brown skin, even now, in September, and dark floppy hair. But mostly he just has this way of looking at me, like he's looking inside my head.

'What are you reciting?' I ask him, swallowing down the bread.

'Boris Pasternak's "February".'

'I thought he was anti-Soviet now?' says Valya, the girl sitting next to him. Valya's pretty and clever, but she's really mean. I don't know why.

Slava shrugs. 'His poetry books are still in the library.'

'You'd better learn them *all* off by heart then, because they won't be for long,' says Valya. 'And I don't think he's a good writer at all. I don't think you should be reciting that. Does Vera Stepanovna know?' Slava shrugs again. I bite my lip. Valya's an Activist. She's always telling on anyone who says or does anything anti-Soviet. I don't like her much. I like everyone else, but just not Valya. Not much, anyway.

'Shut it, bitch!' says Masha, pushing her plate away. 'Peanut here can recite what he likes. Well, c'mon, shipwreck, let's get back into that bathchair.'

I can hear Valya saying in a nasty, shouty sort of voice as we're leaving '... and how did those two get on the bathchair rota when they can run like rabbits?'

And then I think I hear Slava saying, 'Masha always finds her place in the sun.'

## October 1964

### Olessya comes out of the San, and tells us about the school

'Olessya!' we both squeal as we see her being let through the gates.

We're sitting in the corner, on the steps, with Sunny Nina next to us and Little Lyuda on our lap. Olessya comes over and hugs and kisses us, and we hug and kiss her, and we're all of us laughing all over the place.

'Are you b-better?' I ask. 'You were in there forever.'

'We thought they'd married you off to one of the doctors,' says Masha, grinning.

'They keep you in for ages after you're well,' says Olessya. 'I was going crazy with boredom. Come on, let's go sit behind the laundry room and you can tell me everything.' Masha tips Lyuda off our lap, then pushes Sunny Nina off the steps in a friendly sort of way, and we paddle off in our bathchair.

'Can't believe you're actually here!' says Olessya, as we squeeze in behind the hut they do the laundry in. It's the only place you can sit and no one can see you. It's warm and dusty, even though it's October now. It hardly ever rains in Novocherkassk. Masha's squashed me against the fence, so Olessya has to sit next to her, not me.

'How come they let you two leave SNIP?'

'The Minister of Social … Social … whatever-it-is, said we had to go because everyone in Moscow had got to hear of us …' says Masha, all excited.

'… Deputy Minister of Social P-Protection …' I put in.

'No one else wanted us to leave, not Aunty Nadya or Mikhailovna or Anokhin, but Popov did. He's gone too from SNIP now. Retired. He knows the School Director here, but we haven't seen him yet …'

'No, he goes off to lots of Party meetings and gets funding,' says Olessya.

I wish I could snuggle up to Olessya, like Masha is. Her hair's grown even thicker and blacker and her eyelashes have too. She looks so beautiful. I wonder if she likes Slava, or if he likes her? Probably. They're both really clever. I'd just like to snuggle with anyone actually. Masha and I are too far apart to do that.

'Still got a knife under there?' asks Masha, pointing to her trolley.

'*Nyetooshki!* Don't need it here. The kids are all nice.'

'Valya, the Ice Queen's not nice.'

'She's just bitter, Masha, that's what it is. She was a Healthy up until two years ago. She swung on an electric wire and lost both her arms, so she was sent here. She can't accept that she's in with the Defectives, and she's always going to be stared at by the Healthies, and what's worse is that, now, she can't even marry one.'

'Is she a Reject?' asks Masha. I think she sort of hopes she is.

'Yeah. Her parents rejected her when she lost her arms. She's got two healthy sisters. It was too far for them to come and visit …'

'And what about her precious Slava?' says Masha, jerking her thumb at me.

'Precious?' Olessya looks at me in surprise.

'Not *precious*, that's just Masha being … Masha. We're b-both top of the class is all.'

'Teachers' pets,' says Masha, and rolls her eyes.

'Slava, yeah, he's a Congenital, but he's not a Reject. His mum visits almost every month, he's a family kid, they bring him a food parcel of milk and eggs and fruit. His family live in a village. He always shares his food though, he's nice like that. He's really nice. I like him.'

I bite my lip. Of course she likes him … We get food parcels too, from Aunty Nadya. She sends us little tins of cod livers and boiled sweets from Moscow. There's no sweets at all in Novocherkassk, but Masha doesn't share anything. She just unwraps them and pops them in her mouth when we're in the dorm and goes *mmmmm* as she sucks them, so everyone can hear. She sometimes gives me one though.

'Yeah, and his dad comes on a motorbike, with his brother Grisha in a sidecar. All the girls here are in love with Grisha. You should see them swooning around the courtyard when he's here, like dead flies on a windowsill …' she laughs. I laugh too, but secretly I bet Grisha's not half as handsome as Slava. I wouldn't swoon over Grisha. 'The teachers are all nice,' Olessya goes on. 'Vera Stepanovna's pretty strict, but she's honest. She makes sure all the State funds go where they should and aren't stolen along the way. But the best teacher of all is Valentina Alexandrovna. She's young and she only came last year. She's so healthy! She wants every one of us to be the best. The Best of the Best in the Best of All Possible Worlds, as she says!'

The bell clangs for afternoon lessons.

'I f-forgot to ask – what class are you in?' I say as we squeeze ourselves back out into the courtyard.

'I'm in class 7, how about you?'

'Class 6,' I say, and it's stupid but I feel all good and warm inside that she's not in our class, even though I really like her. I *should* want her to be in our class, but actually I don't. 'Yeah, we're in Class 6,' I say. 'With Sunny Nina and Little Lyuda. And Slava.'

## We get drunk with Petya and Slava, who likes my hair

It's evening time and we should be in the dorm, but we've sneaked out to smoke papirosas and get drunk. There's four of us hiding behind the cobbler's workshop in the school yard.

'Go on,' says Petya. He's in year 7 with Olessya, but he likes Masha because he says she's dirty (although she's not, we both wash all the time with soap. Masha says I scrub us both so much there'll be nothing left of us by the time we're twenty).

'Take a drag, go on, quick,' says Petya. Masha sucks on the papirosa she's found on the ground here. It's got lipstick on its cardboard end, so it must be from one of the kitchen staff. The teachers don't smoke because it's not cultural. Slava's here with us, so it must be all right, but we might get caught. My heart's banging around like a drum. Petya kissed Masha on the cheek a week ago and she slapped him. But now he's got a bottle of cheap wine because he wants to kiss her some more. He bribed Aunty Klava from the kitchen to get it. He's not a Reject and he gets five roubles a month from his family to spend, so he bribed her to get it from the Vegetable Shop in town.

Masha keeps on sucking on the papirosa and coughs like a mad thing, like she's choking to death or something.

'No, no, you've got to suck and then hold it in your mouth, and then slowly breathe it in,' says Petya. 'Go on.' Masha does it again and this time she doesn't cough so much. Petya laughs. 'See? It's easy. Go on, go on.' Masha keeps sucking until I feel all dizzy, and almost fall over backwards. Petya laughs like mad. 'Dasha fell over first! You two are crazy. Fuck – Dasha's such a lightweight, she didn't even take a drag!' He thinks that's the funniest thing ever. Slava laughs too and picks me up by pulling on my arm.

Masha told me that boys go crazy for a kiss. She says that's all they ever think about in their stupid little heads. She says girls can get them to do all sorts of stuff for them, like getting this bottle of wine, if they let them have a bit of *seksy koo koo*. Anyway, it's called Red Sunrise, the wine is – not because it's red, like I thought, but because of the dawn of Communism. Slava and Petya have been drinking it, and Masha's been drinking it too, but when she does, she just throws it straight back up. I won't drink because Aunty Nadya says the Consumption of Alcohol Degrades the Personality. That's what all the slogans say too. Slava's drinking, but then he's a boy, and men need to drink. But women don't.

It's October. Lessons have all finished for the day, but it's still not completely dark. And it's still quite warm. Slava can't stop laughing, and is taking swigs from the wine bottle. And he's looking at me all the time. He really is. He's looking at me *all* the time. It's really stupid, but I keep thinking about him. It's like nothing else matters. It's like everything, like our third leg, and the people outside the gates, and Icy Valya, and even Masha have all been pushed out of my head to make way for all these millions of thoughts about just Slava. How can you even think about one person all the time, and not think any other thoughts hardly at all?

'Go on, Mash, take another swig, get it down you.' Petya shoves the bottle at her and she takes another few gulps. We stand around looking at her and waiting; and then *Khryoosh!* up it comes again. Petya laughs and laughs. 'She keeps throwing up! Hey, wait, wait, think about it … think, think …' He points a finger at his head and then at Slava's head, and then falls back against the wall. 'Think … Masha takes a drag and Dasha falls over. So if Masha can't keep it down, let's get Dasha to *drink!* Right? Right?' He looks around at us, swaying all over the place. Slava's swaying too.

'Great idea!' shouts Masha. 'Get it down! Get it down!' She takes the bottle, grabs one of my pigtails and tips my head back, pushing the bottle into my mouth. I try and shut it, but she's got the neck of the bottle right down my throat and it's going down, all sweet and nice. 'Swallow, swallow!' shouts Masha. I swallow. I shouldn't, but I do.

'More! More!' cheers Petya. '*Davai!* C'mon, Dashinka, get it down! Quick!' Masha's still holding my head back, and forcing the bottle down me so I keep swallowing. It's all right really. It's sweet. Then suddenly, I feel like there's a hand grabbing the back of my neck. Only there's no hand there, even though I look round. And then I start feeling sort of like they're all going into the distance and I can hear them laughing like it's from miles away, and Slava's still looking at me; all I can see are his big black eyes. I'm not me at all.

'*February!*' he says, still looking at me. '*Take up your pen and weep.*'

'Fuck me! Trust Slava to start spouting morbid poetry …' Petya's voice sounds miles away. Miles and miles. Petya takes the bottle off Masha and lifts it to his mouth again.

'*Write of February through your tears while the burning black slush of spring thunders at your feet …*' It's the most beautiful poem in the world. He has the most beautiful voice in the world. Really, really beautiful. *Write through your tears.* I start to cry a bit. I love Pasternak. I love …

'Hey, wrong fucking sister, moron!' Masha slaps Petya's hand off my leg. 'Oooh, wait, it's working, it's working, it's fucking working!' She waves her hands in the air. 'I'm drunk! Whoop whoop! Have some more, Shipwreck!' She gives me the bottle and this time I tip it back and drink it myself.

'Your hair's soft, Dasha, all soft,' says Slava. I don't think the other two can hear him. Just me. He has dimples like Yuri Gagarin, but Slava is a million times better looking than Gagarin. His eyes are shining and they're looking right into mine, so there's only his eyes in all the world. He reaches round Masha to touch my hair.

'Oi! Keep your greasy hands off of her!' Masha slaps his hand. 'She's not a fucking tar barrel that you can get all stuck to her. She's mine, see. All mine.' The bottle's finished. Petya's on the floor and Slava's staring at Masha now, like he wants to slap her back, right across her face. 'C'mon you, c'mon, Sheep,' she says to me in a distant voice. 'Back to the Home Front. Back to the dorm. C'mon. I'm fucking getting out of here. I've fucking had enough. You're mine. All mine.'

And then I think I fall over too …

## Masha decides to cut our hair

We miss our lessons in the morning, saying we're sick, which we are. Sick as dogs. But I don't care a bit because now I know for sure that Slava actually likes me. He kept looking at me all the time, and tried to touch my hair last night. I can't believe it; I just can't believe someone like Slava actually likes me. But he must, mustn't he? Yes. He said my hair was soft. He wasn't touching

Masha's hair; he was touching *mine*, and looking at me. I lie in bed with my hands under my head just thinking over and over about what it would feel like if he kissed me on the cheek – like Petya kissed Masha. And if he kissed me, he'd be my boyfriend, and then maybe we could go to his village and meet his mother. At the weekends. And maybe go on a boat on the pond … or maybe …

'Hey, you!' Masha's sitting up and kicking my leg. 'Get up.'

I manage to get myself up, and sit on the edge of the bed. My head's still going round and round. It's so strange. She opens our side cupboard and takes out some blunt scissors she found in the skip. She's got all sorts of stuff from the skip in there, like bent needles and glue pots and leather cut-offs from the cobbler's workshop. Or old nail varnish which she can't open.

But now she just wants the scissors.

'C'mon.'

'Where are we going, Mash?'

'You'll see.' We go down all the dark corridors because there's still no electricity, and out into the courtyard. She makes for the secret place where we meet Olessya behind the laundry room, but Olessya's not there. No one's there.

'Stand still,' she says, and gives me the scissors. 'You cut my hair off and then I'll cut yours. Cut it short though, like a boy. It gets in the way.' She shoves the scissors into my hand but I just stand staring at her, not understanding a thing. Why? 'Well, go on then, start cutting,' she says, all sharp and sniffy. 'Really short.' I look at the scissors in my hand, as if they're a knife or something, and she's asked me to saw us in half. I can't let her cut off my hair. It's all long and dark and silky, and Masha brushes it for me, or plaits it, and then I plait hers. I love my hair. Slava loves it. I can't.

'*Davai!*' she says angrily. 'Go on!'

I lift my hand and start cutting. *Snip, snip*. With every cut I tell myself over and over that she's right. Masha's always right.

We spend ages washing and brushing it. I don't know what I'd do without Mashinka. *Snip.* It's thanks to her that we're here and not buried in a hospital ward all our lives. *Snip.* It's always getting knotted anyway. *Snip.* I cut right down at the roots, so it's all sticking up. She runs her hand over her head, then nods.

'OK. Now you.' I bow my head as she starts cutting. I watch all my shiny hair fall silently over our feet, and my stupid tears fall silently too, and make it even shinier. When she's finished, she blows in my face but the hair's all stuck to my wet cheeks, so she wipes it off with the palm of her hand, then she wipes my nose with her sleeve. She pushes all our hair under the fence, with the tip of her boot, and we go into the food hall for lunch.

Everyone goes all quiet when we walk in. Olessya opens her mouth and then closes it again. 'What?' says Slava, and shakes his head a bit, like he can't believe his eyes. As if my hair was the only thing he liked about me. And it probably was. 'What ...?' he half asks again.

Masha looks at me quickly, waiting for me to speak. 'It g-got in the way,' I explain. 'So we decided to c-cut it short.'

## Age 15
## Spring 1965

### We see other identical twins and Slava writes an essay about me

It turned out Slava didn't mind at all. He said it showed off my face, neck and ears.

'What about *my* ears, Peanut?' Masha had said. 'If hers are little seashells, what are mine? Sea monsters?'

'Yeah, yours are great big conches, which hear every wicked whisper. Your ears are scary.' They have this banter back and forth, him and Masha. I'm glad, because if she doesn't like someone, we don't go near them, but Slava jokes with her all the time. He still hasn't kissed me, or tried to touch me, and it's spring now. But he looks at me. He looks at me like he's trying to talk to me just through his eyes. Perhaps he doesn't try to do anything more, like kiss me, because he knows that Masha might get angry again, and then we wouldn't be able to hang out together at all. So it's been six months since we got drunk that time, and we haven't got drunk since. Masha started running around with Vanya after that, but he's a Reject. He doesn't have any money for wine.

We're hanging over the wall now, which runs all round the school, looking into a neighbour's back yard where this little girl, Manya, lives. She's only six, but we lie here when it's warm, watching her play, like two salted fish laid out to dry. Manya chatters to us all the time when she comes out, so we're just waiting to see if she'll be out today. She can't see we're Together. She tells us about all these crazy things, like how she has a dragon inside the house, who's a pet but hides in a cupboard, and how the dragon taught her how to do a magic whistle, which brings all the little lizards out of their cracks to listen. She says there's hundreds of them, all different colours and sizes, who come wriggling out when she does this whistle. But when Masha asked her to show us, she said the dragon would burn the house down with fire if she did.

We've both got our cheeks on the warm wall. It's nice to be warm after the winter. There wasn't any snow, but it was colder than in SNIP, because quite a lot of the time the heating or hot water went off so we froze like blue icicles in our bed.

I don't know what Masha's thinking about, I never do – maybe she doesn't think about much at all – but I'm thinking about Slava's essay. I think about that a lot when Masha's not talking or running. It was in our Russian class. We were asked to write an essay called *My Best Friend*. I wrote about Olessya. I wrote that she likes me and understands me, and seems to know things about me I hardly know myself. She knows what I'm thinking when even Masha doesn't. Masha wrote about Vanya, who can run like a rat. She didn't write that he scrumps apples from the neighbours' garden for her, and got bitten on his bottom by their dog once. Everyone thinks he's got rabies now and keeps away. Except Masha. We're not supposed to go over the wall, but Vanya does. When the teacher pointed to Slava, he said his essay was about Dasha Krivoshlyapova. I couldn't believe it, I really couldn't. I think I know it pretty much by heart from that one reading in class.

> *Dasha Krivoshlyapova is my best friend. She is clever and studies very diligently in order to get her school diploma and thus be able to work with all other citizens of the Soviet Union to build Communism. Dasha is not only very bright and hard working, but she is kind and thoughtful too. She irons the pinafores of girls who have no arms. She helps other girls make their beds in her dorm, and she always cleans up after class and wipes the board without being asked. She does everything she can to help anyone. Dasha never has a bad word to say about anybody, and she never quarrels with anyone or gets involved in gossip, denunciations or rumours. This is because I believe she is incapable of being unkind to anyone. Why? Because she always understands how other people feel, whatever that person's situation is, and she sympathizes with them and finds a way to admire and respect them. Dasha Krivoshlyapova is the best person I know. That is why she's my best friend.*

He put his piece of paper down after he'd read it and there was silence in the room. I thought they were all going to laugh, I really did. I thought Masha would be the first to start laughing. But she didn't and they didn't either. After what seemed like ages, they started smiling and nodding and even clapping in the end. That was the best moment of my life. It really was. Slava never actually *says* anything nice to me. Not actually anything nice to my face. Not ever. I still can't believe it. I wanted to ask him if I could keep it, but Masha said that would be stupid, and she's probably right.

I thought Masha might be cross, as it was all about me, but she had three of the boys in our class dedicate their essays to her, and I only had this one. Besides, Masha's just been voted Class Leader and she's been on the Most Popular Pupil of the Week board in the school's Lenin Corner for three weeks in a row. Everyone think she's so funny. And she is.

After the lesson, as we were going out, I said, 'Thanks, Slava,' because I thought I should say something, and he just sort of shrugged.

'Hey, Manya! Cuckoo!' Masha's waving at Manya, who's come out with her little pram, with a dolly in it.

'I've got friends today,' she says proudly. 'I've got friends who are twins like you two. They look just the same. They're Denticles too.'

'What's Denticles?' asks Masha.

'*Foo!* Denticles is when you look the same. Even *I* know that.'

Her mum comes out and shouts at her to stop talking to us. Her mum doesn't look at us, she just goes back in, and then two little girls come out pushing prams too. One each. They follow each other down the grass path, in between the rows of vegetables. One of them stops and takes a pretend bottle out, to feed her dolly, and the other one walks on. I know Masha's thinking the same as me. She thought that Denticles would be twins who were Together like us. They *look* the same as each other. But they've got a whole body each, not a shared one.

They're dressed the same too, like me and Masha. I wonder if they got separated? How can you have two people looking like one person? It's amazing.

I stare and stare at them walking up and down different paths, with their prams.

'Masha, can't we ask someone why we're Together and not apart like them? I mean, ask a grown-up?'

Masha doesn't look at me. 'Why? We just are. You're not going to change anything by asking are you?'

'But don't you want to know? Don't you want to know if loads of people are born Together, or only us? Or is it only one in each country, like Ronnie and Donnie in Amerika? And if it's only us, then why?'

She shrugs and wipes her nose. 'Not going to make us single, is it? Not like them.' She nods at the twins, who are in different parts of the garden now.

I suck my bottom lip while I'm thinking. There are lots of Polio or Palsy or Sclerosis kids, but no other Togethers. The senior kids are all Doing It with each other. I don't really know what 'Doing It' means, to be honest, except it's more than kissing and it's *nyelzya*, but it's the best fun you can ever have. And you can get babies from it. Olessya says Mila was sent off to the San to get rid of her baby and never came back. She didn't know why. Maybe she died.

'But, Mash, don't you want to know if you and me … if you and me can Do It like the others do, and have babies? Can't we ask someone?'

It comes out in a rush because I've been thinking about it loads, but Masha doesn't talk about stuff like that. She thinks boys are much better fun than girls, but only because she runs with them, and swears, and smokes and jokes like they do, and she says girls are gossipy, boring geese like me. I like girls better, mostly. Like Olessya and Little Lyuda and Sunny Nina. And I only like one boy. I want to get married like everyone does, and push my baby in a pram. But if I *can* have babies, will they be Together too? Are we like a breed or something? Is that why Anokhin said we should marry Ronnie and Donnie? I don't want to marry one of them. I want to marry Slava.

'*Foo!* I'm not Doing It with anyone, ever!' She spits over the wall in disgust.

'Well, we might want to, Masha, some day. We can ask, that's all ...'

'Who're you going to ask? High and mighty Anokhin? Might as well try and call the Queen of England.'

'How about Zinaida, the School Nurse? She's young and not stuffy. She'll tell us.'

Masha watches the three kids all getting their dollies out of their prams and giving them bottles in the sunshine. She shrugs again.

'Yeah, could do. But don't stutter. You make us sound like a couple of morons.'

It starts raining then. Just warm little drops now and then, but the kids all scream and run into the house, leaving their dollies behind. Me and Masha drop down off the wall and look up at the sky. The raindrops splish on our faces and into our open mouths and Masha laughs and grabs me, and we go dancing round and round in the rain like mad things, dancing round and round and round with our mouths open, catching the rain together.

## Age 16
## April 1966

### We finally ask our School Nurse if we can have sex and get pregnant

It's taken me exactly one year to work up the courage to do it.

I'm so embarrassed I want to curl up and die, but I've asked everyone else I can think of. Olessya said whether or not we can conceive and give birth is a medical question, but she didn't see why we couldn't have sex. Masha was so disgusted by *that* idea she got up and walked right off. But how does she think we're going to have children if we don't have sex? I keep telling her it would be me down there, not her, because we've got one *pizdyets* each, but she still shudders at the thought. And I tremble at the thought. I tremble whenever Slava so much as looks at me, let alone touches me, let alone …

'Well, we've run out of people to ask,' says Masha. We're standing in front of the shiny green medical room door. 'Aunty Nadya looked like she'd swallowed an elephant when you asked her …' Aunty Nadya comes down to visit us every year and bring us food parcels. She just sniffed when she first saw our short, spiky hair and said, 'Teenagers will be teenagers. No accounting for taste.' But when I asked her if we could ever have children, she got so angry she stormed out of the room and slammed the door on us. I can still hear it slamming.

'She still sees us as children,' I say.

I do feel terrible though, for asking her. That's why I'm so nervous now.

'So, the only person to ask is the nurse.'

'*Da-oosh*.' I take a deep breath and knock on her door.

'Come in! Oh, it's you two. OK, sit down.' Zinaida points to a chair. She's perched on the front of her desk, dressed in her white coat, painting her nails red. I wish I could paint my nails red too, but I keep chewing them, so they're only stubs. Masha's nails are long as anything. Good for scratching people in the eyes, she says.

Zinaida's hair's all piled up, like it's tangled in a great big bun. Like spiders' webs. You do it with a comb, Olessya says, pushing and pushing your hair back up so it looks all big and thick. I wish I could do that too. She reaches for a pack of Zenit cigarettes and lights one up. I don't like the smell of smoke, but it's better than horrible surgical spirits, which is what this clinic smells of. That just made me want to be sick when we walked in.

She's got shiny tights, not woolly ones, and high heels. She swings one leg while she puffs smoke at us.

'If you want another sick note, Masha, it'll have to be cholera or leprosy you've got. I'm not doing 'flu any more. I know you sit on the radiators to bring your temperature up.'

'Dysentery?' asks Masha with her head on one side. 'The pox?'

Zinaida looks at her watch. 'Well, I can't sit here wasting my time,' she says.

'W-we w-wanted to ask you s-something.' She looks at me and raises a pencil eyebrow.

I can hear the first-year kids in the Hall for Extra-Curricular Activities, practising a song in English, for International Women's Day. The window's open, so we can hear them clear as anything. *My dear, dear Mummy, I Love you Very Much. I want you to be Happy, on the eighth of March.* Masha's looking up at the ceiling and sniffing. She's waiting for me to say it.

'Zinaida. We're sixteen now and w-we w-wanted to know why we're not having a period like all the others? And C-c-can we have intimate relations? And, and, and, can we have a b-baby? Ever?'

Zinaida forgets her cigarette. It just burns down slowly while she stares at us, sticking to her red lip, in her open mouth with the ash dropping off it. The kids are still singing. *Be happy, be happy, on the eighth of March!*

She kind of wakes up then, and takes her cigarette out, stabbing it on the desk. Stab. Stab. She looks at us, then stabs again. Then she says:

'Look at yourselves!'

'There aren't any mirrors in school,' snaps Masha grumpily. This isn't the answer we wanted.

'No, I mean just look at yourselves. It's, it's ... impossible.'

'Why, why? What p-part's imp-possible?' I say.

She stands up, goes round to the back of her desk and sits down with a thump.

'Every part. It shouldn't even enter your head … heads.'

'B-but why?'

'Why? Why?! Well, if you don't know yourselves …'

'W-we don't.'

'That's why we came to you,' says Masha. 'Stupid idea.'

'W-why though, why?' I insist, feeling Masha getting up to go. I have to know. I have to.

'Because … because …' She looks wildly around the room, opening and closing her mouth like a fish. 'Because … you'd bleed to death, that's why. That's what would happen. And then I'd be for it, for telling you it's all right.'

'*Why* would w-we b-bleed to d-death?'

'I don't know! You just can't have sex, you can't. You're not … like everyone else. You can't!' She's pacing around the room now, all upset. Then she comes to a stop in front of us, shakes her head and says again, but this time to me, in a low voice, 'Look at you.'

'Right,' says Masha, all angry, tugging at me. 'Thanks for that, I look at her all the time. Great advice. C'mon, you, let's get out of here.'

She gets up then and we walk out. Masha's furious.

'Told you not ask,' she says, ignoring the hoots from the gate as we cross the courtyard. 'You and your stupid questions.'

'What makes her think that just because we're Defectives we can't fall in love or feel passion and make love? That's what she was saying, wasn't it? Wasn't it, Mash?'

'She was saying we'd die if we did. That's what she was saying, and she's the nurse so you can stop your mooning about love right now. You wanted an answer and you got an answer.'

'But that means I can never have sex, never have a baby …'

'*I* don't want sex or a *yobinny* baby, I've got one hanging off my side day in, day out. I should never have given in to your nagging.'

I follow her inside, almost tripping because she's stomping so fast, but I'm thinking that I don't believe Zinaida. I don't think she really knows. But if she doesn't know, then who does?

## Putting up a propaganda poster on care of Defectives

I feel like screaming sometimes. No one in the world will tell us anything. No one knows anything about our parents – or if we even have them. Or if we were split in two, or were just two people who fused together somehow. Or if we'll really die if we have sex. *Someone* must know.

But I won't think about that right now. We've got Valentina Alexandrovna as our class teacher. Olessya's right, she's the best teacher in the school, she really is. Everyone thinks so, not just me. Masha does too. Me and Masha are helping her put up this banner across the whole of the school. It's massive; it goes on forever. We're up a ladder, putting one end up. Well, it's sort of been put up already, but Masha said it didn't look straight, so we're up here straightening it. Uncle Tima, the caretaker, is nervous as a box of cockroaches. He's standing at the bottom of the ladder with Valentina Alexandrovna, saying he'll be fired if we fall. The banner says *We Are Systematically Perfecting Forms and Methods of Social Care for Defectives.* It's a high ladder, really high actually, and I want to get down. But Masha likes taking risks. I mean, we could fall and smash our skulls, so I'm holding on and she's banging a nail in with a hammer, but it won't go in, so she keeps banging and banging. I really don't think she needs to. The banner looks pretty secure to me. But she wants to, so I just don't look down.

'You hold on, goose, and I'll do the man's work,' she says. I can't even talk, I'm so scared, we're so far up. I can't even look, I really can't. I'll think of something else. I'm good at that.

Valentina Alexandrovna's great. She says we can all achieve whatever we want to in life. She's going to be our class teacher right up until we graduate. We're her first-ever class and she's really young for a teacher, maybe twenty? Or twenty-one? She says I can be an accountant because that's what I want to do now. Masha wants to be a cook, and Valentina Alexandrovna says she can do that too. We'd just have to find time to do everything one by one. She says that just because crayons are broken, it doesn't mean they can't colour in. Actually I don't think we're broken. We're just two crayons in one. With different colours each end. And then she said Communism needs every single crayon to form the Great Painting. It's really exciting. I think I'm going to be better even than the Healthies. I really am. The Best of the Best. I'm the cleverest in class. Cleverer even than Slava now. He wants to be an accountant too. He was saying we could both be accountants on a Collective Farm in the Novocherkassk region. The same Collective Farm. That's what he said. Masha changes her mind every week about what she wants to do. Yesterday she piped up in class and said that me and her were going to be coal miners and we'd over-fulfil all the quotas because they'd be getting two for the price of one. Everyone laughed at that, even the teacher.

'Stop dreaming, for fuck's sake!' Masha pulls at my arm. 'I said, let's get down. How can I get down without you?'

'Oh … sorry, sorry, Mash. I was thinking.'

'You're always thinking. Stop thinking and start moving, otherwise we'll be up here all night, and Uncle Tima will have our arses for dog food.'

## May 1966

### We go off to Summer Camp, but Slava doesn't want to come

'Mwaah! It's like being in Africa today ...' Masha wipes her face, which is all wet with sweat.

'It's only May, you wait 'til it's July! Then you'll be dripping into a puddle,' says Slava. He rubs the palms of his hands over the cobbles in the courtyard. He has nice hands. I don't know why, they just are. Brown with white, flat nails.

'Bit stupid that you're not coming,' Masha says to him. 'To Summer Camp.'

He shrugs.

He's not coming. I thought he would be, so I've spent ages and ages thinking about what we'd do when we were all alone, us kids, in the woods, in Summer Camp, with the wood fires and the river and swimming and boating and everything. All the kids say that the Educators who are sent to look after us there are drunk most of the time, so you can do what you want. The kids get together and Do It a lot because you're not watched like you are in school. That's what they said anyway. We've never been before because we get sent off to a Sanatorium in Crimea every summer. We hate it there. It's for Defectives and it's by the sea but none of us are allowed down to the beach, of course, and there's nothing to do there except stupid exercises in the high-walled courtyard. It's more like a prison camp than a Sanatorium and all the staff there want to do is take photos of themselves sitting with us, one by one, to show their families. So we just stay in our room all the time and play cards or stare out of our window at everyone swimming in the sea. Masha calls it the Crematorium. I don't even like to think about it. I don't know why we get sent there instead of Summer Camp, but this year it's different. Slava always goes to Summer

Camp, but this year, the one year we're being allowed to go, he's not.

I don't want to be sitting here at all, waiting for Slava's mum to come and get him. We'd all of us been looking forward to Summer Camp like mad, every single day for months, and then Slava said, two days ago, on Tuesday, that his mum and dad wanted him home for summer, so he was going home instead. I don't care. I really don't. If he's stupid enough to want to stay at home with his mum and dad, instead of with us, then I'm not going to be stupid enough to care. That's what Masha says, and she's right. She's always right.

Anyway, Masha's so excited about going she's ready to burst. She wanted Slava to come because he's a laugh. But she's got Vanya and Petya and Little Lyuda and all the others. And I've got Olessya. She's coming to camp too. So that's all right. It'll be healthy.

'Here's my mum then,' says Slava as his mother walks through the gates. They've boarded the gates up now, so people can't see through. His mum waves, but Slava doesn't look that happy. She runs up and hugs and hugs Slava, and tries not to cry. I look away. Masha spits.

'So, girls,' she says, looking at us, after all that hugging and trying not to cry, and starts wiping her tears away with her sleeve. 'I've brought you some marmalade sweets.' I don't want her stupid, sticky marmalade sweets at all, but I thank her, and she gives them to Masha, telling her to save them. She won't though. I think marmalade sweets would make me sick. I feel sick just looking at them. 'Are you looking forward to Summer Camp then, girls?' Masha's already eating them and can't talk as her mouth is all gummy and gooey. It's going to be ninety-eight days until we get back. I counted.

'Yes,' I say. 'Yes. I can't w-wait.'

'Bye then,' says Slava. It's so hot, I can't even move.

'Bye, Peanut,' says Masha, with her mouth all full of marmalade. 'See ya.'

I don't even want to look at him. He could have come to Summer Camp if he'd really wanted. He always went before. He could have said to his mum that he'd rather go to Summer Camp with us lot than go back to his stupid village.

'Bye then, Chimp,' he says, because that's what he calls her, but he doesn't move. He might even change his mind, right now, and get on the bus with us instead. I would. I wait. I'm looking down at the cobbles. 'Bye, Dasha. Have a nice time.' I just nod and pretend I'm trying to dig one out. One of the cobbles, that is. With my fingernails. I have this great ball in my chest, the one that's always there somewhere, waiting for the right moment to push up into my throat and make me cry, and if I look up at him, it'll do it, and I'll just start crying all over the place. And I won't do that.

I don't look at him at all as he goes.

We get up then. I'd really like to go and find Olessya and talk to her, but Masha doesn't like me talking to someone else about feelings. I don't need to talk to Masha about them. She mostly knows how I feel anyway. Without me saying.

We go off to the place behind the laundry room in the shade, and sit down.

'If he doesn't want us, we don't want him,' says Masha, and tucks my hair back behind my ear.

I nod, but I can't talk because the ball has just popped up, and I can't do anything about it, I start crying like an idiot. Like I'm never, ever going to stop. And Masha just keeps on tucking my hair back behind my ear.

## We take the bus to our Summer Camp by the Don

'Look, look!' Masha's bouncing up and down on the front seat of the bus, on the road to Summer Camp. 'Watermelons! A whole mountain of watermelons! Stop, stop, I want one!' The bus driver's used to her telling him to stop every five minutes, and ignores her. Olessya's sitting behind us with her boyfriend Big Boris and she laughs. I do too. Little Lyuda's on our lap and she keeps nearly falling off every time Masha bounces, so I'm holding her tight.

This is the first time we've been outside the school since we got here, and everyone's so happy, it feels like the whole bus is bouncing. I don't feel that happy, myself, because every kilometre post we pass is leaving Slava further behind, and each one makes me ache more, right down in my stomach.

The little kids in the back are singing the Pioneer Song, '*Let there always be Sunshine, Let there always be Blue Skies, Let there always be Mummy, Let there always be Me!*' It's a stupid song, but they keep on singing it over and over again. It's driving me mad. Why is every single song for kids about their stupid mummies?

'Look! Look! It's the Don! I was first to see the River Don!' says Masha, jumping up and leaning over the driver's shoulder, tipping Little Lyuda on to the floor. He bats her away. You can't help being a bit happy though, when Masha is. And the Don looks so beautiful – it's so big and blue, like the sea in the Crimea. We can see it through clearings in the trees now.

'The camp! There's our camp!' she shouts. Everyone crowds to the windows and looks out. There's this big, white, stone archway that leads along a pink, paved pathway, down to a round flowerbed, just bursting with all sorts of flowers, and in the middle there's a white statue of a Young Pioneer blowing a bugle. I can make out rows of neat little red-brick blocks in the woods, with red pennants flying on top of them.

'Not yours, love,' says the driver, swinging the bus past the archway and going on down the road. 'That's for the Healthy kids.'

A few minutes later we turn down a dirt track to a gate with a hand-painted sign, which says *Strictly No Entry*. There's an old man in a baggy suit, hung with loads of war medals, sitting outside the gate by a pile of watermelons. He gets up when he sees us, and opens the gates slow as anything. We drive in and stop by a row of low army tents. The Educators are standing around, watching us as we get off – they're big, fat women chewing sunflower seeds and swatting flies with branches from the pine trees.

They just sort of look at us, without smiling, as we tumble out.

'Good thing they pay us double for this lot,' says one, spitting out a husk.

'Come on then, you busload of cripples,' says another, stepping forward. 'Let's get you to work. *Davai, davai.*'

Once we've put our bags in our tents, they divide us off into groups to go and collect wood for the fire, and bring water for the cauldron from the river, and peel potatoes.

'Yeah, yeah – get to work, everyone! *Davai!*' shouts Masha, running off to the woods for sticks. 'Bags I light the fire!' The Educators are standing around with their arms folded, shaking their heads a bit, but they're sort of smiling. I think I'll be all right. Me and Masha. We'll be all right.

## June 1966

### Uncle Vova wants to take us to his village and Little Lyuda tells us why she was rejected

We've been here a month now and it's healthy, even though I can't stop thinking about Slava and what he's doing. I still have fun, living in the woods like this and cooking our own food. It makes me feel useful somehow. And we get lessons in the morning and spend the afternoon outside, doing our washing and cleaning and cooking for supper. It's a very strict regime, like in school, and we're all fenced in, but we get time to play and pretend stuff, like we're the Reds hiding from the Cossacks. And although we're not allowed to swim (Masha's just desperate to go swimming) we can paddle when the Educators are celebrating something and getting drunk on vodka. They're always celebrating something, the Educators are.

They've been drinking since lunchtime today, because it's a Sunday, and they've all gone down to the river to paddle, dressed in nothing but their baggy knickers. They don't think of Defective boys as being real boys.

'C'mon,' says Masha to me. 'Let's go and talk to Uncle Vova by the gate.'

'We're not supposed to, Masha. They'll kill us, if they see us.'

'They can't see anything beyond their saggy tits right now,' says Masha, and she goes running up the dirt track, and knocks loudly on the wooden gate. Uncle Vova does odd-jobs in the camp like mending things if they're broken, so Masha always talks to him, because she likes mending things too. We hardly ever meet men. He opens the gate a crack.

'Well, you're a couple of naughty monkeys, aren't you?' he says, when he sees us wriggle through to him. 'Fancy a slice of watermelon?'

'I fancy *ten* slices of watermelon,' says Masha, and he laughs.

'Tell you what,' he says, after a bit, watching us wiping all the juice off our faces. 'If you let me take you on my motorbike, in the sidecar, up to my village, I'll give you all the watermelons you want. Come for just half an hour. They all think I'm lying like the devil back there. I'd show 'em if I turned up with you two in the sidecar. I really would.'

Masha takes another big bite and nods happily.

'Done then,' he says, smiling, with all his gold teeth as bright as his medals. 'Come up next time the grown-ups get drunk, and we'll be off.'

* * *

'But I don't want to, Masha,' I say, when we're back at the camp. We're so stuffed full of watermelon, we can only lie on our camp bed. I didn't have half as much as her, but it's all come down to *my* side of our tummy somehow and I feel like popping. 'Everyone will just stare. I don't like watermelons *that* much.'

'I do,' she says.

'Do what?' says Olessya, coming into the tent with Little Lyuda.

'Uncle Vova says he wants to show us to his villagers,' I say, all in a sulk.

'*Nyetooshki*,' says Olessya, shaking her head. 'He only wants to exploit you. He'll probably get them to pay him, for looking at you. And what if he keeps you up there, and the Educators find out? You'll be sent back to the Crematorium.'

Masha frowns.

'Don't, don't!' says Little Lyuda, jumping on to her bed, which is pushed next to ours for our legs, like at school. 'I don't want you to be sent away!'

Just then it starts thundering, and there's this great flash of lightning.

'See, it's Father Stalin telling you not to,' says Little Lyuda, and scrambles over to our bed laughing. 'Let's tell stories.'

'Tell us about you, if you like,' says Olessya. 'You never talk about you.'

Little Lyuda shrugs. 'All right. My mum was only sixteen when she had me. I was Healthy as anything, but she had to reject me and send me to a State Baby Home cos she was just a kid herself. I was adopted when I was two years old by this really nice couple in Moscow. He's an engineer and she's a doctor.' The lightning flashes again and we all sort of huddle together.

'They were the ones that named me Lyuda, and they loved me loads. They were really kind. But then, when I was nine, I was playing in a bit of wasteland behind our block of flats, digging away with a stick, looking for treasure, when I heard this crashing sound and realized the old crumbly wall I was under was giving way. I tried to get away but it all fell on my legs and crushed them. My parents didn't visit me once in hospital, and when I got better, I was sent to an orphanage. They wrote the Rejection letter to the militia while I was in hospital, but they didn't write to me. I didn't even get to go home to say goodbye.' Her eyes are all white and staring, but she's not crying or anything. 'I still write to them though. I've been writing for years, telling them what I'm doing, you know. But they haven't written back.'

We all just sort of sit around, not saying anything. We've all got history.

'Not yet anyway ...' she adds. I know how she feels. I kept writing to my real mummy, right up until we left SNIP. But I don't any more as there's no one to send my letters for me. And there's still no address. In any case, Masha keeps saying Aunty Nadya just put them all in the bin.

I wonder if it's better never to have known your mother, like us, and to imagine her, or to have known her, like Olessya and Little Lyuda, and been rejected.

I can't quite decide.

## August 1966

### We get the best surprise ever

Twenty-one days to go.

Me and Masha are lying on our tummies, on the dock today, doing our washing. I've done ours and I'm washing Icy Valya's too, because she can't. Masha says I should just let it float away with the current and serve her right.

It's August, and so hot, I feel I could melt and drip down into the cool, blue water. I wish Slava was lying here with us. I think about him as much as ever, maybe even more now he's not here, which sort of makes up for it. Every time the thought of him comes into my head my stomach flips, every single time. Masha's used to it now. She doesn't know what's causing it but she says it's like me hiccupping inside. She thinks I've got never-ending tummy hiccups.

I like washing things. I like to be useful. I'd like to spend my whole life washing Slava's clothes for him ... Masha's just dabbling her hands in the water, seeing if any fish will come up and nibble her.

'Dashulya! Dashinka!' We both turn to see Lyuda scooting down the dock on her trolley. 'Guess what? Guess what?!'

'What?' we say together.

'Slava's come! Slava's here! He's just come with his dad, in the sidecar of his motorbike.'

Slava!

We jump up so fast I almost lose all the clothes in the river. Slava!

I can see him. He's there, under the pine trees with all the kids around him, talking away at him, and laughing like mad. We jump up and run to him, pushing through the others, and then just stand there panting, looking at him.

'What's up, Peanut?' says Masha, all cool and everything, but really excited too. 'Been a bad boy?'

'Nah, what the hell, it was boring back home. My brother's got a bicycle now, so he was never there, and if I poked my nose out the door, the village kids chucked stones at me ... you know how it is ...' We don't because we've never lived on the Outside, so we haven't been stoned yet, but I nod my head all over the place. 'Sooo ...' he goes on, and then shoots me that dark look of his that makes my insides turn over and over, and his mouth turns up in a smile, 'so, that gets a bit boring after a while ...' I nod again and think my heart's going to burst right out of my chest, it suddenly seems so big. So big that it's swallowed up the big black hole that's been in there all summer. 'Yeah, so I thought it'd be more fun here. Right, Dasha?'

I nod again, smiling all over my face. 'Right, Slava.'

## The best day of my life: Slava rows us out on to the Don and kisses me

The next day's a Sunday, and it's so beautiful I can hardly believe it. We're sitting under the pines with Olessya and Boris. And Slava. He chucks a pine cone at the small wooden Rescue boat which is rocking a little way out.

'Why don't we take the row boat out?' he says.

'No one can row,' says Olessya. 'The Educators said if you can row, you can take it out, but none of us can.'

'Of course, Masha here told them *she* could,' says Big Boris. 'So her and Dasha sat in it, and went round and round in circles, bashing each other on the head with the oars, while the Educators stood on the shore laughing their heads off.'

'I was just getting the hang of it when they pulled us back in! It was worth a try though – you know what they say: you can't fetch wood if you don't go into the forest.'

'I can row,' says Slava. 'Dad taught me on the pond in our village.'

We all stare at him, then Masha yells: '*Ooorrah!* – I'm going boating!' We jump up and run off to get changed into our bikinis while the two boys go and ask for the oars. Ten minutes later he's rowing us out into the Don with the Educators standing watching, to make sure he *does* know how to do it, from the bank. And he does. He's just in his shorts and he's got these big muscles in his shoulders and arms. He rows really well.

The water's flat as glass, and to start off with, we're all whooping and splashing each other as we go further and further out into the wide river, watching the bank growing smaller and smaller. The Educators turn and go back into the woods, leaving us. It seems to me we're rowing away from the world, right out into real Russia where everyone else lives, able to go wherever they want, whenever they want.

It's strange, but when we went from the walled school to the fenced camp, it was sort of like being taken from one enclosure to another. But now I feel free, right out in the open. Slava stows the oars and we all lie back, Big Boris and Olessya at the front are curled up in each other's arms, and me and Masha are at the back. Some geese fly overhead in a V shape, flapping their wings with a whooshing sound, flying away. I close my eyes and wonder if Slava's watching me.

After what seems like hours, I open my eyes again. Masha's asleep with her head half hanging over the edge of the boat. Olessya and Big Boris are asleep too. Slava's not. He's looking at me. Then very quietly he moves over towards me, still looking at me all the time. He pushes in next to me, the other side to Masha, not waking her. I can feel his warm, bare skin on mine and I sort of gasp. I don't mean to, but I can't help it. He makes me tingly and melting and throbbing all at the same time. He keeps just looking at me, like he can't ever get enough of looking, and then he tilts his head towards me and his lips touch the corner of mine, and then he kisses me little by little, over and over on my lips and my nose and my cheeks. My whole body goes limp, and even though his lips are cool, they burn my skin. He puts his hand round my neck and pulls me in to him, so I can smell his sweat and his breath all mixed up with mine. It's like nothing I've ever felt before; it's a million times better than anything I've ever felt before! Everyone's right: sex is the best thing ever! His fingers push under my bikini top and touch my nipple … I want to explode. I'm throbbing in between our legs where my *peezdets* is. I can't breathe, my heart's pounding and pounding …

'Ei! Ei! Ei! What?! Cut it out, *Moodak!*' Masha's woken up. We weren't touching her or anything, it must have been my stupid,

stupid heart banging through to her. 'Leave my sister alone, you horny bastard,' she yells, pushing him off me. 'Or you'll get an oar up your arse!'

He looks like he wants to kill her then. She knocks him into the bottom of the boat and he glares at her with his lips tight closed, breathing through his nose. Then he puts his head in his hands and closes his eyes, and just sits there, still breathing hard. Olessya and Big Boris have woken up but they're not saying anything, just watching us. After a bit Slava looks up, and he's different. He's in control again. 'Oh yeah,' he says, pulling himself on to the middle seat, 'and how you gonna row back then, Chimp?'

'You'll just have to paddle with your arse,' says Masha, calming down too when she sees he's not going to get into a fight about it. 'C'mon, get back to your work post, and we'll go catch some crayfish.'

Later on that evening, Masha and me are sitting behind our tent. She's trying to carve her name into the bark with a fork but I can hardly see what she's doing, I'm so happy I just feel like laughing all the time, like it's all bubbling inside and trying to pop out in loads of little laugh bubbles. He kissed me! He kissed me! I'm still tingling all over, right from the soles of my feet, and every time I remember him starting in to kiss me on the corner of my lips, my stomach flips right over and sends sparks all through me. And this is only the start, the girls say. It gets better and better until you just explode in pure pleasure … I can't imagine anything being better than this, but I can't wait. I hug myself, all smiling inside.

Masha stops stabbing the bark and looks at me. 'So,' she says. 'Trying to sneak some Do It time with Peanut, were you?'

'It was just a kiss, Mashinka. *You* kiss all sorts of boys and I don't mind. Not at all.'

'That's not real kisses. That's just to keep them sweet.' She stabs at the bark again. 'So. Just to make it clear, don't even *think* about having real Do It time, right? I mean, apart from the fact you'll kill us, what am I supposed to do? I can't send you off into a corner, can I? I can't close my eyes and think of Lenin, can I?'

I stare at her then, and it's as if all the air has been thumped right out of my body. Like she's just thumped me hard in the chest. I can't breathe.

'What?'

'Yeah. I've been thinking about it. I don't want you having some boy climbing all over me to satisfy his needs with you and leave us in a pool of blood.'

I get my breath back and stare at her, feeling sick. I *can't* not have him, now I've had some of him, I can't, I can't! The more I think about what Zinaida said, the more I think it's a lie. I know it's a lie. I've told Masha that. I've told her Zinaida thinks only Healthies should have sex. 'It's not some boy, Masha, it's only Slava, and it's *my* needs, and, like I said, there's two of us down there. You can't feel it when I touch mine, we've tried. It wouldn't be you, Masha, it would be me. You *must* let me, you must, you don't understand how—'

She pushes the fork into my arm. 'Listen, you. I'm saying this once. I'm not having you Doing It with anyone. Not Peanut. Not anyone. Got it?'

I don't even nod. I hate her. Why do I always have to do what *she* says? I hate her. I put my head in my hands. I'll never talk to her again. She can't *make* me not make love to him. She can't. She can't!

Can she?

## September 1966

### We go on a trip to the zoo

'The zoo! The zoo! We're going to the zoo!' Masha jumps out of bed and starts pulling on our clothes. 'I want to see the snakes and crocodiles the most – do you think there'll be crocodiles, Aunty Zoya? Do you?'

The nanny, Aunty Zoya, nods and smiles. 'Wouldn't be surprised, Mashinka, there might be bears and tigers too, so you'd better keep your distance.' She picks Little Lyuda up under her arm to take her down to breakfast and looks back over her shoulder before she goes down the stairs. 'You'll make a nice double helping if that lot gets peckish.'

'Make sure they don't put you in with the chimps, Mash!' shouts Little Lyuda as she's carried down.

We've been back in school for three weeks now. Slava stayed in camp until we all left, but Masha watched us like a wolf with two goats, and made sure she never dozed off again. I don't care. Slava likes me. That's all that matters. I'll find a way to get round Masha. I must. I just must. Slava looks at me now in this hot, hungry, secret way. But only when Masha's not looking. It's our way of talking without talking. He's not going to the zoo today and neither's Little Lyuda or Olessya, because they don't want anyone on trolleys in case they scare the animals. It's a travelling zoo, which has camped outside town, and our Director, Semyon Konstantinovich, has come to an arrangement with the zoo's Director that he'll close it to the public so we can visit.

We all pile into the bus and everyone's singing *Africa has Gorillas, Africa has Sharks!* But I don't think they'll have those in this zoo. Svetlana Petrovna, the biology teacher, stands up at the front of the bus when we're all settled down.

'Now then, children. Those with crutches, do not poke them through the bars. No feeding the animals. We will alight from the bus and walk in pairs through the gates, quietly and calmly.'

'Please, please, Svetlana Petrovna!' Masha's jumping around like a flea, with her hand up. 'Can I be paired with Petya? Dasha can go with Olessya.'

'Very funny, Masha. Sit down. And remember, children, be quiet and orderly. You will be a credit to the school, understood?' She glares at Masha.

It's already warm by the time we drive up to the scrubland on the outskirts of town. Everyone wants to be the first to see a giraffe, or even an elephant, but there's this high wooden fence all round it, so we can't see in at all. When the bus door opens, we can smell a strong, stinky African smell, which makes the girls all scream like mad.

There's a couple of boys from town hanging around when we get off the bus, and they stare at us like all their dreams have come true as we line up, waiting to go in. As we all file in through the gates, I can see the boys legging it back to town, whooping.

The zoo Director is waiting for us inside. I can tell he's nervous but when he sees Masha and me, he almost topples over backwards. He's thin, with a long scraggly neck and has a crumpled suit on.

'This is Anahit Tigranovich. Say thank you, children.'

'Thank you, Anahit Tigranovich,' we all chirp, like parrots, but he just backs away as if we've bitten him.

'Come along then, first we'll see the wolves, shall we?' says Svetlana Petrovna quickly, and we all run off after her. The wolves are thin as anything with their ribs sticking out and they're pacing up and down their little cage, like that's all they've been doing for hundreds of years. There's even a groove in the cement floor where they walk, and their fur's sticking out in tufts.

'The Big Bad Wolf will come one day – to grab little Masha and take her away,' chants Big Boris in Masha's ear. Mummy used to sing us that when we were little. It wasn't scary when she sang it. It's a lullaby. Masha goes to bite him on the arm.

'Come along, come along,' says Svetlana Petrovna, 'no playing around. On to the snakes.'

'Oooh snakes – healthy!' shouts Masha. 'I want to hold one – can I hold one?'

'Certainly not. They're behind glass and probably poisonous …' Svetlana Petrovna glances around to see where the Director is, but he's gone. Good, he's creepy. We spend ages pressing our noses against the glass, looking at the lazy snakes staring at us with their unblinking eyes, until one of the girls says she thinks they're just stuffed and not real, so we all start dancing around to see if they'll move. But they don't.

'That's quite enough of that. Next is the monkey cage.'

'Put Masha in with them!' laughs Big Boris when we get to their cage, and see them all sitting on the branches staring out through the bars, but not looking at us. I know that, because I looked into their eyes really carefully. They're looking beyond us, as if there's something out there. But there isn't. It must be more fun for them outside their cage, back in the jungle. Maybe that's what they're looking for. The jungle.

'She'd cheer them up!' Boris says. 'Throw Mashinka in! Go on, go on!' Masha laughs and grabs the bars, rattling them, but the monkeys still don't move.

'Are there lelephants?' asks one of the younger boys. 'I want to see a lelephant.'

'I don't believe there are, Dima, but look, here are some zebras.'

'Those stripes are painted on, they're painted!' says Masha. 'Look' – she licks her finger – 'I'll get in and wipe them off.'

'Stop right there, my little beauty, and behave. Silence!'

We all stop talking, and it's then we hear it. A shouting coming from the entrance. The Director is standing by the wolf cage, wiping his forehead with a handkerchief and one of the zoo staff is saying '... hundreds of them ... more than we've had all week ... make a fortune ...'

Svetlana Petrovna can hear too. She strides up to him. 'I forbid you to let anyone in.'

'Sorry, comrade, have to make a living, can't be a parasite on the State ...'

He goes off to the gates then and opens them. Him and the zoo man can't take money off everyone fast enough as they all come in and run towards us in a big wave, surrounding us with their stinky breath and sweat and fat bodies, pushing us back against the zebra pen. I want to be sick, I can't breathe. There's loads of them, spitting at us and shouting in their stupid loud voices, saying stuff like: *There's the mutant, there it is! It's not a girl with two heads, it's a boy, they've mutated further, should be killed ... aaakh! ...* Svetlana Petrovna is somewhere behind them, but Big Boris pushes in front of us, so we're right behind his back, pressing into him and holding on to him, round his waist. He's shoving them back. I can hear Svetlana Petrovna's voice somewhere in the distance saying over and over again, 'Comrades! Look at the animals! Comrades, please, please, look at the animals!' We're going to be crushed to death, Masha and me, it's the end, I can't breathe, being squished against the pen. But then suddenly Masha pushes out from behind Boris, and steps right out in front of him. She starts screaming at them, waving her arms, shoving them back herself with her two arms and yelling, '*You're* the fucking mutants! *Moodaki, Blyadi!* Who asked you to come and insult us? Get the fuck away from us!' They all stop shouting like she's cast a spell over them. They take a step right back, when she starts in yelling at them like that, waving her arms all over the place. Then Svetlana Petrovna pushes through to us and the driver's come from somewhere too, and is shielding us all as they both herd us back to the bus with Masha still yelling her head off, swearing like crazy. 'Go home to your stinking holes in the ground! Us? Killed? I'll see the fucking lot of you dead and buried before I think of dying. And you know what? Know what? I'll come and dance on every one of your *yobinny* graves ...' Svetlana Petrovna's trying madly to shush her, but she won't stop until we're on the bus and the door's closed behind us all. I'm crying and trembling and all the little kids are bawling too, but Masha just starts thumping her fists on the window and keeps swearing until Svetlana Petrovna pushes her down hard into her seat and we drive off.

'Disgraceful! Disgraceful!' Svetlana Petrovna's all red in the face and standing at the front supporting herself on the driver's chair. 'How *dare* you, Masha! How *dare* you humiliate us, speaking in that language to townspeople! It's disgraceful. *Pozor!* It's humiliating. You will be punished for this, I can assure you.' Masha has her hands balled into fists and just sort of stares back at her angrily. But she doesn't talk back. You don't talk back to Authority.

## We get punished for Masha swearing at the Healthies

'Aaakh, girls, girls! What am I to do with you? What am I to do?'

Vera Stepanovna, the head teacher, has called us into her office, and we're standing on this red rug with lots of whirly patterns on it, while she's pacing up and down in front of us.

'But, Vera Stepanovna,' says Masha, 'they said we should be killed and not go upsetting people. I couldn't just stand there—'

'*Molchee!*' She comes to a stop with all her pacing, right in front of us. 'Do you really not understand by now? It is your duty to be patient with those who are traumatized by your appearance. To understand and forgive. It is your duty, Masha, to behave with dignity, and not dishonour our school with your vulgar, unforgivable outbursts.' Masha looks sulky.

I keep looking down at the whirls on the rug. That's exactly what Lydia Mikhailovna said to us that time after we went into the grounds and got shouted at by the passers-by. She said we should try and understand them, but I just can't do it. Not yet.

Then I remember Aunty Nadya telling me once to remember that if there's just one person who loves you for who you are, it doesn't matter if a hundred thousand people hate you for what you look like. And Slava said I was his best friend.

'Remember the words of the great novelist Nikolai Ostrovsky, crippled and deformed like you …' Vera Stepanovna's still going on at us. But we're not crippled. Just deformed. She steps back, looking beyond our heads, up at the portrait of Brezhnev all shiny with his rows and rows of medals. '"Man's dearest possession is life. It is given to him but once and he must live it so as to feel no torturing regrets for wasted years …"' We've heard all this a million times before. '"… to so live that, on dying, he might say: all my life, all my strength was given to the finest cause in all the world – the fight for the Liberation of Mankind!"'

She looks back at us, and I can see she doesn't think we're very hot on Mankind at the moment, so she goes back to looking sad and disappointed in us.

'I will have to punish you, of course.' She starts up with her pacing again. I hate being punished. They strip us to our vest and pants and make us sit on a chair in the corner of class facing the wall. I hate that Slava can see me like that. He never gets punished because he's not naughty. But then I'm not naughty either. It's Masha who's naughty. And sitting in your underwear like that makes you feel so sad, I just want to crawl into a crack in the wall. And they make us sit there for hours and hours. 'Yes, you will have detention every day all next week for an hour after class, and write one hundred times on the blackboard *I will accept that my deformity traumatizes others. Accept and understand. I will remember my dignity.*'

Lines. That's a relief. Even though I know who's going to be doing all the writing on the blackboard as punishment for swearing at the Healthies. And it's not Masha.

## Olessya gives me some advice

Olessya comes over to our bed that evening. Masha's playing *Durak* with Little Lyuda, slapping cards down and shouting, so she doesn't much notice her.

No one really talks about what happened at the zoo. What's there to talk about? But Olessya's heard about it.

'Don't be upset by those idiots, Dasha,' she says quietly. 'Being a Defective doesn't make you worse than them; it makes you better, because you have to work twice as hard to succeed in life. And you have to be ten times as strong as them to put up with their prejudice.'

I can't even look at her. I just keep bunching our blanket up in my hands while Masha slaps down cards.

'You know what I think?' She touches my arm. 'What I always tell myself?' I do look up at her then. 'Defects are given to ordinary people to make them extraordinary. That's us. You and me.'

I nod, but deep down all I want to be is ordinary without defects. Like everyone else. I don't feel extraordinary in any way at all. I just can't think the way Olessya does. Or Masha.

'*Ei!* What're you two mice whispering about?' says Masha.

'I'm just telling Dasha how you cheat,' says Olessya with a laugh. 'Look, you've got one up your sleeve ...' and she goes to tickle her under her arm. Masha bats her off but we all laugh then. Olessya's like Slava. Olessya knows how to deal with my Masha, so she can stay friends with me.

## Masha gets the whole class to play truant

'I hate Maths,' says Masha as I'm washing our nappy in the morning. 'First lesson too. Makes you want to puke.'

'I like it. Valentina Alexandrovna's really good at explaining the hard bits. I'll help you.'

'I'm not going.'

'What?' I stop washing and stare at her. 'We've got to go. Zinaida won't give us any more sick notes.'

She's leaning against the wall, balancing us. 'I'm going to bunk off, that's what. The sun's out.'

'The sun's always out. And you can't, Mash, we'll miss the next stage in algebra. I can't do that. I'll never catch up …'

'All right then. I'll get the whole class to bunk off.'

'Whaat?! No, no. They won't go! No one will go, Masha. That's crazy.'

Ten minutes later we walk into class. Valentina Alexandrovna's not in yet.

'Right, everyone out,' says Masha, clapping her hands to get attention. 'Class Leader Maria Krivoshlyapova,' she points at herself, 'is giving you an order. Everyone out. This is officially the last sunny day of autumn, and we need our vitamin D.'

Everyone just stares at her, so she starts pulling them off their chairs. 'C'mon, c'mon, it's a beautiful morning, follow me, quick, quick!' I look across at Slava but he's smiling.

'OK. We've got to do what the Class Leader tell us to, right?' he says. Everyone starts giggling then, and like a whole flock of sheep, we rush out into the morning sun and over to the patch of grass behind the kitchens where the pear trees are. Masha starts picking them off the tree and tossing them at everyone.

'Breakfast of fresh fruit, last pears of the season, eat up!'

It's *nyelzya* to pick the fruit. Masha's going crazy. But I eat one anyway because everyone else is. It doesn't take long for Valentina Alexandrovna to find us.

'And what exactly is the meaning of this?' she says, standing there in her sharp high heels and knee-length skirt. I didn't want her to be upset, or get into trouble, but she looks more surprised than angry.

'It wasn't my fault, Valentina Alexandrovna,' pipes up Masha in this high, little girl voice she has when she's getting round someone. 'They all wanted to go out and I couldn't stop them, I tried … I tried, I did … as Class Leader I really tried …'

'A very likely story.'

'Besides,' goes on Masha, 'Ostrovsky says we must live life so as to feel no torturing regrets for wasted years …'

'I believe that quote lies within the context of fighting for the liberation of Mankind. Lying in the sun stuffing yourselves with forbidden pears hardly constitutes that.' We all keep staring up at her, not knowing if she's going to report us or punish us, but after a while she says a bit stuffily: 'Well, since you're here, I don't see why we can't have one lesson outside without our books.' And she kicks her heels off, which are sinking into the grass, and sits down on a log. 'But on the condition that this little trespass against authority is never to be repeated.' We all nod like mad. She's the best teacher ever. She really is. And Masha's the best sister ever. Most of the time.

## Age 17
## January 1967

### We're given our passports – or rather, passport

'Well, girls, this is a momentous day for you.'

We've been called into Vera Stepanovna's office again and we're standing on the red rug. But she's not angry with us for once. She's all puffed up and proud.

She comes round to the front of her desk. 'I have the pleasure of announcing that you are now officially citizens of the Soviet Union.' She picks up a shiny red passport, and hands it across to us. Masha takes it, all excited. It says on the front in thick gold letters *Citizen of the Union of Soviet Socialist Republics.* She opens it quickly and flicks through.

'This is Dasha's,' she says, giving it to me. 'Where's mine?' She holds out her hand.

'There is only one passport.'

'But where's mine?' She's still holding out her hand.

'I told you, Masha. There is only one. You have both been issued with one passport.'

'But there's two of us.'

'Yes. I know that. But you are considered to be one citizen in the eyes of the State. And in a way … you are … aren't you … I mean … you have one body.' She's not looking at us. She's looking up at Brezhnev again.

'No. We have one body but we're two persons.'

'People, not persons. And that's enough of that, Masha. The State has made a decision.' Masha takes the passport back from me, and looks through it again, not saying anything, but I can feel her getting all tense, while Vera Stepanovna gives us this speech on our duties as citizens and the great honour of being a part of the movement towards Communism spreading across the world like wildfire. I actually think she's going to get us to sing the Soviet anthem or something, but she finally winds down and goes back behind her desk and sits down. Masha's still staring at the passport and I'm still looking down at the whirls on the rug, but I can feel her all balled up inside.

'You may go,' says Vera Stepanovna, and picks up a pen.

We leave her office and walk out into the courtyard. We don't say anything at all for a bit, then Masha suddenly spits on the passport. '*Foo!* What the *fuck?* Why do *you* get the passport? Like I don't exist or something! Like I'm just a bit of you?'

She thrusts it into my hands and I stare at it, thinking, are we just an *it* too? That's what people on the Outside call us – it – not them. And now the State has confirmed, officially, that we're only one person. 'But, Masha, we're not … are we?' I'm starting to cry, I wish I wouldn't, but it just comes over me. 'Vera Stepanovna thinks we are too … she said so, she said we were—'

'Stop bleating! Course we're not! We'll go to Valentina Alexandrovna.'

'This is outrageous,' says Valentina Alexandrovna, turning the passport over and over in her hand like it's going to bite her or something. 'Insulting! Now please stop sobbing, Dasha, it's a bureaucratic mistake. It happens. I shall call your Aunty Nadya and she'll sort it out, you'll see. She'll sort it all out for you and get things straight. It's a mistake. I'll call her right now.'

She picks up the phone and after a bit we can hear Aunty Nadya on the other end of the phone shouting down the line. 'Scandalous! Are they to get one wage? Will they give them one plate to eat off? One ration book? Put it in the post to me immediately and I shall deal with it! One person indeed! *Pozor!*'

## April 1967

### Aunty Nadya goes to the top to get us two passports and we have an anti-Soviet conversation in the cellar

Three months later and we're down in the cobbler's cellar, with Olessya, Big Boris and Slava. It's a Sunday so the school cobbler, Vyacheslav Tikhonovich, isn't normally around, but today he's lying in a corner, dead drunk, with an empty vodka bottle by his head.

Aunty Nadya brought Masha her own passport last week.

'See? I've got one too now!' Masha's waving her passport around like a flag. 'I'm a person too now, see? It's a miracle! Maria Krivoshlyapova – welcome to the world!'

Slava's got himself sitting right next to me. I can feel the heat coming through from him. People say he looks just like me with his big brown eyes and dark hair. They say he looks more like me than Masha does even. When I'm right next to him like we are now, I start trembling, because I want him to kiss me so much. It's stupid, but I can't stop it, I want to just hold him as tight as anything, and never let go. If Masha wasn't here, we'd do nothing in the whole world but touch and hold each other, I swear.

Normally I'd feel a bit lonely when Aunty Nadya leaves, but with Slava around I don't feel lonely at all. She stayed for a week in the lodgings in town and visited us every day. It really was a miracle, getting that passport.

To start off with, she queued for three days at the City Passport Office, and when she finally got to see the official, he didn't even look up from his desk. He just told her we only have one birth certificate, so even if we had *ten* heads, we'd still be one person. That's exactly what he said. Ten heads. Then she got an appointment with Anokhin, to see if he could do anything to help, but he just told her what Maternity Hospital we'd been born in, and said she should check the files to see if there was another birth certificate for us. She went off to the hospital then, but there wasn't. It seems when we were born they issued us with just the one. I don't know who named us Masha and Dasha, perhaps it was our mother? I don't think Aunty Nadya asked about who our parents were when she was there – she didn't say anything to us about them at any rate. And we didn't ask. We've learnt not to ask questions. We just get told off and they never get answered anyway.

The Maternity Hospital Administration said they couldn't issue another certificate, so Aunty Nadya went back to Anokhin to ask him to write a formal letter saying we were two people for the Maternity Hospital. But he just told her not to bother him any more with it, so she went to Professor Dolyetsky instead, who's known us since we were babies apparently. He was the one who was supposed to amputate our leg. He agreed to write the letter and got some other important professors to sign it. The letter explained that since we had two mouths and two digestive systems we needed to be provided for by the State as two people, which meant two passports. 'Forgot about the two brains, hearts and souls, didn't they,' Masha had sniffed when Aunty Nadya told us.

So then she took the letter to the Maternity Hospital Administration saying they needed to send the application to the State Registry office for a certificate because Masha was a person too, but they refused. She didn't give up though. She kept fighting for us. She wrote to the Minister of Health, and he didn't reply. Then she wrote to the Minister of Social Protection, and he didn't either, so then she wrote to Anastas Mikoyan himself, explaining we were two girls who just happened, unfortunately, to be joined together, and by some miracle he wrote back on Kremlin stamped paper with one sentence, saying: *Issue Maria and Daria Krivoshlyapova with two passports.* And signed it himself.

'Who's Anastas Mikoyan?' Masha had asked. But I knew. Everyone knows. Except Masha. He was Lenin's comrade, then Stalin's, then Khrushchev's, and now he's the Chairman of the Presidium of the Supreme Soviet. Or at least, he was. That's almost as important as Brezhnev himself. We couldn't believe our ears when she told us that Mikoyan knows about us and took the time to write that line. 'Yes,' Aunty Nadya told us proudly, 'and when I took that letter to the Passport Office, they pretty much carried me right to the front of the queue over everyone's heads! And that rude official, who hadn't even looked up before, was turning somersaults to get the second passport issued as quickly as possible. He started grovelling and stammering as if I were a Presidium member myself! So you see, there is some justice in the world.'

Vyacheslav Tikhonovich groans and turns over, and we look at him to see if he's going to wake up. But he doesn't. He just starts snoring really loudly. Masha throws a few tacks at him.

'So anyway,' says Slava eventually, 'I thought you'd need a pardon from Brezhnev to save you last week, Mash, after you refused to answer the question about how Nikolai Ostrovsky is your ideal.'

'Well, why should I write a whole exam essay about why he's my ideal, when he's not? We're all supposed to love him to bits because he wrote that stupid novel and was crippled in the War.' I bite my lip. I didn't think it was *that* stupid; in fact I quite liked *How the Steel Was Tempered*. It was … I don't know, so passionate somehow. I wonder if Slava liked it. 'He just married that young fool of his,' Masha goes on, 'and bullied her into doing everything for him. She had no life; she was his slave. It's plain selfishness to shackle someone to you like that … And he was given his big apartment in Moscow, and his villa in Sochi, and juicy sturgeon steaks to eat every day. Just for writing about how great everything was.'

'It's not all great, though, is it …' says Slava slowly. His hair falls over one eye. Olessya looks nervously up the steep wooden steps leading to the courtyard. He shouldn't be saying stuff like that. 'Well, Masha's right, isn't she?' he goes on quietly. 'Why are we all told to think Ostrovsky's our ideal? Why *don't* we have a choice? Why do we have to listen to the Red Army Choir night and day,' he points at the little transistor radio he carries around everywhere, which is playing Soviet marching music, 'when there's this English group called the Beatles that everyone else in the world's listening to?' He's whispering now and we all lean in closer. 'Why can't we listen to the Beatles? Why not? And *Pravda* is packed full of propaganda about achievements and goals and quotas and heroes and honesty and sobriety and plentiful food. But you can't leave a kopeck lying around for two seconds without it getting pinched. And half the nation seems to be drunk.' He waves at Vyacheslav Tikhonovich. 'You can see them all collapsed in the street outside our dorm. And my mum queues for eight hours for toilet paper or sugar. You can't buy meat or butter or milk anywhere on the Outside – you could queue a lifetime and not get that.' Olessya glances up the stairs again. If Icy Valya is hiding up there and listening … 'And you can't find fault with anything. You can only agree that we live in the Best of all Possible Worlds.'

'Unless you're Masha,' says Big Boris.

'Yeah, but the only reason *she* wasn't put on trial in the Young Communist court was because Valentina Alexandrovna rescued her.' He looks at me and smiles. As soon as Masha said that she wasn't going to write the essay, Valentina Alexandrovna swooped in without batting an eyelid and said she'd actually prepared two questions for the two of us because Masha 'has a tendency' to copy from me. No one, not even Valya, dared say anything.

'What about *us* then?' says Big Boris in a low voice. 'The newspapers don't say anything about criminals and drunks and dissenters and shortages, because that's all bad stuff, and can't be talked about. But they don't say anything about Defectives either. Us lot. What does that make us? Bad stuff too?'

'No, no, not at all!' I sit up straight. 'You've got it all wrong. No! We're the *p-p-privileged* ones, we are. *We* get milk and b-butter and b-bread. Well, sometimes we do. We get an education. The State is Systematically P-Perfecting Support for us all the time. Remember the b-banner. We should be G-Grateful. Don't you understand?' I look round at them pleadingly. I want them to stop talking about things I don't want to hear. 'In Amerika cripples have to b-beg on the street or humiliate themselves by dancing in side-shows for kopecks,' I go on. 'But here in the Soviet Union, we're cared for by defectologists.' Masha nods. 'We have nice teachers, and p-people who cook for us and do our laundry and, and … mend our shoes for us,' I say, pointing at Vyacheslav Tikhonovich. 'And we have extra-curricular activities like d-dancing and sewing and orchestra and choir.' (Although we don't do any of them because Masha doesn't want to.) 'The State looks after us, like p-parents. We're special. We *are.* Maybe there are some things they don't tell us, but it's for our own good.' Slava's looking at me with his dark eyes, but I can't see what he's thinking.

'That's right.' Masha's nodding but the others aren't. 'The less you know, the sounder you sleep.'

Olessya shakes her head. 'I'm not so sure, girls. I think I'd sleep a lot sounder if I knew the truth.'

## New Year's Eve 1967

### New Year's Eve party with Slava

We always have this party on New Year's Eve in school. It's held in the Hall for Extra-Curricular Activities, and the nannies lay a long table of food, which is the best ever food we have all year. They make potato salads with salted cucumber and peas, and we have salted herring, and slabs of lard with white bread. There's grated carrot and raisin salad, grated beetroot salad, and even sliced tongue, if we're lucky. We're not allowed alcohol, but Slava's smuggling in some vodka for him and me. We're going to get really, really drunk, and then we're going to Do It for the first time ever. We haven't talked about it, of course; we can't do that because of Masha. But we both know. We've said it with our eyes. I don't care if I die. But we won't. Olessya says Zinaida was only trying to stop us doing it to protect herself. She says Zinaida doesn't know a heart from a brain.

'Right, I'm going,' says Masha. We're lying on our bed under the duvet because the heating's off, and it's minus twenty outside, and piled sky-high with snow. We've got a heater, but all the girls are crowded around it at the other end of the dorm. They're not talking to us. Or rather not talking to Masha, so that means me too.

She gets upset with people, and when she does, she bears a grudge forever. Her big mistake was making an enemy of Icy Valya. She got it into her head that Valya had stolen our food parcel from Aunty Nadya about six months ago. I don't know if she did steal it, but Masha took her to our School Komsomol Court to be put on trial. Valya wasn't found guilty because there wasn't any proof, but now she's turned everyone against Masha. If I'm honest, I think they were turning anyway because the others don't like the way she beats me up at night sometimes. I'm used to it and I understand why she does – it's because she can't stand me always being there, and being so weak, not strong like her. It's upsetting for her. But the kids don't like her for it. Olessya and Little Lyuda tried to stop her to start with, but that made her even angrier. They both still talk to us, but they're the only ones now. They're sitting snuggled up together under the duvet in Olessya's bed, reading a book.

Masha gets out of our bed.

'I'm not lying here watching those *yobinny* idiots tarting up,' she says loudly. The girls have managed to get some lipstick and mascara from somewhere and they're making each other up, and giggling. I'd love to wear lipstick and mascara too, but Masha's not into anything like that. Not at all. She doesn't care what boys think. We're not even wearing our nice blouses. Just our plain flannel shirts and trousers. 'Come on, we'll go to the Hall and wait. Get our coats.'

I don't care. Not tonight. Slava's got vodka. His brother dropped it off last week, and he's been keeping it at the bottom of the woodpile. Masha's fed up with everything so she wants to get blind drunk. We haven't talked about me and Slava, but I think she knows because my heart's been racing like a mad thing all day.

'You're early, girls! No one's here.' The nanny, Aunty Traktorina, is laying the table. There are only two nannies looking after us and Valentina Alexandrovna is in charge, but she must still be in the kitchens. Masha puts her icy-cold hand down the back of my neck to warm it up. I shiver. He'll be here soon. The boys are in their dorm getting ready too. I can't think of anything but Slava. Not being able to have him makes me want him all the more. It's like being starving hungry and having a steaming plate of the tastiest food in the world sitting right in front of you. You can smell it all the time but you can never eat it. Masha lets us sneak a kiss sometimes, when she's in a good mood, but as soon as she thinks it's getting too heavy, she pushes him off. 'A bit of a kiss is all right, but I'm not having you falling in love. You're mine, all mine,' she always says. I can tell Slava's frustrated. There's this new girl, Anyootka, who's just come to our school. She's really pretty. And sweet. And clever. She's in our class and of course she likes Slava. And poetry.

Masha's got her leg over my knee and is jiggling it up and down angrily.

'Thank goodness there are boys here,' she says. 'Boys aren't bitches. Girls are bitches.'

I look up at the frosty window, and blow on my hands. Masha would never let me put my cold hand down *her* neck. Slava would. I'm worried though, because if Slava ever gets too fed up of not being able to be with me, he might start seeing someone else. Like Anyootka. If he did that, I'd die. I would – I'd die, I know it. Sometimes it feels like I'm just waiting all the time, every stupid second of the day, for him to stop liking me, and start liking her instead. It's torture.

'I should set Uncle Mikoyan on them ...'

I sigh and push her hair back over her ear. 'That's part of the problem, Mash,' I say. 'When you started going on all the time about how he really *was* our uncle, at least our real great-uncle, it got them all angry. I mean, you did go on *all* the time about it ...'

'They're just jealous.'

'Making people envious doesn't make them like you, Mash. It makes *you* feel better, but not them ...' She's not listening. 'It does the opposite,' I add quietly. Sometimes I don't think Masha understands what people think – or cares. I hear a noise and look over at the door again, but it's only Valentina Alexandrovna coming in. Masha does think up all these really crazy things, like she tells everyone now that we were created in a laboratory by Professor Donetsky and Anokhin, and that when we graduate with our diplomas we'll be taken on a trip all over the world as one of the great Soviet Achievements, and get awarded the Order of Lenin. If I'm honest, she believes these things so hard that she gets me half believing them too. I don't want to be taken away from Slava though, not ever. Not for anything.

The door opens again, and this time the boys all come in, laughing and whooping when they see the food. They've already been drinking. I'm afraid for a moment that Slava's not there, but he's right at the back, and when he sees me, he comes straight over to us.

'All right, girls? C'mon then, let's go somewhere quiet and sort this out.' He taps a bulge under his shirt. Vodka. Masha laughs.

Midnightish, dark, very very dark and swirly-wirly … soooo drunk can't see … Masha laughing'n'laughing'n'music's thumping thumping'n'Slava kissing kissing … his hand 'nder my shirt on my breasts. Mmm, can smell his breath'n'sweat … reaching down and down to touch me, feel me … heavy on top of me … inside me … 'n' I hold him so haaaard, so haaaard, can't breathe … joined in one, him'n'me … together … Slava … Slava … at last … aaakh … Slava!

# Age 18
# Spring 1968

## Sitting under the pear tree discussing our future

Masha doesn't know I'm not a virgin any more. I didn't bleed at all. I was beautifully throbbingly, sore, but she wasn't. Obviously. I don't remember what happened after we had sex, or even how long we did it for. All I know is that when me and Masha woke up, in our bed, she had a headache but no memory of me and Slava. But I did. Oh yes, it was all a bit muddled, but I did … he was so hard and his lips so soft …

The sun's all warm, even though it's evening time, so we're all sitting on the grass under the pear tree listening to music on Slava's transistor radio. He gave me a hot secret smile when we walked up to meet them just now. He always gives me this hot secret smile. Masha wants Aunty Nadya to bring us a transistor radio next time she comes. Last time she visited, Little Lyuda asked her to look up her parents, to see if they were still at the address she was writing to. She thought maybe they'd moved, but they hadn't. Aunty Nadya did go. She's kind like that. She knocked on the door and said she'd come from Lyuda in Novocherkassk but they wouldn't even open the door properly. They kept it on the chain and told her through the crack that they'd adopted another daughter now. They said that they'd named the second one Lyuda too, and to go away.

I knew I wasn't going to get pregnant because we haven't got our periods yet. I smile inside. I've had sex! Masha said we couldn't, but we have. *Kha!*

We're all sitting here together, Masha, Slava, Olessya, Little Lyuda, Big Boris and Anyootka. She's sitting next to Slava. We're talking about the Medical Commission. We all get graded by how defective we are when we're eighteen years old, by this panel of defectologists. No one talks much about the grading system, but everyone hates it.

Top grade is Four. That's for the kids like us in the school, who are clever and can walk and work for a living. It goes down to One for the totally paralysed who can only be dumped into full State Care and treated like rotting vegetables.

'What are you going to d-do, Olessya, when you leave SNIP?' I ask. She's leaving school in two months. So are Little Lyuda and Big Boris, because they'll be graduating. She's leaning back against the tree trunk with her eyes closed.

'If I get top marks in my diploma, I'm going to apply to the Moscow Technology College,' she says, without opening her eyes. 'And live in a student dorm.'

Big Boris is registered to live in Novocherkassk, so he'll have to study and work here, but the two of them don't seem too bothered about splitting up. Valentina Alexandrovna wants him to apply for the Engineering College, and then maybe go and work in the Locomotive Factory. Little Lyuda's not sure where she's registered now.

'I hope it's Moscow,' she says. 'Because that's where I lived ...'

'Do you think we'll get Grade F-Four?' I ask no one in particular, and no one in particular answers. 'I mean we can *do* everything. It doesn't make any d-difference being Together. Right?' Anyootka looks up then, but she's looking at our third leg, not us. Then she just looks back down again to her stupid book of poetry.

Olessya opens one eye. 'Why don't you ask Valentina Alexandrovna, Dasha? She'll know.'

'Yeah,' says Masha, who's been quiet up to now. 'She's on night duty. Let's go now; she'll be in her study.' I don't want to leave Slava and Anyootka alone, even though I really think he wants me more than ever, now we've Done It, but I have this ache, sort of chewing away all the time inside me, which is me being afraid

I'll somehow lose him. 'C'mon, scarecrow. Let' s go,' says Masha. And pulls me away.

## Taking Valentina Alexandrovna's advice on our third leg

We knock on her study door and walk in. She's looking through some essays, but she gets up with a big smile, and goes over to the samovar of hot water. We often come in to sit with her, just for a chat, now that Icy Valya's gang aren't talking to us.

'So how are you doing this evening, girls?' she says, and waves her hand at the chair we always sit in. It's a cosy armchair. All around the room there are vases of flowers that she's been given for International Women's Day, so it smells like a garden in here.

We sit down and Masha looks at me in her *Go on then* way.

'W-we just w-wondered,' I start, 'if you knew w-what grade we're likely to get for the Medical Commission?'

She gives us a glass of sweet tea each, and sits down herself. 'Well … hmm … it's always difficult to tell what their criteria is, you know, about the severity of the disability, even though it's all set out in the rules. Of course you're perfectly agile and intelligent, so it should definitely be a Grade Four … I would easily give you a Grade Four myself, everyone here would …'

'B-but what about the Commission?'

'Well, I have heard some rumours, just rumours you know, that there's been some law passed, tightening up the criteria. So, I know it doesn't get in your way or anything, but maybe your leg might make a difference to them … it shouldn't, of course, it doesn't make any difference to *you*, and that's the main thing, but they're assessing whether or not you can go out to work, you know, in the workplace, at desks or in factories. I just wonder …'

I stare at her with the tea halfway to my mouth. I know what she's going to say. I just don't want her to say it.

## March 1968

### We go back to SNIP to have our third leg amputated

'It feels strange being back,' says Masha. She pokes at the pillow. 'Same old blue stamp, *Property of SNIP* on everything. Same old staff, same old routine right to the minute with all the bells. And Mikhailovna looked almost pleased to see us. Cracked half a smile, she did.' I nod and look around our isolated room. It's the same one we had when we first moved in. 'It feels strange, not having our leg too,' says Masha, and goes to shake it, but can't. I laugh.

'Thank goodness they used general anaesthetic,' I say again. I still can't quite believe we've actually done it.

'I wasn't having you ruin it for us again. Coming all the way up here just to be humiliated by my worm of a sister.'

'And it doesn't even hurt much now, does it?'

'Speak for yourself. I'm in agony.'

'No, you're not. I wonder what people will think? Back at school?'

What I actually mean is, I wonder what Slava will think. We've been here two weeks and we've got two more to go. I can't bear to think of him and Anyootka together every day, sitting next to each other in class, and under the pear tree. Olessya wrote us a card but she didn't say anything about them. He hasn't written any cards. Not one. I miss him all the time. *All* the time. I can't wait to go back. Today's the first day we can get out of bed and start walking again.

'I'll tell you what they'll think, they'll think we're idiots. It won't make any difference to them, will it?' says Masha. 'I mean, the kids don't care if we've got five legs. It's all for the *yobinny* Medical Commission. We have to go and mutilate ourselves, don't we? We have to go and lop bits of ourselves right off, just to please the morons on the panel.'

'I was thinking, Masha … you know how they're all defectologists on the panel? Well, I was thinking maybe we could study to be defectologists ourselves? You never see any who are actually Defective themselves. It makes sense though, doesn't it?'

'You can study whatever you like. I'm going to be a trapeze artist in a circus, now we haven't got the leg.'

I laugh. 'I'm not going up any trapeze! I'm scared of heights!'

'And I'm not training to be a defectologist. I'm fed up of seeing scarecrows like you day in, day out!'

The door bangs open and Aunty Nadya comes in. Aunty Nadya! We smile and hold out our arms to be hugged. We all laughed so much when she brought us back to SNIP, in the very same room. It's like Masha says, it's really strange. So much has changed in us since we left. I never thought that my life would be filled with the thought of one boy instead of thoughts of being Together, and of Masha. Slava has pushed all that into a corner.

'Right then, girls, on your feet!' she says, not even hugging us. 'Today's the day we get up and walk.'

'Get up and *run*, you mean!' shouts Masha. 'Run and run!'

'Well, let's do the walking bit first, shall we,' she sniffs. 'Right then, legs over the bed, up we get, arms round each other and …'

*Plookh!* We fall right over, flat on our faces. She picks us up, laughing.

'*Ladno* … try just standing first.' She lets go of us and *plookh!* down we go again, head first. It hurts. 'Hmm, your balance is going to be a bit different now, girls, the leg was heavy, fifteen kilos—'

'I wanted to keep it, why wouldn't they let us keep it? I wanted to pickle it in a jar.'

'*Aaakh*, Masha, you say the oddest things,' says Aunty Nadya, shaking her head. 'I suppose you'd have it on display by your bed? Well, enough of that. Right, this time try and lean back to compensate for the leg. That's it. *Aaakh!*' She shouts as we're over again with even more of a bang. I can't keep us standing up, not for a second. Not even for half a second.

'I'm s-scared.' I look up at Aunty Nadya. 'What's wrong? What's h-happening?'

'Now, now, none of that talk. Remember, it took us months to get you to walk. It will just take a bit of time, that's all.'

'I'm going to be black and blue, and have two broken arms by that time,' grumbles Masha, as Aunty Nadya lifts us back on the edge of the bed.

'Right. We'll start off with a chair, like we did when you were little. Here you are.' She pushes one towards us, and we grab the back of it. '*Tak* … I'll hold you from behind and you stand up … *Aaakh!*' This time we fall over, right into the chair, and she catches us just in time to stop us breaking our noses, but we all three end up in a stupid heap on the floor.

'It's as if every time we try and stand, something's p-pushing us down,' I say. 'As if someone's p-pushing us right down flat.' I won't cry. I look at Masha. She'll tell me to stop being a sheep. She'll tell me everything's going to be all right. But she doesn't. She just looks up at Aunty Nadya and bites her bottom lip.

## 27 March 1968

### We hear on the radio of an important death

The next day we're sitting in bed not talking much, waiting for Aunty Nadya to come back for more physiotherapy. The State radio speaker in the room is playing really sad classical music, going on and on and on, with no talking in between, and not even any news every half hour, like there always is. The music's playing exactly the same tunes as the funeral orchestra plays when it passes the School with a body in the back of a bus on its way to the cemetery at the end of Red Decembrist Street. There's this little brass band that walks behind the bus, playing the same depressing thing.

'I wish they'd stop playing that *yobinny* music,' says Masha, after we've been listening for what seems like hours. She bangs her fist on the bed. 'You'd think someone had died.'

We don't talk to each other until the cleaner, Aunty Vladlena, comes in to mop the floor.

'Someone's died,' she says, pointing her mop up at the speaker.

'Wh-who?'

'Dunno, Dasha. Some big pine cone. Someone from the Presidium or the Central Committee, most likely. Not Brezhnev though, he's too young. Could be any of the others though.'

'Wh-why don't they say who it is?'

'They will. Eventually. Not likely to be poor old Khrushchev either. He's been banished, so he wouldn't get the whole funeral music treatment.'

'I don't care who it is,' says Masha. 'I just wish they'd drop it.'

'Last time someone important died, we had three days of this music, so get used to it, love.'

She's mopping under our bed by the time Aunty Nadya comes in carrying a pair of crutches under her arm.

'Well, Vladlena, who do we think's died then?'

She's not looking at us.

Crutches? Me and Masha stare at each other and then back at them. What do we need crutches for? We haven't needed those since we were first learning to walk.

'Could be anyone, Nadezhda Fyodorovna.'

'Not Brezhnev though.'

'*Nyet* … Too young.'

'Wait a minute. I think it's stopped.'

They both stand there, looking up at the speaker, waiting for an announcement.

*It is officially announced*, says the deep, slow voice of Mayak State Radio … we all hold our breath. Except Masha. She doesn't really care who's died … *that the Hero of the Soviet Union, Yuri Gagarin, the world's first cosmonaut, has perished.*

I feel like someone's punched me in the stomach. Gagarin? No! No, no, no! How? Aunty Vladlena claps her hand over her mouth. We can't stop staring up at the speaker. *The announcement of Colonel Gagarin's death has just been made by the Communist Party's Central Committee, the Presidium of the Supreme Soviet, the Soviet Council of Ministers* … on and on he goes about who's made the announcement that Gagarin is dead, but he doesn't say the most important thing – how did it happen?

'P-Perished? What d-does that mean?'

I look up at Aunty Nadya, but she's gone completely white. 'It means killed,' she says after a bit. 'But who killed him? How? What?' And then, she and Aunty Vladlena run right out of the room, leaving us alone.

When they've gone, I see she's dropped the crutches on the floor.

Our crutches.

## April 1968

### And with Gagarin's death the hope for Communism fades away

You'd have thought the world had ended that day. In a way it had. Everyone just seemed to lose heart somehow.

'You really shouldn't take this so badly, girls, you really shouldn't.'

Aunty Nadya's sitting in the chair by our bed. It's been two weeks since we first tried to walk. Two weeks since Yuri Gagarin was killed.

'How can we not take it badly? That we'll never walk again? Not by ourselves, at any rate,' says Masha, thumping the pillow.

Masha cried a week ago when Aunty Nadya told us that amputating the leg had altered our balance so much, we'd probably never be able to walk without crutches. The last time I saw her cry was when Lucia left SNIP. Lucia had hopped into our room to say goodbye, and had given Masha a slap on the shoulder, saying, 'Right, back to the Home Front. If I don't run away again, I'll write,' and when she'd gone, Masha had put her head under her pillow and cried and cried and cried, all muffled. We never talked about that. And she did again, a week ago. She hated herself for crying, but she couldn't keep it in. We weren't cripples before, we were just … Together. At least I know it won't make any difference to Slava. As long as Anyootka hasn't stolen him away from me …

'Now come along. At least you can learn to walk with crutches. Look on the bright side.'

'What bright side?' Masha's all knotted up inside. 'We did the amputation to look better for that stupid Committee, we did it so we'd be graded Four, and now we're on crutches they'll probably grade us Three. We've just gone and assassinated our chances of a good future …'

'Now, don't talk such silliness, Masha. We've got to leave tomorrow … assassinated your chances, indeed …'

'Talking of assassinations,' says Aunty Vladlena, walking in through the open door. 'Did you hear it was the Americans that killed Gagarin?'

'Well, so they say … Vladlena, we really shouldn't believe rumours—'

'What else are we supposed to believe, when we don't get told nothing?'

'The less you know …' says Aunty Nadya, getting up with a sigh.

'It's like the whole country's died with him, isn't it?' goes on Aunty Vladlena, 'just like the whole country's been shot in the heart somehow, like Gagarin was by Uncle Sam.'

'Please stop that, Vladlena, I'm having enough of a problem with the girls. Dasha can't stop sniffling about him and neither can any of the kitchen staff. We've had salty soup all week …'

'*Da-oosh!* Well, whatever you may say, Nadezhda Fyodorovna, it's like we've not just lost Gagarin, it's like we've lost the will to go on and fight for everything, you know? He was our shining light. Those *yobinny* Americans! We should nuke the lot of 'em.'

'That's quite enough, Vladlena – as if Masha's language isn't bad enough as it is. I do believe you've been drinking. Now off you go, shoo, shoo.' She shuts the door on Vladlena, turns back to us and sighs again. We all know Aunty Vladlena's right, though. Everyone's going around looking like deflated balloons. The Soviet Union just doesn't seem to be the Best of all Possible Worlds any more without Yuri Gagarin in it. I hate the Americans more than ever now. 'Come on then.' Aunty Nadya gets up and shakes her head. 'Let's try to walk with those crutches again.'

## We learn a bit more about the Comrade Healthies on our trip back to school

'Two heads, two passports, two tickets,' says the official at the boarding desk. She's supposed to be processing our tickets for the Aeroflot flight, from Moscow to Rostov-on-Don. She goes back to shuffling papers, and doesn't look up when Aunty Nadya leans over the counter with our three passports.

'Don't be ridiculous, comrade! They don't need two seats. They need one!'

We got here really early, to avoid queues, but I can see out of the corner of my eye that other people are catching sight of us and slithering up to look.

'Now you just listen to me, comrade,' she goes on, waving the passports at the official. 'The Ministry of Social Protection has allotted enough money for only two air fares. Mine and theirs. They were given one ticket between them on the train up here because they lie on one bunk. Now they are post-operational amputees and must fly, but again, they only sit on one seat. Are you going to question the Ministry of Social Protection?'

The woman doesn't look up. She just says loudly: 'Next.' Aunty Nadya elbows the next passenger in the chest as he tries to get past, and turns back to the official.

'They're tiny, see? Like children, and they have one bottom for one seat. Turn round and show them your bottom, girls.' We do, but I don't think the woman is even looking at us. Everyone else is though. 'And the flight is in less than an hour. I demand you let us through.'

'*Nyet*,' says the official.

'What do you mean, *nyet?*'

'I mean *nyet*. Like I say, two heads, two passports – two tickets. Buy another one or stay behind.'

'*Pozor!*' She angrily digs in her handbag and hands over her own money for our extra ticket. That must be a month's wages for her.

Masha gets to sit by the window in the plane and I put my head on Aunty Nadya's lap. She's still cross as a box of cockroaches, but Masha's bouncing up and down, all excited to be flying, forgetting that we can't walk by ourselves any more, and that the Commission is next week. And that Aunty Nadya's had to pay for another ticket. I wish I could forget things, like Masha does.

'You'll be seeing your Slavochka soon, and Olesskinka, and Lyudinka,' says Aunty Nadya, stroking my head. She's still stroking me when I fall asleep.

When we land, we let everyone off first because there's an ambulance coming to meet us, to drive us from Rostov-on-Don to Novocherkassk. The two women paramedics get on, to help us off, but when they see us walking down the aisle, holding the seats for support, they just back away. Further and further away, 'til they're almost falling out of the plane door.

'Come along, comrades, here are the girls,' says Aunty Nadya crossly.

'We're not taking that,' says one of them.

'Whatever do you mean? Help them off immediately.'

'*Nyetooshki*.'

'Don't be ridiculous. Why can you not take them?'

The two of them look at each other, then one says, 'Well … for a start, it can walk, can't it? Ambulances are for people who need to be stretchered. This is a waste of State time and money, that's what it is.' They're getting angry themselves now. I've noticed when people are afraid, they do that. 'If it can run down the aisle it can run to the bus station.' And then they almost tumble backwards down the steps in their hurry to get away from us and back to the ambulance.

Aunty Nadya stamps her foot angrily, but there's nothing she can do, so we walk out through the airport to the bus stop and she sits us on our suitcase on the pavement.

'Oh, for goodness sake, comrades, get away from them, just get away! You're like flies round a dustbin!' She bats at all the usual crowds of stupid, gawping people who are pointing and calling us the same old names. Masha doesn't say anything. What's the point? We both cover our faces with our hands to keep off the flies. I wish it wasn't so hot. I wish there was some shade.

We sit there, for what seems like all day but Aunty Nadya says it's only been two hours, when our bus comes.

'Here it is at last, girls, here's the bus. Up you get. Hey, comrades! Comrades! Let us through, I have post-operational amputees, please show some common kindness. Comrades!' But it's no good; they've all pushed past us with their bags. By the time we get on, there's only one seat left. We stand looking at this one little seat, and then around at the fat, sweaty, stinky passengers, who are staring at us but not getting up. They all want their seats.

After a bit, Aunty Nadya sits down with a puff, and pulls us on to her lap facing her. The man next to us is chain-smoking papirosas and has a cage of hens on his lap. We rest our heads on her shoulders and hold her through the bumpy, two-hour ride. It's so hot I think I'm going to melt into a puddle. Masha's sick into a plastic bag.

'Right, girls, well done. Well done. Off we get.' She helps us off and sits us on our suitcase again while she looks for a car to flag down.

There aren't any at all on the streets. 'Don't worry,' she says, wiping the sweat off her face. 'Every car moonlights as a gypsy taxi, so we'll be home in no time.' She sounds cheerful, but she's looking tired. 'No time at all.'

Finally a red Zhiguli comes round the corner, and she stops it and bends down to talk to the driver. 'I have post-operational amputees here,' she says. He doesn't even look at the two of us. Some people do and some people don't. 'We need to get to the School for Invalids on Red Decembrist Street.'

He spits on the ground. 'Ten roubles.'

'Ten! That's ridiculous, it's five minutes from here. That's a day's wages.'

'I'm the one with the car.' He spits again.

'I only have five roubles left, comrade. Please take us for five. They're very weak, and just learning to walk on crutches. It's hot and we have luggage. Please, comrade. Please.'

He shrugs. 'There's a shortage of petrol. No one will take you for five. Let them walk.' And he drives off.

'Very well, girls. Very well,' she says, straightening up. 'Walking it is then. Pick up your crutches. Off we go. It won't take long. Not long at all.'

The back streets are all uneven, with cobbles and potholes, and we haven't gone twenty metres before the crowds come out of nowhere. She's right, they're like flies lured by the stench of rotting food. Aunty Nadya's struggling along with our suitcases, and there are dozens of men behind us, and no one offers to take her bags, and we're trying to balance with the crutches so as not to fall flat on our faces in front of them all. And it's still so hot. I keep thinking of Olessya and how I've got to be extraordinary and telling myself that I'm walking to Slava. Back to Slava. I won't cry, I won't. Some of the kids start throwing stones at us.

'Remember your dignity, girls,' hisses Aunty Nadya. I think she's afraid Masha's going to start throwing stones back, but she's too tired to do anything. 'Remember your dignity.'

## May 1968

### We go before the Medical Commission to get graded

'Right, you, no stuttering. They'll think we're gibbering idiots if you stutter. Got it?'

I nod. Me and Masha are waiting in the anteroom to the Room of Relaxation, where the panel of the Medical Commission is sitting. Masha keeps fiddling with the button on her trousers.

'But can't you answer their questions, Mash? Just this time? In case I *do* stutter?'

'In c-case you st-stutter? You're doing it now! Listen to yourself!' She slaps me on the cheek. 'No, I can't fucking well answer all their questions, you're supposed to be the clever one. They'll ask us algebra and history, and all sorts of trick questions too.' I nod again. I wasn't stuttering. She's lying. I only stutter when I'm with someone. 'And about what we want to do, and stuff like that, so you'd better say you want to be a doctor or something.' I nod again. 'And *don't* stutter!'

The door opens and we're invited in. We get up and tuck our crutches under one arm each. The three of them are sitting behind a long wooden table right at the end of the room, so we have to walk right up to them. They watch us approaching, then they look down at their papers and start writing.

'G-good m-morning,' I say after a bit, thinking I should be polite.

'You may go,' says the one in the middle, still writing. Go? I don't understand. Neither does Masha. Go where? The woman looks up then. 'I said you may go. Do you not understand plain Russian?'

We turn around then and walk right on out.

'How come you all got asked questions and we didn't? How come?' Masha's staring at Olessya and Little Lyuda, like they're in some sort of conspiracy against us. We're all sitting on our bed that evening. After the Commission.

'I don't know, Mashinka,' says Little Lyuda. 'They asked Sunny Nina questions too and Big Boris, and all the boys. I don't know, I really don't. But maybe it's a good thing. Right?'

I don't think it's a good thing at all, but I don't say anything.

'Anyway,' says Olessya slowly. She looks a bit sad. 'Anyway, I've got an exam tomorrow. I've got to get top marks, so I'd better do some studying.'

'We've got an exam in algebra tomorrow too,' says Masha. 'Can you help me, Lyudochka? Help explain to your little Mashinka the rules of algebra again? My scarecrow here doesn't explain it like you do. Pleeeeze?'

'Yes, of course I can,' she says, smiling. 'We can do it now if you like. All together.' Little Lyuda is so healthy. And Slava hasn't even been talking to Anyootka. He's been with me all the time.

He touches me, just a little touch, whenever he can. And he looks at me with his deep dark eyes. Everything's going to be all right.

### We get our grades, then Masha scares me

'Grade One?! Grade *One?!*' Masha can hardly speak, she's so angry.

'I can't understand it, I can't,' says Olessya. She's got her head in her hands. We're outside on the wooden ramp leading down from the school door. 'And I can't understand how the rest of us got Grade Two. That means we'll be banished to closed institutions for the rest of our lives, doing nothing except staring out of the window. Why? Why? What happened? What's happening?'

'Well, at least you're *yobinny* Grade Two. I'm Grade *One!* How can I be Grade *One?!*' says Masha, thumping her fist on the steps.

Big Boris is sitting on the dusty ground. We're all in shock. Slava's just shaking his head. Sunny Nina's with us. She started off in our class, but she was put up to the one above because she's so bright, so she's graduating now. Sunny Nina got Grade Two as well. She wanted to be a geologist. Now none of us can be anything. Don't they *want* us contributing to the Socialist work force? After all they've done for us? Don't they *want* us to work to a Communist future?

'It's because she stuttered, isn't it? Isn't it? My moron?'

'Shut up, Masha,' says Olessya.

'But Grade One!' she goes on, ignoring her. 'That's Total Defectives. That means paralysed and not being able to think, or move, or do anything for yourself. It means imbecile. And all because she stuttered. It means peeing yourself, it means—'

'Shut *up*, Masha.'

We sit there for a bit then, none of us saying anything. Slava's got his transistor radio on, like he always does, and there's this stupidly happy Soviet song on, with the singer shouting *Further and further! We will strive to succeed even further!* And there are these stupid cymbals too, clashing, and the orchestra almost bursting right out of the radio, it's so … so *triumphant*. It's as if everyone in the world's laughing at us for thinking we could be part of their perfect society. We sit there listening, and I'm just thinking that Grade One means you might as well be dead. Grade Two means you might as well be dead, but if you're not, you can earn some kopecks by putting cardboard boxes together for a living in an asylum. I'm also thinking we could go and live with Slava in his village with his parents. Because the only thing worse than being kept in an asylum is being without Slava.

He's not coming to Summer Camp this year either. He wants to, but his mum won't let him again. She says he needs some extra looking after. But he's staying on at school until we leave, even though it's summer holidays now. He wants to be with me as long as possible.

We keep on all sitting there in the sun on the ramp, not talking. 'So … where will you g-go then, Olessya?' I ask, after we've been sitting for ages. She's leaving on Friday. That's in three days.

'I'm going back to Moscow. The Ministry of Protection's assigning me to some Home for Old People for the rest of my life. I can't even choose which one. I got top marks. I got the best diploma … I tried so hard … I thought … I believed …' She shakes her head and balls her fists up tight like grenades.

There's a kids' choir singing now on the radio. *Everyone on the planet should laugh with the children, should laugh with the children, everyone on the planet should be friends, they should! They should! They should!*

'Turn it off, Slavochka,' says Olessya wearily. He leans over and switches it off. I look around at Big Boris and Sunny Nina and Little Lyuda. 'What about you three?'

'We're all being sent to a Home here in Novocherkassk,' says Lyuda in the smallest voice ever. 'The green bus is coming for us tomorrow. To take us away. They said not to bother to pack. But I will. I'll pack just in case.'

'Well. Come back and visit us,' says Masha. 'If you're going to be living here in town. Come back and visit.'

'Yeah. Class of '68. Don't forget us, will you, eh?' says Big Boris. He picks up a twig and throws it at the wall. 'Don't forget us while you're here, playing in the orchestra, and dancing, and swotting like crazy for your *yobinny* diplomas. Write about us in your memoirs.'

We sit around on the ramp after that, still not really talking, then Masha says it's too hot and picks up her crutch and goes in.

'Well, I'm not staying locked away in some stuffy, boring asylum doing nothing all my life,' she says, as we walk back to the dorm. My heart goes cold. I can't leave Slava. Not ever. We've got another year here. I won't mention staying with him in his village after we graduate. Not yet. I've got a whole year left to soften her up.

'At least we have another year of school. Things might change, Mashinka.'

'Another year of school!' She spits on the floor. 'What's the point of studying if we can never work?'

'They might change the rules on Defectives again. Or Brezhnev might die.'

'I'm not staying in a school where everyone's a hateful *pizdyets* waiting for Brezhnev to die. *Nyetooshki*. I'm off.'

'What?!' I stop and tug her back. 'What do you mean – off? We need to graduate, Masha. We can't *leave*. We need to get our diploma.'

'Why do you need your *yobinny* diploma now? It's all a stupid fucking lie. Everyone's been shitting themselves trying to pass exams – you're a nervous wreck by the time it comes to sitting them – and what for? Tell me that? What fucking for?'

'We can't just *go*,' I say stupidly.

'We can. If I want to.'

'No!' I start pulling at her sleeve. 'No! We can't! I won't!' I'm shouting at her, and she stares at me like I've gone mad. 'I won't go. I won't leave Slava!'

'Slava?' She turns and looks hard at me. 'What's Slava to you? Eh?' I just stand there, panting. 'Olessya left Big Boris, didn't she? And Sunny Nina left Vanya. Everyone leaves each other. What's so special about you and Peanut?'

'I won't leave him, Masha. You can't make me.' I shouldn't have said that. I knew it as soon as it spilt out.

'What?! Why? Have you gone and fallen in love or something?' Her eyes start going black. 'With Peanut? *Nyet, nyet, nyet.*' She shakes her head slowly, still looking at me like that snake in the zoo did, and then she grabs my upper arm so tight it hurts. 'I told you, I told you, didn't I? You can mess around a bit, but you're never to fall in love with anyone. I should never have let him kiss you, I knew I shouldn't. I'll kill him! I'll kill you!'

'No, Masha, no! … You've … you've got it all wrong.' I hold her arm too, so our two arms are wound together. 'All wrong.' Quick! Think! Think! 'It's not that. I haven't fallen in love. He's just … he's fun; you think he's fun too … I like hanging round him, is all. The kissing's just a laugh. Everyone kisses.' Think! Think! Don't let her know what *I'm* thinking. 'When I said I won't leave Slava, all I mean is that the three of us are having a laugh. That's all.' She keeps looking me in the eye like I'm still crazy or something, but after a bit, she slowly releases my arm.

'All right, c'mon then, but just remember – me and you are what it's all about.'

'Yes, Mash.'

'Just me and you.'

## Not going on the end-of-term trip

I'll have to wait, that's all. She'll come around to the idea of me and Slava in a year. Just as long as I can keep her here. I wish the other kids were nicer to her, but they don't like her *chortik*. That's what Mummy used to call the Little Devil that rises up inside her when she's angry and takes her over. It's when her eyes go black as if there really is the shadow of a devil passing inside her head. It scares me.

I won't think of that. This morning is the day of the end-of-term school trip. We have it every summer and we all love it. Last year we drove along the banks of the River Tuzlov, and watched the swans flying over the golden-domed churches. It was all like something out of a real Russian fairy tale. We always sit next to Slava. Everyone's already on the bus when we go running up to it, because I had to wash our nappies, so we're a bit late, and when we clamber on, we see he's saved a seat at the back for us. He's got himself on the right side of the bus, which means I'm the one pressed up against him. We sit down and wait for the bus to start. Everyone's so excited, it's like a real holiday.

'*Nyet.*' Mikhail Ivanovich, the driver, is standing at the front and pointing at us. 'You can't sit in one seat when there's two of you.' He only came to work here a few months ago, but he doesn't like us. That's what happens. Some people just like us, and some people just don't. Masha says it's their problem, not ours.

'B-but we always sit on one s-seat.'

'Not with me you don't.'

Icy Valya's at the front and she starts tittering into her friend's shoulder. Then her friend starts tittering, and soon the whole little bus is laughing at us.

The driver smiles. 'Right, anyone offering to give up their seat for these two beauties?' He knows they won't.

'I will,' says Slava, and starts to get off his seat, but I push him back down and Masha's so angry she doesn't even want to go any more. We stand up slowly, and walk back down the aisle of the bus, past everyone, all watching us, and get off.

When the bus has driven off, we walk straight to the empty Hall for Extra-Curricular Activities without saying a word. We go into the middle of it, hold each other's arms and dance slowly round and round. Without a word, without music. We just dance.

## 1 June 1968

### We hear what happened to our school friends who graduated

'There's nothing to do here. Let's go and sit with Valentina Alexandrovna,' says Masha, throwing the blanket off our bed and climbing out. It's strange seeing Little Lyuda's bed next to ours, all empty now. And Olessya's and Sunny Nina's empty too. The others are back from the school trip and are all yapping at the other end of the dorm about what they saw, as if it's the most amazing trip they've ever been on or something.

'OK, Mash,' I say. I like it when Valentina Alexandrovna tells us about her boyfriend (he's called Slava too), who's an engineer in the Locomotive Factory, and how they go out at weekends to his parents' dacha, and play with their dog Tima, or walk down to Baba Kira who keeps a cow to drink the fresh milk. '*Foo!*' Masha had said. 'Milk straight from a cow's tits!' Valentina Alexandrovna had laughed at that, and said it was all warm and frothy.

We knock on her door. There's no reply but we can see a light from a crack under the door and there's a strange noise coming from inside.

'Go on, open it,' says Masha.

'We can't just barge in, I'll knock again.' There's still no reply so Masha goes and opens the door a crack and tells me to poke my head around. She's sitting at her desk with only the table lamp on, leaning over awkwardly with her head bent. I think she's crying.

'What is it?' whispers Masha and pushes the door open some more so she can see too. Valentina Alexandrovna looks up then, and sees us.

'Girls! Oh, girls!'

She says it like her heart's breaking in two, so we take a step back into the shadows. It's scary.

'Come in, come in!' She gets up then, and comes walking, well maybe more staggering really, over to us, with her arms open, and hugs us so tight she almost knocks us clean over. She smells strongly of sweet cherries. She said Baba Kira made her own cherry liquor infusion … is she drunk? She can't be. Nice, educated, intelligent women don't get drunk.

We all kind of stagger over together to her desk, because she's still clinging on to us, then she sits down with a thump in our armchair and puts her hands over her face.

'I saw them, girls, I went to visit …' Her voice is muffled, but me and Masha can hear anything when we want to. 'I wanted to see if they needed anything. The guard wouldn't let me through the gates. He said I needed a special pass from the Ministry of Social Protection. It took me three weeks to get it and by then I was too late … too late …' She starts crying again. She just can't stop.

'Too late for what?' says Masha, getting up and shaking her by the shoulder. 'Too late for what?'

'Oh, girls, girls, it's not a Home at all, it's an Asylum for the Unwanted. The conditions there … like a Madhouse … the stench, metal beds crammed into small rooms, excrement, people lying on the floor, the elderly there starve to death, and the wailing, the wailing, it's hell in there … the staff are little more than beasts … they beat them for nothing, I saw them, they don't feed those who can't feed themselves, so they're skeletons … death is everywhere …' She keeps sobbing, and talking, and then sobbing again. Her face is all blotchy and puffy.

'Little Lyuda, our Little Lyuda, must have known somehow, or suspected. She took a bottle of insecticide with her from our storeroom … I found her alone in agony. It took her twenty-four hours to die, my Little Lyuda … Little Lyuda … the Director refused to have her hospitalized. He said she'd just keep on trying, so best to let her go first time. That's what he said: "Let the little poppet go first time."'

We don't move, me and Masha. We can't move. I feel dead with shock.

'I got them to call her mother in Moscow, the one who adopted her before she had her accident. She flew down the next morning, she was weeping over her and pulling out her hair, saying: How could you punish me like this, Lyudochka? How could you punish me? And all Lyuda could say was: *I didn't want to live in a world without love. It's not so terrible to die among strangers.* That's what she said. And her mother wept even more, and said she did love her, she said she'd always loved her, and had always missed her so much it broke her heart, which is why she cut off all contact. But it was too late to save her then. Oh, girls! Girls! What have we done?' She looks up at us with her eyes all smudged and wild like she's been possessed. 'What have we done?'

Masha and I take a step back.

'I had no idea … no idea …' she goes on, babbling like she's mad. 'The other teachers here, they didn't say, they don't talk about it … they've never visited … Aaakh, Sunny Nina, pretty blonde little Nina, she hanged herself from the window latch with her belt. Boris has gone, he escaped somehow, but if they catch him – and they will – he'll be sent to a prison for invalids … I had no idea … the other teachers suspect, but they don't go and see for themselves because they only want what's best for you, girls, they want to believe it's all for the best … Are we wrong? *Aaakh!* Are we wrong?'

We take another step back, and then turn and just run like mad, out of the room. We run and run, our crutches clattering on the wooden floor, leaving the sound of her crying behind. We run out into the courtyard and around the walls of the courtyard, until we get to the closed gate. And then there's nowhere else to run, so we climb down to the cobbler's cellar, and sit down with a thump on the floor among the sawdust and leather cut-offs, panting. I look at Masha. Her eyes are glassy, like she's not seeing anything. And then I start crying, like I'll never stop, bent over forward with my head in the sawdust. While Masha just sits very still and stares at the wall.

## We tell Slava about the others and that everything was a lie, then we get drunk

The next morning the bell goes and we get up, just like we always do. We get washed, I scrub our nappy clean and hang it up. Just like I always do. We go to breakfast and we eat our curds and whey. Slava looks across the table at us. He knows something's happened.

When we go out, Masha and me sit under the pear tree.

'So shall we tell anyone?' asks Masha. 'About what happened? What it's like when you leave here?'

I shake my head. 'No. They're right. We don't need to know … they're right …'

Slava comes out of the breakfast room and looks over at us. 'Except Slava,' I say. 'He's our best friend and he's got family. He won't have to go there.' What I'm really thinking is, he won't let *me* go anywhere like that either. He'll want me to stay with him, in his village, where there are ducks and hens and cows, which give warm, frothy milk straight from their udders. I'll cook and clean for his family, I'll …

'Hey, girls. What's happened?'

'Slava,' we say together. He sits down and then I tell him everything, just like Valentina Alexandrovna did. When I've finished, his expression hasn't changed.

'We need vodka,' he says in a quiet voice. 'Get us some vodka.'

Me and Masha get up then, and walk down to the kitchens.

'Morning, girlies! What have you two come to scrounge today?' Aunty Shura is fat and greasy and smells of cabbage, but she always gets us a bottle in exchange for letting some of the townspeople come and look at us. We don't do it often. Masha's always ill after we drink, and I only do it so Slava and I can kiss a bit without her minding. We've never had sex again though. Masha hasn't been drunk enough. The townspeople pay Aunty Shura to see us and she spends some of it to buy us cheap cigarettes or vodka, and keeps the rest for herself. An hour later, we're in the cold pantry, stripped to our pants and vest, with three of Shura's clients circling us. They want to see everything, so we keep undressing down to nothing, but it only takes ten minutes and Aunty Shura is always there and won't let them touch us. She looks after us. Masha always says that if Ronnie and Donnie, the American twins, can get people to give them hundreds of American dollars to look at them, why shouldn't we get a bottle of Russian vodka?

We get dressed afterwards and walk out, with the bottle tucked under my shirt.

'What about Olessya?' I say.

'What about her? She never liked us doing this, but she's not here to slap our wrists now, is she?'

'No. I mean we must get Aunty Nadya to find out where she is. Make sure it's not like the place here. Olessya hasn't written, and she said she would.'

'Aunty Nadya can't save everyone. She's ours.'

I sigh. Sometimes I just want to take her head in my hands and squeeze and squeeze until it cracks like a nut and let some pity for other people seep in. I worry so much about Olessya and Masha doesn't worry at all. I'll ask Aunty Nadya anyway, I'll just come out with it, then Masha can't stop me. Masha can't read my mind.

Slava's waiting for us and we go down to the cobbler's cellar. He puts his transistor radio on the floor and turns the volume up. It's the Red Army Choir singing a marching song. He takes the first swig. 'To Big Boris, wherever he is,' he says.

I take the next gulp, screwing up my eyes and fighting down nausea.

'To Sunny Nina,' I say. And then I take another small swig and say, 'To Little Lyuda.'

'To us!' says Slava loudly, over the music, as I hand the bottle back to him.

'To survival!' says Masha, even louder, taking the bottle and handing it to me. 'To winning!'

'To life!' I take another gulp.

'To love!' Slava has a gulp.

'To forgetting …' My gulp.

'To Dashinkaaaa!' Slava has another long swig.

And then he leans in to me. But we're not drunk enough yet. The bottle's only half-empty. It won't have properly reached Masha and we need a double dose to his single one. He usually understands that …

'Dashinkaaa,' he whispers in my ear. He's grasping my knee tightly as if he's drowning and I'm a life raft. 'To life and love …' I can hardly hear him '… seize it while you can …'

Masha leans over and pushes him off.

'Whadjuh do that for …' he says, trying to focus on her and frowning. 'Leave us alone.'

'You leave *her* alone, *moodak*. Have you no respect for the fucking dead?' He sits back and takes another wobbly swig. Masha sniffs, then tips my arm to get me to drink as well. More and more. I feel the vodka swilling through my veins and mashing up my brain, taking away the pain. I can feel his warm hand on my back too, under my shirt, I can smell him. God, I wish we were alone. I want to live. I want to have him … just once, just once before I die … alone … and with him and forget …

*Kryaaaak!* Masha smashes him in the face with her fist and he goes flying on to the floor. 'Fuck off, *pizdyets*!' she screams. The marching music bangs on victoriously as he lies there on his back, not moving. We both stare at him. Then slowly he sits up. His eyes are blazing, black and angry. He's going to hit her back. I really think he's going to hit her back. He's swaying, or maybe it's me that's swaying. None of us say anything, and then finally, after what seems like hours, the music ends with a triumphant clash and he says in a slow, horribly quiet voice:

'What have you done?'

I go cold all over.

'What've *I* done?' yells Masha. '*Me?* You mean what've *you* done?! Keep your dirty black hands off my sister, you hear? She's mine, all mine, my sheep, my slave. All mine!'

Then he speaks again in that whispery, crazy cold voice. 'You don't know what you've done, d'you? *Nyet*. You don't know what you're doing to us, d'you? The three of us? Because you don't know *shit*, Masha Krivoshlyapova. We're in this t'gether, see. We're all fucked, and we may all stay fucked, and there's no time … no time … but there'r still things thad make life worth living. Bud you can't see it can you, you selfish, psychopathic *bitch*.'

'No! P-Please! P-Please don't, Slava!' I hold both hands out to him trying to get him to stop talking, to stop saying things that will mean we can never be together. If he does, then this is the end.

'And you …' He turns to me, his eyes glittering like he has his own *chortik*. 'You're weak, a feather, you won't stand ub to her, nodeven for me. Nodever. Will ya? Will ya?' He glares at me like he hates me.

I look at Masha, who's white with rage, and then back at him, who's black with rage. I'm shaking all over.

'I c-can't …' I stutter.

'You can!' he shouts. 'Do it now! Do it! Do it for me, do it for you, do it for us! Stand up to her!'

Masha's getting up. She reaches for her crutch so I reach for mine, automatically, and we almost fall over backwards. I can't look at him. I can't do it. He must understand that. I can't force Masha to let him and me be together. I can't force Masha to do anything. She's the strong one. She's in control. He's right, I'm weak. A feather blown in the wind. I'm scared of her. I can't suddenly stop doing what I've been doing all my life – doesn't he understand that? 'Slava … p-please, Slavochka …' I say and reach out to him again, but Masha tugs me back.

He grabs the bottle off the floor by the neck like he wants to throttle it.

'Go'way then, Dasha,' he says. 'Just get out of my life.' Then he tips it up, drinks it to the dregs, and the last thing I hear as we go up the steps is it smashing against the wall.

## I make an important decision

We go back to bed. Masha's banging her crutch around, trying to break everything. She realizes we've lost our last friend here in the school and she blames me. I lie back. The room's going round and round but I can hear her, the other end of the bed, still raging.

'I'm not staying in this fucking place with these *blyadi*. I'm gonna call Aunty Nadya and she'll come as soon as she can and take us back to Moscow. I'm out of here. I'm leaving this shit-hole and all the arseholes in it. We'll go back to live in SNIP, you can say goodbye to your *yobinny* sprat of a lover. You can say goodbye, that's what you can do.'

But I already have, or rather he has. And now I know what

I'm going to do. I knew the moment he told me in that cold voice to get out of his life. I knew as we were falling all over the courtyard and up the stairs to our dorm. I know now, clear as a bell what to do.

It's just a question of how.

## I decide to hang myself

The next morning is sunny. Good. We can put the washing out on the line, standing on the upturned washing basket. I've got it all worked out. I'm going to hang myself. Just like Sunny Nina did. Well not just like her. Not from a window latch with a belt. I'm going to do it with the washing line, which we knot around a branch of the pear tree. Slava told me once that one of the other girls did it, before we came: she hung herself from the pear tree. No one knows why. She came out at night with a rope but I can't do it at night, because Masha mustn't suspect anything.

'Not eating?' she points at my bowl of buckwheat porridge.

'No. Not hungry. You eat it.'

She does, without asking any more questions, and then we go out into the courtyard. Slava's sitting there under the pear tree with Anyootka. Their dark heads are bent together over a book of poetry, and as we walk past, I see that it's Pasternak. That should hurt, but strangely it doesn't matter. It's as if I'm so sad I couldn't get any sadder. I'm just looking forward to stopping it all by dying. I'm looking forward to feeling nothing, ever again. He doesn't look up at us. Good. That makes it easier. We walk to the laundry room. It's our turn on the rota. They like to teach us how to cook and clean in school so we can be independent.

'We're well rid of the little rat,' says Masha. 'Sitting there with his next morsel, on the grass. See how much he cared for you?' She snaps her fingers in my face. 'This is how much. We'll find a job in SNIP, that's what we'll do. In Moscow. We're special, we are. Not like these morons. We'll start again.' She looks across at me, and I nod, feeling dead already.

Maybe Masha will be all right when I kill myself. It's only *my* neck that will break. They'll probably just amputate me, like they did our leg. They'll give her another prosthetic leg in SNIP instead of mine, that's what they'll do. And if she isn't all right ... well I don't care. I won't know. I hate her.

It was quick, apparently. That's what Slava said, when this girl hung herself. Snap. Like falling under a train. Or a bullet through the heart. It doesn't hurt. I wouldn't want it to hurt, like the poison with Little Lyuda, but if it did, I'd do it anyway. I didn't choose Masha. I chose Slava. But I don't want to hang myself right in front of him. I don't hate him. Perhaps they'll move away?

We walk to the laundry room. I pick up the wicker basket and throw the washing in. Then I pick up the washing line – it's rough, so I know the knot won't slip – and place it on the pile of washing. We walk back out into the sunshine. Everything seems to be in slow motion. It's hard to balance with our crutches and the heavy basket full of wet washing, but we manage it. We manage everything, Masha and me.

I have to make a noose. She won't notice because she doesn't suspect and I'm so strangely calm that my heart isn't even beating fast. Odd really, that we do everything in perfect physical harmony, and yet she doesn't know I'm about to kill myself. The birds are singing fit to burst, and there's the usual tinny music coming from Slava's radio. Music for Anyootka now, instead of for me. We walk to the pear tree. The two of them are on the other side, with their heads still dipped together. They haven't left. I'm sorry that they'll have to see me die. We empty the washing on to a plastic sheet on the ground, and then turn the laundry basket over to stand on it. We can stand without crutches now – Aunty Nadya was right, it was all a question of balance. We got there in the end. Everything looks sharply in focus. I can see a tiny ladybird up there on the branch, as if it's right in front of my nose. I throw the rope over the branch and tie a knot. Then I tie a noose. Then I put it over my head, lift my leg and kick the basket out from under us.

## I get told off by Vera Stepanovna for being insane

It didn't work.

The knot didn't hold and the noose slipped right off over my head. I'm an idiot, and I'm still here, standing outside Vera Stepanovna's office waiting to be given what the kids here call 'the suicide talk'. Turns out she gives it a lot. But I didn't know that. They don't tell us about the attempted suicides.

Masha's so furious I think she's going to kill me and save me the trouble.

'What the *hell* were you thinking of?' she says for the millionth time. 'You didn't think what would happen to *me*, did you? Your sister?' She's trembling. She may be angry, but she's in shock too. 'Well? Did you? If you'd known what you were actually doing with that noose – fat chance of *that* – we'd be goners.'

I shrug. All I can feel is this dull, aching despair that I'm still alive. 'I thought … I thought they'd amputate you or something,' I say in a sort of croak, 'and then you'd be free of me.'

'I don't *want* to be free of you, moron! What would I do without you? Who'd wash our nappy? Who'd do everything for me? Who'd … who'd … always be there to talk to? I'd be alone, see? All … *alone*.'

I shake my head, thinking, *And I just go on living half a life in your shadow?* I think it. But I don't say it.

'Don't you *ever* try anything like that again, you *hear*?' She shakes her fist in my face. 'I'll be watching you now.' I remember the Director's words at the Novocherkassk asylum: *She'll just keep trying, so best let the little poppet go first time.* Masha probably remembers too. But it was easy for Little Lyuda and Sunny

Nina. They weren't Together like I am. How can you keep trying to kill yourself when you're Together?

The door to Vera Stepanovna's office opens, and we're told to come in and stand on the red rug.

She's furious too, of course.

'*Pozor!* It's a disgrace for the school, Dasha, a disgrace! To have one of our pupils try to take their own life? You are lucky I'm not sending you to a psychiatric institution for the insane. That is the normal procedure for those who attempt suicide. One must be insane not to want to live in the Soviet Union. We have done everything for you, cared for you, educated you and this is how you show your gratitude?' She's doing her usual pacing up and down. Now she stops in front of us. 'As Ostrovsky said, 'we have been given this life only once, to live to the full …'

I squeeze my eyes closed and wish I could put my hands over my ears. I really don't want to hear about Ostrovsky and Mankind right now.

What I want.

Is help.

'Did you hear her? Did you?' say Masha. We're walking back from Vera Stepanovna's office. Vera Stepanovna's called Aunty Nadya, to tell her to fly down and take us away as soon as possible. She doesn't want suicides on her books. 'If you try anything like that again we'll be put in a Madhouse. That's even worse than the Home here in Novocherkassk. And you'll be sure to muck it up again …'

'I don't care. Maybe we'll both want to kill ourselves if we get put in a Madhouse …'

'I'll never want to kill myself. I love life.'

'Even this life?'

'What's wrong with it? Life is what you make it. We've just got to keep trying until we find the right place and the right people. To never give up trying. *Never.* D'you understand? Do you?'

I nod, but I'm thinking that the only place with the right people is somewhere together with Slava.

## I say goodbye to Slava

The next morning at midday, we're sitting in the shade of the pear tree waiting for Aunty Nadya to come. The other kids are lounging around, but I can't see Slava. He probably asked his mother to take him back to the village. I can't blame him. What's the point of saying goodbye?

It's almost as if my sadness has seeped right through to Masha for once, so we're both sitting there, not talking, and not doing anything. Not even thinking.

'Girls!' We look up as Aunty Nadya walks through the gates. She holds out her arms, but neither of us jump up to run to her like we normally do. We both just sort of sit and stare at her with this dull, dead look. She's come to take us away. But to what? She walks up to us then, quite slowly, with her head on one side and then leans down to kiss us. Masha first.

'*Nooka?* Look at the state of you. Miserable as two damp socks. I won't ask why you did it, Dashinka. Let's just go and get you packed. The car will be here to take us away soon.'

All we've got to pack is our toothbrushes, our comb, our thermos flask, our spare nappy, one spare pair of socks and our spare shirts. I fold them all into our string bag. I put our red Pioneer scarves and passports in too, but I leave our school uniform behind.

'Where's our envelope with the photos in? The photos of all of us?' Masha asks, rummaging around. I look in the side cabinet, but it's not there. And under the pillow. I can't see it anywhere. Masha loves looking at photos of us. I hate it.

'That *yobinny* Valya has taken them. I know it! Just like her.'

'Well, come along, girls. I'm sure they'll be found and sent on to us,' says Aunty Nadya, fussing around us. 'The car will be waiting, come along.'

When we get outside, the Director is waiting at the bottom of the steps. He shakes our hands. This must be about the second time we've seen him in four years.

'Goodbye, girls, goodbye. I'm sorry you didn't stay to finish your schooling and get your diploma, but if you change your mind, we're always here.' He smiles this big smile at us, but I know he's lying. He doesn't want potential suicides in his school either. Besides, Masha will never come back. 'You're always welcome. If not, I wish you the very best in life. Yes. The very, very best.' Masha's sulking because of the photos, and I couldn't smile if my life depended on it, so he just nods a bit, then turns to Aunty Nadya. 'Look after them, Nadezhda Fyodorovna. Keep in touch.'

Icy Valya and her gang are leaning up against the school wall, giggling and doing this stupid slow handclap. The Director doesn't seem to hear or understand; he stands aside and my heart jumps right into my mouth as I see Slava waiting behind him near the car. Just waiting. We've got to pass him to get to it.

'Slavochka!' says Aunty Nadya, seeing him and getting all excited. 'There you are, girls! At least someone's come to see you off. Say goodbye to Slavochka and we'll be gone.' She doesn't know anything about him and me. None of the grown-ups do.

We walk towards him. Why's he here? Is he going to say anything? Shall I just walk past and not look at him? We're getting closer. Can't breathe. Can't look at him.

'Wait,' he says as we come up to him. Masha sticks her nose in the air and makes to walk right on by, but I stop. I can't just walk past. I don't lift my foot, so she can't move. She's rooted there by me. I look at him. 'Don't go, Dasha,' he says quietly. His eyes look big and he's sort of rubbing one hand over the other, which is balled into a fist as if he's holding something precious, and he suddenly looks thinner and paler. I just stare at him with

Masha tugging angrily at me. He doesn't want me to go after all? He wants to be with me, not Anyootka? After all that's happened? He still loves me and only me? Aunty Nadya's the other side of the car, tapping her fingernails on the roof.

'I … I … we've got our flight booked …' I say.

'Well, come back after summer. Come back to school. I'm sorry. Masha,' he looks right at her then, but she's got her head turned away. 'Masha, I'm sorry for what I said.' Masha keeps ignoring him, so he looks back at me. 'Come back after summer.' The clapping from the girls is getting louder and we can hear them chanting *Get lost, Masha, get lost, Dasha …*

'I'll come back to this hellhole when I hear a crawfish whistling on a mountain,' Masha sniffs. 'Have a nice life.' She never forgives an insult.

I still don't move though. 'Dashinka?' He looks straight into my eyes. 'Dashinka. Be strong. Be strong for me and come back.' He's telling me to stand up to her. All I want to do right then is grab his hand and run away with him, just run and run and run, him and me and no one else in the world.

'I'll write,' is all I can say, even more quietly than him.

Masha snorts. 'Just you fucking try it!'

'Come along then, girls,' says Aunty Nadya. 'Come along.' And so we do.

# TWENTIETH HOME FOR VETERANS OF WAR AND LABOUR, MOSCOW

## 1968–88

> 'The best weapon in the ideological work of the Party is the truth and the truth alone.'
>
> Leonid Ilyich Brezhnev

## Age 18
## September 1968

### We move to Moscow

'*Nooka?* Got everything, girls? Yes, I'm sure you have.' Aunty Nadya's bustling around her flat, looking in every corner as if we've left something vital behind, but we're sitting on the sofa looking at the blank TV. We're holding one plastic bag each. That's all we have to take with us to the Twentieth. All our worldly possessions for our new life.

It's been three months since we left Novocherkassk. Masha wouldn't let me write to Slava. I tried to because I don't care how much she hits me – let her kill me, if she wants – but you can't write a letter when someone's pulling the pen and paper out of your hand. And I couldn't ask Aunty Nadya to write it because Masha's always sitting there listening. Valentina Alexandrovna sent us a postcard, addressed to Aunty Nadya at SNIP, but Slava hasn't sent anything.

When we first got back to Moscow, Aunty Nadya took us straight to SNIP from the airport. She said we'd talk to Lydia Mikhailovna about getting us admitted to an adult ward, but the guard on the entrance gates wouldn't even let us in. It was the Director, he said, who left instructions that we shouldn't be allowed anywhere near the hospital. Aunty Nadya was a bit shocked, but she couldn't very well leave us under a bridge, so she had to take us back to her flat. That's when she told us Uncle Vasya had died two years ago. We always used to ask after him, and she always told us he sent all his love. She said she didn't want to upset us. She wanted to protect us. She must have been so sad, and she didn't even show it. Or share it.

'Well now, everything's beautifully clean as usual, well done, well done,' she says, reappearing from the kitchen. I can tell she's nervous. So are we. 'I won't have my little helpers any more, will I? Not a speck of dust anywhere.'

I look out of the window. I cleaned those too, with vinegar and screwed-up newspaper, but I had to do it with the lights out, at night, so no one would see us from outside. Poor Aunty Nadya's a nervous wreck having us here, because it's illegal. We don't have a *propiska* permit to live with her and she says if the authorities knew, she'd be fired from her job and probably put in prison too. Masha's loved it here, living in a proper flat, with home cooking and the TV and the bath. The bath! We spent so much time lying in the bath I'm surprised we haven't grown fins. After a week of being locked up inside the little flat with the curtains drawn, Aunty Nadya started taking us outside, but only after midnight and with a rug thrown over us, just to get some fresh air. 'Like we're criminals in hiding,' said Masha. 'But what's the crime?'

We still don't move from the sofa, even though she's got our crutches now and is standing in front of us waggling them. The dresser behind her has photos of Uncle Vasya and Little Vasya, in frames, but there's none of us. They're all tucked away in a drawer. We're not saying goodbye to Little Vasya. He's sixteen now and taller than her and sleeps on this sofa while we sleep on a mattress on the kitchen floor. He's hardly ever here though.

He's out on the streets getting into trouble most of the time. He hated having us back and ignores us. He ignores Aunty Nadya mostly too – when he's not talking back to her. Him and Masha got into a fight about that. So much for adopting Little Vasya instead of us …

'Come along, girls, come along,' she says again. 'The taxi will be waiting. No use sitting here like daisies waiting to be watered.'

We get up then and take our crutches from her. If only we could stay here, but she can't even apply for a *propiska* for us because that Grade One life sentence means we have to be kept in a State Institution.

We go out to the landing, get into the lift and go down to the waiting taxi like we're being taken to the executioner's block. It's raining. Moscow looks exactly the same as it did when we went out on our trip to the Mausoleum. Grey blocks of flats, wide, empty streets and lots of bright red slogans.

The Ministry of Protection assigned us to the Thirteenth Veterans of War and Labour Home. That's where Olessya is. We went to visit the Home, but even though there were nice grounds with bushes and flowers and some other Defective kids our age there for company, Olessya seemed as if she'd somehow lost her spirit. She didn't even say much when she saw us again. She didn't complain – after all, it was nothing like the asylum in Novocherkassk, it was all quite clean, and the staff weren't too mean. I really wanted to go there, to be with her, and I think she wanted it too. But Masha didn't. It was a Closed Regime Home, so they don't let you out at all, and don't let anyone in to visit either, which means Aunty Nadya couldn't have come to see us and bring us food and treats. And the rooms were communal. Masha said she didn't want to share a room with stinky old babushkas.

We're driving past the Red October chocolate factory now. There's a big poster of a sweet, pink-cheeked girl in a headscarf on it. Alyonka, her name is. That's what the most popular chocolate bar is called, apparently, but it seems there's still no chocolate in the shops. When one of Aunty Nadya's doctor friends came for supper one night in the flat (she can keep a secret), they were saying that all the chocolate goes to the special 'Beriozka' shops where only important Party members can shop. I suppose that's why Anokhin always has it … I don't know anything about politics, but I don't think Lenin would have wanted chocolate to be only for the children of Party bigwigs …

Masha wanted a room to herself, with a toilet and sink in the room, so she didn't have to trek off down the corridor and queue for hours and wipe everyone else's shit and pee off the seat. That's what Masha said. So she refused to go to the Thirteenth. 'Mashinka needs her place in the sun,' she'd said. Then Aunty Nadya sighed and said she'd do what she could to get us in somewhere else.

So that was that. No Thirteenth.

None of us say anything until we draw up outside the barred gates of the Twentieth Veterans of War and Labour Home. It's the best Home in Moscow. The best in the whole of the Soviet Union. It's a Show Home, visitors from abroad are taken around. We're really lucky. It's the only one in Moscow that has rooms for just two inmates, with a toilet and sink, *and* it's Open Regime. Aunty Nadya went to talk to the Director to see if she could get us a room, but he said, flat out, that he wasn't having something like us in his precious Home. He said he'd never let a Defective in yet, let alone Category Ones, and he wasn't going to start now. So Aunty Nadya asked Lydia Mikhailovna (who's the Head Doctor now of all of SNIP) to write a letter to Soldatyenko, the Deputy Minister of Protection. And, wonder of wonders, he told the Director, Barkov, to let us in here. I suppose he just wanted to get rid of us. We were born in Moscow so we're registered to live in Moscow. We couldn't live anywhere else unless we had an official job. Or got married. Soldatyenko would have sent us to Siberia if he could, but he couldn't. It's the law.

The gates swing open in front of us and then close behind us with a clang. Slava will still be in his village. It'll be sunny down south.

## The Twentieth

We walk into the echoing entrance hall and the guard tells us to sit down and wait on the bench for someone to take us to our room. Masha gives me her plastic bag to hold and Aunty Nadya sits with her handbag on her lap. We all look straight ahead and don't say anything. It's quite dark in here. There's a row of portraits of all the shiny members of the Politburo looking out to our shiny Communist future, with shiny medals on their chests. They're old. There are a few people shuffling around in the shadows. They don't notice us in the corner. They're old too. We're sitting next to grimy green pot plants, which look like they've been growing for a hundred years. It smells OK though. It smells of nothing.

Masha crosses her leg over mine and starts jiggling her foot up and down.

I wonder if Slava's thinking about me back in his village. I wonder if he's going to bother to go back to school now he knows there's no point in getting a diploma … or will he stay with his parents? If I wasn't Together with Masha I could be there with him now in the sun. Him and me. Not Masha and me … but I won't think about that.

'It's very nice here, isn't it?' says Aunty Nadya after a bit. 'Very nice indeed.'

'Yes,' I say, because she did everything in the world to get us in here. 'It's really very nice.' I have this stupid ball in my chest again, at being left here without her.

'And I'll come and visit every week. Bring you whatever you want.'

'Yes,' I say again. 'Thank you.' Masha just goes on jiggling her foot.

After what seems like hours, there's a sharp tap-tap of heels and a woman's suddenly there, standing in front of us, casting a shadow. She's tall and heavyset with a face as angry as a walnut. She reminds me of Nasty Nastya, the cleaner from the Ped.

'Masha and Dasha Krivoshlyapova?'

'Yes,' we say together.

'My name is Iglinka Dragomirovna. I'm from Administration. Come with me.' We all shuffle to our feet and she turns sharply to Aunty Nadya.

'You can leave now.'

Aunty Nadya looks for a moment like she might argue, but the woman is so fierce, she just nods.

'Ah, *ladno*. Well, I'll say goodbye to you now then, girls.' I grab on to her hand. I'm asking her with my eyes please, please, please, don't leave us here for the rest of our lives. 'Goodbye then,' she says. 'Be good.' I start to cry then, right there in front of the stupid Administrator and the guard and everyone. I can't stop myself. Masha doesn't even slap me because I think she's trying not to cry too. Aunty Nadya turns around and walks right on out without stopping to kiss us. I think she's almost crying as well.

'Come along.'

We go up a clanging lift to the sixth floor. When we walk out into the corridor, the stench of urine and disinfectant and old, old people hits us. Masha holds her nose. The walls are painted dark green. There's brown, warped linoleum on the floor that we keep tripping over, and there are two surnames written on a card on each door. With our two passports we get one room for both of us. I look at the blue ink on cardboard on each door. Dyogtina, Yermushina, Zolina, Ivakina and then Krivoshlyapova.

She pushes the door open. It's a very narrow room and painted dark brown. I suddenly feel there's not enough air in here and I start panting for breath, my heart's going faster and faster. Masha almost gets knocked sideways by the way it's suddenly pounding, so we sit on the single metal-framed bed with a thump.

'Room all to yourselves. *That's* a one-off anywhere you care to name,' says the Administrator. My heart's still pounding away like we've run a thousand kilometres and my stomach has turned liquid, so Masha stands up and we try to get into the toilet, but can't. The doorway's too small, and we could never both fit on the seat in there anyway.

'There's one down on the first floor you might get into,' says the Administrator with her arms on her hips, watching us. She sniffs. 'This one's not made for ...' she wants to say *urodi*. But she doesn't. 'So. The basics: supper on ground floor at 18:00. Don't be late or you won't get anything. Every room has a balcony, but there are bars, so no jumping off.' She smiles nastily. 'Similarly, the door to your room does not lock, so staff can enter at any time in the event of illness or attempted suicide. Our statistics for suicide are the best in Moscow, so if you intend to die, we shall ensure it's of natural causes. There's a list of rules and regulations in the Lenin Corner but to summarize: in the rooms there must be no music, no smoking, no drinking, no food, no fraternizing with staff, no soiling, no kettles or sharp instruments, no raised voices, no singing, no photographs and no pictures on walls. Any questions?'

We both look at her blankly.

'Well, you two teenagers are going to be here for the next sixty-odd years, I'd say, so a few might arise,' she says. 'I just hope you enjoy each other's company.' And then she smiles again and goes.

We sit there on the bed looking at the brown wall. The sheet has stains on it and I move over. We've been sitting there for maybe an hour, not saying anything, when the door's pushed open and this old woman comes in and stands staring at us. Then another one comes in and another until the room's full of them. They don't say anything at all. Just stare and cross themselves.

'Go away, you dandelions!' shouts Masha suddenly. 'Go away.' She waves her arms at them but they keep on pressing in to look at us. They've got fluffy grey hair and they're all thin as a stalk. They're dandelions ready to be blown away by the wind. One of them starts dancing round and round with her arms out, singing.

We get up and push through them, on to the balcony. It's cold out here. We both grip the bars and breathe in and out. It's getting dark, but we can see a stack of empty coffins piled up by the side entrance. We don't say anything to each other, but we turn around together and push past everyone again and then walk straight out to the lift, and press the button.

When the doors open, we stand there, not going in. After a bit I say:

'We can't run away, Masha. There's a guard on the gate and dogs. And if we do escape, they'll catch us, and send us to a prison or Madhouse.' She nods. The doors close in front of us. 'We can go back though,' I say quietly. 'We can always go back to school.'

'No, we can't. They don't want Suicides like you.' She turns to go back to our room. 'Anyway, rather you and me in a Home full of daft dandelions, than you and your sprat, in a school full of bitches.'

And so that was that.

## Age 19
## 20 March 1969

### Slava writes to me, I write back, he writes back, and we meet in Moscow!

'I knew I shouldn't have let you reply to his card. I should listen to myself more,' says Masha. We're sitting on the bench in reception, in the Twentieth, waiting for Aunty Nadya to take us to see Slava, in SNIP. 'This is how it ends up,' she goes on, sniffing. 'Just a couple of letters and here he is, rolled up on the doorstep like a rotten cabbage.'

I'm so excited I can't think straight. I feel like an unexploded bomb. He's here! Slava's here, in Moscow, and he's waiting for us to visit! I know Masha's excited too, despite all her moaning. She's great at making friends and we have some nice ones now in the Twentieth, but she's still bored as anything, locked up in this dark block of musty corridors. If we didn't have each other, I think we'd go mad.

'I was just so fed up with your lovesick sighs and tears, I couldn't stand it any more. I was weak, and see where it's got us?'

'You weren't weak, Mash, you were kind.'

'Kind – *foo!*' She spits on the floor. 'I wasn't thinking of you, you can be sure of that. It was like walking round with a corpse hanging off me; you might as well have gone ahead and hung yourself for all the life in you. It gets to a person, that does.'

I feel in my pocket for his card, which we got on our birthday in January. It had a bunch of beautiful purple violets on the front and inside he'd written: *To Masha and Dasha, wishing you health, happiness and every success.* I take it everywhere because if I leave it in our room it might get stolen. It gave me a tiny spark of hope that lit me up again.

'Anyway,' I say. 'If you hadn't let me reply, I'd have strangled you. Hey! That's an idea, I could always strangle you – I'm stronger than you.' I laugh.

'So you'd be free to run off into the sunrise with Peanut? *Nyetooshki.* I'll poke your eyes out first!'

We both laugh then. I was so happy that Masha relented and let me reply to him. I sent a letter back to him, and then I waited every day – well, every minute and every second of every day, for a reply. It came in March. I've got that in my pocket too. I take it out and look at it, even though I know it off by heart.

*3 March 3 1969*

*Hello girls,*
*Greetings from Slava! Thanks for your letter. How is your health? What's new? I'm sorry we couldn't talk before you left. I didn't know you were going so soon. We had the end of year party and Vannya got drunk as a priest and had to be taken to hospital. Dasha, don't be upset. I wanted to talk to you and give you something, but perhaps you didn't know that. I'll try and come up and see you when I can. Perhaps Aunty Nadya can get me a bed in SNIP to be treated? I'm living at home now with my mother and don't want to go back to school. Have you found a Home in Moscow yet? How is Aunty Nadya?*
*Write to me,*
*Slava*

'All he wants from you is to get his treatment in SNIP, you know that, don't you?' grumbles Masha. 'If there's one thing I've learnt in life, it's that everyone in this world is out for themselves.' Masha sniffs and looks up at the ceiling. '*Gospodi!* When's she coming then? If I have to look at those stuffed frogs lined up in the portraits any longer, I'll start throwing eggs at them.'

'Shhh, Mash!' I look around nervously, but there's no one within hearing distance. We're sitting between two greasy palm trees and a bust of Lenin. She's right though, I revived like a wilted flower in water after I got his birthday card. Olessya always used to say that happiness lies in three things: having someone to love, something to do and something to hope for. At least I've got the first and the last. But having nothing to do except sit and stare at our shiny brown wall, means I go over and over every look, every touch, every word and that last New Year's love-making in my head, like I'm on some crazy hamster wheel.

I stare at the gloomy reception with its dark walls and yellow linoleum and wonder for the millionth time why he isn't going to school. Could it be because I'm not there? Or is he sick? And what did he want to say to me? What did he want to give me? What? What?

*... We now require the mobilization of all possible forces, highest possible labour productivity, improvement of discipline ...* Mayak State Radio is droning on, and I yawn. I'm so nervous I just can't stop yawning. *Not one working day, not one working hour is to be wasted ...* we've been sitting here on this chair for ages ...

'Hey, girls!' Sanya, the cleaner, bangs in through the front door for the start of her shift. 'What are you two doing, looking like two geese trussed up for dinner? What's the gossip?'

'Juliet here's off to see her Romeo,' says Masha.

'Ooooh! Kept that quiet, didn't you, Dashka. Handsome, is he?'

He's the handsomest boy in the USSR but I don't say that, I just smile happily.

'Well, I want all the gossip, including intimate contact and whispered secrets. Got it?' She wags her finger at Masha, who winks at her. Sanya and Masha hit it off as soon as she walked into our room with her bucket and mop. She's quite young and plump and cheerful. She comes from Siberia, but she gets to share a communal room in a barracks in Moscow in exchange for working in a Home. She lives off gossip. So does Masha, come to think of it. They're two of a kind. (Except Masha would die rather than mop anyone's room for them.) 'OK, girls, have fun. If you can't be good be careful,' and she waddles off.

I put the card and letter back in my pocket, then take them out again, then pat my hair.

'For God's sake, stop fiddling, you're turning me into a nervous wreck,' says Masha, slapping my arm. 'And your hair looked fine before you kept running your fingers through it and turning it into rats' tails.' I stop smoothing back my hair then, and start biting my nails instead. I haven't seen him for a year. How long will he be in SNIP for? Will he come and visit us when he's better? Will we be able to talk? To … to kiss? My stomach twists inside me and Masha slaps me again.

'Ei, girls!' Ivan Ivanovich, the guard who sits in reception, has come out from behind his desk and is standing stretching in the doorway. 'Are you two running off to get married?'

'No, Van Vanich, we're waiting for a proclamation of love from you!' chirps Masha.

He laughs, showing his two rows of gold teeth. He's quite old, he must be at least forty. 'If you can cast one of your death spells on my old lady, I'm all yours!'

'Bring her on!'

We all laugh together then. The death spell thing happened when we were down in the canteen in the first week or so after we got here. All the old *babas* were gawking and asking the usual questions like, how do we Do It with a man, and did we have the same dreams and the same thoughts, and if we had children would they be Together too …? And then this one *baba* came up and stuck her face in Masha's and asked if it would be painful for the one left behind to die, and how long it would take? Masha just went crazy then. She pointed her finger right between this old woman's eyes and said, *Yooou are going to die before I do, granny, mark my words*, which actually wasn't rocket science, because she was like a hundred years old, and we're only nineteen, but this old woman looked like she'd been struck by lightning and her eyes all bulged out in horror, because there's this gossip going around that we're the spawn of the devil or something and have evil powers. The next thing we knew, she'd had a heart attack and was lying there dead as a doormouse at our feet. So now all the *babas* keep away from us, like we're real live witches.

'Oh yes, Van Vanich, beware the Magic Finger!' says Masha, wagging it at him. Sometimes I think she actually believes she *does* have magic powers. She'll sit there and hold her finger up and just look at it.

'Girls, girls!' Aunty Nadya bangs open the doors and rushes in. We jump up and run over to her. 'Right, right, that's quite enough of the hugs, thank you very much, get off, get off, let me breathe. Have you got your day-release passes?'

'Yes! Yes!' We flash them at Ivan Ivanovich.

'Don't try and escape, will you?' he says. 'Who'll I have to play cards with, when you're gone?'

'You'll find a nice sprightly granny or two,' shouts Masha as we jump outside into the warm spring sun.

The car from SNIP's waiting and the journey is only ten minutes, but seems to last an age. We're led up the back stairs, like we were the first time we got here, and then we walk along the corridor to his door. When we reach it, Aunty Nadya looks at us both and says that we look thin as weeds, so she's going to get us some fresh vegetables from the kitchens and leave us alone with Slava.

We stand there outside the door for a bit, not saying anything, then Masha looks at me and I nod. She pushes the door open and we walk in. He's sitting on the bed with his big dark eyes staring out of his white face. He looks like I feel.

'*Yolki palki!* You look like you've crawled out from under a stone!' says Masha, as we walk over and sit on his bed.

'Thanks, Mash, just what I need ...' He relaxes and smiles then, and glances at me. 'You two look good. Pretty as pansies.'

'Don't get fresh with me.' Masha punches him on the shoulder.

'Ouch!' He rubs his arm then smiles. 'S'pose I should be thankful it wasn't a slug in the face, given your usual form. Near broke my nose, you did.'

'Should've knocked your head off, but there's always a next time.'

'Not if I see it coming ... So, how's things?' He cocks his head on one side.

'Yeah,' says Masha, 'so we've got a room to ourselves, with our own toilet, and we've just about worked out how to climb into it – one at a time, like a crab squeezing into a crack.'

'*Kha* ... bet I know who gets in first ...'

'... yeah, Dasha knows her place, and that's behind me. So our room may be small but it's clean and dry, which is all I care about, and we've got our transistor to listen to all day, though the batteries keep running out, and there's a shortage of batteries, so Aunty Nadya has to stand in queues for days when they appear in the shops.'

'Which is never,' says Slava. 'We haven't seen batteries or stamps in Novocherkassk for months, that's why I didn't write sooner ...' He flicks a quick look at me and my heart starts flapping around like a bat.

'So the Director, Barkov, he's nothing like our School Director,' goes on Masha, twiddling her button, 'he's just there to skim off as much State money as he can. Sanya, our cleaner, says he's got two Volga cars, and a dacha off the Rublyovsky Highway, with gardeners, cleaners, drivers – you name it. He nabs the money meant to buy a TV set for every floor, and trickles it into a private sauna at his dacha. You know what it's like.'

'Yeah. Everyone's on the make, inside and out.'

'Well, not everyone. We've got this crazy Komsorg comes in every week – she's like an Activist for the Komsomol Young Communist League and she's got a funny name, what is it … hmm … anyway, she's only about twenty herself, and she comes round to us to make sure our Socialist morale is all topped up with cherries. Doesn't she? Hey, Sheep. Doesn't she?'

'What?' I realize I'm just staring at Slava's brown hands with the square, white fingernails, wanting to touch them. 'Oh, yes, yes …'

'So the room's clean and dry, which is all we want, and they feed us regularly, and the staff are OK if you chat them up. Some of the inmates are OK too. My Scarecrow here gets them talking about their lives, the Great October Revolution, Civil War, Reds and Whites, Peasants and Cossacks, all that crap.'

'At least they lived a life …' says Slava quietly, and looks at me again.

I want to talk to him alone. I want to touch his skin and his hair.

He sighs. 'So it's all right then? In the Twentieth?'

'Yeah, yeah, it's all right. Come visit.'

And it's then that I get what's happening. I look from him to Masha, and then back again. Masha wants him to come and live with us. He's fun, he banters with her and makes her feel good. It's been a year since they quarrelled; normally she'd bear a grudge forever, but she needs him. She knows I'd be happy, she might even let us …

'So it's all right there, is it, Dasha?' He's looking at me.

'Yes,' I say, nodding like mad. 'Yes, it's healthy!'

It's not though, it's like all the inmates are sad and bitter and waiting to die, and we're bullied by most of the staff, especially the Administrator and the Director. But if Slava was there with us, it would be fine. Everything would be fine.

'What about you?' I say. 'Why don't you want to go back to school?' There. I've said it.

'Why? Because I got graded down to a One like you, by the Medical Commission, that's why, so I'll never be able to take any real work on. What's the point in studying?'

We hadn't known about that, so we sit there, not saying much, because he's right.

'Being a One sucks,' says Masha eventually. 'But hey, gotta make the most of things, right? Winners see a problem and fix it – losers only see the problem. *Gospodi*, I'm starting to sound like fucking Olessya!'

'Yeah,' laughs Slava. 'But you're right. I thought if I went back to live with my mum, I could get some work on the side, but that's not worked out.' He looks down at his hands. 'I can't do much being like this. It's hard for my parents. They both work full time and I need sort of ... looking after, I suppose. Grisha, my brother, he's graduated from school and is studying now in a PTU technical college, living in a dorm.' I'm breathing quickly, in and out, in and out. *I'd* look after him. I would, I'd care for him every minute of the day and he'd care for me until we were old and bent. We'd fix everything. Every single problem. I'm sitting there, willing him to read my thoughts, because I can't say them out loud. I think at him, as hard as I can: *I'll look after you, Slava, I will, I will, forever.* And when he looks at me, I think he's heard me. I'm sure he has.

There's a silence, then Masha, who's been gazing up at the ceiling suddenly says:

'Dazdraperma! That's her name, the Komsorg – it's short for Long Live the First of May! And it suits her, I can tell you. She almost swallowed her Komsomol badge when she got an eyeful of us for the first time. She couldn't believe that we were hidden away in a dark corner of an Old People's Home. So turns out Brezhnev's got this new mentoring scheme for the Komsomol. She's an Activist – active as a squirrel she is, too. She's found out that she can get tutors in to teach my fool here maths and science and Russian literature so she can finally get her precious diploma.'

'Really?' Slava looks at me quickly and I smile and nod.

'It's only one tutor for an hour a week, but she'll give me homework. I've got plenty of time – not that I need the diploma now …'

'Dazdraperma can't believe how brilliant my Einstein here is. And she's going to bring me magazines to read. And there's this other girl, Gulgunya, who works in the kitchens, she's one of them blackies from Azerbaijan or some other dirty Republic down there, but she's really nice too. You know what Princess Turandot here is like,' she waves at me, 'she can't bear the thought of eating out of a badly washed soup bowl, so Gulgunya lets us keep our own bowls and our own cutlery and mugs. Caused a revolt down among the babushkas, I can tell you, but I cast a spell on one of them, Slava, I really did, and she dropped down dead. So now they think I'm a witch and keep their mouths shut.'

We all laugh and while Masha's chattering on, I very, very slowly move my hand across the bed until the tip of one of my fingers is touching his.

## June 1969

### Slava visits us in the Twentieth to see if he wants to stay with me

'I wish you'd stop scrubbing and polishing, I'm knackered!' Masha's balancing us against the door, while I scour the toilet bowl for the hundredth time. It's no good though, the stink just seems to come up from the pipes. 'It is what it is,' says Masha.

'I don't want him to think … I want him to …'

'Like I say, it is what it is. If he wants to stay with us, he will. A sparkling toilet won't make any difference.'

It's been three weeks since we saw him in SNIP, and he's coming to see us before he goes back to Novocherkassk.

'Does the corridor really reek of toilets more than usual, or is that just me? Do you think he'll notice? Do you, Mash?'

'Yeah, it does. And of course he'll notice, he's got a nose, hasn't he? Just our luck all the babushkas have come out today of all days, and are creeping about like spiders. And I haven't even got a fag to smoke. *Yobinny* Dragomirovna and her spot checks.'

Masha hides her cigarettes behind the toilet roll but somehow the Administrator found them straight away. And we had to bribe Uncle Styopa to get them for us. That was our ten-rouble monthly pension gone. But the worst thing was that she pushed us up against the wall like a battering ram and screamed into my face. I hate it when people do that. I'd rather she actually hit me than screamed at me like I was an idiot child.

'I thought she was going to kill me, Mash … you could at least have told her we both smoke, instead of blaming it all on me. Considering I don't smoke at all …'

'Stop bleating, don't you think I was upset too? I hate being humiliated. C'mon, stop fishing around in that toilet, he'll be here any moment.'

I wash my hands and we sit down on our bed. I keep brushing non-existent crumbs off the cover, but it's so stained, a crumb here or there wouldn't matter. We're not allowed our own sheets, let alone a bedspread. Masha's sulking. She's still upset about the telling off. And she's nervous, I can tell. And I'm so nervous, I feel like I'm going to tremble myself into pieces.

Our clock, which Aunty Nadya bought us, ticks slowly on the *tumbochka* bedside table. Two of the babushkas in the corridor have started a fight right outside. He's being brought up to our room by one of the nannies, I hope she's a good one, I hope it's …

I stop breathing. *Tic, tic, tic.* The door's opening. We put tacks in the floor so we get some warning when someone's coming in. He's carried in by Inna, the worst nanny possible, who's holding him like he's a pot of urine. She pitches him on to the hard chair across from our bed, and leaves. He just looks down at the floor and not at us. He's already decided, I can tell. So can Masha. We all sit there, not saying anything, listening to the yelling outside and the wailing pipes as the babushka next door washes her hands for the millionth time that day, moaning to herself through the thin walls.

After what seems like years, he shifts his weight a bit on the chair. He's still looking at the floor when he says:

'I'm sorry, Dasha.'

That's all. Just, I'm sorry?

I feel a hard lump of anger inside me.

'Dasha,' he adds, quietly. 'I can't.'

I feel the lump getting bigger and bigger, rolling up from my stomach. He doesn't love me enough to live here, in our room in the Twentieth. The anger turns to grief and I can't help it, I just burst into tears then, and I'm crying like I've never cried in my whole life before, as this crazy, hopeless sea of despair washes right over me. I can hear myself yelling at him, as if someone else is shouting the words, *Go then! Go on! Go back to your village!* Masha starts screaming at him too, telling him not to keep on hurting her sister, and then Inna runs back in, swearing her head off, to take him out. But before she can, he leans towards me and pushes a scrap of paper into my hand with a terrible look in his eyes. And then he's taken away.

Masha's looking around for something to throw and is screaming, 'Bitch with Balls! *Pizduk! Zalupa! Yobinny stik!*' She hasn't even noticed the note. I just can't stop crying my heart out though. I can't do anything but wail.

Later, when she's gone to sleep, and I'm lying my end, on the pillow covered in snot and tears and still hiccup-sobbing, I uncurl my fist and read it.

*Dasha, I'll find a way for us to be together. I promise. It's our secret. Please wait.*

I wipe my eyes with the back of my hand and heave a great, juddering sigh. And then I lie back.

And start hoping all over again.

## November 1969

### Love among the inmates

'Get a move on, you've got a thousand pipettes in that box.'

'I'm trying, Masha, but my fingers are cold. It's not easy, getting these rubber bulbs on. If you tried it, you'd know …'

We've just had another box delivered. They pay us kopecks, but it keeps Masha in cigarettes, which we now hide beneath a loose tile under the sink and even Iglinka Dragomirovna with her X-ray eyes hasn't found them. Masha sniffs and goes back to looking at the recipes in her magazine, *Krestyanka* – Peasant Woman – which Dazdraperma brought her.

'I should be doing my history studies, not this,' I say.

'Stop whining.'

It's been five months since Slava left, and I haven't heard from him. Not yet. We haven't talked about it, Masha and me. She just said if he ever showed up again she'd smash him to a pulp. But she's forgiven him before, and she'll forgive him again. Meanwhile, I'm waiting and waiting, and thinking of what plans he has for us to be together. It must be in the village … with the hens and the pond, and …

'Aunty Nadya had better hurry up with getting those new batteries, my transistor sounds like a can of snakes.'

She jabs me to get an answer, so I say, 'Doctor Golubeva said she'd look for some too.'

It gave us the shock of our lives (haha) when Dr Golubeva pushed open the door two weeks ago. We half expected her to have the helmets in tow, to fry our heads again, but all she had with her were home-made sour cream buns. She said she thought about us often and would we mind if she started visiting? Masha said if she kept bringing sour cream buns she could come as often as she liked. But I thought it was odd somehow … Our old doctor from the Ped turning up with gifts.

'Yeah, old Golubeva. I thought we'd be falling over Anokhin next, down in reception,' says Masha, turning a page of her magazine to an article on vegetable plots.

'No chance of that. Anokhin's lost interest in us … everyone's lost interest in us …'

'Ei! Don't say that, girls! I still love you!'

Uncle Styopa, one of the inmates, has pushed open the door and is standing there, waving a little padlock and chain. 'See what your old Uncle has got for you!'

'*Ooraa!*' Masha jumps up, knocking my box of pipettes over. 'Now we can lock up our thermos flask.'

'You have to chain everything down in this place, girls. Sooner you learn that, the better. How many have you had stolen? Three? Well, the best place is the leg of your bed, here we go.' He gets down on the floor and starts chaining the thermos down. He was wounded as a teenager in the Great Patriotic War and was put in here nearly twenty years ago. He likes us. He knows what it's like to be nineteen and locked up for life.

'Heard from your girlfriend then?' asks Masha, grinning. 'She was the only one worth talking to in here.'

'*Baba* Yulia? Nope, haven't heard from her. Gone from the eye, gone from the heart.' He shakes his head. 'Shame.

Bright as a scythe, she was. That's a rarity in this House of Rejects …'

Baba Yulia lived on the corridor below, and we used to visit her every day because she was so cheerful and interesting. Her husband was killed in the War and she brought up their baby son, Dima, in a communal flat until he got married. Then Dima went to court and had her put in here, so he could have the room to himself. She still loves him though. She says you never stop loving your own child, whatever happens … blood is thicker than water.

'If I'd been her, I wouldn't have gone back to that *moodak* son of hers,' spits Masha, balancing me while I hang off the bed trying to pick the pipettes up from the floor. 'He only took her in because of that new Decree of Brezhnev's saying war widows living with families could get a two-room flat.'

'She was so h-happy though, to be going to live with her f-family and g-grand-daughter.' I look up at Uncle Styopa.

'Yes, yes, and I'm happy for her,' he says. But he doesn't look happy, he looks sad. They were the same age and really liked each other. And she hasn't written to him for months. Once people get to the Outside, they forget about us lot on the Inside. 'Well, she made the right decision. Better than staying here,' he says. 'No one usually leaves the Twentieth on their own two feet. They leave it feet first.'

'Got any vodka for her, Uncle Styopachka?' says Masha in her little girl voice. She points at me then tips her head on one side and opens her eyes wide. He shakes his head.

'My brother got caught last time with two bottles down his felt-boots. Now they virtually strip-search him.'

I've recovered all the pipettes and go back to popping the rubber bulbs on. I'm glad for Baba Yulia. I wonder for the thousandth time where our own mother is. If she's still alive, she must be about forty now. Maybe she's got other children? I sort of imagine her as a doctor. Maybe she's operating on someone right now? Or maybe she's sitting somewhere, thinking of us? Looking for us even? Does she know our names? Did she name us, or did …

'*Nooka?* Want some gossip?' Sanya the cleaner has popped her head around the door. She sits down on the chair with her mop between her legs and pushes her headscarf back, nodding at Uncle Styopa, who's still on his knees by the leg of our bed. 'Baba Agafia went so crazy in the queue for the kettle in the kitchen that she hit out at the old crone in front and knocked her clean out. Before she knew what was happening, the nurses were on top of her with their syringes and she woke up in Stupino! Serve her right. Right mad 'un, she was.'

'Stupino?! *Chort!*' say Masha and me together. It's the prison for Rejects. We know all about Stupino. You don't live long there. If you're not killed by another inmate, you're killed by the guards. And you don't need to stand before a judge and jury to get sent there. It's up to the Director of whatever Home you're in. We're all scared stiff of the threat of Stupino. You can get sent there for anything, from Spreading Slander to Unacceptable Behaviour.

'Ooh, and did you hear that your Baba Yulia's coming back?' We all look at her with our mouths open. Uncle Styopa rocks back on his heels. 'Yes, that monster of hers, Dima, has moved his wife's parents into the flat and kicked her back in here.'

'B-but he c-can't do that!' I exclaim. 'He got the flat because of h-her! So she c-could stay there!'

'Course he can do that. And I bet you anything, he'll be round here, cap in hand, shaking with the White Fever, and begging her for vodka money from her pension. Just like he always used to. Bet you anything.'

Uncle Styopa jumps up now, looking all excited. He keeps running his hands through his hair and pulling his ear.

'Well, well, better be off,' he says, smiling all over his face. 'All done, girls.'

'*Mwaah*, you're running back to the girlfriend – and I thought I was in with a chance there,' says Masha, pretending to look upset. He laughs and runs out.

Aunty Sanya shakes her head. '*Da-oosh*. Little children bring headaches, and big ones bring heartaches.'

'Well,' says Masha. 'If I had a mother who hadn't thought I was a monster and left me to die, like ours did, I'd help her through every bog and burrow. Not stick her in here to suffocate in her old age.'

'There are monsters and there are monsters,' says Sanya, and then goes over to look at Masha's *Krestyanka* magazine with her. And I go back to fixing the rubber bulbs on to the pipettes.

## Talking about sex, tales from the Twentieth, and another letter from Slava

'Do you think they have sex?' I ask Masha. It's the same evening, and dark as death outside. The transistor has finally died and I'm halfway through the box now. Masha's been fiddling with her button for the last half hour, yawning. She looks at me.

'Who?'

'Baba Yulia and Uncle Styopa. Do you think they do?'

'Course not! They're like, what … forty, fifty years old?' I shrug. 'Anyway,' she goes on, sniffing, 'what's the big deal about sex and all that kissing stuff? I've never wanted it and never will.'

'But don't you feel … you know, urges, down there? Like it's this little thumping box or something, waiting to be opened and explode with … with, I don't know, fireworks or something?' She stares at me as if I'm mad. 'And didn't you like it,' I go on quickly, 'when you used to kiss those boys in school? Didn't you feel like you were just melting and hot and wanted to go on and on doing it because it felt so good? That you wanted them, you know, right inside you?'

'*Foo!*' She spits at me. 'Of course not! When I kissed those rats it was only to get something out of them. I'd rather have been kissing a toilet seat.'

'Really? But don't you feel a sort of *need* for boys and for getting with them? Like a proper ache?'

'Are you talking about when you rub yourself down there, like you're trying to scratch an itch? I wish you'd lay off that, it's disgusting, and don't think I don't know you're doing it when I'm half asleep.'

'There's nothing wrong with it, Masha. It's natural, isn't it? Why should I not want sex, just because you and me are Together?'

I pop another bulb on the pipette. I do rub myself and she's right, I know I could explode if I only knew how. I get close when I think of me and Slava. But I don't. Perhaps because I can only do it when I think she's asleep and have to be careful because we're so close together down there. 'It's just strange that you don't feel anything like that too ...'

She shrugs. 'I'd rather be me, than you, sitting there, miserable as a cow with colic, waiting for your kisses and sex from that little prick. You can't think straight, you lot can't, once you start feeling. Look at Uncle Styopa, running about like a headless chicken. You should be like me – Masha's the only one I love.' She keeps flicking through the magazine pages, looking at the patterns for making clothes, and the recipes, then, after a few minutes, she says she wants to go and see Ivan Ivanovich. 'He's on duty tonight. I'm bored stiff.'

We go down in the lift, and find him in the dark reception hall with his feet up at his desk, reading *Sovietskyi Sport* newspaper and half watching a film from India on his black and white TV. We squeeze in.

'Ooooh, can we watch the film with you, Van Vanich, can we? We'll hide under your chair if anyone comes! I love watching those beautiful dark Indian women in those sparkly, silky dresses. Their teeth are so white!'

He chuckles a bit and nods. He's got a kind face, like an apple. 'All right then, girls. Man the fort while I slip out for a fag.' Masha puts her face in her hands and settles down to watch the film. I look up into the pigeonhole box under the letter K to see if there's anything there. There is! Slava! But there are about fifty of us with surnames beginning with K. It's probably not for us. No, probably not for us at all. But my heart's thumping like mad.

'Calm down, you pervert,' says Masha, not taking her eyes off the TV set, 'he's not *that* handsome.' I look at the screen and see a young Indian man in a turban, dancing and singing. No, he's not handsome; he's nothing like Slava. I look up at the box again, just as Ivan Ivanovich comes back in.

'Oh yes, almost forgot, there's a letter for you two. Came yesterday.' He reaches up for it. It's a blue airmail one, and when he hands it to us, I can see from the writing it's from Slava! Masha can tell too. She grabs it and opens it with her thumb, while my heart goes on pounding. I'm sweating. She leans away from me so I can't see it, and starts reading it. I watch her face and her eyes, but she has no reaction. When she's finished, she tears it in half and then tears those pieces in half, and drops them in the waste-paper bin.

'That's what *he* thinks,' she says. 'He might as well be asking us to go and see the President of Amerika.'

Ivan Ivanovich doesn't look up from his newspaper, and she goes back to watching the TV. After a bit, when she's laughing at a dance scene, I lean down slowly and pick up all the bits of paper from the bin, and then piece them together on the desk. She doesn't look across or say anything. She doesn't stop me.

*3 November 1969*

*Hello girls, greetings from Slava!*

*I hope you are well.*

*I'm still at home but doing some studies. I was sorry to leave you that way. I hope you forgive me. To be honest, I still don't want to go to school but it seems I must. Everyone thinks it's for the best and I suppose it is, though I'll be put down a year now. Can you come for the end of year school party? How are you? How is your health and how is Aunty Nadya? She's told Vera Stepanovna that I can come up for treatment in SNIP, so I'm planning on coming next spring. Maybe you could come and see me? I expect Aunty Nadya will tell you the exact date.*

*Mother sends her love. I don't see the village boys much now, as they have motorbikes.*

*Write to me,*
*Slava*

I put the pieces in my pocket. I'll find a way to stick them together later. New Year. That's only a few weeks away. Just a few weeks. If I can only persuade Masha to let me go.

## Age 20
## January 1970

### Another letter from Slava, Masha gets her beloved Lydia, and we visit the privileged eighth floor

*Nyet.*

Masha didn't want to go down to Novocherkassk for the New Year's party. She said she wasn't doing that long trip to see an icy bitch who'd stolen all her photographs and a little *pizdyuk* who'd insulted her sister. I couldn't say anything to change her mind. I felt like I'd been hollowed out with a spoon. Slava went to the party though, and he started back at school after New Year. He sent us a card for our twentieth birthday. It was a bit late. I expect he couldn't find stamps ...

*6 January 1970 Internat.*

*Hello girls, greetings from Slava. I'm enclosing a card from Vyacheslav Tikhonov. As well as your photos. You thought that someone had stolen them but in fact no one did because I found them in a Russian textbook. You often used to put your photos there for safekeeping and you just forgot about these. So there you are ...*

*Well, how are you? Probably same as ever. I'm sorry I haven't heard from you.*

*How is Aunty Nadya? Give her my love. Vanya sends his love and the Director, Konstantin Semyonovich also sends his love. He keeps talking about you and asking after you and asking how you are, what you're keeping yourself busy with and so on.*

*Irina Konstantinovna sends her love.*

*I'm still hoping to come up in spring if Mum can spare the time. Well, OK, for the moment that's all I can think of to tell you. I hope to see you in spring.*

*Slava*

Everyone sent their love. Except him. Masha didn't tear up this letter but she wouldn't let me write back. And he didn't come in spring, because his mother couldn't spare the time in the end.

But he'd given me his promise in that note. After he gave it to me, I crumpled it up until it was soft and then flushed it down the toilet when Masha was getting out of the door.

I just have to wait. I wish I could write back. I want to write back so much it's like a physical pain, I want …

'*Ai! Ai!* Ouch! That hurt, Masha!' I suck my bleeding thumb.

'You should concentrate then.'

'You did it on purpose. You always do it on purpose.'

Masha's happy as a sparrow nowadays, because we've been given a sewing machine to hem muslin nappies with. It's a real honour (there's only a handful of people in the Twentieth can be trusted with a needle) and it pays more too. Masha's christened the machine Lydia. She just loves turning the handle while I push the nappy through, but sometimes she jolts it hard, just for fun, so the needle goes right into my finger or thumb.

'I slipped,' she says.

'No, you didn't, you did it on purpose. Look – now this nappy's a reject, it's got blood on it as well. We'll get that docked off our pay. If there are too many rejects we'll get the sewing machine taken away too …' I keep sucking my finger.

'No, we won't, because all those nice, new sheets are still there on *our* balcony.'

'I know.' I look at my finger to make sure it's stopped bleeding and pick up another strip of muslin. I still can't believe that the Twentieth got a delivery of bed sheets. Aunty Nadya says they haven't been on sale in Moscow, let alone anywhere else in the Soviet Union, for twenty years. There must be another foreign delegation due – not that *we* ever see them.

'As if any of those sheets will end up on *our* beds … they'll all be nicked by the staff to sell on the side,' sniffs Masha. 'Or sent to the *blatnoi* inmates who can afford to give the Administration bribes.' I nod and stick my tongue out as I carefully edge the corner under the needle. We're hoping to go up to the eighth floor today where the privileged inmates live. We've not been before, but I've heard it's wonderful. I can't wait. That's where they take the visiting delegations from abroad, to show how well looked after we 'all' are. They'll get new sheets up there, that's for sure. Or perhaps they even have their own? 'It was funny though, wasn't it,' Masha goes on, turning the handle slowly, 'when Inna got caught in that strip-search by the inspectors?' I smile. I'm glad Inna got caught and fired. She was the one who brought Slava to our room and dumped him on the chair. Apparently she'd undressed, wrapped one of the new sheets around her naked body, and then dressed again. But they caught her. They catch nearly everyone, the inspectors do. Except Dragomirovna. I finish the nappy and pick up another. Dragomirovna will sell the ones she's hidden on our balcony on the black market for a fortune. Four days ago she pushed open our door and walked in with a whole box of sheets; there must have been twenty of them. New, clean sheets. Never been used. A dream come true. She didn't even look at us, just marched right through on to our balcony, plonked the box in a corner and dusted off her hands.

'If the inspectors come to your room,' she'd said, when she walked back in, 'sit on the box and make faces or something. Not that you need to do that to scare the living daylights out of them.' And then she'd walked out. So now I go to sleep every night, squirming on my stained sheets, and the last thing I see is the box of new ones on the balcony.

'Stop going so fast with that handle, Masha, I almost missed the corner!'

She pats the sewing machine. 'At least we got our Little Fat Lydia here as a reward for hiding her precious sheets.'

'You treat Lydia like a pet or something.'

'And you lust after those sheets every minute of the day. I keep seeing you gazing out at that box like it's Slava covered in chocolate.'

'All I want is sheets that no one's ever lain on, Masha. Not our old grey, threadbare ones with all the nasty stains that might be from Uncle Garrik who has open tuberculosis, or Aunty Faina who's got weeping leg ulcers …'

'… or Baba Alla who sawed herself to pieces in bed with a knife …'

'Urgh! Masha, I forgot about her.'

'Well, you can forget about those clean sheets too. They might as well be sitting in Amerika.'

I shrug. I'll have clean sheets in Slava's village. I'll wash them 'til they gleam.

'Right, last nappy. Time to go and meet Uncle Styopa and see if he can get us to that old doctor, on the eighth floor. My back's killing me.'

We get up and I pack everything away neatly.

'It seems stupid that the nurse here doesn't know what's wrong with you …' I say.

'She's about twelve years old, and she's from Tobolsk. What do you expect? She asked us how many hearts we had, for fuck's sake … we're joined at the waist, not the neck.'

Uncle Styopa's waiting by the lift. He's happy as anything now Baba Yulia's back. He doesn't even get drunk any more.

'Come along, girls, I don't have all day.'

'I'm in agony here, Uncle Styopa, take pity on your little Mashinka.'

'That's what I'm doing, isn't it? So right, just so you know: obviously none of us lot are allowed on the eighth floor. You're gonna get an eyeful, believe me.' He presses the button for the lift. The doors open and there's the lift attendant sitting on her stool in the corner looking like a toad with her bulging eyes and warts. She's the one that presses the buttons.

'Which one?' she says.

'Eighth,' says Uncle Styopa, and just as she's about to spit and say *nyet*, he gives her a box of Zefir meringues. I gawp at it. Zefir meringues! Where on earth did he get those? 'For the grand-children,' he says, and winks. She sniffs and presses button number eight.

'*Yolki palki!*' says Masha as we walk out. 'It's like the Kremlin up here!' We stand gazing around. It's bright and light with white walls and wooden parquet floors, and loads of shiny pot plants and white lacy curtains, which flutter in the clean windows. The corridors smell sweet and clean too and … of fresh air.

'Here we are. This is a taste of what Communism will look like,' says Uncle Styopa.

'There's even a buffet!' says Masha. There is too. A proper buffet, selling green Tarzan mineral water and little white sand-wiches with sliced tinned ham. As we walk past, I see the buffet attendant is standing by a long window that's slightly open, so there's a cold puff of fresh air coming in.

'*Gospodi!* An open window,' whispers Masha. 'And no bars. They can even kill themselves up here if they want to!'

'Come on, come on, we don't want to get caught,' says Uncle Styopa. 'Here, this is his room.'

We knock on the door, and a deep voice says 'Enter'. Yemil Moseyevich is at his desk writing. He turns around and smiles like we're normal guests. He has kind little eyes and a large nose with lots of hair sprouting out of his nostrils, and he's wearing this funny purple waistcoat with yellow flowers on it.

'Sit down, girls, and you, Stepan Yanovich, do sit down.'

He's only just moved in but already he's got his walls all covered from top to bottom with photos and pictures, and he has bright curtains and a bedspread from home.

'So, now then, how can I help?'

'Well, it's M-Masha,' I say. 'She's got this p-pain in her back, just here,' I point at the bit where we join, 'and since you're a d-doctor, we wondered if you'd l-look at her?'

'Certainly, certainly, lie down on my bed here, my dear, that's right.' He pushes and prods her a bit, and asks her some questions, and then sits back and says he thinks it's a large kidney stone that she can't pass.

'You'll need to see a urologist urgently. I know a very good one who will come here and see you at no cost. A good man. I'll organize it. Tea, anyone?' He gets up and puts a kettle on. A kettle! In his own room. And a TV set. All to himself.

'So why are you in here with us lot, Yemil Moseyevich?' asks Masha, feeling a bit more relaxed now.

'Well now, Mashinka, I married a War Widow with a baby son, you see. We brought him up, but when she died, my stepson, who has a growing family now, decided there was no room for an old fool like me … rightly so, I'm sure … and a doctor like myself, you know, earns less than a welder in our Worker's State. No doubt that's a good thing, no doubt it is. Wonderful, all this equality. So we decided on this option, instead of me staying in my flat. Must make way for the young generation, you know. My time is past. But I do like my creature comforts. I couldn't do without those, I'm afraid. And the others on this floor are generally from the … ahh … intelligentsia, so very pleasant to converse with.' He smiles. He's got a rug on the floor and loads of books too, all stacked up on a bookshelf. He sees me looking at them. 'Your body can be imprisoned, my dear …' he's looking right into my eyes '… But not your mind.'

Masha sniffs. 'Got a TV too. All right for some. I'd watch Spartak footballers playing day and night, I would.'

'Yes, yes, I'm very lucky. My stepson is deputy director of the Mikoyan Meat Factory – hence the eighth-floor option.' He winks at us. 'He's very good to me, my stepson is.'

We nod, but I'm thinking that throwing your stepfather out of his own flat isn't being very good. Meanwhile, Barkov's getting paid in all the meat chops that he and all his cronies need, while we get boiled bones and cabbage.

'Now then,' he says, once we've got our Georgian tea – in proper glasses too, not cracked tin mugs – 'how about a little game of chess?' We nod again although neither of us have ever played chess before. I could stay up here forever. It's like being back in Aunty Nadya's flat, it's cosy, it's like ... being on the Outside.

'I expect you know about the great chess match,' he goes on, 'the USSR versus the Rest of the World? Hmm?' We shake our heads this time, and I feel stupid. He pats his purple jacket. 'Ahh, well, we won of course. Of course we won. We always win. Now then, here's the board, let me see, black or white? Do you mind if I have a cigar? Since I've got my smoking jacket on, eh?' He smiles and pats his silky waistcoat again. He reminds me of Professor Popov. He starts puffing on his sweet-smelling cigar and tells us about how he used to train dogs in the Great Patriotic War to run under the wheels of oncoming German tanks with explosives strapped to their collars. 'We used to always feed them under tanks you see, working on Pavlov's theory of conditioning.'

'Poor dogs,' I say.

He shrugs. 'Well, they weren't told, were they? What you don't know can't harm you, they say ... And it was all a sacrifice for the greater Soviet good. Better dogs than people ...'

Masha winces in pain. I hope he gets us that urologist.

## A tale of Soviet reality

We couldn't work today. It's been a week since we saw Yemil Moseyevich, and Masha's getting worse. She keeps groaning and moaning, and clutching at her back, and she's been sick three times. We went to Katya, the nurse, for painkillers, and she wanted to take her to hospital, but Masha wouldn't go, so now we're just sitting here, hoping this urologist is going to turn up soon.

'I really think you should've gone to hospital, Mash, you look green, you really do.' We're just sitting on the bed, staring at the shiny brown wall.

'I don't want to be laid out on a slab and mauled by perverts, even if you do. I'd rather suffer in silence.'

'Hardly silence. Our entire floor thinks you're being tortured.'

'I *am* being tortured. By this *yobinny* kidney stone. All right for you, sitting there like a cat on a cushion.'

'I'm not, I'm worried about you.'

'Like *fig* you are, you're just being smug, because you got your precious diploma.'

Yes. I finally did it. I got top marks – one hundred per cent. One hundred! Dazdraperma cried when she brought me the diploma. She said my physics teacher cried too. They were crying because it was such a waste. Such a waste of an incredible brain, they said.

'Waste of space, more like,' Masha had muttered. 'Dear Dashinka, lovely Dashinka, clever Dashinka, pretty Dashinka … makes you want to gag.' Dazdraperma had looked a bit shocked at that. And left. I asked her to take the diploma with her, in case it got stolen.

We both look up as the tacks on the floor go *tic tic tic*. But it's only Sanya, not the urologist.

'I was just going home, girls, but thought I'd drop by for a bit of gossip.' Masha perks up a bit then. 'Right,' she goes on, 'so I've got three really juicy bits for you today. Ready? First off, Nyusha – you know, the tart from accounts who's been having it off with Viktor Vladimirovich, the head accountant?' We both nod, no one has any secrets in the Twentieth. 'Well, he chucked her, so she tried to blackmail him. She said she'd tell his wife and kids if he didn't siphon off something from the Twentieth's pocket for her. And what do you think he did?'

'What?' we say together.

'He went straight to Barkov and told him everything. Informed on her, he did.'

'What about Nyusha?' I say. 'Did she go and inform on *him* – to his wife?'

'Yeah, but turned out the wife was having an affair with her boss too, so she couldn't care less.' I shake my head. If I married Slava, I'd never cheat. And neither would he. No, not if … when … *when* I marry Slava. I clench my fists. He'll write soon. I'll deal with Masha. I *will.* I'll be strong.

'So next up is Baba Keesa, the old bag who's in with Baba Yulia. She makes funeral wreaths, right?' I shiver. That's the only other job we're allowed to do here, along with the pipettes and the nappies. We can make funeral wreaths. But I won't. We see dead bodies in here all the time, either laid out in their rooms, or being wheeled around on gurneys, or even outside in the yard in open coffins. I won't make wreaths.

'So she made one for herself, see, a really fancy one, took her forever, and then she refused to take any food or water until she shrivelled away and died. Yesterday it was, that she went. No one's gonna force-feed you in here, are they?'

'What's number three then?' says Masha, wincing again. The pain seems to come in bouts.

'Yemil Moseyevich, that snooty doctor on the eighth floor.' We both stare at her. What? What? 'So, turns out his stepson stopped supplying Barkov with his steaks or whatever, so he's being moved down to the third floor. He'll have three roommates there – nice little *troika* they are, I can tell you. One's a *zek* ex-con who'd bite your arm off soon as look at you, the other's an *alkash* who's always thrashing around with the White Fever because he can't get vodka, and the other's got less sense than a duck.'

'No!' We both say it at once.

'Yeah. Why, what's the big deal?'

'He's getting me a urologist,' says Masha, 'that's the big deal. He might forget or something if he's down there. He might …'

We both know what Yemil Moseyevich might do.

'Yeah, well, he won't be able to put all his pretty pictures up on the wall on the third floor, I can tell you that.'

When Aunty Shura's gone, me and Masha try to get up to the eighth floor to see him, but the old toad in the lift won't let us. So we go back to our room and sit there on our bed. Neither of us feels like going down to the canteen for the evening meal. It's still warm out, so after a bit, we both stand up without saying anything and go on to the balcony. It's strange, but we always do that – get up at the same time and do the same thing, without even talking about it. Masha thinks it's because we read each other's minds, but it's not exactly that. She can't read my mind. I think it's just when one starts moving it's like, I don't know, instinctive for the other to move too, and we don't even know which one started it.

We both hold on to the bars and look up into the blocks of flats around our courtyard wall. It's dusk and we can see the Healthies coming out on to the balconies to smoke, or take in washing, or put a baby in its pram out to sleep in the fresh night air. Some balconies have flowers, and some have sledges, car-tyres, ice-hockey sticks, Spartak football banners, bicycles …

'He shouldn't be moved down there. It's all so wrong,' I say after a bit, pressing my forehead against one of the bars. 'How can these things happen?'

'How does it happen that my little budding atomic physicist here is stuck sewing nappies?' snaps Masha. 'Or Miracle Masha the Trapeze Artist is trapped behind bars? Shit happens.'

She doesn't seem to care, but I can't stop thinking what state of mind Yemil Moseyevich must be in right now. I just can't stop it. We can hear music from over the wall. It's not Soviet marching bands or ballads or the Red Army Choir. It's *popsa* music.

'D'you think that's the Beatles?' she says.

I remember Slava talking about the Beatles. Masha starts tapping her fingers on the bars to the beat. She likes it.

Just then we see something fall to the right of us, about three rooms over. It looks like a piece of sacking someone's getting rid of. But it's not. When it hits the ground with a thud it moves around for about two or three minutes, which is when we know it's a person. And when the yard lights go on, we see it's a person wearing a purple waistcoat with bright blobs of yellow on it.

## March 1970

### Slava comes back to Moscow to see me

The next morning Sanya told us that after Yemil Moseyevich was informed he was being moved, he wrote a note to his step-son, smoked a last cigar, tidied his room and then walked on to his balcony with no bars, and tipped himself off it. I can't bear to think of him, still moving down there on the ground. I can't bear to.

That afternoon we got a visit from Mikhail Ilyich, a urologist who says he received an urgent call the day before, from a friend who asked him to come and see us.

He examined Masha and told her she did have a kidney stone and he massaged her a bit to try and help her pass it, then told her to drink three litres of water a day and if that didn't help, she'd need to come into hospital.

'I'm going to pop if I drink any more,' she says, screwing up her face as she forces more water down herself.

We're sitting on our bed the next morning. She still doesn't feel like doing any sewing, so we're just sitting there. We've done our morning exercises in the narrow space between the bed and the wall, we've been down for breakfast and now we're back here, with nothing to do all day. Except imagine. When Masha's not talking, I go into this other world I have, of living in the village with Slava. I'm not Together with Masha there, and Slava and me are both Healthy. He works as an accountant and I'm a science teacher in the primary school. I can picture it all in my head: the stove, the tables and chairs, the rug on the wall, the books we have and the vegetable plot in the garden. I have all these different situations I think up and I go through the conversations, word by word, in my head. It's my other world. My real world.

'Girls! Girls! I have great news!'

Aunty Nadya bursts into our room all out of breath and red in the face. We weren't expecting her.

'What! What!' we say together.

'Slava's here! Slava's in SNIP. His mother sent him up for urgent treatment and he didn't want me to say anything until he was actually here. He wants you to visit.'

I look across at Masha.

'*Nyet*,' she says, and looks out of the window.

There's this shocked silence, which bounces off the walls.

No, she can't do this. No! Slava! Slava's here! She can't stop me going – she can't! Not this time, not now he's here, just ten minutes away, waiting for me!

'What do you mean, *nyet*?' splutters Aunty Nadya. 'Of course you're going. The car's waiting outside. Get up this minute!'

'*Nyet*.'

'*Da! Da!* I'm going, Masha, I'm going.' I struggle to stand up, but she doesn't move, so I grab her arm and tug at her, but she still won't budge. She's like a dead weight. I keep trying to get up, and end up half on the floor. Aunty Nadya picks me up and puts me back on the bed. I'm sobbing now and still pulling to go, lifting my arms to Aunty Nadya for help, but it's no good. Masha's made up her mind and we both know it.

'How can you be so … so … selfish and heartless and cruel!' shouts Aunty Nadya, going even redder in the face. 'They want to see each other, can't you see how you're hurting her? Can't you see what torture this is for her?'

'You haven't seen her crying every time *he* hurts her!' Masha shouts back. 'You haven't been together with her when she's tearing herself into a million pieces with her pain! *That's* torture! *He's* the one who's torturing her and he wants to do it again. He thinks he can whistle and she'll just crawl back into the boxing ring, to get punched to the floor again. I can't go on seeing her being mutilated like that all the time – she's my sister, I love her. I'm not going! You couldn't get me to see the little *moodak* if you chained me to a locomotive.'

'No, Masha, no! You don't understand,' I sob, still pulling at her, 'not being able to see him is the torture. He only hurts me because you and me are Together, which means *we* can't be together … him and me … it's so hard for him, can't you see that? Can't you?' I'm trying to talk through my tears, trying to get her to understand. 'I *must* see him, I *must* talk to him … he promised …'

'Promised what?' She looks at me sharply. 'And why would you believe his stupid promises anyway?'

'He … he …'

'I'm not letting him make you miserable as sin all over again. It's like dragging the devil along beside me …'

'If you don't let me go I'll be so miserable you'll wish you were *dead!* I will, I will, I swear I'll never talk to you again!' I thump the bed. 'Let me make my own mistakes!'

She looks back out of the window. '*Nyet*.'

'Well, Masha,' says Aunty Nadya, going almost purple in the face now, 'if you can't see that you're burning down the house to get rid of the mouse, there's only one thing for it. I'll tell the little lad to come here to see you. That's what I'll do.' She nods firmly at me and stalks out.

When I finally stop crying, hours and hours later, I won't talk to her. I'll show her what our life will be like if she doesn't let me see Slava when he comes here. It's the only thing I can do. I'll stand up to her, I will. That's what I'll do. I'll stand up to her. Just like he said.

'Finally stopped all that bawling?' she says. 'About time too. Here's me, downing all this water, and you're crying it all out again as fast as it goes in.' She's trying to be funny, thinking a stupid joke will make it all right again. I hate her. I turn the other way.

By evening Masha's passed her kidney stone and wants to go and see Ivan Ivanovich down in reception. I don't want to do anything she wants to do, but I also don't want her to ruin Slava's visit, so I get up.

He's watching *Vremya* news.

'Heard the rumours, girls? About the Americans having landed on the moon?'

'That's just rumour, spread by Uncle Sam, everyone knows that,' sniffs Masha. 'No one except us can land on the moon. And we'd have read about it if they had. Or it would be on the news.' She points at the TV set.

Ivan Ivanovich shrugs. 'Not everything gets reported in our news ...'

'They just hate us because we're better than them,' says Masha angrily. 'They want to drop one of their atomic bombs on us. They're bullies. And they're jealous.'

'All right, all right, Miss Politics. You should join the Politburo,' he chuckles. 'That'd shake them up.'

We sit and watch the news for a bit. It's all about our Five-Year Plan and more Over-fulfilled Quotas and Brezhnev opening the biggest dam in the world, which has just been built here in the Soviet Union. I wonder if Slava will come tomorrow. I wonder how long he's been here. I wonder why he needed urgent treatment.

Masha yawns.

'Well,' she says, 'back off to the cell,' and she gets up to go. We tap across the dark hallway to the lift. The doors open and we step inside. Then, as if as an afterthought, she holds the closing doors and pops her head out.

'Van Vanich!' she shouts. 'If someone called Slava Dionego comes to visit us, tell him we're busy, OK?'

He nods and goes back to watching the TV.

The lift doors close on us.

## December 1970

### I punish Masha by not talking to her and she relents, then we down wine on the floor of the balcony

'I wish Aunty Nadya would hurry up. I need a drink like a camel needs water,' says Masha.

It's December now, and we're sitting in reception on two chairs pushed together with a rug over our legs. Barkov has said we can't come down here any more, unless we sit on the two chairs with this rug, as he's had complaints from visitors who were traumatized. There are hardly any visitors in the Twentieth though, because all the inmates here are unwanted. So I don't know who we managed to traumatize this time.

'I hope she's got that sweet port wine again,' I say. 'It's easier to drink when it's sweet.'

She rubs her jaw. 'Getting drunk is the only way to stop this pain. The only thing I eat nowadays are *yobinny* painkillers with my toothache, not to mention these kidney stones I get every two minutes.'

I tuck her hair back behind her ear and stroke her cheek with the back of my hand. I get toothache too but I don't think it's as bad as hers.

I didn't talk to Masha for eight whole weeks after she told Ivan Ivanovich not to let Slava in, and when I started in on the ninth she gave in and apologized. It was a Monday evening. 'All right, *all right*,' she said. 'Listen, please, please, please, just stop it. I'm sorry, OK? You're driving me mad with your silence!' I turned to look at her then, but I still didn't speak. 'For God's sake,' she went on, 'what are you going to do? Ignore me for the rest of my life? Isn't it bad enough in here, without you being an enemy to me too?'

I turned away. I still wouldn't talk. She'd tried everything over those eight weeks. Beating me up until she was exhausted and me not caring. Yelling at me. Telling jokes. Tickling me. Then beating me up again. She broke my nose twice but none of the medical staff in the Twentieth asked any questions. They know Masha and me have our problems and they don't get involved.

I talked to other people, of course, but I didn't talk to her. It drove her crazy but it was the only thing I had left in my power to do.

Then, that Monday, after supper, we'd gone back to our room and I'd just sat there and stared at the wall while she went prattling on about who'd died and who'd been brought in. I still wouldn't speak, so then she took my hand and squeezed it. 'Dasha. Stop this. Just fucking *talk* to me again! Tell me what you want, all right? Just tell me.'

And then I did speak.

'There's something you've got to understand, Masha,' I said slowly. 'I've always done everything for you. I wash you, I comb your hair, I play cards when you want to play cards. I go and see whoever you want to see. I do everything you want to do and you don't do anything *I* want to do. I don't even bother to ask you any more. I've never asked for anything. Until now. If it was you who wanted to be with someone else, I'd be happy for you. We'd all be friends. We could all be friends.'

She'd looked up at the ceiling then and sniffed, like she does. 'All right then. If that's how it is. All right. Write to your Peanut. We'll see what happens …'

But before I could write, we got a letter from him.

*10 June 1970, Novocherkassk*

*Hello girls, greetings from Slava. How is your health? What's new? How is Aunty Nadya doing? I'm fine and my health is OK. Listen, girls, I'm sorry I didn't write before but I'm just getting used to settling in at home for the summer holidays.*

*Dasha, before I left Moscow I did call in to see you but they told me that you were busy and weren't to be disturbed and they wouldn't let me up to see you. I was sorry you didn't come to visit me in SNIP.*

*Give my love to Aunty Nadya. I don't see the staff or the other kids any more. I want to ask Vera Stepanovna to come and visit me. It seems I have to go back to school this year to get my diploma since I missed so much. But now I'll have to go down again into the class below. I wish this would be over and done with as soon as possible.*

*Dasha, don't be upset. I gave you my promise, didn't I? And I won't ever tell anyone. I can't write any more on that subject in this letter.*

*Slava*

'What promise?' Masha asked when she read the letter. 'How did he give you a promise? Where was I?' I didn't tell her. It's the only secret I have from her. That we're going to be together. I'll do my part in getting Masha to agree. And he'll do his in getting us to live with him. I'll be strong.

Everything was all right again after that. I wrote straight back to him. It's been so long since I've actually seen him now, that the Slava in my imagination, living in the village with me, is becoming the real one. He didn't write back so I wrote another one.

*2 September 1970, Moscow*

*Slava!*
*Greetings from Masha and Dasha. How are you? How is your health? We haven't heard from you since June so it seems as if you've stopped writing. Perhaps you're busy at school. We are OK and have made some more friends among the staff and a few of the inmates. There are some nice people here. Olessya writes to us from her Old People's Home, which isn't far away but it's a Closed Regime one, so she's not allowed out to visit and of course we're not allowed in. She doesn't sound that happy, but there you are.*

*Aunty Nadya said you wanted records so we bought them. We hope you enjoy them. Aunty Nadya will send them but I wonder why you need them? Doesn't your transistor work? How is school and everyone there? Give our love to Maria Petrovna, Valya Starozhika in the kitchens and the rest. And especially love to Valentina Alexandrovna, if she's still there. If anyone comes to Moscow please tell them to visit us.*

*Masha and Dasha*

I waited and dreamed and waited but he still didn't write back so I sent him a card of congratulations on October Revolution day. Finally, he sent us one too on 7 November. It just wished us health, happiness and a long life. The usual. I was a bit disappointed, but there you are. At least there's hope again. All I need is hope.

A visitor comes out of the lift and walks across the hall, stopping by the bust of Lenin to do up her coat and I pull the rug a bit further over our legs. She doesn't even glance at us.

'I'm never going back to the dentist who comes here, Masha, not ever. I almost went through the roof when he dug that drill into me.'

'What about me? He said he'd only just stopped himself from drilling right through an artery after I jumped two metres in the air. Maybe Aunty Nadya can get us some novocaine from SNIP ...'

'She's cross enough about bringing us wine when it's against the rules. It's only because she can see how bored we are. Good thing that even Igor Semyonovich never dares to look at the bottom of her bag.'

'That *svoloch*,' she mutters under her breath. Ivan Ivanovich was fired for not noticing that Uncle Styopa's brother had smuggled in another two bottles of vodka. I shiver. Uncle Styopa got so crazily drunk that he went on the rampage and got sent to Stupino. We'll never see *him* again ... Or Ivan Ivanovich.

Sanya comes down, dressed in her felt boots and wrapped up in a rabbit fur coat. It's the end of her shift. She sees us sitting there and sticks her nose in the air as she goes past.

'Bitch. Thinks it's OK to go stealing our money ...' mutters Masha.

Sanya and Masha aren't talking any more. We used to give her money from our pension, to buy cigarettes, but Masha got it into her head that she was buying cheap cigarettes and telling us they cost more so she could pocket the difference. We don't know the prices Outside. Maybe she was. Sanya got so angry. 'It's all right for you,' she'd said, 'waited on hand and foot here and lying back in your bed reading magazines and listening to music all day. I have to work, I do. I have to get up at dawn and slave away for you lot, living off the State like parasites.' Masha was furious but didn't reply. She never gets into an argument, she just refuses to talk to people who anger her. She refuses to talk to them ever again.

I go back to looking at the front door, waiting for Aunty Nadya. It's what Masha would do actually, keep some money back, that's why she suspects Sanya. But it's against the rules to buy them for us and sneak them in, so Sanya was doing us a big favour. She deserves a few kopecks for that, and she does work hard, but she doesn't understand I'd like nothing better than to be *allowed* to work. All I want is to be useful, to have a purpose in life. But Masha can't see it. She doesn't trust anyone, Masha doesn't.

'I wish you hadn't just turned against her like that, Masha. You always do that.'

'Don't you start. Everyone's out to get us. I hate this place. I hate it.' She puts her head in her hands and says fiercely, 'Where *is* she?!'

It wouldn't be so bad if they hadn't taken Masha's beloved Lydia away from us.

It happened a few months ago, after Barkov called us in. We hardly ever see the Director, but this one time he called us in to his office, which was about twenty times the size of an inmate's room and all panelled in wood. Three people could have laid end to end on his desk, it was that big. We sat on a high-backed chair on the rug in front of the desk. He's fat like a pig. And pink. And bald.

'So, girls,' he said, tapping a pen on his desk. 'I need to know if there is any slander going on among the staff or inmates.' Barkov has this way about him that makes everyone shrink. Olessya used to say it was the Party way – Authority makes you shrivel like a salted slug. By slander we knew he meant criticism of the way he runs the Home. 'I intend to crush dissent from within,' he went on. 'Crush it.' He balled up a piece of paper in his fist to make his point. We just kept looking at him, not really knowing what to say. 'And in order to do that, I need to have someone from within to give me information.' He knows Masha lives for gossip. We both realized then that he wanted us to be informers, but everyone knows who the snitches are in an institution like this, and they're despised. They get perks from the Administration, of course, but they're despised by everyone for their denunciations.

I looked down at the floor.

'I don't know anything, Igor Nikolaevich,' said Masha. 'I sit in my room with her and her books and we don't hear anything. We don't see anything either. Nothing.' She looked up at the ceiling.

He drew his breath in through his nose, picked up a pen and started rapping it on the table like a machine gun.

'Is that your last word?' He looked at Masha. We all three knew what was happening then. Masha nodded and kept looking at the ceiling.

The next morning Iglinka Dragomirovna came and took our sewing machine away.

I stare, for the millionth time, at the row of portraits of the Politburo members glowing with medals. They never change. Or perhaps they do but still all look the same. I wonder what it's like inside the Kremlin Palace where the Tsars used to live, and now the Politburo do. All golden, probably. The door clatters open.

'Here she is!' We throw off the rug and run to her for a kiss. If we didn't have Aunty Nadya, I don't know what we'd do. She comes to see us every single week.

'I can't stay long, girls. I've brought some cabbage pies and a jar of pickled cucumber. How are you doing?'

'My teeth are killing me,' moans Masha as we get into the lift, still hugging her as she tries, with pretend anger, to push us off.

'Well, and whose fault is that? How many times have I told you to brush your teeth?' she tuts. 'What do you expect when you drink sweet tea and don't brush?'

She comes up to our room, empties out her bag, tells us a bit about her new patients in SNIP, then kisses us both on the top of our heads and goes.

As soon as the door closes, Masha hands me the wine bottle and gets me to push the cork down with my thumb. She's excited.

'C'mon, c'mon! *Blyad!* I want to get drunk so bad!'

'I'm trying. It's stuck.' I want to get drunk too … It's shameful, but I do. When I drink I forget. I forget we're here, I forget who I am and I forget I'm with Masha. I've got it on the floor now and I'm pushing and panting. At last the cork pops in. The only place we can drink and not be seen is out on the balcony, lying down. It's freezing outside but it doesn't usually take me long to drink it. Two minutes. Maybe three.

'Finally …'

We go out on to the balcony. The snow is knee-deep but I lie down anyway, and I haven't even got a coat on. No one can see us from the courtyard, and if someone comes into the room they won't see us through the window either. I don't care about the snow. When I'm drunk I don't feel the cold. Masha pushes my elbow to get me to start, and I tip it up and start drinking it in one, stopping for the occasional breath. So I'm lying there in the snow, glugging it back, with Masha still shoving my elbow, and suddenly I think, Wait – how did this happen? How did I end up here, aged twenty, lying on the floor of a barred balcony, downing a whole bottle of wine like a common alcoholic? I need rescuing … I need … Slava … But before I can get too sad or ashamed or lonely … that wonderful wave of drunken forgetfulness seeps into my blood, washing right over me and sweeping me away with it to a world of numbness and nothingness.

## Age 21
## February 1971

### We arrange to leave the Twentieth to go and live with Slava in the village

*12 December 1970, internat.*

*Hello girls, thank you for your letter and a big thank you for the records. I liked them very much.*

*Sorry about the delay in replying but I couldn't find a stamp. I had to ask someone to get one for me but they were a long time in fulfilling the order as there's such a shortage. My health is OK. I'm not doing too well with my studies. Never mind. I've grown used to my new class.*

*Dasha, no, my transistor hasn't broken but I don't listen to it because I can't get batteries. Does your transistor work?*

*Dasha, thanks for your card of the 7 November. I expected a letter but there you go. Alla sends her love and Nadezhda Lazareva, remember, who works in the kitchens? How's Aunty Nadya? Send her my love.*

*Dasha, have you read any poetry books?*

*Dasha, could you come down to see me in the village next summer? I would come up to Moscow if I could, but it won't be possible because my mother will be working and my brother will be preparing for his entrance exam to university. So you must come here to me. You can stay as long as you like. Mum says I need company.*

*Will you?*

*Love Slava*

'Well, everything's going according to plan, yes, yes.' Aunty Nadya's in our room and I'm holding his last letter as if it's a straw and I'm a drowning man. 'Yes, yes, Slava's mother has written back to me and she says that Slava's very much looking forward to it and so is she. Yes. And I've just been given your leave of absence form, from Barkov ...'

'Yeah, I bet he couldn't write that fast enough ... he hates us,' says Masha cheerfully. 'Thinks we're some sort of cancer in the body of his precious Home. Well, we're getting away from this hell-hole, we are – Masha's off to dance around the village pond.'

'Well, yes, I had no problem at all in getting it. And I told Slava's mother that you have no special needs and that you're very clean and well behaved. I didn't think I needed to inform the Ministry of Social Protection as this isn't considered, you know, permanent ... as yet ... just a holiday ... and you will have your invalid pension to buy food and such like.'

'We don't eat much,' I say. 'And we'll eat anything.'

'Well, just remember to brush your teeth. And you've written back to Slava?'

'Yes, I sent him a birthday card,' I say. 'It was his birthday on January twenty-seventh.'

'That's right. His mother said he was having a party in the village for the children from school.'

'I told him we can come to him first thing in summer, in May. I told him we're arranging it all.'

'Good, good, well, I'll be off.' She stops at the door. 'I must say, I'm so very pleased to see the difference in you both. I'm glad you finally came to an agreement. See how happy it's made you? See what good things can come in life if you both just agree. And never give up hope ...'

The next day we go down to reception. The crows outside are going *kaaa kaaa* mournfully and it's raining, so the snow's melting into a slush. February. I remember our poem. *Take up your pen and weep*. He asked if I was still reading poetry in his letter. Well, we'll read it together now. In ninety-nine days from now. I wonder if he still has that book of poetry by Pasternak. *Write of February through your tears, while the burning black slush of spring thunders at your feet* … And he wrote 'Love Slava' in his letter. For the first time ever, he wrote Love.

'Letter for you two,' says the new guard.

We jump at it excitedly. Masha snatches it, of course, but I can see it's not from him. I can tell from the writing it's not him. It might even be from his mother. Masha opens it and stands, leaning on her crutch while I fidget, wanting to see it too.

'Who's it from? Who's it from, Mash?'

'Valentina Alexandrovna. Shut up.' She starts reading and then all of a sudden I feel her heartbeat punch through to mine like a cannon ball, and I rock back. She draws in a quick breath but reads on and then she hands it to me.

*2 February 1971, Novocherkassk*

*Hello girls. Greetings from Valentina Alexandrovna!*

*How are you? How is your health? We are busy at school here but we often think of you up in Moscow.*

*Girls, I wanted to write to tell you that Slava had a birthday party at his home. He invited all his friends from school to his village and we took the school bus out there. It was a lovely affair and everyone had such a nice time.*

*Dasha, Slava said that he wished that you could have been there and that he was looking forward to seeing you in summer.*

*I'm very sorry to say that he died the next day.*

*I thought I should write and tell you, or you might not have known. And you might have been waiting for his letters. And planning your trip.*

*I think I should say, and I hope I don't upset you, that Slava was the nicest possible pupil. He never complained.*

*Anyway, I'm sorry to bear such bad news, girls, but I had to write.*

*Valentina Alexandrovna*

> 'Flaws should no longer be concealed.'
>
> Mikhail Gorbachev, General Secretary of the Communist Party 1985–91

## Age 38
## October 1988

### Olessya is transferred to the Twentieth

'Morning, my Dashinka …' Slava leans over me and kisses my cheek as we lie in bed. 'Time to get up and make breakfast for the kids. I'm starving.' He pushes my long hair out of my eyes, and kisses me again. His lips are warm and soft, and he smells of sleep. I yawn and stretch. 'We'll go into the woods and pick mushrooms,' he says. 'It's a lovely sunny day. The meadows are full of flowers.'

'Mama, mama!' Lyuba bursts open the door in her flannel nightie with her curly hair all knotted, and jumps into bed between us to snuggle up. She kisses me too, and pushes her little head into my neck while Slava tuts and tries to smooth out the knots.

'Is Marat up yet?' he asks.

'Course not, he'd sleep 'til the cows came home …' she says.

'That's what being a teenager does for you … good thing it's a Sunday,' I say, hugging her. 'What shall we have for breakfast then? Ground rice with butter?'

'And honey! I'm going to get some more from the hives today. I didn't get stung, not once, last time.'

'Fuck me! That's enough for today,' says Masha, and flops down on our bed. We do our exercises for fifteen minutes every morning, and while I exercise, I go on with my life with Slava and our two children Lyuba (age six) and Marat (age fourteen). I go on with it through the day too, whenever there's time to dream, which is a lot of the time. It's like Yemil Moseyevich said, that time we visited him: your body can be imprisoned, but not your mind.

'Can't believe Olessya's been moved here,' says Masha. 'It's gonna be so healthy having her here.'

'Except she's in the Lying Down Block next door, so we can't visit ...'

'She's allowed out though. We can meet her outside every day for as long as we like.'

'It's minus twenty out now.'

'For God's sake, stop moaning. I thought this would cheer you up for once in your miserable life ... C'mon, let's put our coats on, she'll be waiting.'

When Brezhnev died six years ago, everyone thought the world was coming to an end. Like when Gagarin died. Just like I thought the world was coming to an end when Slava died. It wasn't though. More's the pity. We've got a new General Secretary now, Gorbachev. He's much younger. 'Not going to keel over dead as soon as he's sworn in like the two old horse radishes before him,' Masha had cackled when we heard the news. We've seen him on TV promising changes and condemning the old order for not telling the people the truth. For concealing flaws. Flaws like us. He has kind eyes, Gorbachev does. But then, so did Stalin. So life goes on, and me and Masha play cards with each other, day in, day out.

But now Olessya's here. My Olessya. I haven't seen her in twenty years.

As we go out of the back door into the walled yard, we pass Uncle Zhenya, sitting bolt upright on the bench.

'Ei, Uncle, you'll freeze to death sitting there!' Masha pokes him but he's fast asleep. '*Yobinny stik*, stay there then, I'm not your nanny.' Masha pulls her scarf over her nose, and we crunch into the snow, careful not to slip over. The Lying Down Block (called the Goners Block by the staff), for inmates who can't walk, is at the far end of the Home. One of the kitchen staff, Lala, is acting as our go-between and we don't even have to bribe her to take messages. She's sweet, Lala is.

'You should've let me put those plastic bags on over our socks, Mash. My foot is freezing already …'

'Stop bleating … c'mon.'

We pick our way along the path, packed hard with ice. I can hardly believe Olessya is waiting for us just around the corner. We don't know why, but she's been transferred to the Twentieth with lots of other Defectives – except they call us invalids now. There still aren't any proper Homes for adult invalids, because it seems that officially there are still no invalids in the Soviet Union – so how can there be Homes for them? There are still only perfectly formed citizens in our country. I'm sure Olessya will have something to say about that. Olessya hates injustice.

'Look! Oh my God! There she is! Olesskinka!' I squeak, and start laughing and laughing.

We run up to her through a snow drift, almost falling over, and then all hug and kiss and laugh some more.

'Well, girls, how many winters has it been? Twenty? You haven't changed a bit, you really haven't.'

'Neither have you, Olesskinka,' I say. I mean it. She's just as beautiful as ever with her soft skin and big dark eyes. Like Slava's eyes.

'Look at you in your fuck-off wheelchair!' says Masha, laughing. 'What happened to the trolley with the sheath?'

'You know me, Mashinka, I know my rights. I get the Komsorg in the Thirteenth to bring me the latest decrees from the Ministry of Protection and it said we can get one wheelchair per five invalids.'

'B-Barkov's dead set against inmates having wheelchairs,' I say.

'Yeah, I know. He says the Lying Down Block means you lie down and stay there, so it was a battle to bring it to the Twentieth. But here I am. With a wheelchair.'

'I want one,' says Masha. 'Why can't I have one?'

Olessya laughs. 'We'll work on it, Mash. So what's been happening then?' she asks. 'Two decades in the Twentieth … what's been happening? You hardly ever wrote to me.'

Masha and I look at each other.

'Nothing,' we say together.

'We get up,' says Masha, 'we eat, and we go to bed. Every day. Over and over again.'

'I d-don't want to talk about it,' I say. 'But now *you're* here, Olesskinka!' I lean down and hug her again.

'So why did they send you and all the other Defectives over here to the Twentieth from the Thirteenth then?' asks Masha, rubbing her cold nose. 'Did they run out of rooms? Or run out of patience?'

'Bit of both. It's all those young soldiers coming back from the war in Afghanistan with bits of them missing. Thousands of them, and nowhere to put them. So they've had to start transferring us Congenitals to Homes that wouldn't have taken us before. Shame, in a way – some of those lads were gorgeous …' She smiles slowly. Her teeth are still white and even. Ours are awful. All brown and rotting. 'But as soon as those poor boys saw what they were in for, they were topping themselves so fast they couldn't get enough coffins in. These Homes take some getting used to when you've lived life as a Healthy.'

'Well, my shipwreck here was born Defective,' says Masha, nodding across at me as if she wasn't, 'but she'd be topping herself too, given half a chance. You heard about Slava?' Olessya nods and glances at me with those eyes that still see right inside me. 'Well, after we got that letter from Valentina Alexandrovna, she wouldn't eat. Got it into her head she could starve herself to death, so I had to stuff my face all day and every day to keep us going until she realized it wasn't going to work. Just as well – I'd have ended up like a lard balloon!'

Olessya smiles but puts her gloved hand on my arm and tips her head on one side.

'I'm sorry, Dashinka. Slava was a good boy. Aaakh …' Her breath puffs in a cloud around her head. 'It all seems so long ago now … But you know what they say: death leaves a heartache no one can heal, love leaves a memory no one can steal … right?'

Masha rolls her eyes but I whisper, 'Right.' I'm not sure she is, though. Memories are painful. The only time I've ever felt really alive was when I knew Slava. Since he died, I've been living half a life.

'Oh, *gospodi*, don't remind her, she'll be at it again – trying to end it all,' says Masha. 'First it was boric acid powder. Swiped it off the kitchen counter, she did, and was tipping it down her throat before I knew what was happening. That was two days of torture for me, being turned inside out while she threw up after all the emetics they gave her. Then it was a knife, the idiot; she tried to cut her throat, but I got to her first that time. Just about. Don't know why I bother.' I rub the scar on my neck. Olessya's shaking her head. 'And her next little stunt,' Masha goes on, 'was when we managed to get up to the eighth floor to get chocolate from the buffet, and what does my moron here do? Only tries to chuck us out of the open window. If I hadn't grabbed on to the curtains, we'd be two metres under by now. Lucky for us they didn't send us to a Madhouse for attempted suicide. *Both* of us. And what am I supposed to say if we're put in front of a psychiatric panel? Am I gonna stick my little hand up and quack: "But *I'm* not depressed, comrades. I'm sane. I love Socialism, just like everyone else – so send *her* off to your Madhouse, please do; but not me, comrades. No, not me."' We all smile and Olessya shakes her head again.

'Same old Masha.'

'Life's just a constant process of waiting to die for her. And if she *had* chucked us out of that window, chances are, knowing our luck, we'd just be maimed, so then we'd be in a Goners Block like you. I have to have eyes in the back of my head to keep her from ending it all. I was scared to go to sleep, Olessya, I tell you I was, in case she strangled me. No offence and all that, but there's three things I'm frightened to death of – being in a Madhouse, being in a Goners Block and waking up dead.'

Olessya smiles again and shrugs. 'We're all afraid of the Madhouse – and Stupino, come to that – aren't we? That's how they keep us in line. And as for the Goners Block, yeah, they die like snowflakes in the sun in there. But the worst thing is the humiliation.' Her eyes flash. 'It's run like a prison camp and the staff treat us like animals, just because we can't walk. The Administration drags in the cheapest possible village idiots from god-knows-where, instead of employing professionals, and then they pocket the difference in wages for themselves. And what makes those peasants think they're so superior to us? Just because they have straight legs and don't squint?' She bangs her mittened fist on the arm of her wheelchair.

'Yeah, you're right,' says Masha. 'They think we have porridge for brains if we look different. And Dragomirovna barks at us like a mad dog if we so much as fart.'

'Exactly! They treat us like subhuman pigs!' Olessya bangs her fist against the chair again. 'There's all this talk about this new Openness of Gorbachev's, but no one writes about invalids in the press – the so-called Organs of Enlightenment.' She snorts. 'That's a laugh.'

'Or they could at least change the management,' I say. 'Barkov and Dragomirovna have been here forever. Everyone knows they're crooks. And cruel. Everyone. They must have both been here since Stalin …'

'Gold sinks and shit floats,' says Masha.

'And you know what they say in their Organs of Enlightenment?' goes on Olessya. I shrug. We don't read the newspapers. 'That the campaign for human rights is an imperialist plot to undermine the foundation of the Soviet State. What crap! Giving us wheelchairs instead of trays with wheels is an imperialist plot? *Chort!*'

'Well, Gorbachev might change things …' I suggest, and blow on my hands. It's freezing out here. My eyelashes have iced over and my nose is going numb. I rub it, then rub Masha's nose and pull her fur hat down over her ears. (We always wear men's hats and men's clothing because she likes them better.) 'He seems different … Gorbachev does.'

'He *is* different,' says Olessya. 'I've heard one half of his forehead is covered by a red birthmark – that's enough to get you put in a Home from birth. He must have had one strong mum.'

'But Gorbachev *hasn't* got a birthmark,' I say, frowning. 'We see him on TV in the guard room. And his portrait's up with all the rest of the Politburo in reception. He hasn't got a birthmark.'

'They airbrush it out, that's what they do. He's got one, all right. But if he's flawed himself, you'd think he'd help the Defectives, wouldn't you? Not hide his own defect. He's like all the rest of them; if you can crawl out of the dung heap into the garden you stay there … it's one big cover-up …'

'Shhh …' Masha says, looking around. An old woman is shuffling about in the snow not far away, muttering to herself. 'You should be careful, Olessya, you'll get put in the Isolation Hut for slander. You won't survive a week in there.'

'I don't care. I'm going to get a petition up to have the food improved. We get fed slops a dog wouldn't eat here. It was much better in the Thirteenth.'

'A petition?' I say, gawping at her. 'No, no – don't do that, Olessya. We'll get Aunty Nadya to bring you oranges. And tomatoes.'

'I want *everyone* to have oranges and tomatoes. Not just me. And bananas and green beans too – fresh ones.'

'Well, don't get *me* involved in your little uprising. I'm not signing any bananas petition,' says Masha. 'It's hard enough keeping our heads below the parapet as it is.'

'Good for you, Olessya,' I say. 'Someone's got to do it.'

'As long as it's not me,' says Masha. 'I look after Number One, I do, and that's a full-time job. Well, I'm freezing my tits off out here. Let's meet tomorrow, yeah? Same time?'

Olessya nods. 'OK, OK … Just give me a hand up the ramp, girls. Forward to Communism. Haha! That'll be the day.'

As we walk back, I feel things are getting better. I feel things can change. Olessya's inspiring. She always was.

'She's crazy, Olessya is,' says Masha. 'Getting up a petition, for God's sake! Where does she think we are – Amerika?'

'But maybe she's right. Maybe this is the—'

'Hang on a minute – how long's Uncle Zhenya been out here?'

She's stopped in front of him by the bench. He's only forty-seven but after he was crippled in a car accident his wife put him in here and took another husband. A Healthy one, of course. He loves being outside in the yard. He's in the Lying Down Block because he's crippled, but he always sits on the bench outside our Walking Block as if he thinks one day he might simply stand up and be invited in. We sometimes sit with him and listen to him talk about his old life in his country *dacha* where he had a log stove and grew giant marrows and taught his kids how to ride a bicycle. Like me and Slava … in my dreams …

I lean down and push his dog-fur hat back. He's dead. We both realize it immediately – we've seen enough corpses. Masha shrugs.

'You can't teach a fool how to die well.'

We walk away from him then, and up the steps. It's a common enough way for the men to go here. Drink a lot of vodka, and then go and sit outside and hope to freeze to death.

'It's terrible,' I say as we step inside, into the warmth.

'What's so terrible about it? Haven't you seen enough people die?'

'Yes.' I stop inside the door. 'That's the point. It's not terrible about Uncle Zhenya, it's terrible that I don't feel anything any more.' I look at her in growing alarm. 'I'm like you.'

'Thank God for that. Not feeling saves your sanity,' says Masha shortly and starts us off walking again, past the Politburo. 'You torture yourself in these places if you allow yourself to feel everyone's pain. Or allow yourself to feel something for someone. Because they always go, one way or another … like Lucia … and Slava.'

I stop her again.

'But, Masha, compassion makes you human. Doesn't it? Have they killed my compassion?'

'Compassion makes you weak,' she snaps, and pulls us over to the lift. 'If it's gone, then good riddance to it.' The door opens. The Toad is still working here and she watches us walk in with her cold, loathsome eyes.

As the doors close I feel empty. I feel that they've won. Because when I think of Uncle Zhenya, a frozen block on the bench, I feel indifference.

## We meet Olessya again and learn something shocking

When we go back outside the next day, Uncle Zhenya's still sitting there, but now he has a sack over his head. There's a militiaman next to him, because the cause of death was unknown. He's smoking a papirosa.

We've seen this militiaman before at other deaths, so Masha says in a friendly way, 'Hey, you keeping him out here all winter then, Fedya? 'Til he thaws out?'

He spits tobacco on to the snow. 'No hurry, is there? He's not going anywhere.' Then he looks away. We disgust him, I can tell. I don't care.

We walk on. Olessya's out there with a group of her friends who were moved with her from the Thirteenth. They're all laughing. I'm so happy she's here. I've been lonely in the Twentieth.

'*Yolki palki* – I think our Olessya has a boyfriend,' says Masha as we make our way slowly towards them through the snow. The narrow raised path of packed snow is still icy and worn down by footsteps, but our crutches sink deep into the snowdrifts either side, so we're wobbling all over the place.

'Yes,' I say. 'Look – he's got his hand on the back of her neck. He's not bad-looking, is he?'

'She could do better, but a starving dog makes do with scraps. And just look at him standing there like the king of the farmyard.'

'I'm pleased for her.'

'Wonder if she's Doing It with him?'

'Well, why not? There aren't many pleasures in life ...'

By the time we finally get close, they've all rolled back indoors except Olessya, who's sitting waiting for us, rubbing her nose with her mitten to warm it up.

'So who's the cockerel then?' cackles Masha.

'Him? Garrick. He's OK, we have fun.' She smiles her slow, white-toothed smile, showing her dimples.

'Good in bed?'

'Good enough, Masha, thank you for asking, good enough.'

'Aren't you afraid of … you know …' I bite my lip, not sure if I can really ask her about getting pregnant, but it's still our Olessya, so I do.

'Pregnant? That's a laugh. They sterilize all Defectives in Institutions as soon as they get the chance. Can't be having any more little Defectives, can we? Not in the Best of all Possible Worlds.'

'Sterilize?' I stare at her.

'Of course, *gospodi!* You two are so naïve, it's like you've been living in a hole … well, in a way you have. But yes, we all have sex, but we never get pregnant. Remember the summer camps at school when everyone was Doing It? And almost no pregnancies – unless you were *really* young? You two might have had it done when they took your appendix out in SNIP. Or maybe even when they amputated your leg. They never tell you. Why should they? It's none of your business. It's the State's business. And if they don't do the op, they give you birth-control injections. They inject us all the time anyway with sedatives and vitamins and stuff, so how would we know?'

I stare at her.

'Wait …' says Masha. 'So how do *you* know?'

'I asked the nurse back in the Thirteenth why I never got pregnant; why *none* of us ever get pregnant, and she told me. Very proud of herself she was too. "So you have nothing to worry about," she said. "It's all taken care of for you."'

I want to sit down, right there in the snow. I feel weak. Am I never to have children? Never? We're thirty-eight, we have periods, I still have a school group photo with Slava (Masha says it's hers, but I can look at it) and I sometimes fantasize about him when I feel that throbbing and pounding down there. Somehow I thought that I'd have sex again with someone, anyone really, just to have a baby. And now there are Defectives my age, in the next block … I want to be a mother to someone who loves me more than anyone else. I thought it was still possible … a little baby …

'What's wrong with you? You've gone limp as a dishcloth.' Masha squints at me.

'I … I just thought …'

Olessya understands and leans over to hug me but Masha starts trying to slap some sense into me, cuffing my hat right off my head. I don't try and stop her. I feel winded and helpless, as if the child I always wanted has just been snatched from me.

'For fuck's sake, that's all we need, a *yobinny* babe-in-arms in this hellhole. Are you mad?'

'Even if they didn't do it, and they might not have done, and you *did* get pregnant, Dashinka,' says Olessya softly, 'they'd make you have an abortion … And if somehow they didn't notice, and you had it, they'd take it away.'

'And if they didn't,' says Masha angrily, 'I'd bash it on the head and shove it down the rubbish chute. So you can stop dreaming about your unborn child and get real. Who do you think in a million years is going to father your sprog? The King of Spain? None of the old goats in here could get it up, and I'd not let anyone within a hundred metres of you anyway, even if it *was* the King of Spain. No. We've lived here twenty years, just you and me, and we'll live here another fifty, so get used to it.'

'No, you won't,' says Olessya. 'You won't be living here forever – I've got news!'

'What?' we both say together. I use my scarf to wipe my face and start hiccupping. Masha's right … I'd never find any man. And Olessya's right too. A baby would be taken away. I'm being stupid. Stupid, stupid, stupid. I have my little Lyuba and Marat in my other world. I'll always have them …

'Well, Rita the nurse told me this morning that the Twentieth's being reprofiled. It's being turned into a *psykhooshka* – Psycho-Neurological Home.'

'A Madhouse? What? When?' Masha leans forward and tugs at Olessya's scarf. 'When, Olessya? Are you sure? When?'

'Yes, I'm sure. They're bringing in a Medical Sanity Commission to assess all the inmates next week. It's happening fast. If you pass, you get transferred to another Old People's home – away from Barkov and Dragomirovna – and anywhere's got to be better than being here with them!'

'Medical Commission?' I swallow nervously. I remember the last one, where they didn't even let us speak. 'What happens if you don't pass?'

'Then you stay here with the crazies. But don't worry, as long as you can say your name and know which country you live in, you're fine. I mean, you have to be certified mad to stay in a *psykhooshka*. Shrieking mad. Or anti-Soviet, of course.'

'Leave? We're leaving the Twentieth?' Masha shouts, hardly able to believe it. She's so happy that I look across at her and start laughing, and then we all start laughing. 'Let's just make sure we stay together, Olessya,' says Masha. 'You and us, and your cockerel – we've only just found you!'

'Yes, they say we can even apply to whichever one we want, instead of just being assigned. There's a new one, the Sixth, which has a view of a lake and everyone gets their own room. Imagine! Everyone! Forwards to the Communist dream at last!'

I nod at her, still laughing now, instead of crying. Yes, I'll imagine, all right. I'm good at imagining.

## We go before the Sanity Commission

'OK, calm down, you'd think we were lining up before a firing squad, not a Sanity Commission.'

We're sitting in the anteroom to the hall where the interviews are taking place. It's full of other inmates muttering to themselves or chattering about what questions are being asked.

'I'm worried I'll stutter. Why do you want me to do the talking, Mash?'

'Cos you're the clever one. How many times do I have to tell you? What if they ask us what fifty-seven divided by three is? I can barely manage two times five.'

'I just keep remembering the last commission …'

'That was a lifetime ago, and it was assessing us physically. They thought being Together was as bad as it gets, so we got a One. This is only to check we're not crazies.' She taps her head. 'And we're not. Olessya said the hardest question was, what season is December in? And everyone's passed so far, even the daftest dandelions. They tell you straight away.'

'Maria and Daria Krivoshlyapova.' A voice comes from the interview room. My heart flutters like a trapped bird as we get up and walk in. We've washed and brushed our hair and have clean shirts on. There's three of them, a defectologist, a psycho-neurologist and a speech therapist, sitting behind a long desk. They have little signs in front of them saying which ones they are.

'So, good morning, girls. Which one of you shall we start with then?' says the psycho-neurologist who's in the middle. I put up my hand. 'Very well, and what is your name?'

'D-D-Daria K-K-Krivoshlyapova.'

'How old are you?'

'Th-th-thirty-eight.' It's getting harder to get the words out. I can feel it. Masha's stiffening by my side. She's angry and that makes me stutter even more.

'And in what year were you born?'

'N-n-n-nineteen f-f-f-f …' I can't do it. I feel like bursting into tears, it's like I have a splinter of wood in my tongue.

The speech therapist is tapping her pencil on the table, and interrupts me, asking: 'Why do you stutter?'

'Be-be-be-be-c-c-c …' I still can't get anything out. I look like an idiot. I sound like I'm mad. I should be in a Madhouse. The speech therapist takes off her glasses and looks at me. She's got grey hair and quite a kind face so I try again, but this time I sound even worse so I just stop.

'Hmm … Do you both stutter?'

'No!' Masha's voice is high and angry and it rings around the big hall. Their eyes swivel across to her then. 'No. I don't stutter, and she only does it because a dog jumped out at her when she was little, and bit her, that's all.' I gawp at her. She's always making stuff up. 'She does it when she's nervous,' goes on Masha, 'and she's nervous now because we don't want to end up in here, once it's re-profiled. We have to battle every single day to prove that we're sane, just because we're Together, but if we're left in here, we'll have lost that battle. No one would believe us. We'd be *driven* insane in here.'

None of the three women say anything. Masha's got her arm around me, and mine is around her, like we always do when we're standing. She pulls me to her with a squeeze and the wooden floorboards creak as I lean into her.

'She does it because she's soft, that's all, like a peach. She bruises at anything. That's the only thing wrong with her. And that dog, it almost killed her, it did, almost savaged her to death in front of my very own two eyes, and she had to have all these rabies injections in her stomach afterwards.' I think the speech therapist is smiling but the other two just look a bit amazed. So am I. She's making the whole thing up. 'She's clever, she is,' goes on Masha, glaring at them all, 'she got top marks in her diploma, she got one hundred per cent, you can check, you can, and her tutors here said she could have been an atomic physicist or … or a professor if she wasn't Defective … they said—'

'Thank you, thank you, that's quite enough, Maria, we do have others to see, you know,' interrupts the psycho-neurologist, holding up her hand. Then she glances across to the speech therapist on her right and the defectologist on her left and they nod. I can scarcely breathe. What has Masha done? What have *I* done? They're going to say no …

'That's fine, girls, I think we can safely say you're as sane as any of us.' She smiles. 'You've passed. You may leave.'

## We're crazy happy then suffer a setback, but my Masha never gives up

'This is the best news ever, the best ever,' says Masha, bouncing up and down on our bed. Olessya's sitting across from us in her wheelchair because everything's going crazy in the Twentieth with the changes and she's allowed in our Walking Block. Van Vanich, who's been reinstated as the guard on reception, after the other one got drunk on duty, let her in. It's so wonderful to have him back, we couldn't stop hugging and kissing him, and he joked that his wife would leave him if she ever caught sight of the three of us all in a huddle like that.

Barkov has gone off to some conference today for a week, and Dragomirovna is off sick. Masha thinks they're having an affair and have run away together to the Crimea. That's what she's telling everyone anyway. Masha's crazy. Sanya's here, too, leaning on the balcony door. She and Masha made up in the end because Masha got bored without her to talk to, although it's never quite been the same. But that's OK. As Masha says, Friendship stays green with a hedge in between.

'The Sixth has got grounds with flowerbeds in it that the inmates are allowed to walk in,' Olessya's saying. 'Not like here, where the garden is only for foreign delegations. And they've got two hundred and fifty rooms, single rooms with toilets, all empty. I've already got a place. You should apply as soon as you can, I bet they're filling up like water in a bath.'

'It's OK. We put in our f-formal request for a transfer to the S-Sixth straight away, the very next day,' I say.

'I got my confirmation two days after I put the request in,' says Olessya. 'Almost everyone got passed by the commission. The *babas* are all dithering around like sheep in a pen.'

'Well, I've applied for a job at the Sixth too,' says Sanya. 'Gotta give the Director there a bribe, of course; but a box of chocolates, if I can find one, should do it. I'm not staying here to mop up after dribbling loonies, I can tell you that.'

'I'm not staying here either,' says Masha. 'No *yobinny* way. Mashinka's off out to dance in the flowerbeds by the lake!'

Just then the door opens and Nina from Administration hands us a yellow note.

'It's the confirmation,' says Olessya.

Masha grabs it and starts reading it out loud:

*Dear Comrade Inmates!*

*We confirm receipt of your request for transfer, which is refused.*

*With Respect,*

*Administration of the Twentieth Home for Veterans of…*

Her voice trails off.

'*What?!* You've read it wrong.' I stare at her. It's one of her stupid jokes. I take the note of confirmation from her. *We confirm receipt of your request for transfer, which is refused.*

'It *can't* have been refused,' says Olessya. 'On what possible grounds? No one's been refused. Not one person. Why would they?'

'Why would *he*, you mean,' says Sanya putting her hands on her hips. 'It's Barkov, isn't it? He hates your guts.'

'We know he does. He always h-has,' I say, 'so why k-keep us h-here?'

'To make your life a misery. He'd love that,' says Sanya. 'It would give him a little kick every day to know you're both festering in here with the crazies. I know that man. He'd rather wish for his neighbour's cow to die than have his own cow brought back to life. It's peasant mentality.' She pushes back her headscarf complacently. Masha's still staring at the little yellow note. 'What can we do?' she says eventually in a small voice, and looks up at Olessya. 'Olesskinka, what can we do?'

'Ask Aunty Nadya to talk to Barkov?'

'You could try. But I don't think that would help,' says Sanya firmly. 'He'd just love to see her humiliating herself, begging to let you go. He'd make her squirm for a century. And besides, she's got this strange respect for him, hasn't she? She never disagrees with him about anything, just sort of bows and scrapes like a serf before the master. I've seen her. He has that effect on people.'

We sit there then, not saying anything. I feel icy cold.

'What about writing to the Ministry of Protection?' says Masha slowly. 'We've got to do something. He can't be allowed to do it. The commission passed us. Olessya? Can we write to the Ministry?'

'I'm not sure … they're all in cahoots now, aren't they, these bureaucrats. And the deeper you two are buried away, the better – *they* don't want you out and about, dancing round flowerbeds, I can tell you. But you can try …'

'I will, I will! We *can't* stay here, we can't!' shouts Masha. 'I won't! What about all this Openness?'

'Yes, yes, what about that organization you t-talk about, Olessya – the D-Defence of Invalids Group?' I look at her pleadingly. It was set up a few years ago by Healthies who'd had an accident and ended up crippled and were shovelled aside like compost at the bottom of the Socialist garden, as Olessya puts it. 'You said they have this campaign against the incarceration of invalids. Can't they help us?'

Olessya shakes her head again. 'They can't even get them-*selves* out, Dasha. They organized a breakout from the Homes and marched down to the Town Hall in protest a few years ago, remember? And what happened to them? They're all in Stupino. Even a Madhouse is better than that …'

'*Chort!* You're powerless, girls,' says Sanya. She sits down on the bed next to us and looks at us as if we're already dead and buried.

'Anokhin?' asks Olessya.

'He died years ago,' we say together.

Anokhin. He came to visit us, unannounced, here in the Twentieth, not long after Slava died. We weren't expecting him, we were just sitting on our bed with our box of pipettes when we heard the tacks on the floor clicking and we looked up and saw him standing there, all shrivelled and crumpled in a suit. He didn't stay for long. He sat down on our creaky chair and looked at us. We didn't say anything. What were we supposed to say? So after a while he said, 'I thought I'd come, girls, to see how you are … We had good times, didn't we? You and I?' Masha just glared at him, but I nodded, because I thought we ought to be polite. 'Yes, yes, good times,' he went on, shaking his head. Then he looked around our room for a bit, like there was a nasty smell somewhere, and got up. He put a hundred-rouble note (we'd never seen one before) on the bedside table. 'Just for old times' sake, girls. Buy yourself some chocolate,' he said. And then he left.

Two months later Aunty Nadya came in with a copy of *Pravda*, dated 8 March 1974. There was this big photo of Anokhin above a headline: *Pyotr Kuzmich Anokhin – Soviet medicine has suffered a great, irreparable loss.* And then it went on for pages and pages about how he had won the Lenin Prize and was a Hero of the Soviet Union or something, and had studied under the great Doctor Pavlov and how wonderful and revered and wise he was. Masha tore it into strips, and we used it for toilet paper. No one needs heroes like that, she'd said.

'He can't help us from the grave,' says Masha now.
'He wouldn't have h-helped us anyway,' I add.
'Then there's only one thing more I can think of,' says Olessya. We all turn and look at her.

## We look for our mother

I tried to get Masha to look for our mother a few years after Slava died, once I'd stopped trying to kill myself and resigned myself to living instead. But Masha just kept saying she'd abandoned us, and if she didn't need us, we didn't need her. Masha's proud like that. Or stubborn. So that was that. But now we *do* need her. We need her desperately.

'OK, will you two stop pacing up and down like tigers,' says Sanya. 'You're going to give me a heart attack just looking at you.'

We're down in reception on a Sunday when no one from the Administration is around. There's only Van Vanich, who's outside sucking on a papirosa. Sanya's going to call her up. Our mother. She's going to call our actual mother up on the phone in reception.

'It's her doing the *yobinny* pacing, not me,' says Masha angrily. 'I'm the one who's gonna get the heart attack.' It's true, I can't stand still, my heart's leaping around like a cat in a bag. Masha doesn't get nervous like me, and she's cross when I do, because she says it gives her palpitations. But I can't help it.

Sanya was right, Aunty Nadya refused to go with us to Barkov to ask him to change his mind. She said it was probably for the best that we stayed here after it was re-profiled. For the *best?* In what world could it possibly be for the *best?* Neither of us could understand it at all. Sanya says Aunty Nadya often goes in for meetings with Barkov when she comes to visit. We never knew that. There was this one time when we were down in reception waiting for her and as she was coming in, he was walking out through reception, like a Tsar sweeping past the peasants. He'd stopped and talked to her though, by the door, and it was odd the way she stood there and smiled and nodded, wringing her hands. It's the salt on a slug effect he has. She's always done everything in her power to help us, and now she's telling us he's right. But as Olessya always says, 'Obstacles are stepping stones to success.' If Aunty Nadya hadn't refused to help us, we wouldn't be calling up our mother now. Masha would never have done it.

We had to bribe Katya in the Medical Room to look at our birth certificate and tell us which district we were born in, so Sanya would know where to look to find out where we were born in Moscow. (Aunty Nadya wouldn't tell us. She's doesn't want us to find our mother either. Maybe she's jealous?) It was Sokol District. Sanya looked up the name Krivoshlyapova and there was only one in Sokol. It's such a rare name, she said, it's virtually the only one in the whole of Moscow, so it must be her. It *must*.

'So. You ready for this?' says Sanya, picking up the receiver and looking over at us. Masha nods and Sanya starts dialling. We go and stand behind her.

'Hello? Is this Yekaterina Alexeyevna? Yes? Krivoshlyapova?' She nods across to us. 'This is a cleaner at the Twentieth Home for Veterans of War and Labour. Did you give birth to twins who were born together thirty-eight years ago?' There's a long pause and then Sanya puts her hand over the receiver and mouths across to us, 'She's crying.' Raising her voice, she shouts into the receiver. 'They want you to visit them. This Wednesday. They live here at the Twentieth, number 12 Obrucheva Street … Yekaterina Alexeyevna? Hello?' She pauses again and then puts the phone down. 'She just kept crying,' she says, looking up at us. I don't know if she heard me. You'll have to wait and see …'

## We meet our mother

It's Wednesday. We've been waiting all morning. It's nearly 2 p.m. and no one's come.

'If she doesn't come today, Mash, we'll have to call again. She just didn't hear, that's all.'

'She heard, all right. It's easy enough to find the Twentieth without an address if you've got half a brain. If she doesn't come, I'm not calling again. And that's that.'

She has to come. We've washed our hair, put on clean shirts, scrubbed each other's faces and combed each other's hair. And now we're sitting on the bed, looking at the door. Masha's fiddling with her button. We don't know anything about her. Is she still married to our father? Is she a doctor, like I imagined? Or does she work in a Ministry? Is she a member of the Communist Party? Why did she agree to come and see us if she abandoned us as babies? Does she feel guilty? Did she ever think of us? There are so many questions swirling in my head I can hardly breathe.

There's a little tap on the door.

Two elderly women walk in. One of them is old and hunched, with her grey hair pulled back in a bun and tucked under a dark green headscarf. She's wearing a shapeless woollen dress. The other one is younger and smarter and is holding a handkerchief over her nose. You don't notice the smell in the Twentieth when you live with it. She has a little green beret on, and a grey suit. They stand there staring at us, and we sit there staring at them, not saying anything. Then the old one in the headscarf takes two steps towards us, bends down and kisses me softly on the cheek, and then she kisses Masha.

And it's only then I realize that this is my mother. The mother I'd written all those undelivered letters to in SNIP. (Aunty Nadya finally told me she *had* just put them all in the bin. She had no idea if we had a mother or not, or where she might be.) This is the mother I imagined wearing a flower-print dress, with hair the colour of corn, and eyes as blue as the sky. The mother who was going to come to SNIP, take us in her arms and carry us back home.

Masha flinches when she's kissed, and the old woman sits back heavily on the chair. The other one just stands there, holding her bag in front of her like a shield. Our mother has tears in her eyes. She can't take her eyes off us, she keeps shaking her head and saying under her breath, 'Alive … how can you still be alive … how?'

'*Nooka*,' says the other woman, as if waking from a dream. She puts her bag down on the floor with a thump, and tucks her handkerchief in her pocket. 'We'd better introduce ourselves. I'm your Aunty Dina – Katya's younger sister. Well, well, *yolki palki*, I had no idea you two existed until last Sunday when Katya called. No idea … Katya didn't ever mention … so there we are, and you were here all the time. *Tak, tak,* so you have a room to yourselves, do you? That's very nice, isn't it? And a balcony and your own toilet, goodness! Better conditions than most of us on the Outside, I can tell you!' She laughs cheerily, but a bit nervously, and keeps chattering on in a friendly way, while Masha looks sullenly at our mother, who's sitting, slowly wiping her tears away and still shaking her head.

Mother. She has a kind, placid face and pale blue eyes folded in wrinkles. She's older than I thought she'd be. She looks about eighty, and she still hasn't said a word to us. Aunty Dina's talking on and on though.

'Yes, well, I'd heard rumours, you know, about the girl with two heads in Moscow – those rumours have been going around for years and years, but I never imagined … not for a moment …' she looks over at Katya, who's still staring mournfully at us. 'So I don't expect you knew that you have two younger brothers, Seriozha and Tolya? No, of course not. Well, Seriozha hasn't been sober in ten years, but Tolya's a good boy. They're both in their thirties, and live with Katya in her flat. It's only a one-roomer, but at least it's not communal. We've winterized the balcony so Tolya sleeps there, and Seriozha crashes wherever he crashes. Usually in the stairwell outside! So you see, you two have got it made here, living for free off the State. Marvellous. Marvellous. Isn't it marvellous how they care for you?' She can't stop talking. I can feel Masha hating the whole situation. 'Your mother here survives on cabbage soup,' she goes on. 'What with her pension being so small. That's what you get after a lifetime of service, wearing yourself to the bone on a factory floor. But there you are. There you are indeed. Much cosier to be cared for in here, I'd say. Marvellous. Wonderful that you decided to contact her after all this time. Really wonderful.' She looks around our tiny brown room with its bare walls, narrow bed and bedside *tumbochka* and tries to smile.

Masha's not saying anything, just watching and listening as we see our only escape route slowly closing off. Two brothers and a one-room flat. And a factory-floor mother living on a State pension and cabbage soup. No room for us then.

'So yes,' goes on Dina, 'your father passed away in 1984 – a drink too many, you know, a drink too many. Misha, his name was; yes, he led your mother a merry dance with his wicked ways – if Katya won't mind me speaking ill of the dead. But there you go … he was an army driver, drove the officers around in the Great Patriotic War. In the Far East, wasn't it, Katyoosh?'

But Mother isn't listening. She's looking at us with those sad blue eyes that just keep on filling with tears.

Eventually, Aunty Dina stops talking, and a thick silence fills the room. After a while Mother heaves a sigh.

'*Dochinki* – my little daughters, why didn't you come to me before? Why did you never come?'

'We didn't need you,' says Masha coldly.

Dina looks a bit nervous then, and shifts from one foot to the other, smoothing down her jacket and patting the pockets.

'Right, yes, well perhaps we should be off then. Things to do, you know …' At that, Mother stands up and takes a step towards us. She kisses my cheek again, but when she goes to kiss Masha, she jerks away to avoid her touch. Mother looks startled but then turns to me.

'What can I do, now that we've found each other, *dochinki?* I can do your laundry, and you can tell me what you need me to buy for you.' Neither of us say anything. What we really need is to be rescued from the Madhouse. 'Yes, just tell me and I'll buy it for you, if I can.' We still say nothing, so she says, 'Well, I'll bring you my home-made cabbage pies next time.' Then she gently strokes my hand. 'I'm sorry,' she says quietly.

And then they both leave …

I look across at Masha. She's gone all black like she does with her *chortik*.

'Sorry? *Sorry??*' she shouts once the door has closed. '*Chto yebyot!* Sorry for *what?*' She thumps her pillow. 'Sorry for being a peasant woman as stupid as a tree stump? Or sorry that she buried us in that maternity hospital and left us for dead?'

'We don't know that's what happened, Masha … She didn't say that.'

'Well, what else did she do? Why didn't she at least come and see us when we were little? Why didn't you ask?'

'I wanted to. I wanted to, but I couldn't bring myself to ask. I thought … I thought it would upset her.'

'Upset *her*?! For fuck's sake! Listen to yourself. Haven't we been upset enough for the past thirty-eight years of our lives? Stuck with all the other Rejects, obsessing about their darling lost mothers when we were growing up?'

'Don't swear, Masha—'

'I'll swear if I fucking want to …' She punches the wall. '"Sorry?!" Sorry that she only has one tiny room, which she shares with our brothers, so there's no room for two more? Well, I'd rather live with the crazies than with an old woman who can only wag her head in pity and cry – just like all the other daft dandelions in here. I'm not going to live with a silly old bat and a drunken sot of a brother. I'd never do that. Never!'

I put my hands over my ears.

'No, I liked her, Masha. She's still our mother, she called us *dochinki*, Mashinka, *dochinki* … no one's called us that before. Who have we got to call us that, except a mother? No one …'

'Liked her? What's there to like? You liked her because she's the same as you, sitting there with her eyes welling up all the time. Two of a kind, you are. Two sheep, two idiots. The apple doesn't roll far from the tree. Well, I bet I take after our father. Mikhail, that's a good strong name. Stop crying, see what I mean? Two of a *yobinny* kind, can't stop the waterworks for two seconds.'

'Please, let her come again, Mashinka, if she wants to … please, Mash. She said she'd do all our laundry for us and bring us home-made food … perhaps they'll invite us to meet them all, perhaps one of the family can think of some way of getting us out of here … please …'

She shrugs and gets up to go and fetch the pack of cigarettes she keeps behind the sink.

'What we need is to get out of here,' she says. 'Not meet the fucking family.'

## November 1988

### We meet the family

'Well now, help yourselves, girls, eat what you like,' says Aunty Dina and waves her hand at the spread on the table.

We're sitting in her flat with our mother and our brother Tolya. Our other brother, Seriozha, is late. Masha reaches out for a slice of white bread, slaps a thick slab of lard on it and pushes it hungrily into her mouth. I'm not quite sure how I got her here, to be honest. She said it was only because they'd have vodka. But it helped that Dina arranged for a friend to pick us up in his car and bring us over – any trip away from the Twentieth is a luxury. And deep down, I think we're both holding on to the idea that Aunty Dina might ask us to live with her in this two-room flat she shares with her husband and her eighteen-year-old granddaughter, Kira. It's got rugs on the walls, dark wall cabinets and a fold-out sofa. It reminds me of when we lived with Aunty Nadya. Bit of a squash. Not much room for us … But if Aunty Nadya can't have us, then why should a woman we've only met once fight the authorities to take us in? Is blood really thicker than water?

I look across at Mother, with her grey hair pinned back in a bun. She reminds me a bit of our mummy at the Ped. I wonder what our lives would have been like if she'd taken us home after giving birth to us? Or at least visited us in the Ped and sat there all day by our cot, like Mummy did, singing us *bye-oo bye-ooshki bye-oo* and bringing us presents. And she could have come to see us in SNIP on visiting days, and taken us back home every weekend to play with our little brothers … I'd have looked after them … I'd have …

'*Nooka*, Tolya dear, pass your sisters the potato salad,' says Dina. He looks like he's in a trance and hasn't spoken at all. Dina's husband, Boris, and Kira are 'busy' tonight, so it's just the five of us. 'That's right, help yourselves,' Dina goes on. 'Katya made these cabbage pies, and the *borsch* beetroot soup. No meat in it, I'm afraid, we'll have to wait for Communism to see meat, won't we, haha, but she used a couple of nice meaty bones, didn't you, Katyusha?'

Mother is sitting across the table from us and she nods, smiles and pushes the plate of warm cabbage pies across to us.

'I'm so sorry, girls, I looked for meat everywhere,' she says. 'I asked everyone I knew …' She has this way of taking a deep breath through her nose and then sighing as she shakes her head and speaks. I like it, but I know it'll irritate Masha. All Masha wants is the vodka standing in the middle of the table, unopened. 'But I used the scraps off the bones to make this jelly *kholodets*,' Mother goes on, pushing the dish towards us. I take a wobbly slice. I've never had it before. I push the dish across to Tolya. He's dark like us, and thin, and he's just sitting there, staring at us like he wants us not to exist. I can tell he doesn't want to be here. Neither do I much, now.

'Well, Seriozha should be here soon, no doubt a little worse for wear …' says Dina, all bright and cheerful. Mother shakes her head again. 'But he did promise … that's if he can find his way here, of course … It's the vodka, you know – opium of the masses. Takes after his father; they do say it's in the genes. Tolya here would be the same, but he's sworn off it. Doesn't drink a drop now. He's a tram driver, you know, so he'd lose his job … he's such a good boy.'

'Talking of opium of the masses,' says Masha quickly, 'this one here drinks like a priest.' She jerks her thumb at me. 'She needs her vodka. It's in the genes, like you say. But I'm like Tolya. Don't touch the stuff. Can't stop her, though; it's like trying to hold back the Volga River.'

I feel nauseous at the thought of drinking the oily vodka. And I don't want to get drunk in front of Aunty Dina and Mother. Apart from the shame of it, she won't want us to live with her if she thinks we're alcoholics. Mother looks across at me sadly, shakes her head a little bit and says nothing.

'Of course! Of course! What was I thinking,' says Aunty Dina and reaches for the bottle. 'We must have a toast.' She pours a little for herself and some for me, in two shot glasses.

'She'll have a tumbler,' says Masha and looks all sad and apologetic. 'Started when she was fourteen, she did, and there's no stopping her. I've tried everything.' Aunty Dina looks a bit shocked, but goes to the kitchen for a bigger glass and fills it for me. I feel bile rising in my throat. If only Masha could keep vodka down for more than two seconds, she could do all the drinking herself. I hate it.

After that first visit on Wednesday, Mother came to visit us in the Twentieth two more times and brought a bottle of vodka each time because Masha asked her to. Van Vanich doesn't search her bags. Everything's topsy-turvy in the Twentieth now, with the inmates all leaving for different homes like cockroaches abandoning a burning cellar. Masha's still so angry with Aunty Nadya she refuses to see her, and Olessya's already left for the Sixth. Time's running out. I look at the vodka and take a deep breath.

Just then there's a scraping at the front door and after a bit the bell rings, long and hard. Aunty Dina sighs and gets up to unbolt the door and a man stumbles into the little hallway. It's our brother Seriozha.

Mother stands and leads him to the chair next to her. 'Sit down, *sinochik*,' she says in her quiet voice. 'Sit down, little son, and behave.'

He staggers in so drunk he can hardly see us. He just keeps squinting across at us, all bleary-eyed. I know I shouldn't be, but I'm revolted by him. His eyes are slack, his nose has been half sliced off somehow, years ago, and he's leering at us. Then he sees the bottle and makes a grab for it.

'No you don't,' says Mother, still in her low, quiet voice, but firmly. She takes it and puts it in front of Tolya.

'Needa drink ...' slurs Seriozha.

'No you don't,' she repeats, just as firmly.

He frowns at the bottle, then at us, then at Tolya. 'Zat her then?' he asks him. 'Our sister. The one with all the arms and legs?'

I pick up the tumbler then.

Aunty Dina looks flustered. 'Well then, here we all are, let's have that toast,' she says, quickly picking up her little glass. 'A toast to finding family!' I don't clink glasses with her. I just drink the whole tumbler down in one, while Masha watches me like a wolf to make sure I don't spill any.

## Mother comes to visit for the last time, then Masha plans our great escape

I don't remember how we got home. The next time Mother visited, bringing our clean laundry and jars of pickled cucumbers (but no vodka), she didn't mention the dinner at Dina's. Masha didn't talk to her at all as she sat chattering on in her low voice about how everything was changing in the country. She said that shops and restaurants and even some factories were privately owned now, instead of being run by the State. And that the media was able to publish things that were wrong in society, instead of only the things that were right. It didn't concern us though. Nothing changes for us in here.

She's coming again today and I've been thinking that perhaps I'll ask what happened after she gave birth to us. But then again, perhaps I won't, because we might not like what we hear. Or perhaps she might not want to tell us.

'They're all going, every single one of them,' says Masha angrily as we walk down the empty corridor to our room. We're coming back from the canteen, which was almost empty too. 'They'll be bringing those poor mad bastards in soon.' She clenches her fists. 'By the busload.'

'We'll think of something, Masha, we must.'

'You're all retch and no vomit.' She looks up. 'Oh God, that's all I need. There she is – Mother Misery.'

She's standing outside our room with a string bag, smiling wearily as we tap towards her on our crutches.

'Shush, she's good to us, Masha. And it's a two-hour journey for her to get to us from Sokol by metro and tram. And all with heavy bags of our laundry.'

'If she hasn't bought vodka this time, she's dead to me.'

'Shush.'

'Hello, *dochinki*,' says Mother, smiling as we walk up. 'I didn't want to walk into your room without you there.' She kisses me on the cheek – she doesn't even try with Masha any more. We walk in and she starts unpacking the bags.

'Here's your laundry, all washed and ironed. And the women I used to work with in the factory all had a whip-round when I told them about you, so I was able to get the batteries and coffee you asked for, off the black market, of course, and cigarettes …' She starts taking them out of the bag and putting them carefully on the bed, then folds up her string bag and puts it in her pocket. There's no vodka. I feel Masha tense. 'It's getting empty in the Home, isn't it?' she says. 'Why's that?' We haven't told her about the re-profiling.

'They're dying of boredom,' says Masha coldly. Mother looks confused.

'Well, I got you a toilet brush too, Dashinka, as you asked, and a needle and thread to darn your socks. I can sit and do that now, if you like?' She looks up at me hopefully, with her gentle blue eyes.

'Thank you,' I say. Masha would kill me if I called her Mother or Mummy. Our mummy was Anna Petrovna, in the Ped. We talk about her a lot nowadays, especially now we've found our real mother. We sometimes wonder who she was, and what happened to her. She must have been a nanny, paid to look after us. Paid to be our mummy because ours had rejected us … I wonder where she is now. I wonder why she never did come and visit us.

'Well, give me your socks now, *dochinki*, they're filled with holes.'

I reach over to get them from our clothes drawer but Masha gets up and pulls me out on to the balcony instead, so we just leave her standing there on her own in the room. It's raining and the sky's as flat as a lead lid.

'I don't want my *yobinny* socks darned every week for the next twenty years in here, I just want to get out,' hisses Masha.

'Shhh, Masha, she can hear.'

'So what? Do you think cabbage pies and a tree stump for a mother are going to make life better for us in an asylum of lunatics banging their heads against the wall day and night? Do you? What use is she – pitying us with her charity.'

'*Teekha.*' I look back at our mother, who's just standing there, looking lost.

'It's like having an older version of you around. Life's a tragedy. It's bad enough with the one of you – now I feel outnumbered.'

We stand there in silence. Masha's holding on to the bars on our balcony, Mother's standing in the room, and I'm half in and half out of the door. Eventually, Mother speaks.

'*Dochinki* …' I look back at her. 'Have I done or said something to upset you?'

Masha sniffs and looks up at the sky. 'We've lived thirty-eight years without her,' she says loudly, to me, 'and we'll live another thirty-eight without her.'

There's a pause when no one says anything at all and then I hear Mother start to cry in this sort of hushed way, which I know only too well. It's how I cry. I want to go to her, but Masha's still holding tight on to the bars of the balcony.

'*Meelinki, meelinki,*' says Mother. My darlings, my darlings. '*Meelinki dochinki.*' I pull at Masha. I understand Mother's pain. I understand it all. I can't cause her any more. I want her to kiss me again. But Masha won't move. I look back then at my mother, and her eyes meet mine.

'*Proshai,*' she says, and wipes her nose. 'Farewell. The first time tortured me. And now I have to do it again … Such is fate. May God now take me away from this life.'

Then she picks up her empty string bag and walks slowly out.

After a bit, we go back into the room. I sit on the bed and pull our socks out of the drawer. They do need darning and Mother's left her needles and wool behind so I try to thread a needle but can't because my hands are shaking too much. There's nothing to say really. Masha reaches over for painkillers for her toothache. She takes two and then puts her fingers in her mouth gingerly, to feel her broken teeth.

'Wait!' she says excitedly. I jump and look at her, startled. 'I've *got* it!' She slaps her hand on my knee. 'I have fucking *got* it!'

## 5 December 1988

### We go on national TV to appeal to the Soviet public

We walk out on to the stage, blinded by the bright lights. I can hear all the applause from the TV audience but I can't see a thing. Vlad Listyev, the presenter of *Vzglyad*, this new talk show everyone's watching, takes me by the arm and leads me gently to a plush red sofa. He's smiling and clapping too. When the applause finally ends, he shakes Masha's hand and then my hand, like we're important, respectable people.

'So,' he says, beaming at us, 'my name's Vlad, and you are Masha and Dasha.' We nod. He's got a friendly face and he's wearing these big, round spectacles, and has a bushy moustache. I don't look out at the audience, which has fallen silent now and is watching and listening somewhere out there in the darkness. 'And you are Siamese twins,' Vlad goes on. 'A very rare occurrence in nature – I don't believe many of our viewers will have heard the term. Named after two famous twins, Chang and Eng, from Siam who lived a century ago and were born together, like you.' I haven't heard the term either. And I haven't heard of his Chang and Eng, but we just nod again.

'Well now, girls – I hope you don't mind me calling you that, but you both look so young – why don't you tell me a bit about your situation, in your own words.' He smiles warmly at us and leans in to listen.

I take a deep breath. This has happened so fast I've barely had time to panic. It started a month ago, with Masha's Great Idea to get us transferred to the Stomatological Institute (the 'Stom') for a course of treatment on our teeth. We'd been there twice before over the years, and stayed there for up to two months. Our young dental surgeon, Doctor Shevchenko, always welcomes us with open arms. He's a good man, and so is the Director of the Stom and all the staff. They love us there. They'd help us, Masha said. When they heard what was happening, they'd keep us at the Stom until we found a new Home.

It all worked like a dream to start off with. Barkov didn't suspect a thing. We both went off and cried in front of Rita, the new nurse in the Twentieth, showing her our black stubs of teeth, and the poor girl couldn't get us into the Stom quick enough.

We had a private room there with a double bed, and Doctor Shevchenko did all our treatments in the middle of the night so we wouldn't be seen. When we finally explained the situation to him, he went off and asked some questions and then came back to tell us that all he could do was keep us in for as long as possible. 'It's against the law for you to stay here,' he'd said. 'The Ministry of Protection have decided you should live in the Twentieth. So that's where you must live. But …' We'd both looked up at him from our bed then, watching him pacing up and down. 'But … perhaps you could go to the press? Things are changing now, with Gorbachev and his Openness campaign. There are all sorts of appeals for justice going on.'

Everything kicked off really quickly after that. He introduced us to a journalist who'd won a campaign in her newspaper, *Moskovskii Komsomolyets*, to get a bus stop built outside the

Stom. She wanted to write a story about us, but her editor refused to believe in our existence, even when she showed him photos. He said a freak like that couldn't possibly exist and now that he didn't need to lie to his readers any more, he wasn't going to give them a cock-and-bull story like that. So instead she went to a cameraman friend who worked on *Vzglyad*. That was when Vlad Listyev, the creator and presenter of this new talk show, said he wanted us both on air, live, as soon as possible, and before we knew it, a car had come to pick us up from the Stom and take us to the studios. I was petrified, but Masha kept telling me this was our only chance. 'They'll hate us, they'll spit and jeer,' I'd said in the car on the way here, 'on live TV.' She shook her head. 'No. We'll be amazing. You heard what Doctor Shevchenko said – the Russian people have changed along with the times. They've become more open with all this … openness.' She'd waved out of the window as if it was blowing in the breeze. 'You can do it, you know you can.' I'd taken a great big breath. 'But I'll stutter, Masha, I'll stutter.' She'd squeezed my hand then. 'Even when you stutter, you still sound more intelligent than me, and you always know what to say.' She'd taken my chin in her hand so I was looking right at her. 'I trust you, Dasha.' She never calls me by my name. 'You *have* to do this. Just this once. You *have* to.'

'Girls?' says Vlad again, still leaning in, like we're in his living room or something. There's complete silence in the studio, as if everyone's holding their breath. They clapped as we walked in, they actually clapped. And now they're listening.

'W-we've been kept in institutions all our l-l-lives,' I start. 'H-hospitals to start off with, then a s-school in Novocherkassk. Everyone was very k-kind. We hoped to w-work. But when we were eighteen we were s-sent to a Home, for V-veterans of War and L-Labour.' A sort of collective gasp goes up in the audience, I'm not sure why. Don't they *know* that's where the Reject children go to from orphanages?

'At eighteen?' says Vlad, edging a bit closer. 'Teenagers? To an Old People's Home?'

'That's because we're D-Defective. There aren't any homes for D-Defectives.'

'Of course, of course, because the official line has always been that we have no invalids in the Soviet Union. But now, of course, we're finding out that there are. There most certainly are – but they are still kept out of the public eye. So you two sisters were kept hidden away all your lives?'

'Y-yes. We've been living there for n-nearly t-twenty years. B-but it's being reprofiled into a Psycho-neurological Home for the insane now, and w-we're *not* insane. S-so we don't w-want to s-stay there. We w-want to go to …' I don't finish because there's a little ripple of applause which gets louder and louder, and Vlad's sitting there, looking out at the audience and nodding slowly in this *Aren't they just great?* way and Masha's nodding hard at me too. Encouraging me.

The applause dies away and Vlad asks: 'You want to go where?'

'Anywhere. Anywhere but the Twentieth.'

'The Sixth,' says Masha quickly. 'It's Open Regime and looks over a lake.'

'I see. And that's why you've decided to come here tonight? To appeal to the Russian people,' Vlad waves at a camera with a red light on, not the audience, 'to help you escape from this life worse than death? This terrible injustice?'

'Y-yes.' I swallow. 'P-people have always thought w-we're not right in the head, j-just because we're T-together.' I look at Masha, who's nodding again and fiddling with the button on our trousers. This is her line and she says it along with me. 'All our lives we've had to prove we're normal, but if we stay there, we'll have lost the battle.' When she speaks along with me, I don't stutter.

'Of course, of course.'

'And as for her,' Masha suddenly adds, 'she only stutters because she got savaged by a dog. When she was little. That's the reason she stutters. People stutter all over the place.'

'Of course,' says Vlad encouragingly.

'She got top marks in her school diploma.'

'I'm not at all surprised,' he says. 'It's a travesty to have been locked away like convicts all your lives as punishment for having been born physically different.' He looks out at the audience again, which gives another little collective sigh of agreement. I can scarcely believe this is happening. Where are all the people who shouted at us outside the gate at SNIP? Or the ones at the zoo in Novocherkassk? Perhaps it's because Vlad accepts and likes us? And I like him. He's not asking how we're going to die or how we have sex. He's asking about us. It's as if he understands us. 'And so, girls, tell us how it is that you were able to come on our show tonight? How have you been able to escape the Twentieth?'

'It was M-Masha's idea,' I say. 'We g-got ourselves into the S-Stomatological Institute for dental treatment, but w-we're being sent back to the T-twentieth in three days. We're being sent back. And then we'll never get out. Please help.' I steel myself then and glance quickly out at the blackness. 'Please, please help.'

There's a sort of sucked-in silence in the room. And it's then that I panic. They don't want to help. Of course they don't. They hate us. Like everyone does.

'And how *can* we help, Dasha? How?'

'W-we want to be sent to a Home with our friends. W-we want … to be treated like everyone else, that's all.'

'And what does that mean for you?'

I pause, thinking. There's still no sound from the audience. The cameras are swirling around the stage on wheels. My mind goes a blank. Vlad lowers his glasses on his nose and looks at me over them and I know Masha's staring at me, willing me to talk.

'We w-want our own sheets,' I say. 'C-clean sheets.'

I feel Masha tense then, but Vlad nods understandingly. 'You want to be rescued, so you can finally live a normal life with that small luxury the rest of us all take for granted. Your own sheets.'

I nod.

'Thank you, girls.' He stands up then and looks out at the audience.

'I think we can give these two very brave girls a big round of applause.' We stand up too, but there's still silence. He starts clapping his hands slowly, still looking out at them. And then there's this sound, like the patter of rain in the distance, which gets closer and closer until it's all thundering in my ears. They're applauding. They really are, all of them. But why? What for? I feel as if I've only been talking on that sofa for two minutes. I didn't say enough. I should have told him about how our lives have been good compared to other Defectives in orphanages or asylums like the one in Novocherkassk. I shouldn't have just talked about us. I should have spoken up for Little Lyuda, Sunny Nina and Big Boris. Or told them about Stupino and the Isolation Hut. I feel stupid. But Vlad takes my arm and starts guiding us off the stage, waving his arm and smiling a huge smile at the audience. I want to go back – I didn't even mention Aunty Nadya and all she's done for us … and how there are people like Olessya, fighting for invalids' rights. As I turn in the wings, to look back, without the light in my eyes, I can see them all standing on their feet, clapping and clapping like they're about to burst. And then I think of Slava. I remember him telling me to stand up for myself. And now I have. Not against Masha, but with Masha. Yes, I think Slava would be proud of me.

# SIXTH HOME FOR VETERANS OF WAR AND LABOUR, MOSCOW

## 1988–2003

> 'When I came to power in Russia I started to restore the values of "openness" and freedom.'
>
> Mikhail Gorbachev, General Secretary of the Communist Party 1985–91

## Age 39
## January 1989

### Enjoying a life of luxury in the Sixth!

'One hundred million viewers? One hundred *million*?' Sanya's in our new room in the Sixth, sitting on our bed with her mouth open, repeating the viewing figure over and over again. If I'd known, I'd never have been able to go on. Never. It was bad enough facing the hundred-odd people in the audience.

'Yes, yes, that's what they said,' says Masha, pulling our fancy net curtains closed and then swinging them open again with a flourish. '*Vzglyad*'s the most popular TV show in the country. We're celebrities, we are. Famous!' She swooshes the curtains closed and open again, then looks out at the frozen lake beyond the fence bordering our grounds, as if to make sure it's still there.

'You are!' agrees Sanya. 'I was in the hairdresser's the other day and everyone was talking about it. They were talking about you at the bus stop too, and I could hear them behind me when I was standing in line for fish.'

'Fish! We can buy fish now – we can buy *sturgeon*, if we want. They've been sending money to us like there's no tomorrow. Sending money to poor little Mashinka who needs her caviar. Meow …' We all laugh at that. It's so nice of them.

We moved in yesterday and I still feel dizzy with all the space and luxury. The first thing I did was put all Slava's letters under the pillow. The door to our room locks, so I know they're going to be safe now. Olessya's sitting with us because her room's only four doors down and Garrick, her boy from the Twentieth, has been transferred here too. The large window leading on to our balcony lets in lots of light and we have flowery, textured wallpaper. I want to keep touching it. That's stupid though, so I bend down instead to pick some white fluff off our red rug.

'*Gospodi!* You're gonna break my back if you keep doing that for the next forty years,' says Masha, but I know she loves having a rug as much as I do. A rug just like Vera Stepanovna's or Barkov's. Or Aunty Nadya's … Masha's paced out the room, over and over again and it's five times bigger than the one in the Twentieth. The bed's at one end and there's a sofa with cushions the other end. I can't stop laughing when I look around, neither of us can, it's more than we could ever have hoped for.

It's like waking from a lifelong nightmare.

And that's not all. We have an entrance hall with a big cupboard for our clothes (we'll have to get some clothes) and we have our own toilet and shower, which is so wide and deep at the bottom we'll be able to sit in it together and have a bath. If we had a little kitchen it would be like having our own flat. But this is even better, because we get cooked for and have all our friends and cheerful staff around to chat to. And no one bullies us now we're famous. Fame brings respect.

'Well, I don't know,' says Baba Iskra, shaking her head and sucking in her lips. She's the cloakroom attendant from downstairs, but she's come up to help us move in. We don't really have any stuff to move in actually, so she's walking around straightening the tables and rearranging cushions. 'I never knew anything as splendid as this existed in the Sixth and I've been here since it opened. A proper VIP apartment. Your own kettle, look, and a fridge as big as me – and that's saying something.' She opens the door and peers in before closing it. There's nothing there yet. 'And you'll be able to afford a TV now, to put there, by the bedside table.'

'And a tape recorder. We'll get a Modern Talking cassette and play it all the time, over and over, and dance on our rug,' says Masha. 'And we've got a phone too, see? Our very own phone.' Masha picks up the receiver and speaks into it: 'Kremlin Palace? Yes, it's Mashinka here, could I have a quick word with Comrade Gorbachev?' We all laugh again, even Olessya. She wasn't too pleased that we didn't use that opportunity to talk about the plight of invalids in the country, but she's happy that we got what we wanted. She says we deserve it. We deserve the peace of mind.

'I'm surprised it's not ringing off the hook,' she says, 'with all those journalists wanting to interview you now.'

'They don't give out our phone number to journalists. Anyway, I'm done with that. All they want is to sell their newspapers with a story about the two-headed girl. Besides, we've got our American journalist. One foreign journalist in the hand is worth a thousand of our lot in the bush. We're snug as a bug in a rug now. We don't need anyone.'

'B-British,' I say. 'Joolka's B-British, not American.' Masha shrugs.

Olessya tips her head on one side thoughtfully and looks at our reflection in the three-winged mirror on our dresser. There's three of her from all angles. 'But you could make a real difference now, you know. You have the power to make real changes. People will listen to you.' I can't see if she's looking at me or at Masha; the sun's shining in our eyes.

'Don't start that again, Olesskinka,' says Masha, picking up the kettle and stroking it. 'We've got all the changes we want.'

'Yes, but what about our rights?' says Olessya in her calm voice. 'The right not to be sterilized without our knowledge, the right to live independently, the right to be acknowledged? You two can be a mouthpiece for us. Who's interested in anyone with palsy or polio? They won't listen to us. But they'll listen to you.' She looks straight at me, but she knows it's hopeless. Masha's made up her mind. Masha's found her place in the sun.

'And we should be permitted to work,' puts in Garrick, who's leaning against the wall, lighting up a papirosa. He doesn't know Masha very well so he's not giving up the argument. 'Just because I'm on crutches doesn't mean I shouldn't be allowed to go into an office and ask for work. Or walk into a shop or theatre. Why are we still considered to be such an ugly secret?'

'*Ei*, speak for yourself, and smoke that out on the balcony,' says Masha, clapping her hands at him. 'You'll be even uglier after I tip you off it. We've still got rules, you know. Don't want to be kicked out on our first day because of morons like you with your nasty habits.' He shrugs and goes over to open the balcony door. A cold blast of air hits us.

I wish Aunty Nadya could see all this. I really wish she could. She came in to visit us in the Stom the day after the interview. Our room was full of doctors and nurses, congratulating us on the show when the door flew open and in burst Aunty Nadya, her face as black as coal.

She marched right up to our bed, ignoring everyone. 'How could you do this without telling me?' she'd said in a low voice, standing over us. The room fell quiet. Masha just sniffed and looked out of the window. Masha hadn't wanted to see her again after she sided with Barkov and 'abandoned' us. And then Sanya told us that Aunty Nadya was being paid by Barkov to keep us in the Twentieth, which made it even worse. I didn't believe it for a minute, but Masha did. And then there she was, standing over us. 'How? Without asking me? And how could you not say one word about me? Not one word? And I know it's you, Masha, it's no use putting your hard face on. I know it's you, I know Dasha will be suffering. I know you two inside out. I know you better than anyone and you've just cut me out of your life as if you're deadheading a flower, just like you did with your mother. Well?'

Masha turned to face her then. 'We're not children, Aunty Nadya,' she said coldly. 'We're all grown up. You wouldn't help us, so we helped ourselves. We don't … we don't need you any more.' My heart had lurched at those words. I felt physically sick. Oh yes we do! Of course we do. We'll always need her! She's been more than a mother to us. She's been everything to us. But I hadn't said anything, of course. What's the point? I'd just looked down at the floor. Everyone in the room was listening as if their lives depended on it. I couldn't look at either of them.

After a bit Aunty Nadya said, even more quietly: 'Is that it then?' Silence. 'Now that you have all these new, so-called friends of yours? Now that you're famous for a day?' More silence. 'You think you're just wonderful, don't you? You think you're always right. No one else matters to you, do they? Well, I'll tell you what you are, Masha Krivoshlyapova. You're selfish and arrogant and spoilt and cruel, just like you've always been.' I bit my lip hard but still didn't look up. If I looked at her I'd cry, I just willed her to stop. Masha never forgives.

I could see her boots, the ones she always wears, furry and chunky, which make her look like a teddy bear. And the heavy woollen stockings she always wears too. I knew her eyes would be popping and her face all red. Aunty Nadya … don't let Masha turn you away from me forever.

'And I know you've been listening to Sanya and her petty gossip,' she went on. 'As if in a million years I'd take money from Barkov to harm you. But you can't trust anyone to just be nice, out of the goodness of their heart, can you? Because there's no goodness in yours – it all went to Dasha.' I squirmed. *Please* stop talking. 'Well, so be it. Enjoy the rest of your new life as celebrities without me.' And then I'd heard the door slam and everyone started talking at once. But I heard Masha say under her breath 'good riddance'.

I sit down on our bed, which is four times the size of the one in the Twentieth. I still can't understand why Aunty Nadya wanted us to stay in the Twentieth. All this is wonderful, the new sheets, the shower and the wallpaper. But without Aunty Nadya to share it with us, it's just … I don't know … empty somehow. There's a knock on the door and I look up with a thumping heart, I keep thinking she might …? But it's only Timur, the caretaker, who's come in to put a new lock on the door. Masha wants new keys.

'All right, comrades?' he says, tipping his cap back and looking around the room at us all. 'Come to put the lock on, keep these two princesses safe in their tower.' He chuckles.

'As long as *you've* got a key, Timosha,' grins Masha. 'You can come in and see us any time. We could always do with a strong pair of male hands …' Olessya rolls her eyes.

'Cheeky bitch,' he says, grinning back. 'I'm a married man, Masha.'

'*Zhena ne stena* – a wife is not a wall.'

He grins again and shakes his head. 'Well, won't take me boots off though, I'll just stay out here in the corridor and keep out of temptation's way. Won't be long.'

'Right then,' says Olessya, 'it's supper-time. I'm off to get in the queue.' Garrick gives us a mock salute and follows her.

'Yes, yes, off you all go, down to eat with the starving masses,' says Masha, happily waving them out. 'We're staying up here, we are, to get room service. And Baba Iskra said she'd buy us some apples, if she can find them. And vodka.' Baba Iskra shakes her grizzly old head, but I think that means yes.

'Double lock, Timosha, *da*?' says Masha, standing over him and opening and closing our cupboard door with a *klik, klyak*. He nods and starts telling us about how we should get some nice pot plants in our room. He's the gardener too.

'You'll be getting us a bust of Lenin next, and portraits of the Politburo,' jokes Masha. He laughs and while he works, he tells us a bit about what's going on in the Outside. They've brought ration cards in for meat, cheese and other basics now. Just like in the Great Patriotic War. So much for Gorbachev. 'You're lucky,' he says, talking with some screws between his teeth. 'No queuing for rationed food in here. Just your room service. The only thing there's no shortage of out there is vodka, now that they've stopped prohibition, thank God. I saw grown men dying in agony from drinking turps or cologne.' He takes off the lock and cocks his head on one side, looking at the hole in the door. 'Disaster, that was. The one thing that oils the works in this country is vodka.' He looks round at us and winks. It's nice to talk to a Healthy man for once.

There's another knock at the door and this time it's Joolka, who almost falls over him.

'Ooh, *yolki palki!* Sorry, sorry! I'm Julietka,' she says to Timur, and holds out her hand. He stares at it blankly. 'Yes, sorry ...' She says, taking it back and looking embarrassed. 'Hey, girls, guess what? Here it is – here's the magazine article!'

## Getting to know someone from the West who helps us

Joolka plonks something down outside the open door in the corridor and edges round Timur, who's still gawping at her. He's never seen a foreigner before. No one has.

'Here's the *Sunday Times Magazine*. You're on the front cover, see?' She holds it out to us. It's us, all right, there on the glossy cover. Masha looks at it and sniffs. It shows us walking off across a field, taken from behind. Why didn't they show our faces? Why have us walking off to nowhere, full-length, looking stupid and clumsy? I don't like it. Neither does Masha. We don't know what the words say because it's all written in strange wiggly letters.

'Brought any Western goodies then, *Maht?* In your Beriozka bag?' asks Masha, turning from the magazine. She calls Joolka *Maht* – Mother – because she's just had a baby girl, Sashinka. She says she'll bring her in to see us, but I know she won't. Lots of the staff in the Twentieth and the Stom had babies but they would have died rather than bring them in to see us. So we've never seen a baby before, not even out of the window.

'Yes, yes, here you are, I dropped in on the way here.'

It turns out it's not only Party big-wigs who can shop in the *Beriozka* food shops that are filled with any food and drink you want. It's foreigners too. 'Tinned cod roe, cheese balls, ham and chocolate biscuits, just like you asked.' Masha takes the bag and looks for vodka, but there isn't any. She sniffs again. At least everything's *firmennaya* – goods from the West, labelled in that same squiggly writing. Joolka looks around the room as I put the food in the empty fridge. She doesn't seem that impressed. I wonder what her Moscow flat is like.

'So, anyway, here's the article,' she says, shrugging off her coat and kicking off her snow boots. She pulls her hat off too and runs her fingers through her hair. She doesn't seem to own a hairbrush and her jeans are splattered with paint. We thought Westerners would dress in designer clothes and have manicures and perfect hair, but this one's the opposite. Maybe they all are? She speaks good Russian because she's married to one of us. A Soviet citizen. 'Had the whole world to pick from with her Golden Passport and she goes for one of our cretins,' Masha had said, tapping her finger to her temple.

We first met Joolka back in the Stom. She's a journalist from England. She'd seen *Vzglyad* and wanted to interview us for this magazine. We decided to see her for two reasons. Firstly, we'd never met anyone from abroad before, so when Irina Krasnopolskaya told us she'd been contacted by a Western journalist, it was exciting. Secondly, we'd been in the Stom for a month and although we knew that, thanks to the publicity, we'd never have to go back to the Twentieth, we weren't being allowed into the Sixth. The Director here said it was full and she had no rooms to assign us. She didn't even say we could get on a waiting list, just told us to find another one. But Masha had other ideas.

'Well, we've used the power of *our* press to keep us out of the Twentieth, now we need to use the power of the *Western* press to get us in the Sixth,' she'd said.

Joolka turned up at the Stom in the same clothes she's wearing today. Exactly the same clothes. I wonder if she even washes them? She must though. I wash our clothes all the time. She seemed really pleased to see us, just to meet us. She didn't seem to notice we were Together; she was like Vlad, only interested in what had happened to us and how we'd been treated. When we told her we couldn't get into the Sixth, she went back to her office and called up the Ministry of Protection, just like that, called them up and said she was writing this article and that her colleagues in the BBC and CNN wanted to do a report on us, and exactly *why* couldn't we get into the Sixth? After that, we were told there *was* a room available, after all. The best room. *Smeshno*. We've spent seventy years despising the Imperialist, decadent, Western dogs, but when we come eye to eye with them, we just fawn, as if it's us who are the dogs.

'So, do you want me to translate it?' she says, bouncing on to our bed, next to Masha, and leafing through the pages.

She came back twice to see us in the Stom to do more interviews for the article. We told her about SNIP and the school. Some of it, anyway. We didn't mention Slava.

'*Gospodi!!* What the *fuck* is that? A fucking doll?' Timur jumps back into the room, pointing at the floor outside the door as if he's seen a ghost.

'Oh no, no, don't worry, that's my baby, Sashinka. She's asleep. She's fine.'

'Baby?' He jumps back even further. 'A real live baby? On the floor like *yobinny* Moses in a basket?'

Joolka gets up, laughing. 'I thought you'd like to see her,' she says, looking back at us over her shoulder as she goes to the door. 'She's a bit of a handful but sleeps a lot, thank goodness. Here we are, she's in her car seat.'

A baby! She's brought us her baby? I can't believe it. I can't believe she's actually done it. Babies are kept swaddled in cots, away from germs and people for the first year of their lives. She walks back in, swinging the car seat, and places it between us. I can smell her, the softness and milkiness. She's waking up, she yawns slowly, the biggest yawn ever, and I can see two little tooth buds in her gums and her pink tongue. I slowly reach out my hand to hers and she wraps her fingers around mine, like … like she never wants to let go.

'You can hold her, if you like,' says Joolka, and plucks her right out of her chair like she's a piece of fruit. Masha holds out her arms, 'Me! Me!' Joolka gives her the baby, just gives it to her like that, pulling her little fat fingers off mine as she does, and I want to grab her back and kiss her fluffy head and breathe her in, but I can't. Masha's got her now. Masha holds her out in front of her, swinging her a bit and laughing. *Bye-oo bye-ooshki bye-oo*, she sings, and Sashinka yawns that big yawn again. I'm laughing too. I'm laughing and laughing.

'So anyway,' Joolka goes on, 'I put at the bottom of the article that if anyone wants to donate money for you, to get you a cassette player and TV, you know, that they should send it to an account I've set up in your name.' She looks down at the magazine. 'I'm sure there'll be a big response.'

Sashinka's wearing a soft blue flannel jumpsuit. I reach out to touch her, just to touch one of her fat toes and perfect skin, but Masha swings her away from me. I don't mind, I can't stop laughing because there's a baby here, right in front of me. She looks just like my Lyuba did when she was a baby.

'Well, I'll bring her in every time, if you'd like,' says Joolka. 'She goes everywhere with me. I keep her in a sling mostly. I don't live far away.'

Sashinka starts gurgling and smiling as Masha bobs her up and down in the air, and then somehow we're all laughing, even Timur.

'Yes, I'd like that,' I say. 'I'd like that a lot.'

'That terrible Communist experiment brought about repression of human dignity ... we abandoned basic human values in the name of Communism.'

Mikhail Gorbachev, President of Russia

## Age 41
## 16 August 1991

### Our first trip beyond the Iron Curtain, to Germany where we become invisible

'So ... Masha and Dasha, this is your first time in West Germany, your first-ever trip outside the Soviet Union. Can you tell us what your first impressions are?' Matthius, the German TV reporter, sticks his microphone towards us as the camera rolls. We're standing on the cobbled streets of Cologne. It's a beautiful sunny autumn day and I feel like I've been transported into a fairy tale.

'Well,' says Masha, and he tilts the microphone towards her expectantly. 'I like the bright colours and the shop displays. And it's clean.' He nods encouragingly. 'And there are no queues and everyone's dressed in yellow and red and all sorts of bright colours instead of black. And then there's all these lights everywhere and advertisements, and there's every single sort of thing you could want to buy packed on to the shelves. *Every*thing's different!'

He looks across at me then. 'And you, Dasha?'

I blink at him.

Matthius came to interview us in the Sixth a month ago. Masha said we needed another Western journalist after she fell out with Joolka. That was because of Sanya again. She came in one day and whispered that she'd found out that Joolka hadn't given us all the money from the *Sunday Times Magazine* readers, but had kept half back for herself. Sanya also said Joolka was selling photos that her husband Kolya took of us for the article for big bucks. She was exploiting us, just like Ronnie and Donnie were exploited in Amerika. 'She wouldn't do that, Mash,' I'd protested. 'You can tell by her face, by everything she says, that she wouldn't do that. And she's a Christian, she goes to church, she's good … you can tell … by her face, you just can. And Kolya too.' But Masha had said, 'Everyone's out for themselves, Christians or not. Christians are the worst. All they want is to get to Heaven. *Foo!* Good thing I'm not a naïve spud in the soil like you. Someone needs to protect us.' So that was that.

'Dasha?' Matthius pushes the microphone closer. 'And you, Dasha?'

'Oh.' I gaze around at the people passing us in the cobbled street. 'N-no one looks at us,' I say slowly. 'It's as if we're not Together any more. It's as if we magically stopped b-being Together on the flight over here. We're free to walk around with everyone else. We can s-sit in a café for everyone else. We c-can stay in a hotel for everyone else. Over here, we *are* everyone else. We're n-normal.'

Matthius nods again and turns back to the cameraman. 'Got that, Billy? Great soundbite. Really great.' He gives me the thumbs up and I smile.

After we moved into the Sixth, Joolka took us in her car on trips around Moscow to restaurants and parks and even some shops, all with Sashinka. Now the public knew who we were, they weren't so shocked, but they still crowded round and asked questions. So we got fed up with that in the end and stopped going out. Joolka had raised so many thousands of American dollars for us from her appeal that we didn't even know how much we'd got any more. Enough for Masha to buy an Atari and play all her killing games at top volume all day … They scare me stiff. Enough for a big TV and a video player and a cassette player to listen to Modern Talking on. And enough to bribe Garrick to go out to the nearest shop and buy vodka for us. Olessya doesn't like that either. Baba Iskra looks after us in every way she can, but she won't buy us vodka any more. Neither did Joolka.

Joolka had a second baby, Anya, just before Masha fell out with her. Anya had blonde hair like the fluff on a poplar tree, and blue eyes, as blue as the River Don. Now there were two of them I could hold one while Masha held the other. I didn't mind which one. I loved them both. Sasha was three by then and used to come toddling into our room saying, 'Aunty Dasha! Aunty Masha!' holding her arms out because she loved it when we lay back on the bed and swung her up in the air between us. But then after Sanya claimed Joolka was stealing from us, Masha started slamming the phone down every time she called up and eventually she just stopped calling. And we never saw Anya and Sashinka again.

When Matthius first asked us if we wanted to go to Germany, Masha had said: '*West* Germany, right? East Germany's not Over There. What's the point?' He'd laughed. 'Technically it *is* Over There, now that the Berlin Wall's come down. But yes, Cologne is in West Germany.'

A little girl in a flowery dress walks past holding her mother's hand. She glances at us but that's all.

'Right then, you two,' says Matthius. 'Let's get over to the hospital. We've got that appointment with the urologist.'

'I preferred that handsome psychiatrist,' says Masha. 'Johann, the one who speaks some Russian. He said he'd take us around, he did; said he'd give us a tour of the city.'

'Well, I'm sure he will then, Masha. Fine by me. Right, let's get on. Quick march.'

As we tap down the street I look up at the trees, which are starting to turn yellow. I can look around at everything here. In Russia I just look at the ground so I don't see the eyes. I still get my nightmare about being in the glass well …

'Maybe Johann can take us to the circus,' Masha says to me. 'I've always wanted to go to the circus.'

I nod. 'Yes, that would be nice. We'll be able to sit anywhere we like.'

At first she wouldn't see him – Johann, that is, the psychiatrist. She said she didn't need any shrink trying to scrabble about in her head, trying to prove she's crazy. But he came to our room in the hotel with a bunch of roses one morning and told us his mother was born in Russia and he really wanted to practise the language and would we mind spending a bit of time with him? He's young and fun, with his long blond hair and baggy suit, so Masha said yes.

'Just don't tell him you've always wanted to be a trapeze artist, Mash,' I say with a smile. 'He *will* think you're crazy.'

'I'll tell him whatever I want,' she says. And sniffs. 'Hey, there's a sweetie shop. Matthius, can we go in there and get chocolate? Can we?' He smiles and nods at Billy the cameraman. 'Sure you can. As much as you can eat.'

## We make friends with Johann

We wake up and go to look out of our thirteenth-floor window at the view over the blue river, sparkling away in the sunshine. I'm so happy I just feel like smiling all the time. I feel I belong here. Matthius has been busy with some story brewing back home.

'Probably those blackies in the republics rioting again,' Masha had said to me. So Johann has been taking us around instead. We haven't been to the circus yet, but we visited a cathedral and went for a boat ride on the river, and to restaurants in the evening.

'So,' Johann had said, yesterday morning, 'I've got an interesting trip for you today. It's a Home for the Disabled run by the Red Cross.'

We thought it would be like the Sixth, but it wasn't. It was like a gleaming hotel with all sorts of special equipment to make life as easy as possible for the residents. They don't call them Defectives here, or even invalids. They call them people with Special Needs. 'Told you we're special!' Masha had laughed. We walked through all the rooms with soft sofas and TVs and everyone smiled at us like we were the King and Queen of England rolled into one, and we chatted to Johann about the Twentieth. Or at least Masha did.

Then last night, when Masha ordered vodka for me in the restaurant, she started telling Johann about Slava and how I kept trying to kill myself, and about our mother. He was really interested. Masha talked and talked that evening, while I drank. I don't remember how we got home.

'Mashinka,' I say, pressing my forehead against the window in our hotel room, 'maybe we could stay here, in that nice Red Cross Hotel? Perhaps they'd let us stay there? Then we could live a normal life?'

The sun's twinkling on the river. Masha shrugs. 'Maybe.' My heart jumps. Would she really agree? To live an invisible life? Would she?

There's a knock on the door then, and Matthius walks in. We turn from the window and he nods at us and goes over to switch the TV on. Then he picks up our phone and starts dialling.

'Feel free,' says Masha. 'To use our phone. Why not take a shower in our bathroom while you're at it?' He looks up at her, frowning, not getting the joke.

'Matthius,' I say quickly, before Masha can stop me, 'is there any way, do you think, that we could stay here? In the Red Cross place? Stay here to live?' He looks surprised then and puts the phone down.

'Here? Well … I suppose it might be possible. I could make some calls.'

'Just for a bit,' mutters Masha. 'See what it's like.' She peels back our blanket. '*Ei hande hoch!* – they came to change our sheets yesterday, Matthius. We only slept in them once.' He's picked up the phone again and is speaking into it in German with one eye on the TV '*Ei! Achtung!*' Masha says loudly. 'We're clean, we are! Tell them we have a bath every day. And what about that vodka? My sister here can't go a day without her bottle.' He waves her away, still talking on the phone, so Masha leans over and takes an apple out of a bowl of fruit by our bed. She eats it all, including the core, and swallows down the pips.

Matthius starts flicking through the channels, then stops at one and sits down on the end of our bed to watch. There's a big house by the sea being filmed from above on the screen. His phone rings again and he goes out of the room, talking into it urgently. We keep watching and realize the house is in Russia. The picture keeps flashing back to Moscow. There are tanks. Tanks in the streets of Moscow! But we can't understand a word, so Masha switches it over to cartoons.

Nobody else comes to our room after that, except a maid with a tray of food, and it's only after about six hours that Matthius comes back and sits on our bed. His face is white and he keeps jiggling his foot.

'Listen, there's been a coup d'état in the Soviet Union by the Communist hardliners who oppose Gorbachev's reforms. They've declared a State of Emergency and put Gorbachev under house arrest in his government dacha in the Crimea. Tanks have been rolling into Moscow all day and they've closed down the TV and radio stations. Muscovites are rioting, they're out putting barricades round the White House to protect it from the Army. I have to go back to report on it. My flight's in ninety minutes.'

'B-but what about us? What about our t-trip?'

'I'm sorry, Dasha, we'll have to scrap the documentary. This coup is huge news. It could well mean a return to hard-line Communism. Yanayev, Gorbachev's deputy, has taken control of the country. We'll arrange flights back for you, but it will have to be soon because they might close the borders.'

He goes to the door and stops, then turns to look at us.

'Unless … unless you're serious about wanting to stay here? If they *do* close the borders, you won't be permitted back in anyway, and then you'd have to be cared for here …' There's a pause as he waits for an answer.

I glance quickly at Masha.

'*Nyet*,' she says.

He shrugs and closes the door.

'Masha, why not?' I ball up my hands into fists because I want to shake her. 'Masha, think about it, we could stay here, we'd learn German, we'd be able to work, we'd be treated like the Healthies … We don't have any friends back home. Olessya won't talk to us because of our – my – drinking … we could start a new life, we could travel—'

'*Molchee!* Russia is my home, not Germany. Russia is my Motherland. I wouldn't be able to talk to anyone or joke with them. I'm not staying here forever. What's wrong with you? Aren't you a patriot? Aren't you?' She thumps the bed. 'We're Russian, we love Russia. Russians are the greatest people in the world. What are you? A Nazi, that you want to live here? A Fascist?'

'No, no, Masha, it's just that if the Communists come back in, everything will go back to how it was. We'll lose our room in the Sixth. We might get sent back to the Twentieth … Don't you see, Mashinka? It's all going to go back to how it was. Please? Just this once, just this once. Listen to me.'

Her eyes flicker with her *chortik*.

'*Nyet.*' She turns away from me, and points at our suitcase. 'You'd better get packing.'

'Let's not talk about Communism. Communism was just an idea. Just pie in the sky.'

Boris Yeltsin, President of the Russian Federation 1991–99

## Age 45
## 1995 Summer

### We go back to the Sixth, and reconnect with Joolka and Aunty Nadya

'You know you want it, you've always wanted it …' He pushes her roughly against the hot mud wall of the hut and she gasps faintly, pressing one pale hand to her fluttering heart. She looks past him to the rolling desert sands and feels as shaky as the shimmering heat waves dancing in the dunes. He leans forward and brushes his dry lips against hers, his hard body pressing against her thin dress. 'No, no,' she moans, 'oh no …' But it's too late, far too late … his deep green eyes, flecked with gold, glitter hungrily as …

'Bang, bang bang!! Yay, dead, dead, dead!' Masha jumps up, knocking the book out of my hand. Blood splatters the TV screen and she whoops and presses reverse to play the battle scene again on her Atari.

I pick *The Sheik and the Factory Girl* up again. I want to read more, I wish I could just go away and read by myself. I've got a stack of Mills and Boon books by the bedside table, hidden under some magazines because Masha says it's embarrassing. But I love reading them. Why shouldn't I? I escape in them. I need an escape.

The military coup by Yanayev failed, and after coming back from Germany, I collapsed at the same time as the Soviet Union. Masha says I'm just like the old woman in the fairy tale who keeps getting a wish from the fish her husband catches in the sea but throws back in. First she wishes their hovel was a log cabin. Then that it was a brick house, then a mansion and finally a castle. And she's still never happy. Perhaps Masha's right. But all I really want is to be in a country where I'd be invisible …

Gorbachev was too soft, too intellectual, too weak. That's what everyone said. He was forced out of the way by a battling Boris Yeltsin, who stood on a tank in front of Moscow's White House when it was under siege from the hardliners trying to bring back true Socialism. They shot big black holes into the government White House. I don't remember watching the news at the time, I was a big black hole myself, I think. But it seems that while Yanayev was on State Radio reassuring us all that Gorbachev was simply 'resting' (because 'over the years he has become rather tired and needs to get better'), Yeltsin was on TV, showing everyone that there had actually been a military coup to overthrow the government, and that Gorbachev was imprisoned in his dacha in the Crimea.

They didn't win, though, the hardliners. So we're still here in the Sixth and it seems that now Russia is like Amerika – a democracy. After all that talk about spreading Communism like wildfire across the world, it all went *phuut*, and Yeltsin got rid of Gorbachev and then dissolved the Communist Party. Just like that. The Communist Party! And then all the republics slipped away to proclaim their own independence. So now it seems we're back to being Russia again, like we were under the Tsars, except there's no Tsar now. There's a President.

It was all a bit like our lives, me and Masha. You're hopeful one moment and then disappointed the next. You think everything's going well and then there's some change and you realize it wasn't going well at all. You realize it was all going wrong and that you'd been lied to. So then you start all over again, believing it's all going to be right *this* time. You keep on and on, hoping.

Olessya says hope stops your heart from breaking. Masha says Olessya thinks too much.

'She's coming soon,' she says, switching off the Atari. 'Joolka. She's coming soon.'

'Do you think she'll bring the children? I haven't seen Bobik yet, her little boy.'

'She pops them out like piglets, so she'll probably have a fourth one by the time she gets here.' Masha grins and gets up to put the kettle on. Or rather gets up so I can put the kettle on.

'Don't know how I allowed her to interview our stupid mother though …' she says, sitting back down with a thump.

I was so upset when we had to leave Germany that Masha finally agreed to call up Joolka and Aunty Nadya to 'bring me back to life'. Also, we'd run out of money and Masha missed her *firmenni* food products. Matthius never got back in touch. As for me, I just missed Aunty Nadya and Joolka – and her little girls. I missed Olessya too. She doesn't like my drinking. She knows it's Masha who makes me drink, so I get the feeling she doesn't like Masha much either. Perhaps she never did? She came into our room last month and just sat there in front of our bed, looking at me. I looked a mess, I know I did, all bruised and swollen with dried blood on my eye and lip. After a bit she said: 'Are you ever going to do anything about this, Dasha?' I didn't say anything. Masha normally gives some excuse about how I slipped in the shower, but she doesn't bother to tell those lies with Olessya. 'Well, *are* you?' She looked at me then as if she was as disappointed in me as she was with Masha. What could I say? Because what *can* I do?

She hasn't been back since then, and we haven't been into her room either.

I pick up my *Factory Girl* book again.

'Put that *yobinny* book down; makes me sick just looking at all that sex and mushy love.'

'I don't much like World War Three going on right in front of me all the time either.'

'Stop bleating.'

Joolka called to say that she had a book agent from England who wanted us to write our autobiography – with Joolka's help. Masha liked the idea straight away. She wanted to make more money. Roubles were like pebbles, she said. All the money the Russians sent us just sank to the bottom of the stream, but *greeni* dollars were like sifted nuggets of gold. She wanted *valyuta* – foreign currency. When we first called Joolka up and asked if she'd visit, she was happy to see us again and met us as if nothing had happened. So did Aunty Nadya. Masha had called her on the phone. 'Aunty Nadya?' she'd said. 'It's me. How are you? We wondered if you could come and see us?' There was just a slight pause and then she agreed. 'Well, girls?' she'd said when she walked into our room. 'How many winters, how many years?' And that was that.

## We learn what happened at our birth

Joolka said she'd need to research our autobiography, and that the best place to start was with our mother. She went to see her in her flat yesterday. Now she's here, all excited, holding her tape recorder like a baby. She's on her own though, without the children. This is work.

'Here it is then,' she says, sitting on the floor in front of us like she always does, so she can see both of us. 'Let's listen. It was so interesting, I think you'll both be amazed.'

She switches it on and we can hear Mother's slow, deep voice talking about her childhood in a village in Siberia with her nine siblings. Masha picks up *Krestyanka* magazine and starts leafing through it. Mother goes on to describe how she'd been sent away to live with her aunt in Moscow when she was eight, and lived in their communal flat, beaten by the drunken uncle whenever he got close enough to her, and sleeping on a cot with three other children.

'Breaks my bleeding heart,' said Masha, picking up another magazine.

Mother left school at fourteen and moved out of the flat – to her aunt's delight – to work in a metalworks factory. There were no men left after the First and Second World Wars, not to mention the Great Famine and Stalin's Purges, so she was lucky to get Misha. She talked about how he needed her room in Moscow, in the factory workers' barracks, and she needed a man and father for her children. There was no love involved. It was a transaction. All she wanted by then was babies, and she was already thirty-four. Misha loved life and was a womanizer. He beat her, got drunk and controlled her. Mother fell pregnant straight away. She started her contractions in the middle of a blizzard at night, and the woman in the next room helped her on the forty-minute walk through the snow to Maternity Hospital 16, because Misha was working as a night-watchman in a factory.

*I didn't know I was having twins. I was in labour for three nights and two days. I just couldn't seem to give birth. Finally, I managed it. I remember the doctor looking down at my baby and shaking his head in disbelief: he said he'd never seen anything like it. I was frightened and started crying. Then he held the baby up to show me, but I couldn't see because my eyes were filled with tears.*

*They carried the baby out then – I thought I could hear two cries – and after a while, a woman in a white coat came in to see me. I didn't know if she was a nurse or a doctor but she told me that I'd had* urodi. *She didn't tell me why or what they looked like or even if they were still alive. She just said she was very sorry and walked away.*

'Very sorry,' sniffs Masha. 'I'm pretty sorry we're mutants too, as it happens.'

*I suppose that was their way of explaining to me that they were taking them away from me.*

'Taking them away from her? More like – "Take them away from me!"'

'Will you just listen, Masha. Give her a chance. She's telling the truth.' Joolka frowns and Masha looks up at the ceiling sulkily.

*I* know she's telling the truth. There's no doubt about it. I've known enough liars in my time, Masha among them, to recognize honesty when I hear it. But what happened? Did she just let us go and never ask about us?

*I was told they were still alive but weren't expected to live beyond a few weeks and to forget about them. But I couldn't, how can you just forget your children when you've longed for them so much? From then on I lay with a pillow over my head so no one could hear me weeping. I can't remember sleeping at all. Misha was called in to look at them straight after the birth. He told the doctors they couldn't be his and he didn't want his name on the birth certificate. He refused to see me as well. It was a terrible disgrace for him.*

'Turn it off. Turn it *off*!' Masha thumps the bed. 'I won't listen to this crap, I won't. She's making it all up.'

'Masha,' says Joolka, pressing the pause button, 'I know you've created your own version of what happened as you've been growing up, and that's understandable. It's easier to think you were abandoned, and you've thought that so long, it's ingrained.

But just listen, Masha, just listen to what she says. You can choose to believe it or not when you've heard her speak. It won't kill you to listen.'

Masha takes a deep breath, sucks in her lips and goes back to the magazine. Joolka presses the play button and Mother's sighing voice rolls on.

*So all I had now was my babies, my twins. There was a night cleaner there ... one night, in the early hours of the morning when there were no doctors around, and everyone else was asleep, she walked in holding this swaddled bundle with one dark head each end. They were asleep ... She put them into my arms and I rocked them and sang to them and kissed the top of their little heads ... my own daughters ... my* dochinki ... *they were so perfect.'*

'So perfect she threw us down the rubbish chute. Or good as.'

'*Teekha*, Masha,' says Joolka.

*I never saw them again. It must have been a week or so later when I was better that they asked me to sign the forms rejecting them. I asked what that meant, and they said they'd be looked after by the State. I asked if I could visit them if I signed and they said I couldn't, so I told them I wouldn't sign it then and walked out. I thought it would be better if they were looked after by the doctors than coming back to my dormitory with water on the dirt floor and not a stick of firewood for the stove. But I couldn't reject them – what mother can do that? I went home and I was lying in bed, still weak from the loss of blood, and it was maybe a week after I'd left the hospital when there was a knock at the door and a woman wearing a white doctor's coat walked in, sat on the edge of the bed and told me she was a physiologist and that she was very sorry but she'd come to break the news that my babies had caught pneumonia and died.*

Died? We both stare at Joolka, who's paused the tape and is looking up at us.

'*Foo!*' spits Masha after a bit. 'That's her story, see? Just felt guilty about abandoning us.'

*I went back to the doctors when I was well enough and asked to see the grave, I wanted to put flowers on it, but they told me their bodies had been preserved for science. I even went to the Kunst Kamera of Horrors in St Petersburg to see if they had been preserved in a jar there.*

'That's nice, isn't it? Wanted to see her twinlets pickled in a jar.' Masha's still leafing through the magazine, but she's listening as intently as I am. 'That's just the kind of mummy we *all* need …'

*And then, all those years later, when I found they were still alive – I felt so sorry to have not looked more for them, so sorry that I formed them like that in my womb, and then all I could do when I did meet them was cry. I couldn't understand why the doctors had lied to me. Why did they lie?*

There's a pause, and then we hear Joolka's voice saying 'I really have no idea.'

*Well, and then when that cleaner called me up from the Twentieth, and I met them, I thought they would have been told about me. About how I was lied to. About how much I loved them. Now I think they weren't.*

'No.' It's Joolka's voice again. 'I'm afraid they weren't told anything about you by anyone.'

*I can't understand it, I can't understand why the scientists deprived two children of a mother and let them live and grow up without me. I would have done anything for them when they were growing up, anything. And then, when they found me again, it was the same, I would have done anything to make up for lost time, to make up for having formed them like that, but it wasn't to be. It was too late. They found me and then they rejected me … I lost them twice. Perhaps I deserved it.'*

The tape recorder clicks off and Masha sniffs, then picks up the remote and turns the TV back on.

'You're not putting any of *that* in my book,' she says.

## We go on a family picnic

'I've got a round swimming pool in my kindergarten,' says Sasha, picking her nose while she sits next to me on the grass. 'It's got penguins painted on the sides. It's down in the cellar and you have to climb up a ladder to get in. I'm the best swimmer in my class. I can even swim underwater.'

'Sasha,' says Joolka, 'you're supposed to be helping Daddy find sticks for the camp fire.'

Kolya, Joolka's husband, is here with us. He drove us all here in their red Niva. It was a bit of a squash, but Anya sat on our lap and we just hoped we wouldn't get stopped by a GAI traffic policeman. Even though Kolya's a professional photographer, he doesn't takes photos of us and we both like him for that. We're just friends out on a picnic. Kolya's got a fire going and is cooking skewers of fatty pork. It smells delicious.

'I am, see? I'm finding them.' Sasha leans back and rakes her fingers through the pine needles, looking sneakily at Joolka as she does. 'I'm just quickly telling Aunty Dasha about our swimming pool.' Joolka shakes her head and jiggles fat baby Bobik in her arms. We're all having a barbeque in the countryside outside Moscow. It reminds me of the camp on the River Don, except there are no fences keeping us in, so we can stop and light a fire wherever we like. We're sitting by a little river on a grass verge with a village just round the bend. It's getting on towards the evening but it's still warm and swarms of gnats are buzzing round our heads.

It's been a week since she told us about our mother. Masha won't talk about the interview, but I think it's a shame that she wanted us and we wanted her and we were kept from each other. It's upsetting. But I'm glad I know, because it means that I *was* loved and not rejected. I asked Masha if we could go and see Mother again, now that we know what happened, but of course she said no. One thing I can't understand is why Mother was told by the scientists we'd died. Why? She could have come in and held us. Joolka's sitting on a log now holding little Anya on her knee and Bobik suckling on her breast. All we wanted was to be picked up by someone other than the porter. Mummy – Anna Petrovna – didn't cradle us like that; she kissed us over the bars of our cot. And sang to us. Our own mother, though, our real mummy, could have picked us right up and held us to her.

Sasha pokes me. 'Aunty Dasha, I've got a swing at the dacha, it's so high I can't see the top of it because our *dyedushka* climbed right up to the highest branch of a pine tree to make it, and it swings so far it's like flying.'

'That sounds fun, Sashinka. You're so lucky,' I say. I don't stutter with the children. It's odd.

Masha's tapping her leg to the sound of Modern Talking playing on the car radio and has a twig with a marshmallow on it, which she's poking in the fire. She's not interested in the children any more because the novelty's worn off. It's like with Marusya, my doll. She played with her for a bit and then got bored and gave her to me. It's her fifth marshmallow but the twigs keep burning and the marshmallows drop into the flames and burn. She's irritated because she wants vodka. What's the point of a picnic without vodka? I can hear her saying it in her head. To be honest, I want vodka too. I feel all jittery without it.

Anya and Sasha are a bit afraid of Masha, they can see her *chortik*.

'We've got hens, too, loads of them.' Sasha's still chattering away to me. Even the dogs on the street snarl and bark at us because we're Together, but Joolka's children just see us as Aunty Masha and Aunty Dasha. Three-year-old Anya looks at you like she's looking into you. She's white-skinned and has blue eyes like my Lyuba, and Sasha's dark and dusky like my Marat. No one would believe they were sisters. As different as God's gift and an omelette, they are. And even though me and Masha are supposedly identical, we're just as different as them.

Vodka. I want vodka but Joolka won't let us drink with the children around. She's right.

Sasha pokes me again to get my attention. 'The hens go running after Bobik when he's having an outside air bath. Babushka says that's because they think his *pipiska's* a worm. When Babushka wants to make us soup, she takes them on to the back step and chops off their heads with an axe. The blood goes everywhere, all into her face and hair too. She goes to the back step so I can't see her, but I've seen her do it. I hide, and see her. And she leaves their heads and claws in the soup to make it taste nice, so you have to not spoon them out. We've got pigs too, they're called *Obyed* and *Oozhin*, Lunch and Supper. I wish you could come to our dacha.' She stops talking then and blows her breath out, making both cheeks puff. She reminds me of Masha when she was young. 'But my babushka says over her dead body. I don't know why she says that, she's not even met you. She likes dead bodies. I asked her what she'd wish if she had one wish and she said she'd like to find the dead body of a gangster out on the path outside the dacha, one who'd been gunned down, with wads and wads of dollars in his pockets so she could steal them. My one wish is to find dinosaur bones. What's your one wish, Aunty Dasha?'

I smile at her and raise my eyebrows.

My one wish is to have a child like her.

Instead I say, 'I'd like to be invisible.'

'Me toooo!' she says excitedly.

'Time for *shashlik* then,' says Kolya loudly, waving a skewer of pork meat around. 'Any helpers, Sashkip?'

She pulls a face but goes over to her father. I asked Joolka once, if Sasha and Anya had been born Together, would she have kept them? 'Of course,' she said. 'Just as your mother would, if she'd been able.'

Masha's marshmallow falls into the fire again and she swears and throws the stick in angrily. Vodka makes the world soft and sweet.

Joolka's finished feeding Bobik and she lies him face down along her leg and pats his back, then bends down and kisses the top of his head.

'They're like gypsies, these foreigners,' Masha says under her breath. 'I know they've got vodka in the car.' She glances across at it. 'That baby looks like a poached egg, don't know what all the fuss is about.'

'Would you like to hold him?' Joolka stands up and passes Bobik to me, just like that.

'So,' she says, sitting down in front of us, cross-legged. Anya leans on Joolka's back and wraps her arms around her neck. 'Now we're all settled, here's the latest. I talked to your Doctor Golubeva on the phone, just briefly – I'll interview her properly later – and she said that you were kept in the Paediatric Institute to be studied by scientists. She worked in the Brain Institute with Anokhin and he brought her over sometimes to do that helmet thing on you. She said there were two women doctors who were in charge of you, and one wrote a dissertation about you.'

Bobik starts wriggling in my clumsy arms and then he begins squalling and goes bright red in the face. He wants his mummy. She smiles apologetically, takes him back and tucks him in the makeshift sling she's wearing. Anya's still hanging around her shoulders. He calms down straight away and goes to sleep like a light turning off. It's instinctive to want your own mother. Mothers are like magnets.

'It was Red Level, back then,' she goes on, 'so no one could access it, but now, what with all this democracy and the papers full of scandalous stories about what really happened under Stalin, it's a huge can of worms that's been opened. It's momentous. I mean, all the archives are wide open now, so I shouldn't have any problem getting it. She said it was published in 1959 and was written by Doctor Alexeyeva. It'll be interesting, won't it? To see what it says. But you can't remember anything? No? Just your "Mummy" and some of the other nannies?'

We both shake our heads. Ground rice and butter is what we remember, and Jellyfish, our toy. We had him for one day. Mummy gave him to us. Sasha has swimming pools and swings … I don't care that we didn't have that though. We had Mummy, at least we had her. I do care that we could have had our own birth mother too – if they hadn't told her we'd died.

## We find out why the scientists took us from our parents

'I got it, I finally got it,' said Joolka, bursting into our room two days later. She puts her rucksack down with a bang and fishes some crumpled papers out of it. 'Here it is. I went to the library of the Academy of Medical Sciences and asked to see it. I had the title and the reference number, but they said it wasn't accessible. But you know how it is, I got one of the librarians on her own and said that I'd be "very grateful" and she said, "Well, it *might* be possible to just let you look at it, but not make a copy." So I quietly slipped her a hundred-dollar bill and all of a sudden it *was* possible. She brought it out and I was on my own at the table, taking notes. I tell you, I just couldn't *believe* what was in there. Literally, couldn't believe it. Every page I turned over was more horrific than the one before. No wonder they told your mother you'd died. No mother would have allowed anything like that to happen to her babies. Not in a million years …'

Neither of us says anything. I look at the papers in her hands. Do I want to know? Wouldn't I sleep sounder if I didn't?

'You were a dream come true for Anokhin. It says it all here in the first paragraph, they just saw you as two guinea pigs, or, or … I don't know, microbes in a petri dish. *Unseparated twins are objects of great scientific interest. A most remarkable human experiment created by nature.*'

'Human experiment?' Masha's interested now. She definitely wants to hear what they did to us. She wants to hate them, I can already feel her balling up inside, spoiling for a fight. 'Go on then, *Maht*,' she says. 'What did the *svolochi* do?'

'So,' says Joolka, sitting on the rug, 'it starts off saying: *for six years, P. K. Anokhin and his colleagues carried out experiments on a pair of unseparated twins, Masha–Dasha (ischiopagus tripus, born 1950) in the Institute of Experimental Medicine to establish the separate roles of the nervous system and the blood system on the body's ability to adjust to conditions such as prolonged sleep deprivation, extreme hunger and extreme temperature change.*'

She looks up and bites her bottom lip. That doesn't sound good to me … not good at all.

She looks back down. 'It says that a few days after birth you were kept in laboratory conditions, so you must have been taken straight off to Anokhin's Institute of Experimental Medicine – probably soon after you were brought in to your mother by that cleaner. And this is interesting: *It was noted that, despite living in an identical environment, developmental characteristics such as speech, movement and nervous processes were markedly different from birth.*'

'What's so interesting about that?' snaps Masha. 'We're as different as your Sashinka and Anik. We're different people. We just got fused together somehow.'

'Well … no, Masha, what actually happened is that one zygote – one embryo – was dividing into identical twins but started splitting too late, so didn't complete the division. That's what conjoined twins are, but that means the two of you have identical inherited genes. So if you—'

'That's crap, we're as identical as a wolf and a goat!' says Masha shortly. 'So come on, *Maht*, come on, what did they do to us?'

'Well, it's all written down in this very formal medical-speak, which makes it even more chilling, but it starts off saying: *To study the speed with which the blood travelled from one twin to the other we introduced various substances into the blood of one child, such as radioactive iodine, barium, glucose and sodium methane sulphonate. For example, 2500 units of radioactive iodine were introduced into Masha in her bottle of milk, after which, the levels of radioactivity in the thyroid of both twins were measured with a Geiger counter. The kidneys were observed when sodium methane sulphonate was introduced into the ulnar vein of one child. In thirty minutes a distinct change in the contours of the kidneys of both children were observed on X-rays ...*'

'Bastards! *Blyadi!* Pumping radioactive shit into us, then measuring our organs with Geiger counters and X-rays – they might as well have slit our throats, but then they'd have been sawing off the branch they were sitting on, wouldn't they? Spitting in their own well ...'

'It doesn't sound, from what Golubeva was saying, that they thought you'd live long. They studied two conjoined twins very much like you fifteen years earlier, and they died as babies.'

'Not fucking surprised.'

'So I suppose they thought they could do whatever they wanted while they had time ...'

It's a hot afternoon and even though the balcony door is wide open and the net curtains are fluttering in the breeze, my T-shirt is sticking to my back. But I feel icy cold.

She reads on: '*Their reaction to pain (usually introduced by a scalpel, a needle or an electric shock) ...*'

There's a rushing noise in my head now and the words start running into each other ... I feel dizzy. It's coming back to me in short flashes – waiting for the electric shocks – the ticking noise – it was the waiting that was the worst, knowing they'd come and then crying out in pain when they did, and what was even worse – hearing Masha screaming … trying to stop them, holding out my hands and trying to stop them …

'They put a metronome on before they administered the electric shock, and then found the metronome alone caused the same reaction as the shock itself. They prevented one of you from sleeping for long periods, continually shaking you awake … they starved one of you for nine hours at a time whilst feeding the other every few hours …'

'Fuck! *Yobinny* Fascists! Nazis! And we rant on about Mengeles, claiming our lot were all as pure as the driven snow …'

'And you were hooked up during all the experiments to electrocardiograms to measure your heartbeats, penumograms to measure your breathing, and electroencephalograms to measure brain activity. And your gastric juices were analysed constantly through tubes fed into your stomachs. You must have been a wired-up nightmare to look at, it's just … hideous, too macabre to even imagine …' she falters, shaking her head. 'And seeing the photos you showed me of when you were six, in SNIP, so adorable … how *could* they do that? I'm so, so sorry …' She shuffles the papers with the tips of her fingers as if they're soiled, looking from one of us to the other with disbelief.

'Go on,' says Masha tightly. 'Go on, what else?'

'They … they packed one of you in ice until your temperature dropped to twenty-six degrees – one degree lower and you'd have died of hypothermia. One degree … It says that whenever Alexeyeva came into the room you'd start crying, so they had to carry out the experiments on pain when you were asleep or unawares.'

Beyond the rushing in my ears I can hear children playing by the lake. Laughing and splashing in the sunshine.

Joolka turns a page and keeps reading on and on. And on … *both twins react identically to the heart/eye reflex where the heart is slowed down (and can be stopped altogether) by applying pressure to the eyeball* … I close my eyes and I can see Doctor

Alexeyeva walking in with the porter to take us to the laboratory. I can see her as if she's standing there, right in front of me, I can hear Masha screaming at the electric shocks, I can hear her in that laboratory, screaming and screaming …

'… they burnt one of you and then the other, to monitor your different reactions …' but Masha's not screaming now, no, she's swearing angrily and thumping the bed. My poor Mashinka, I hated them hurting her, I won't think about it, I won't. I'll just black it all out, black it out like I did when we were little. I need her to stop reading this now. I feel sick.

I need vodka.

### We see a film documentary of us as children in the Ped

'I'm not sure I want to see it, Masha. Why would you want to see their documentary? It'll be like a horror film.'

We're outside, pacing up and down the path at the end of the garden. We can't sit still, Masha's consumed with this white-hot anger and outrage. But as for me, I just think what's done is done. We did survive, despite all the odds. We're still here. We're *zhivoochi*. Joolka said there were two doctors in charge of us – Alexeyeva and Kryuchkova – women. Both of them women. She said Kryuchkova was probably the one doing the monitoring behind the machines in the Laboratory, that's why neither of us remember her. I wonder if they were mothers themselves? Did either of them ever feel any twinge of pity or even guilt?

'*Ei*, girls, come and do some weeding! Make yourselves useful …' Timur's standing in the middle one of the flowerbeds with a garden fork, waving at us. Masha gives him the finger and he laughs and goes back to his digging. He's planted roses, red and white roses, just like the fairy tale about Rose Red and Snow White.

And what about the kind nannies – Mummy, Aunty Dusya and Aunty Shura, and the nurses? Did they all know what was being done to us in the Laboratory? No, I'm sure they didn't. Only vetted medical staff would have been allowed in there. Like Pavlov's Tower of Silence. Locked and soundproof.

'It won't be like a horror movie,' says Masha. 'You heard what Joolka said, they cut it. They prettied it up for the foreigners. She says we're as sweet as two chocolate drops in it.'

Yes, apparently they showed the original documentary in London, to a gathering of English doctors and they were so 'disturbed' that the Academy decided to edit it right back and sanitize it. I remember all their cameras following us about in SNIP when we were learning to walk. But I don't remember cameras in the Ped.

There's an old woman teetering along the path towards us. She's new and hasn't seen us before. She stops and puts her hand over her mouth and then crosses herself as we walk towards her. 'It's you, isn't it? Masha and Dasha,' she says as we approach. 'The Together Twins.' We go to walk past, but she puts her hand on Masha's arm to stop her. 'How will you die?' she asks. 'What happens when one of you dies?'

Masha shakes her hand off and snaps, 'One goes to Heaven and the other goes to Hell – why don't you just pack yourself off there too!'

We leave her standing there with her mouth open and make our way back to the entrance. Joolka's coming soon with the video to play on our TV.

She slots the tape into the video player and presses play.

There we are, two plump little babies with dark spiky hair. The crackly commentary is like the voice of Mayak State Radio, deep and reassuring, explaining about our separate nervous systems and shared blood system and how they injected one of us with radioactive iodine. A nurse picks up my foot and cuts my sole with a scalpel. I start wailing – silently – because there's no sound on the film. '*Foo!*' Masha spits. 'Nazis! We're helpless and they just want to see how loud we can scream.' It rolls on, showing another pair of conjoined twins, Ira and Galya, joined higher up their body, who were born fifteen years before us and were also studied by Anokhin. They died when they were a year old. 'Not fucking surprised,' mutters Masha.

We sit there on the bed, me and Masha, watching ourselves as babies growing into small children. We look identically angelic, happy, laughing and loving life. There's a great big cot that I don't remember – ours was small – and a vase of flowers. There are stacks of dolls on the table and we're in flowery smocks. I don't remember any of those either.

I glance across at her. She's frowning and fiddling with the button on our trousers. There are two buttons, one for me and one for her, but hers is all worked loose. 'The difference in character was evident soon after the birth,' says the chocolatey voice-over. 'Masha is more passive … it is Dasha who first sits up, Dasha who first starts crawling … Dasha who moved their third leg.' Then they show me struggling to put a sock on my own foot and Masha being told to do the same but taking it from the nurse and pushing it over the edge of the bed. *Khaa!* Good old Masha! Joolka laughs and we look at each other and smile. The film moves to a scene where we're looking bored with thick tubes down our throats to measure our gastric juices. There's a doctor I don't recognize sitting behind the machine. That must be Kryuchkova. She looks … kindly. But as we get older, our eyes, staring unsmilingly up at the camera, have this haunting black emptiness about them. It makes me shiver. They don't show Alexeyeva at all. We'd probably just start crying if they had her in the same room.

Then we move to SNIP where we're all happy and laughing, learning to walk with two big bows on each of our heads. We look so young and … sweet. Both of us. And there's us laughing excitedly again as we lie on the floor naked, pulling ourselves up the metal pole to practise getting close enough to each other to walk. That was the time Anokhin first came in to see us.

When it's finished, we stare at the whirring blank screen.

I thought it would be terrible to watch but it's not, it's actually quite interesting to see ourselves when we were little. It's like a home movie, except it isn't, is it? It's a medical documentary to be shown to scientists around the world. But we've never seen ourselves as children before. Masha's calmed down. She's thinking the same thing as I am. She gets up to have a cigarette and we walk on to the balcony while Joolka packs up the video.

'The ideal Soviet childhood then,' she says, slowly puffing out a ring of smoke. 'Lucky old us.'

I shake my head. 'Lying to everyone about what really happened to us in there is almost more horrific than showing it.'

Masha looks down at the back of her hand. 'I wonder if we're still radioactive. It's almost like they wanted to kill us, with all the starving and freezing and zapping us. Surprised we didn't have a double heart attack.'

'They must have expected us to die too – like the first ones did.' Masha stubs out her cigarette and puts the butt in a plastic bag she hides behind the pot plant. I sigh. 'But we kept on living.'

And here we are, over forty years later. Totally indestructible, despite all the odds, despite Masha smoking like a steam train and me drinking like a cobbler – a litre of vodka a day, if I can get it. *Zhivoochi.* But death and how it will happen is that nagging question that sits at the back of our minds all the time, like a black dog snapping at our heels, a question which, unlike everyone else who meets us, we're afraid to ask. Shall I ask Joolka now? Before she goes? Quick, yes, do it! Just ask what will happen. How long will it take for the other one to die? Hours? Days? Weeks? Will they be able to operate to separate us? Do I *want* to be separated? Would Masha? And if they can't, what happens when one of our hearts stops beating? Will it be painful? Will we …

'Bye then, girls,' says Joolka, standing at the door. 'I'm going to be interviewing Anna Yefimovna, one of your nurses in the Paediatric Institute, next. And Doctor Golubeva, and Lydia Mikhailovna too. I'll be interested to get her viewpoint.'

'That old carrot,' mutters Masha. 'I know what her viewpoint will be. Darling Dashinka … Malicious Masha …'

Joolka casts a brief glance back at us, shakes her head, and then she's gone.

## We go boating on the lake with Timur

We're lying under the birch trees, looking up through the fluttering silver leaves to the sky, while Lyuba and Marat paddle in the cool river. I have my head in the crook of Slava's arm and can feel his chest rising and falling with his breathing. I can breathe his smell, his unique, sour milky smell. The most wonderful smell in the world.

His fingers are running up and down my bare arm.

'Mama, I'm hungry,' calls Marat from the sandy bank. I lift my head and see him walking out of the water, dripping wet. He looks just like his father.

I smile. 'Well get Lyuba out of the river and I'll put the picnic out,' I call back. 'Run around a bit in the sun to get dry first.'

I sit up and spread out a newspaper to put the hard-boiled eggs, dried fish, juicy Borodinsky bread and lard and zefir meringues out on. I've got home-made compote too, made with the strawberries from our little plot. And a thermos of milk, fresh from our cows.

'Hey, don't go away, sexy,' Slava growls and bites my shoulder, trying to pull me back down.

'I have to feed your offspring. Your son and heir is always starving – like his dad … Besides, I thought you were going to build a little fire …'

'Here's my fire,' he says, and pulling my face to his, he kisses me hard on the lips.

'Ei! Timka! Get a grip – we're going round in circles here!'

'If you're so clever, why don't you give it a go!' says Timur, puffing, while he pulls on the oars.

'All right, I will. Move over and let Mashinka take control of the situation!'

We all laugh as she pushes him backwards off his seat on the little rowing boat and takes his place, almost tipping us both over the side. We pick up an oar each. I can see this is going to be a disaster! Timur's wearing a blue shirt buttoned right up to the collar and a flat cap. He's got nice broad hands and a face all brown and wrinkled by years in the sun. He buys vodka for us and comes up to our room sometimes to share it. He keeps promising to take us out to the lake for a boat ride and today he's finally done it.

'Right,' says Masha. 'One, two, pull! We'll get out to the middle of the lake and just float.'

Just float. That sounds good to me. Then I laugh again as I get splashed by water from Masha's flailing oar. Timur reaches over and wipes the water off my face with his sleeve. Yes, this reminds me of that boat trip with Slava on the Don … the kiss … It's nice to spend time with a man. To be looked after. Masha says he's only after our money, but that's Masha. She doesn't trust anyone. Except me.

We're in the middle of the lake now and we sit at the back of the boat again and lean back, looking up at the blue sky while Timur takes back the oars and sculls gently around.

Masha seems to have forgotten all about the dissertation and documentary film. She ranted for a bit, but then she just turned her attention back to the real horror films she watches on our video player and we don't talk about it now. Joolka managed to bribe her way into getting the whole dissertation though. I've read it now, and I've given it to Olessya to look at. Perhaps if she sees what happened to us, she'll forgive Masha and be friends again. I miss Olessya. I feel lonely without her.

Joolka interviewed Anna Yefimovna, who was a young doctor in the Ped with access to us. She still works there as head of a department. She talked of us as specimens, not children. She said Anokhin was courageous and had been exiled under Stalin for daring to believe that nature as well as nurture might affect personalities. Ours. She also said that telling our parents we'd died was an act of compassion, because we were considered 'non-viable for life' and that no one should be expected to bear the cross of having mutant infants. She insisted the experiments were what she called 'humane trials' and ended her interview by saying she pitied us 'as only a Russian woman can'. Masha was spitting mad the whole way through the taped interview.

'Timka, *ei*, Timik, catch me a fish,' says Masha sleepily. 'Catch me a fish and we'll build a fire and fry it up.'

'Only thing you'll catch in here is an old boot,' he says, peering over the side.

'Well, we'll fry that up then,' says Masha. 'It'll be tastier than the stuff they give us from the kitchens ...'

I dip my hand into the water and it ripples gently over my fingers as we float in slow circles.

Joolka asked Anna Yefimovna if she remembered the nanny who sat with us all the time, called Anna Petrovna, but she didn't. It's like she didn't exist. Perhaps we wanted a mummy so much we imagined her? No. No. She was real. She's probably dead now ... I would have liked to have met her again ...

Joolka talked to Doctor Golubeva next, who worked in the Brain Department of Anokhin's Institute of Experimental Medicine. It turns out that she was the one who was sent to tell our mother we'd died. Golubeva was the one who broke the news. And yet she didn't tell us anything, not when she came with her helmets to SNIP, not even when she visited us for all those years in the Twentieth with her sour cream buns. Perhaps the buns were an atonement ... And they kept track of them, the doctors did, kept track of our parents and our brothers, to see if they'd go on and have more Together twins. They all knew.

I can hear her gravelly old voice now, in my head, as we listened to the tape recorder. *Was it wrong to tell their mother they'd died? And not to tell the girls about their parents? No. They were a perfect living laboratory, an experiment just waiting to happen. We saw them as a miracle created by nature, a dream come true for us! You see, Soviet scientists were under terrible pressure to make pioneering discoveries ahead of Western scientists, so it was a very tense period, but also exciting for us. We were making constant breakthroughs but we were always being pushed to do more and more.*

I sigh. The Soviet Union and its dream of Communism is long gone; now we have capitalism and imperialism, all those things we were brought up to hate. But these women, these doctors, they *still* believe it was right to do what they did. Joolka didn't come and see us yesterday because Anya had her booster jab and was crying and clingy. We had vials of blood taken from us three times a day, every day, for six years.

Masha wouldn't let Joolka play much of the next interview – the one with Lydia Mikhailovna. It started off with her saying: *Masha's childish, spiteful and mean but sets herself up as some icon of morality who protects and loves this so-called degraded sister of hers despite everything, and she's delighted when everyone believes her version – that she's the good sister and Dasha's the bad sister – but nothing could be further from the truth.* I could feel Masha's *chortik* rising up inside her as she listened to that. I held my breath. On the one hand I wanted to hear more – no one apart from Aunty Nadya and Slava have ever said what they think to our faces – but on the other hand I wanted her to stop. *It's Dasha who is good and kind and forgiving, Dasha who is intelligent. You'd think they'd been brought up by different families – Masha by peasants and Dasha by professors. You'd think the clever, intuitive one would lead the other, wouldn't you? But no, it's Masha who bullies, abuses and controls ...*

That's when Masha blew up. 'Turn it off!' Joolka shook her head in frustration, but she did. Everyone does what Masha tells them to. I was glad. They don't realize, none of them, that she's right, Masha is. She's strong and I'm weak. Where would I be without her?

So *that* wasn't going in her book either.

I hear an ambulance siren wailing from the highway. There are so many cars now that there are traffic jams and accidents all the time. The newspapers are full of stories of corruption and the new Russian mafia. And we get all these soap operas from Mexico about love and deception. It's all happened so fast. Aunty Nadya says there's more food in the shops now than you can shake a stick at, but most of it's imported from the West and much too expensive to buy. 'We've prostituted ourselves to them,' Aunty Nadya always says gruffly. 'Gorbachev's fault for letting the Soviet Union fall apart.'

Some crows fly overhead, cawing sadly, and I yawn. None of that really concerns us. We get fed three meals a day by the State, and Joolka, Aunty Nadya and Baba Iskra keep bringing us supplies. Nothing's too expensive for *us* to buy. I'd like to buy *firmenni* food for Aunty Nadya and Baba Iskra too, but Masha says they wouldn't accept it. She's probably right. Masha's usually right.

'*Nooka*,' says Timur, taking up the oars, 'come on then, my beauties, back to Home Sweet Home.'

## We talk to Olessya about being us

As we circle back along the dusty path that leads from the lake to the gates, I see Olessya sitting in her wheelchair just behind the guardhouse. She likes to sit there on her own and look out at the people going past. No one notices her. Sometimes she's there for hours. I'm not sure if she'll talk to us, but she grins as we come through the gates and starts wheeling towards us.

'Still trying to get in his pants, are you?' jokes Masha, waving at the guard. 'Bit young for you, even by your standards!'

'Very funny, Masha.' She's still seeing Garrick, I think.

Timur gives us a nod, flicks his thumb and third finger under his ear to show he's going off to get drunk, and walks away. Olessya turns her chair around and comes back down the drive with us to the Home entrance. It's a warm late afternoon and none of us want to go inside, so we sit on the steps looking out across the fence at the blocks of flats opposite. A huge billboard has just gone up by the side of our road, advertising real estate in the countryside, with photos of bright new red-brick dacha country houses.

'Looks like Amerika, doesn't it,' says Masha, nodding at it.

'Remember when it was "Every Day of Labour is One More Step Towards Communism"?' says Olessya. 'Now it's just buy, buy, buy.' She looks down at the palms of her hands. 'If you can.'

The gates to the Home swing open and the chauffeur-driven black Volga belonging to our Director, Zlata Igorovna, sweeps up the drive and parks in front of us, the engine idling, waiting to take her home. Perhaps to a dacha like the one in the billboard.

We should get back to our room to avoid meeting her, but just as we start to get up to go, the door swings open and Zlata Igorovna marches out. I shrink back, but she sees us and comes striding over.

'So, I hear you two have been up to your usual games.' She has this way of standing right over us. It's what Dragomirovna and Barkov used to do. Intimidation. Power. Authority.

'It's in our genes, Zlata Igorovna,' says Masha, jutting out her chin. 'That's what it is. Our father was an alcoholic and Dasha's inherited his—'

'That's your excuse, is it?' she interrupts sharply. 'Everyone has an excuse, don't they? Well, if I find out who's bringing you vodka, I'll fire them on the spot. And if it's that English woman, I'll refuse her entry.' I nod. (It was Timur.)

'We k-keep to our r-room,' I say. 'We s-stay quiet.'

'Oh yes? And I should be grateful, should I? As if my nurses have nothing better to do than patch you up the next morning, Dasha. It's not even as if you drink yourselves to death, more's the pity, you just keep on going, don't you?' I nod again. We're *zhivoochi*. Sorry about that.

She narrows her eyes at us. I don't think she's ever smiled in her life.

Her chauffeur has jumped out and is holding the car door open for her, so she gives us one last evil look and sweeps off.

'So, how's the book coming along then?' asks Olessya once the car has driven off.

'Good,' I say. 'Joolka s-seems to have got to everyone j-just in time.'

'What do you mean?'

'They're dying like flies,' says Masha cheerfully. 'Joolka wanted to ask Lydia Mikhailovna more about Anokhin, so she called up and was told she'd dropped dead. So's Golubeva. So's Mother Misery.'

'Your mother?' Olessya looks shocked. 'She's died?'

'*Da-oosh*. You'd better not let Joolka interview *you*, Olesskinka. It's like the Curse of the Book – one interview and bang! You keel over!'

Olessya looks at me and bites her lip. 'I'm sorry, girls. About your mother.'

Masha shrugs. 'Good riddance. Finally found her release.'

We heard about her death last week. We'd been sitting on our bed one evening when the phone rang. It's on Masha's side, so she always picks it up. I talk in public and she talks on the phone because only close friends have our number. She listened for a bit without saying anything, and then said: 'No thanks,' and put the phone down. I waited for her to tell me who it was. She picked up the controller for her Atari and turned it on. 'That was Aunty Dina,' she said as it started up. 'Didn't know she still had our number. She says Mother Misery died yesterday and did we want to go to the funeral.' She sniffed and pressed play. I stared at her, trying to take it in. Our mother's dead? I feel as if someone's just kicked my leg out from under me and I'm falling … falling. Our poor, kind, sad mother who lost us twice. Mother with her soft kisses …

'I want to go, Masha,' I said, sitting up. 'I want to go to the funeral. At least we can do that. Call her back and say we're going. Where's her number?' I started scrabbling over her to get at our phone book.

'Stop babbling,' she said crossly, pushing me away from her. 'I'm not going off to stand by her graveside in the middle of a media circus and be insulted by our darling brothers.'

'*I* want to though, *I* want to!' We hadn't seen her in over seven years, but I thought about her a lot and hoped that one day Masha would let us go and visit her. Or let her come to us. But Masha didn't need her any more. I did, though. I didn't know how much I needed her until the moment I heard she'd gone. 'Call her! Call her!'

Masha slapped my face sharply.

'*Nyet!*'

I put my hand to my stinging cheek and the tears squeezed silently out of my eyes. Just like Mother's tears when we last saw her …

But there was nothing I could do. Nothing.

We sit here now on the steps, watching the gates closing behind Zlata's Volga.

'So, yes,' continues Olessya, 'I read the dissertation. It's medical torture. They should be locked up.'

'That's too good for them,' exclaims Masha. 'They should be lined up against a wall and shot!'

I give a big sigh. 'They're dead now, most of them. They were old.'

The sun's setting slowly over the rooftops.

Olessya shifts in her chair. 'I didn't realize … I think I've never understood fully, quite how … hard it must be, you know, to be you two.'

Masha's about to say, 'Try living with this shipwreck for a day …' but strangely, she stops herself.

'It's not just being taken away from your parents and having those things done to you – although it did make me realize how lucky I was to have most of my childhood with my mother and father. They were kind. It's just that after my twin and I got polio, I never saw them again. I suppose at least your mother wanted to see you when you got back in touch …' Masha still doesn't say anything. But she's listening. 'No, it was reading about how different you both were, character wise, right from the beginning. You, Masha, being so feisty and well … defiant as you grew older. Knocking down their bricks, refusing to do their so-called "games" – like being told to press that rubber bulb every time you saw a light or whatever, and throwing it down and telling them "Press it yourselves!" I laughed when I read that. And then you, Dasha, being so desperate to please, you know. Longing so much, even at that age, for approval, wanting so badly to … well, do everything they asked you to and do it well. Even if it hurt …'

We still don't speak, me and Masha, we just watch as a visitor shows her passport to the guard at the gates and then walks slowly up the drive carrying two string bags of goods. Somebody's daughter, I suppose.

'I've always thought of you as being just Masha and Dasha,' Olessya goes on slowly. 'I never noticed that you're Together. None of us did. You were just so *different*, you know – to each other, I mean. And then it turns out you were born like that: different. You didn't become that way.' She shakes her head, as if it's come as a big surprise. 'But that doesn't mean you can't *change*.' The visitor trudges past us into the Home, wearing a blue headscarf and an air of deep despair. Olessya looks at us then, at Masha, at me. She looks right into my eyes. 'You know what they say: life's a journey, not a destination. We can all change, however old we are. We all have to work at making life as good as we can make it every step of the way.'

'All right, Plato,' says Masha, sniffing. 'That's what I'm doing, isn't it?'

'*We*. It should be we, not I, Masha. That's what we're talking about. Life's about compromises. All relationships involve compromise.'

'Thanks, but we're OK. We're like an old married couple,' says Masha, sniffing again. 'We've worked it out.'

'But have you?' She looks at me.

I pause for a moment and then say: 'I think it's easier to find a compromise when one of you can leave the room.'

## Sanya comes in with some more gossip and Joolka tells us something about Slava

'So, you'll never guess what …' Sanya's leaning against the balcony door in our room, picking her teeth with a matchstick – she never sits down in case Zlata Igorovna comes bursting in on one of her spot checks to make sure no one's fraternizing with us or that we're drinking. It's *nyelzya* to lock the door when we're in the room. Only when we leave. It's midday and there are thunder-clouds gathering outside. It's so hot nowadays it thunders every afternoon. I'm soaked in sweat. Most days we fill our shallow shower basin up with cold water and sit in it, fully dressed, to keep cool – and dry off in half an hour. Sanya's telling us what she calls 'a horrific scandal' about the new cleaner, an Armenian girl called Zabel. 'So then her boyfriend, who's also Armenian – can't remember his name for the life of me; those darkie languages are all abracadabra to me – follows her to the hairdressers where she's getting her hair done …'

Masha's leaning forward, all ears, but I'm finding it hard to concentrate. Joolka got back from her trip to Novocherkassk today and she said she'd come over to see us after she'd been home and seen the children. She wanted to go to our school because she said she needed to describe it, even if none of the teachers are still there. She says we can't describe anyone or anything for the life of us. I think she gets a bit frustrated with us. I stopped her as she was leaving our room for the airport, before Masha could say anything, and asked if she could look for Slava's family, just to find out what happened on that day after the party. Or perhaps to find out what he said about us … about me. But most of all, to find out how he died.

Me and Masha, we talk about that sometimes. Especially now – because we're digging everything up with our autobiography. Masha says he wasn't the type to give up and kill himself. And anyway, why would he? He was waiting for us to come to live with him. And he didn't seem too interested in studying after we heard that we were all just flushed down the toilet, as she put it, after finishing school, whatever grades we got. But his dad would have found him carpentry work to do, or even accounting on the side. He could have been happy … and yet somehow, deep inside, I'm sure that he *did* do it. I do think he killed himself. How could he hold a birthday party for everyone and then just lie down and die the very next day? Just … die? What of? He was strong, he never fell ill. He was young. But if he did commit suicide, then he broke his promise to me that we'd always be together. If he …

'Whaat? He *never* did!' Masha leans even further forward with a jerk and I almost fall off the bed. 'He actually pulled out a gun?'

'Yes, yes, he did, Mash! He was so crazy about her, but she'd started sleeping with her hairdresser – a man, obviously – because she needed to get a Moscow *propiska* to stay here, and her Armenian wasn't going to be able to give her that, although he was giving her everything else by the sounds of it. And she was pretty as a poppy, wasn't she, with those big black eyes and red lips—'

'Was? What do you mean "was"?' says Masha, her mouth open.

'I mean …' Sanya pauses for effect. 'I mean … he burst into the salon and gunned her down. *Da-oosh!* Yesterday. Right before everyone's eyes. I tell you, it's like Chicago out there. Everyone dived for the floor, and he walked over, cool as a python, and pumped a few more bullets into her head and then strolled out.'

'She's dead?' I look at her, startled. 'Zabel's been killed?'

Sanya levers herself off the wall and nods. 'Like I say, no one's safe any more, what with the car bombings and the mafia. Anyone can get a gun. It's mayhem. There are signs outside fancy restaurants saying *Please leave your guns at the door.* Seriously, I've seen them. And I was talking to Zabochka just the other day about Igor, her hairdresser. She was telling us that he wanted to marry her, and so I said: "*Nye byot? Nye pyot?*" And she smiles with all those gleaming teeth of hers and says, no, he doesn't drink, or beat me, and I say, "You got a good 'un then … they're rare."' Sanya puts her hand up to her mouth, which is swollen and bruised, and shakes her head. 'Most of them do drink and knock you around – what do you expect? It's a hard life. But it takes a real crazy to kill you in cold blood.'

No one talks for a bit and then Masha asks: 'Any chance of getting us a box of *slivochnaya pomada* sweets, Sanya, like the one you brought last week? I felt like I was having an orgasm with each one of those.' Not that Masha would know what an orgasm is like. Or me, for that matter.

Sanya sighs and shakes her head. 'We're all on rationing cards nowadays, Mashkip. That last box was a stroke of luck. Saw the queue and joined it, quick as a flash.'

I look at Masha, talking happily away about creamy sweets. I'm thinking that Zabel, beautiful Zabel with her dark brown eyes and happy smile, is dead. Murdered. Indifference is one thing, but you have to have at least a last spark of pity. Don't you?

There's a knock on the door and Sanya jumps like she's been electrocuted and grabs her mop and pail, almost falling over them.

The door opens and we can hear Joolka's voice: 'Cuckoo! I'm back.'

Sanya relaxes with a fat sigh. 'Well,' she says, waddling across our rug, 'if I don't get to all the rooms on your floor in ten minutes flat, I'm dead meat myself, so I'm off. Just thought I'd tell you though, let you know. Bye, then.'

We nod. Joolka walks in with her rucksack. 'Hey, girls,' she says. 'All good?'

She looks tired. But excited too. Instead of squatting down cross-legged on the rug in front of us like she normally does, she comes over to sit with me, but Masha grabs her hand and pulls her over to her side, pleased as a cat with butter to have her there. Masha starts kissing Joolka's shoulder and neck and grinning that great big happy grin she has. I relax then, and grin too. It's like Masha's joyfulness always comes bouncing through to me. It really does.

'So, that was an interesting trip,' says Joolka, smiling too. 'The school was much smaller than I thought it would be, and I forgot it used to be a rich merchant's house in tsarist days. It was a lovely old building; obviously, a bit grim inside and crumbling on the outside, but still ... lots of sweet little kids. Shy, but sweet. Still on trollies, by the way, and they still have the green *krokod-ilchik* wheelbarrows to take them to lessons. Hey, Mash, stop that, it hurts!' Masha's nibbling her ear now and she bats her away.

'But you're so pretty, *Maht*, and you never get near me. Least you can do is let me love you a bit.'

'If you were a man, I'd hit you! Stop pawing at me, Mashinka – listen, listen.'

'*I'm* listening,' I say quickly. 'Was there anyone there we knew?' What I really want to know was did she find Slava's family.

The storm clouds have burst and the rain's thundering down on our balcony and against the windows like a wild animal trying to get in.

'Wow, glad I made it before that broke,' she says. 'So, right. There were no teachers still there who knew you, but they told me where Vera Stepanovna, the headmistress, lived and I went to see her. She remembered you very well. She says hello. She lives in a log cabin on the outskirts of town and was sitting in a big armchair, looking small and frail. Also not what I imagined. She says she reads about you in the papers and that she saw *Vzglyad* and you hardly looked any older. But she looks as old as the world. She told me that Valentina Alexandrovna left the school soon after Slava died. She didn't know where she is now.'

'D-did you ask about S-Slava?'

'Yes, yes, I did. She said they all liked Slava very much. She said he was extraordinary.' She stops then and gets some papers out of her rucksack and starts shuffling through them. She looks a bit nervous. 'So anyway, I've got her interview here, but it's still in English so I'll type it up in Russian and then you can read all of it, but I'll just give you the gist.' She's talking quickly, hardly pausing for breath. 'She told me where Anyootka was, so I chatted to her too, only on the phone though – she's moved to Rostov.'

Anyootka. Pretty Anyootka. I can still feel the rip of jealousy. Was she there on his last birthday? Did he spend his last day on earth with Anyootka?

'What's she doing these days?' asks Masha.

'Well, she's married to a Healthy and has two children. Here, here's the interview, but it's in English, so I'll read this little bit to you.

*It was like having two completely different people living in one body, but Masha was totally in charge. I know that was hard for Slava … He said half the time he just wanted to tear them both apart with his bare hands so he could get at Dasha.*

Tear us apart? He didn't tell me that. But how could he, with Masha there? He could only tell Anyootka.

*He told me he wanted to give her a ring before she left the school. It was his babushka's ring, but he didn't get the chance.*

Joolka looks at me then with her head on one side, but I don't say anything. What's there to say? Masha's about to make a joke about putting a ring through my nose, but she doesn't.

'Anyootka said she was like a sister he never had. He said he could talk to her, like he couldn't talk to his mother and his friends. He told her that he gave you a promise and that he'd keep it. He didn't tell her what it was, though. Secrets are just for two people.'

Masha snorts. She still doesn't know our secret. But he didn't keep his promise, did he? And he didn't give me the ring. I remember him waiting in the courtyard as we were leaving the school, telling me to be strong, holding something in his fist. The ring. I could have had his ring to keep with his letters. But no, I couldn't, Masha would probably have thrown it away.

'Anyway …' says Joolka, looking back through her notes. 'Anyootka was lucky to be able to live a normal life. I asked Vera

Stepanovna if she and the other teachers were aware that their pupils were pretty much doomed to a living death in homes for the elderly when they left …'

I want to hear about Slava. I don't want to think about Little Lyuda and Sunny Nina. Masha's fiddling with her button.

'… and she said she supposed they did, but they just didn't talk about it. She never visited the Novocherkassk Home and advised Valentina Alexandrovna against it. She told me that after that visit, Valentina Alexandrovna lost all her passion to teach. Here …' she starts reading from the interview with her. *We wanted to protect them, to give them a childhood with hopes and dreams. But their fate didn't depend on us. It depended on the grade of disability they received from the Medical Commission. So we hoped for the best. We did our best for them. We still do.*

'And S-Slava?' I ask.

'Well, yes, we talked about Slava too. I don't know if you know, I think you don't, that Slava was dying.'

Dying? What does she mean – dying? What of? We both stare at her, baffled.

'He had a lot of … of difficult conditions. Vera Stepanovna listed them all; something like severe kyphosis and scoliosis of the spine, and polio as well, but basically, whatever he had was terminal. No one expected him to live as long as he did. It was like he was … holding on …' She coughs and shuffles the papers again and doesn't look at me. 'Yes, he was in a lot of pain all the time. His parents had a good doctor for him, a family friend, but his body was sort of impacting in on itself. Crushing him really.'

The stupid rain keeps crashing in on the windows so loudly that I can hardly hear her. I clasp my hand on Masha's knee to try and pull myself closer to Joolka.

'Vera Stepanovna knew, but she never talked about it with his parents, or him. But she thinks they must have known too. I went to their village; it's a bit run-down, but still very pretty with rows of painted log cabins, but they don't live there any more. One old babushka remembered them, but she said they moved after Slava died. She didn't know where. I looked in the yellow pages but there were no Dionegos. Anyway, Vera Stepanovna said his parents kept him in the school because he loved it so much.' There's a lightning flash and the rain pounds down even louder, I can't hear her '… friends and … summer camp … and then after you left he didn't really want to go to school any more … they thought it would be good for him though … medical care in Novocherkassk …' The thunderclap comes, rolling right over us, and we all look across at the window and don't say anything.

Then I ask: 'Did *he* know? That he was dying?'

Joolka bites her bottom lip and looks back at the papers. But the answer's not there.

'Well, the thing is, Dashinka, I just don't know. Kids weren't told anything about their illnesses or prognosis. You should know that, if anyone should. Good God, even parents weren't told. And the teachers only guessed because of their experience with disabled kids. But I think maybe … he did know … deep down, don't you?' I don't say anything, neither does Masha, but we're both thinking he must have known. 'He would have been suffering a lot, I imagine,' Joolka adds, and looks at me sadly. 'And there would have been a lot of pressure on his heart and lungs.'

'Tea?' asks Masha.

'OK,' says Joolka.

We get up and put the kettle on and then strain the tea leaves through the silver spoon strainer, and I think, looking at it, that I can see every tiny hole in the strainer really, really sharply, just like I saw the ladybird on the leaf before I tried to hang myself.

'Sugar?' says Masha.

'Sugar,' agrees Joolka.

We sit back on the bed with our glasses of tea.

'So, I'll come back first thing tomorrow and give you copies of the interviews. We've got this deadline to write up your book, so we'd better get a move on.'

## I read a medical report on Masha

It's four in the morning and my mind's buzzing like a nest of wasps. I've taken his letters out from under the pillow and I'm holding them on my chest. If he did kill himself, was it because he didn't want me to see him die slowly? Or perhaps the pain was just too much? Or he might have died of heart failure after the party? If he did commit suicide, wouldn't he have written me a note … but he would have known that Masha would read it first. Masha … A suicide note could never have been for my eyes only …

I want to stop thinking and turn over, but I can't. I can never turn over.

Why, why, *why* did we have to be born Together?

I look up at the black ceiling, and try really hard to stop thinking. I want a glass of water, but I can't get up because Masha's asleep. I could get up, but she'd be angry. And I can't make her angry. *Stand up for yourself.* That's what he said. I want a drink so badly. Vodka. I'm all jittery, I can't stop twitching. If I'd stood up for myself, then I could have stayed at the school for another year. And then gone to the village. I could have spent those last few years with him. I might even have had my Lyuba and Marat with him. How do I know we were sterilized? I don't. And I could have done all those things if I wasn't Together.

Masha stirs in her sleep and I feel like hitting her. No. I couldn't stand up to her, I just couldn't. I still can't. I can't even bring myself to wake her up to get a glass of water. Asking me to change and be strong is like asking me to look at rail tracks set in cement and tear them up by willpower alone. It's not possible. We were born like this, we've lived forty-five years like this. How does Olessya think I can get Masha to compromise, as though it's as easy as flicking a light switch? Besides, what's the point?

Stop! Stop thinking!

I thump the bed and she stirs again. What's the point of regrets? Tears pour salt on a wound. Masha was strong, Masha got us to the school in the first place. She got us into the Twentieth, and she got us here.

Stop thinking!

I squeeze my eyes closed and take a deep breath. I need to disappear into my world of fantasy in the village, the log cabin, the stove … yes, get up, put wood on the stove … Slava going out to the meadow. But wait, *that's* why he couldn't come and stay with us at the Twentieth, wasn't it? Because his body was slowly crushing him to death. He needed his family doctor and pain control and medical care … more than he needed me? I would just have been his carer.

Sleep, oh please, let me sleep … *Gospodi*, I need a drink. Vodka is the only thing that makes everything go away. Vodka is that delightful, black, ink-out paint that stops everything hurting. Vodka gives me black, dreamless sleep. Like death … like beautiful suicide.

'Up we get then, rise and shine. Greet the new day!'

I must have fallen asleep eventually.

Masha's pulling me off the bed. 'Put the kettle on, come on, get a move on. Mashinka wants her sweet glass of tea, and what Mashinka wants, Mashinka gets.'

I asked her, after Joolka had gone, if we could call Anyootka. We were sitting on the sofa, tying the laces on our boots before going down to the entrance hall to talk to Baba Iskra in the cloakroom. 'Just to chat about old times,' I'd said. 'It would be nice. She might even know where Slava's parents are.' Masha stood, and picked up our bunch of keys. 'I don't need your precious Anyootka and her tearing-them-in-two talk.' We walked through the corridor to the door. 'She never liked me anyway. And I bet all that sister stuff was rubbish. She fancied him, anyone could see that. She wanted to take him away from you, and now you want to get back in touch. *Foo!*' She opened the door and we walked out. 'Please, Masha, just one call.' She closed the door with a bang and I knew what that meant: *Nyet*.

We've put a Modern Talking tape on and Masha's boogeying to the music while I'm getting our breakfast out of the fridge when Joolka comes in, looking nervous again. She kisses us both on the tops of our heads, like she does.

'I swear, I'm never going to be able to listen to Modern Talking without thinking of you two,' she says with a smile as we all walk over to our bed. She sits next to Masha instead of me on the floor. That's odd.

Masha's pleased though. 'See? You can't get enough of me, can you, *Maht*? You want Mashinka's kisses.'

'Bites, more like – I've hardly got any ear left after yesterday.'

They laugh.

'So, here are the printouts in Russian of Vera Stepanovna and Anyootka's interviews. One for you, Masha, and one for Dasha.' She bites her lip and won't look at us. 'Here, read it and tell me what you think as you go through it. I'd like your reaction.'

Joolka gets up and puts the papers next to me on the bed, then sits back down with Masha. I pick them up and start reading. But I don't understand. It's not the interviews at all. It says in small type at the top: Psychological Assessment by Doctor Johann Weber, Cologne. He's the psychiatrist we met in Germany. I look up at Joolka questioningly, but she shakes her head quickly at me. Masha's got her nose in her own papers.

I look back down at the assessment.

*Having studied Maria and Daria Krivoshlyapova, a pair of ischiopagus tripus twins, my diagnosis is that Maria ('Masha') displays all the character traits typical of primary psychopathy – a stunted paralimbic system present from birth, which also entails disorders in …*

I put it down. I shouldn't be reading this. It's disloyal, it's deceitful; we have no secrets, me and Masha. But yes, yes we do. Slava's secret. I pick it back up again. Masha would kill us both if she knew I was reading this.

*Primary psychopathy is a deeply ingrained constellation of personality traits and behaviours, the symptoms of which reflect an emotional processing disorder, with a strong genetic foundation. This might seem extraordinary, given that these twins are genetically identical, but I believe that, somehow, 'genetic memory' is at work here. From conversations with the twins it appears that their father may well have had psychopathic tendencies and their mother may have been clinically depressed.*

'Haha! See?' exclaims Masha. I jump, but she's pointing at her printout. 'Seems Vera Stepanovna did like me after all. See?'

Joolka laughs too. 'Of course she did, Masha. Who wouldn't like you?'

'Look,' she goes on, cackling, 'look – she says I was a bit of a monkey, but that I was one of the most popular kids in school. She says I made everyone laugh. You can put *that* in the book.'

'Yes, and see what it says here …' says Joolka, and they lean in over the papers with their heads together. I'm still reading mine. My heart's beating fast. I hope Masha doesn't notice. Psychopath? Masha? A medically certified psychopath? I remember Lydia Mikhailovna calling her that when we were hiding under the desk in SNIP. And Slava called her a psychopath once, but it was just a throwaway word and he only meant she was a bit … controlling. And cruel. Didn't he?

> *The vast symptoms of the condition of primary psychopathy exhibited by Masha include the following traits: superficial charm and wit; lack of empathy; callousness; manipulation; pathological lying; arrogance; blame shifting; total control of a partner; persistent devaluation of a partner; aggression/violence; impulsivity; parasitic lifestyle; lack of anxiety but angers easily …*

It's all Masha. Every single one.

She's laughing at something Vera Stepanovna said about how we balanced each other out perfectly. How Masha was tough and I was soft. How Masha always had a big smile on her face and how I was more thoughtful. How Masha supported me through difficult times …

'See?' says Masha, looking across at me. 'Have you got to that bit?' I nod and smile, then look back down quickly, leaning slightly away from her.

> *From my brief interaction with the twins it became clear that Masha displayed every symptom of primary psychopathy. And Dasha, with her suicidal tendencies and persistently bleak outlook on life, displayed symptoms of clinical depression. She was less vocal and therefore less accessible for superficial diagnosis. Depression can be treated by medication, psychopathy cannot.*
>
> *Psychopaths are unfamiliar with and unempathetic towards the emotions associated with depression. Hence we have a situation where two sisters have inherited the personalities of two warring parents – the father being psychopathic and the mother clinically depressed – yet*

> *these two are condemned to share the same body. A psychological tragedy.*

A tragedy? Why has Joolka given me this? If Masha *is* a psychopath, if she really is, it's untreatable. What am I supposed to do? How am I supposed to feel? I want to give it back to her. To cry, but I don't. I keep reading.

> *People who are trusting, empathetic, sensitive and forgiving tend to fare worse in these connections and are often profoundly traumatized by the experience. It is very important that those in a relationship with a psychopath know what they are dealing with. Psychopaths are unable to experience love, which they consider to be a weakness that creates vulnerability.*

I need help – not to feel helpless. How will it make me feel better, knowing that she's, she's, what? A monster? She's not. She's strong, she loves me. Has she ever told me she loves me though? No. Never. She … she doesn't need to. Do I love her? Of course I do, despite everything, I do.

> *It is advisable for the victim to leave the psychopath. However, in the case of conjoined twins this is impossible. One of the best approaches for compromise and restoring a balance in the relationship is limited re-parenting, where the therapist – in this case Dasha – takes on the role of a mother figure.*

Compromise. Re-parenting. One of the best approaches is to take on the role of a mother figure. The one we never had. Is that possible? Is it? Can I? Do I want to? Aren't we happy as we are? Am I happy never being able to make a decision? Being controlled like a puppet on a string?

I fold up the sheet of paper and put it on the bed beside me with my head in a whirl. The interviews, the ones Masha has, were underneath it. Joolka gets up quickly, takes the assessment and pops it in her rucksack.

Then she puts her hand on my shoulder and gives me a little nod.

## Age 48
## Summer 1998

### We go to a Modern Talking concert in the Kremlin Palace

I can do this, I can do this. One foot in front of the other, mine then Masha's, as we walk over the long, wide pedestrianized bridge to the Kremlin. Olessya's on one side in her wheelchair and Aunty Nadya's on the other, holding our tickets. Mind over matter. Face your fears. I have my eyes on the ground. It's not far now. When Masha heard that Modern Talking were giving a concert in Moscow, she was mad keen to go. I sometimes think the only thing Masha and I have in common is loving Modern Talking. Their music makes us both feel happy at the same time. We sing along to all the English lyrics even though we only know what the words mean because Joolka translated them for us, otherwise it's all just abracadabra. I didn't want to go at first, because who wants to take the world's freakiest body out into the public eye?

I think I could have stopped Masha if I'd really wanted to. It's working, this mothering thing. It's slow, like a constant drip, hollowing out a stone, but it's working. It would be easier if we didn't drink. Every time we do, I'm not me any more, I lose myself and when I wake up all battered by her, it seems we're right back to where we started.

But in the end, I decided to do it. I decided to come out to this concert.

'Do buck up, girls,' says Aunty Nadya as we pass under the red Kremlin walls. 'Stop dawdling.'

I'm not dawdling though, I'm going as fast as we can. Aunty Nadya got a taxi to bring us here but the driver can't take us over the bridge. We have to walk all the way. Step by awful step. I keep my eyes down. We haven't been out in public for a long time, so this is a trial. If we had a wheelchair and a rug like Olessya, no one would notice us, but we can't fit into one. The Kremlin bells ring out as if to herald our coming. It doesn't take long for people to realize what's happening and the whispers rise to a babble as they come closer, circling round us. I don't look up, so all I can see are their feet. I feel the familiar nausea rising in my stomach and the trickles of sweat running down my back. How would *they* like it? How would they like to be us? Won't they *ever* understand and just leave us alone?

'That's right, take pictures, you morons!' Masha's shaking her fist at them. 'Show the grandchildren you saw the great Masha and Dasha!' She can't help shouting at them, Masha can't. Well, good for her. I can hear the clicking of their cameras and even though it's still sunny, flash bulbs keep going off in my face.

'Do calm down, Masha!' hisses Aunty Nadya. 'Remember your dignity.'

'Where's *their* dignity?' growls Masha. 'If someone comes up and spits in your eye, you spit right back.'

Aunty Nadya tuts but she starts waving away the bystanders saying, 'Comrades, leave them in peace. Where is your compassion?'

I'm worried that when we get in the concert hall everyone's going to forget Modern Talking and focus on us, but when we finally make it across the terrifyingly open Kremlin Square, and go through the doors, it's almost empty. We got here early on purpose. We run down the aisle, whooping, and get settled in our soft blue seats, right at the very front, with Aunty Nadya on one side and Olessya in the aisle. I'm getting excited now, and Masha's forgotten the crowds outside and is fiddling with her button and singing *yo ma khat, yo ma sol* and clapping. We all laugh. It's a huge conference hall where all the Party congresses were held. We're all half in love with Thomas and Dieter; even Aunty Nadya is, I think, though she'd never say so. Modern Stuff and Nonsense, more like, she said.

Masha's jiggling her foot up and down. 'Let's go backstage, come on, let's nip up those steps and say hi to the boys!'

'You'll sit right there in your seat and calm down, my beauty,' says Aunty Nadya sternly as Masha makes to get up, and she puts her hand firmly on her knee. We didn't even drink before we came out because we thought they might not let us in if we did.

I look around. People are starting to trickle into the hall. It's nearly all women. I can't believe we're actually here, I can't believe Modern Talking has finally come to Moscow! Slava would have loved this, he'd have loved their music. I wonder if he ever got to hear the Beatles before he died?

There's one more reason that I decided to steel myself and come to the concert. Sanya. Hearing the news about Sanya made me realize that we should take our pleasures where we find them. Baba Iskra came into our room about two months ago to tell us what happened. She knocked. She doesn't normally knock. Masha had been playing a game on the computer and I was reading one of my Mills and Boon books: *The Surgeon She's Been Waiting For* – funny how you remember little things when something terrible happens. We could tell straight away something was very wrong.

'Bad news I'm afraid, girls.' She sat down with a thump in the armchair by the bed. 'Very bad news.' Masha turned off the computer and I put my book down. We waited. She sighed heavily. 'It's about Sanya. I'm afraid she's dead.'

'Dead?!' We both stared at her. Not Sanya, not dead. No, no! 'She's our age, she can't be dead,' exclaimed Masha. Baba Iskra shook her head.

'It was that bastard of a husband of hers that did it. He came in, drunk as usual, apparently, and didn't like the fact she hadn't cooked him supper. So what did he do?' We both keep gawping at her. What? 'He picked up the empty frying pan and took an almighty swing at her. She went down like a felled tree, she did. But he didn't stop there, he kept on battering her with everything that came to hand, just to make sure. The iron, a chair, even the butter dish. Seems he always used to beat her – but we knew that, didn't we? She'd come in bruised as a fallen apple most days towards the end, but he always stopped himself before he did her to death. Something must have just clicked in his head.'

'H-How – h-how do you know?' I asked, still not able to believe that she's gone. 'About the butter dish and everything?'

'Their daughter was there in the flat, hiding behind the door, watching her mother being smashed to a pulp on the kitchen floor.'

'*Yobinny moodak!*' Masha thumped the bed with her fist. 'Vicious fucking bully! How could she put up with that? What sort of a person puts up with that?'

Baba Iskra shrugged. 'A Russian woman.'

I felt an icy-cold chill run through me as if someone had walked over my grave. Sanya, our Sanya, dead? We see the inmates dying all the time. And poor Zabka was murdered – it was Sanya who told us that news …

'Oh fuck,' said Masha, maybe thinking the same thing. 'No more gossip from Sanochka. You'll have to fill us in now, Baba Iskra.'

'Masha,' she said, frowning. 'Show some common decency.'

Masha just shrugged. 'If I cried for everyone who died I'd be a puddle on the floor.'

Baba Iskra shook her head and wiped some of her own tears away with her hand. Then she got up to go because Masha had turned the computer back on. After she'd left, I got to thinking that Masha could take anything to hand when she beats me and we're blind drunk. She could take the heavy telephone, the thermos, even a knife, but she never does. She only ever uses her fists and nails. She can't kill me with those. And then I realized that, however drunk she is, however angry, however vicious, she never *wants* to kill me. Because then she'd be killing herself.

There's a low excited buzz behind me as the concert hall fills up. Olessya puts her hand on my arm. 'All OK, Dashinka?'

I nod. Olessya seems to see right into my mind, just like Slava did. More than Masha ever could. She's been trying to help me in all sorts of ways. She came into our room and showed me a site about stuttering to see if I could learn to get better. It was all about taking control. The site was for children, because most of these sites are, it seems, and talked about the 'stammer monster' which is crafty and wants you to fight him because he knows he'll win – he thrives on taking away your power and humiliating you. But like all bullies he has a weakness – he's secretly terrified that one day you will find out that he needs to be fed fear in order to exist. And that fear is only in your head.

I'd sat there, looking at the screen with her while Masha flicked through a magazine on black and white magic, running her finger down all the adverts from witches and wizards hawking their various spells. Fear. Fear is only in your head. Only? The head is an important place. But thinking about the stammer monster as being secretly terrified of me helped. I concentrate on that thought, over and over again. And it's working.

'Oh my God, are you crazy, Dieter is to die for, just to die for. How can you like Thomas? I'm going to orgasm as soon as Dieter comes on stage! Literally, I'm going to come as he comes on!' Two girls have sat down behind us and are giggling and squealing together as they settle down. Olessya grins at me and

Masha's clapping again and singing, 'The Night Is Yours – The Night Is Mine'. The hall's filling up with people who love them like we do. I suddenly feel a part of them, like a bee in a hive, part of a happy, humming community. It makes me feel invisible, like everyone else here in the hall, looking up to the stage, waiting for the curtains to open. I have a sudden blinding flash of recollection of me and Masha up on the stage in SNIP at Anokhin's conferences. That's all in the past though. I won't think of that.

The hall darkens and everyone screams. Masha screams and I laugh and scream too. The music starts thumping so loud and so deep that I feel it deep down inside of me, like a heartbeat. And then we hear the opening bars of 'You're My heart, You're My Soul' and everyone screams even louder and stands up together in a sort of fanatical ecstasy. I'm so happy! I don't think I've ever been so happy in my whole life! Everyone's waving their arms and cheering in a frenzy of excitement and love, waiting for them, and then, there they are! Right in front of us! Walking on stage with the cone spotlights following them and they take the microphones, smiling and clapping and then like some miracle from Heaven they start singing the song we know so well, the song the whole of Russia knows better than our own national anthem and I feel like I'm bursting with joy. *You're my heart you're my soul ... deep in my heart there's a fire ... I'm dying in emotion, it's my world in fantasy, I'm living in my, living in my dreams ...* Girls are rushing past me to get to the stage and give them bouquets of flowers and they're saying *spasibo* in Russian, which makes everyone scream even more, and then they start singing 'You Can Win If You Want', and Masha grabs my hand with hers and lifts them up high, waving them from side to side. We're here, we did it, we're happy! I sing along at the top of my voice, like everyone else in the whole hall is singing along: *I'll be holding you forever, stay with me together.*

> 'I ask you to forgive me for not fulfilling the hopes of those people who believed that we would be able to jump from the grey, stagnating, totalitarian past into a bright, rich and civilized future in one fell swoop.'
>
> Boris Yeltsin's resignation speech, 1999

## Age 49
## August 1999

### We try to stop drinking

We decided in the end not to publish the book in Russia. We haven't been giving interviews to the press, but that doesn't stop them printing mean and hurtful articles in our new tabloid press, based on gossip and lies. Times have changed so much in the ten years since we appeared on *Vzglyad*. That kind presenter, Vlad Listyev, was shot dead in his stairwell four years ago. Who knows why people are being assassinated everywhere nowadays? Usually because of money, I suppose. Masha wanted to go to his funeral but we didn't in the end, of course. I didn't want to be among people any more. There's no one as loyal and loving and kind as a Russian who *knows* you like Aunty Nadya, Baba Iskra, Slava, Olessya, Little Lyuda and Sunny Nina ... But if you're Together you can't be loved for you alone, you're a Mashdash–Mishmash.

And if they *don't* know you, they may pity you, but not for long. The mood has changed here and the sheep have turned into wolves. Everyone out for their own. So much for Communism.

Money. We've got more money than we can count. That's what Masha wrote the book for. But all I wanted from our story is to show Healthy readers that Defectives are people too. Because what I've learnt is that if you don't know one, you can't really understand one, so I want readers to know us.

We can give bribes to members of staff to get us vodka now. Bribes big enough to make the risk worth their while. It's not good, not good at all. We've been drinking almost every day. A litre. Sometimes two, if I can get it down quick enough not to pass out. But I know now that the only way to take back control from Masha is to take control of the drinking.

It was after the Modern Talking concert that we decided to stop. We'd woken up the next morning needing a bottle and I'd said, 'Listen, Masha. We're not going down to find someone to get us vodka. We can be happy without it. We can do so many things if we're not shaking from a hangover or the White Fever. We have our life ahead of us.'

To my surprise she nodded and said, 'Let's try.'

Everyone wanted to help us. Aunty Nadya, Olessya, Joolka. But it's like being madly in love – all you can think about every minute of the day is the bottle. It makes your heart race, it beckons you. You need it so badly it sometimes feels like life's not worthwhile without it. We never knew it would be this hard.

'I'm proud of you.' We're sitting in Olessya's little room, on her armchair. We bought it for her out of our savings. That was Masha's idea. 'I'm not crippling myself on that hard wooden chair of yours any more,' she'd said, with a sniff. 'I'm used to a bit of comfort, I am.' But we both knew she wanted an excuse to do something nice for Olessya. Things are changing with Masha, slowly but surely. All we need to do now is to stop drinking.

'I know it's hard,' Olessya goes on. 'They say it's much harder for women alcoholics to give up than men. But you can do it. I know you can. So is this doctor good?'

We shrug. 'I don't know much about her,' I say. 'She called up Zlata Igorovna and said she was a n-narcologist' (the stammer monster fears *me*) 'and had a new method of curing alcoholism and that it was one hundred per cent guaranteed and free. She said she wanted to help us.'

Masha sucks on her teeth and raps her fingers on the arm of the chair. 'Everyone's just sooo sweet,' she says tightly. 'Like Edouard.'

She's remembering the last narcologist who promised to cure us: Edouard. He came all the way from Omsk and sewed ampules into our arms containing a chemical that would react with alcohol in our blood and kill us. Getting 'sewn up' is a common enough cure, but it didn't work on us. Neither did the hypnotist, or the *koldoon* sorcerer who came to put a magic spell on us. Masha found him. Masha loves reading about all the witches and extrasensories there are now, but I was cynical, even though Joolka says they employ them as members of staff in polyclinics nowadays.

But the ampules didn't stop us drinking. We held out for a month of White Fever – throwing up, shaking all over, sweating, seizures, our heads filled with monsters – until even death seemed preferable, so we got a bottle and drank. And we woke up the next morning alive and kicking. And then Edouard wrote an 'exposé' in the newspapers all about how we'd fallen off the wagon. About how degraded we were. A hopeless case.

'He seemed so nice …' I say.

'Your Timur seemed nice too …' says Masha.

'It was you who told him where we'd hidden the cash.'

'It was you who invited him up for vodka.'

'That was us. Not me, Masha. *Us.*'

She sniffs and looks out of the window. 'Can't trust anyone in this world. They're all out to grab money now, in whatever way they can.' I still miss Timur. I still find it hard to believe he'd do that – steal our thousand dollars we kept hidden in a tea caddy – after he got us dead drunk. And then he quit his job. We never reported it. What's the point? And of course we never saw him again.

So when Zlata Igorovna walked in yesterday to tell us she was sending the narcologist to us this afternoon because she was fed up with her Home being notorious for harbouring the world's only conjoined drunks, we agreed.

'So tell us what's happening out there, Olesskinka,' asks Masha, waving at the window, 'in the land of the living.' Olessya picks up her pile of newspapers and opens it at an article she's been reading. She reads newspapers every day and listens to the news programmes on her radio, but we just let it all pass us by. We can't change anything out there.

'How's our glorious drunken President then?' asks Masha. 'What a great example he is to us all. Has he fallen off any more bridges lately?'

'*Pozor!* Russia's a great country, troubled but great. The greatest country in the world and yet, after Lenin, we had that tyrant Stalin, then the peasant Khrushchev who everyone laughed at after the shoe-throwing incident, then that old stuffed goose Brezhnev, another laughing stock, then a series of Party faithfuls on their deathbeds, and then Gorbachev, who was so weak he let the Soviet Union slip through his fingers like mushy peas. And now we have Yeltsin, a drunken buffoon.'

'*Ei*, calm down!' Masha laughs. 'Stalin was The Man. All we need is another Stalin.'

'You were tortured under Stalin,' says Olessya coldly.

'And look how well we turned out! Cheer up. I only asked what's happening. *Gospodi!*'

'Well, OK, in a nutshell,' she rustles the newspapers again, 'since you ask, all Russia's gas and oil and wealth has been sold off for kopecks to the New Russian gangster businessmen for paltry bribes to the government. In fact, everything's being sold off: factories, airlines, steel plants, land. It's not very different to the Red Army looting the palaces after the revolution. We've gone from so-called altruistic Socialism with the distant goal of Communism, to dog eats dog. The country is being torn apart and the chunkiest, meatiest bits go to the most savage.' She pauses for breath and we stare at her in surprise.

'Um … Altruism?' asks Masha, not really understanding much Olessya's said. I'm not sure I do either. 'What's that?'

'It means selfless concern for the wellbeing of others. Communism. That was what it was all supposed to be about, wasn't it? But it got corrupted. That's why Sunny Nina, Little Lyuda and Big Boris died. That's why I'm in here with my one hundred per cent diploma doing nothing except sitting by the gates looking at the world go by. That's why Dasha with *her* one hundred per cent diploma is drinking herself to death. That's why you, Masha, with your energy and drive and spirit, are sitting in a room all day playing war games. It's because we're arrogant, we Russians are. We're a great people, a cultured people, I truly believe we're the best people in the world, but we're fatally flawed by our own pride and arrogance. Do you know what arrogance is? It's fear of thinking others are better than you. It's vulnerability. We wanted to be the best, we wanted our country to be the best of all possible worlds, so we desperately hid our flaws. Like us. The Defectives!'

'Wow, calm down, Olesskinka,' says Masha, waving her arms. We know Olessya gets political, but she seems particularly fired up this morning.

'I won't calm down! It's such a *waste*. Such a *waste* of a great people. We should be led by a woman, not by men with all their screwed-up patriarchal weaknesses. Why did Gorbachev never tell us about Chernobyl and let everyone get irradiated? All those children splashing in puddles under the invisible radioactive cloud? Everyone in the world knew, except us. Why didn't we know about the Novocherkassk riots either? We were living there, for God's sake. Now it's in the history books. The biggest riot in Soviet history, and did we know anything about it? No. And Chikatilo, the mass murderer who killed fifty-two children, *children*, down in the Novocherksassk region. He was happily killing away for fifteen years, while we were there. And the reason he could keep on murdering then was because no one was told. No one. Those mothers let their children wander around alone because they weren't told, because having a mass murderer in your midst would have been a flaw, and Russia. Does. Not. Like. Flaws.' She emphasizes each word with a thump on the side of her wheelchair, and then balls her fists up and looks down at her legs.

We can hear the black and white crows of Moscow cawing outside in the first snow squalls of winter. Cologne had birds that chirped in the branches of the cherry trees, tiny little songbirds. All we have in Moscow is crows. Slava said they had sparrows in his village, and cuckoos.

'So … anyway, Olesskinka, how's Garrick doing?' asks Masha, trying to change the subject. 'We haven't seen him around much recently. Is your cockerel up and running?'

'Garrick died,' she says flatly, and opens the newspaper again. 'Didn't you hear? Seems he had lymphoma but they told him it was flu. Until he died. Now it turns out it was lymphoma.'

## Meeting the narcologist

'Fuck. Poor Olessya. I need a fag,' says Masha when we get back to our room.

'You put them in the tea caddy. Here. Have one quickly and then spray that antiperspirant around.'

She digs out the hidden packet, covered in tea leaves, shakes it, and we go out on to the balcony, looking down at the early snow powdering the grounds.

'Why was she sounding off about this Mother Russia stuff then? What was all that about?'

'She's angry. Angry that Garrick's gone and that they lied to him. *Mensha znaesh*.'

Masha leans on the balcony while she sucks on her cigarette. She throws the butt over the edge and sighs. '*Krepcha speesh.*'

We've just gone back inside and Masha's spraying the antiperspirant over her clothes and then mine when there's a knock on the door and Doctor Lazareva, the narcologist, comes in. She holds her hand out with a big smile.

'So, it's great to meet you at last. I mean, it's been hard to get to you, to be honest. Like trying to get through to the Kremlin! My name's Ksyenia, but you can call me Kisska. That's what my friends call me.'

She has short blonde hair and a sweet smile. She doesn't seem too put out by the way we look and we both like her immediately. We all sit down and chat for a bit about the Sixth and her Narcology Centre in Moscow. She says she'll give us after-care, which is vital apparently, and we're all nodding and happy until she digs down into her nice leather bag and brings out a bottle of vodka.

'Yes, so this might seem a bit odd, but I've brought vodka.'

'Vodka?' I frown.

Masha starts bouncing up and down. 'That's the sort of narcologist I like!'

'Well,' she says, 'in our practice we like to see how you react to it, you know, and then we can work on your particular case. So let's all have a bit, shall we?' She puts the bottle down on the table. It's a whole litre.

'I don't th-th-ink …' I say, 'I don't th-th-ink that sounds like a g-good idea …'

'You have to trust me, Dasha,' she says, leaning forward. 'You really do have to trust me, if I'm to help you.'

She's brought glasses too. Tumblers. I look at the thick, sickly fluid when she hands it to me with an encouraging nod.

'I feel nauseous, Kisska, at the very thought,' I say to her. 'I hate vodka.'

'Yes, yes, interesting. And you, Masha?'

'Well, what can I do, Kissinka? She's been drinking since she was fourteen … what can I do?'

'Drink up then, Dasha.' She pulls a tape recorder out of her bag. 'I'll need to record what you say. Meanwhile, Masha, why don't you tell me a bit more about your life? Do you have the same thoughts? Do you have identical dreams at night? What's it like to be together? Psychology is all-important when curing alcoholism.'

I look at the glass, then look away. I'm not going to drink it. I look at it again. But I want to drink it. It's calling to me. No I won't, I don't *want* to drink it. If I start drinking I can't stop. She's still holding the tumbler out to me with her nice, encouraging smile. She's a doctor. Trust her. Trust Authority. No. No! But I *need* to drink it. I *have* to drink it.

I drink it.

## Zlata Igorovna brings us today's news – all about us

We're standing with the fridge door open, wondering what to have for a snack when the door bursts open and Zlata hurls herself at us, waving a newspaper.

'Have you seen this? Have you?' She pushes it into Masha's face.

'*Sluts, Drunkards, Losers – Degraded Duo!* – that's just the title of the article. Two full pages. It was that little bitch Lazareva, she was a journalist masquerading as a doctor, writing for that trashy rag *Moskovskii Novostii. Pozor!* You've brought shame on us with your stupid drunken gossip!'

We shrink back into the open fridge, knocking over a bowl of borscht which empties on to the floor in a spreading deep-red puddle at our feet. We don't move.

'You're disgusting, the two of you, that's what you are, disgusting! How *dare* you slander the Sixth! How dare you! That woman was a slimy tabloid hack and you couldn't see it? You took her vodka and then you vomit up this … this … filth?' She shakes the newspaper in our faces again. 'You will pay for this. Oh by God, you will pay for this!' Her eyes are flashing as she towers over us, almost trembling with rage, spitting out the words in our faces as we cringe away from her, bewildered by her rage. Then she throws the newspaper on to the floor at our feet and stalks out, slamming the door behind her.

We stand there panting for a bit, our hearts racing, not understanding what's going on, then I turn, quietly close the fridge door and lean down to pick the newspaper out of the spilt borscht. It's sodden and red but still legible.

We walk over to the sofa and open it. The front page has a photo of us lying on the floor, dead drunk, Masha's laughing and I'm almost unconscious. I don't remember anything of the interview after I started drinking.

*The Rise and Fall of Our Famous Conjoined Twins, Masha and Dasha!*

*Despised by Everyone!*

*Dasha orgasms with men paid for sex while Masha weeps into her pillow!*

What? What did Masha say to her? What on *earth* did she say?
I read on.

*Dasha was too drunk to talk. In a recorded interview, it was poor Masha who, with tears in her eyes, told me of her terrible life. They fear journalists will betray their trust, but Masha opened up with her most treasured secrets to your MN reporter. Their mother fled from them at birth and spent the next two years in a Madhouse, while their tortured father begged the doctors to care for his little girls. He had no choice but to leave them – for he was the personal chauffeur of Stalin's henchman Lavrenti Beria.*

Neither of us speak. I wipe some beetroot off the next paragraph.

*The weak, degenerate Dasha began drinking at the age of fourteen in their school in Novocherkassk where they were bullied constantly by the cruel, taunting pupils and isolated by uncaring teachers. There was nothing Masha could do to stop Dasha – she could only try and support her disgraced, unpopular sister who thought of nothing but sex and where to get the next drink.*

I blink, not quite believing my eyes.

*One boy, Slava, tried to sleep with her for a bet. The other boys brought in townspeople to look at them for the price of a bottle of vodka.*

'What the *fuck?!*' exclaims Masha, making me jump. 'She lied to us! That two-faced bitch lied to us!'

I stare at her with my mouth open. 'Yes,' I say. 'And *you* fucking lied to *her*, didn't you?' Masha looks at me, startled, and I see an odd flicker of fear. How could I swear at her? I never swear at her. But I feel hard with horror. Everyone will be reading this. The children and teachers from the school, Valentina Alexandrovna, everyone in SNIP who knew us. Everyone.

I look back at the article.

*Strong, serious Masha did everything in her power to save her sister, but now she realizes it is far too late to save either of them. Dasha has an endless supply of sexual partners and she orgasms in an ecstasy of quick lust, while Masha buries her head in shame in the pillow.*

My hands are trembling.

*'It disgusts me,' says Masha. 'I've never been attracted to men. I should have been born a boy.' Yet with one vagina she is subjected to sex with hobos who Dasha pays for, from the profits of their autobiography. Men who Masha despises and who pass on the clap. Yet incredibly, she doesn't despise her depraved sister. Blood is thicker than water. And theirs, after all, is shared ...*

I grab the newspaper then and crumple it up into a tight ball, refusing to read any more. The soup trickles through my fingers as I squeeze it, staining my hand red. I feel a hard rock of resentment rising up inside me, of anger and strangely – of a new-found power. I keep the balled-up newspaper in my hand, lift my fist up into the air and look slowly across at Masha. Her head is down and she won't look back at me.

'She lied ...' she says weakly, in a small voice, still with her head down. 'I thought she was a doctor ...'

'Of course I am an absolute, pure democrat. But you know the problem? It's not even a problem, it's a real tragedy. The thing is that I am the only one, there just aren't any others in the world … After the death of Mahatma Gandhi there's nobody to talk to.'

Vladimir Putin, President of Russia, 1999–
(in response to a *Spiegel* journalist who
asked if he considered himself a democrat)

## Age 50
## 6 January 2000

### Our fiftieth birthday

Everything that happens in life is a stepping stone to success. That's what Olessya keeps telling us. After that article, everything changed. Everything. I was never, ever going to drink again. Just like when I was six and decided I was never, ever going to fight back. And I was going to take control of my Masha. That article is online now, word for word. If anyone wants to research Masha and Dasha Krivoshlyapova, they get taken to that link. If they look for an image of Masha and Dasha

Krivoshlyapova, they get taken to the photo on the front page. And whenever I want, desperately, to drink, I go to that link too: a link that will be there for ten years, twenty years, a hundred years.

It's ironic really. Kisska Lazareva, star journalist for *Moskovskii Novostii*, did for us what no real narcologist had succeeded in doing. She stopped us drinking and she made me strong enough to stand up to Masha.

I wasn't too angry with Kisska. She was only doing her job. You've got to admire her in a way for her persistence and for fooling Zlata. And it was all recorded, word for word, on her tape recorder. She didn't make anything up. I'm at fault too. If I hadn't been drunk, I wouldn't have let Masha say all that. Slandering everyone we've ever known. Slandering me. But I mind that Masha lied to Lazareva about our mother abandoning us and going mad. I mind that she lied about the teachers. And I mind that she lied about Slava. His mother may still be alive. But then, in Masha's mind, it wasn't lying. It's what Johann called her 'biological neuro-disorder'. So I forgave her too in the end. But I never forgave myself. I never drank again. And I never let her force me to drink again. I finally found the strength I needed to break our addiction.

'Fifty years old! Fifty! We're in the *Guinness Book of Records*, look, look, here we are!' Masha's laughing and dancing about holding the glossy silver book that Joolka has given us for our birthday. 'Have you got all the food? Did you make your English salads?' Masha's still jumping up and down like a seven-year-old and I laugh. We've only got Aunty Nadya, Olessya and Joolka coming to our celebration. But that's enough. Those three are our trusted friends. Joolka got us medication, which really helps with the White Fever. She got us pills too, which make you so sick if you do go back to alcohol that you never want to do it again. It was hard. It *is* hard. But now we're sober.

'So what do you think of your new President?' Joolka says, pulling a bottle of children's non-alcoholic champagne from her bag. 'That was a turn up for the books, wasn't it?'

Masha grabs a shrimp and pops it into her mouth without peeling it. 'Putin? He looks like Tintin,' she says and spits the shell into her hand. 'What we need is a Stalin, not a Tintin-Putin. He won't last long.' She grabs the *Guinness Book of Records* again. 'Oldest living conjoined twins. Older than those Americans, Ronnie and Donnie, our betrothed. Haha! Aunty Nadya! Aunty Nadya!' Masha jumps up as Aunty Nadya walks in with two heavy bags bulging with food.

'Calm down, calm down, you'll knock me over. Well, where's the table? Let's get these pies and salads all laid out. Get away from me, Masha. Get away this minute!'

The door pushes open and Olessya comes in, holding a bunch of big ox-eye daisies.

'Where did you get those, Olesskinka?' asks Masha, laughing. 'Been rummaging in the hedgerows?'

'*Molchee!* These cost me my pension, these did!'

'Do stop bobbing about like a rubber ball, Masha, and put those flowers in a vase,' says Aunty Nadya crossly. 'Come along, *davai, davai!*'

Masha obediently grabs the flowers and sticks one in her hair. Masha likes being told what to do. All the women she respected and liked were strong: Mummy, Lydia Mikhailovna, Aunty Nadya and even Baba Iskra, who brooks no argument at all. And she despised those who were weak, like Mother and me. So now I'm becoming strong too. It's easier than I thought, because when I really stand up to her, her *chortik* flickers out. Just like the stammer monster.

Ten minutes later, the five of us are seated around the table with a feast of caviar, sliced sturgeon, and *stolichni* salad. Our Modern Talking tape is thumping out the beat of 'You Can Win If You Want!' on our cassette player and

Joolka's bought a cake with five blue candles on it. One for each decade.

'Shall I light them twice, for each of you to blow out separately?' she asks.

'No,' we say together. 'We'll blow them out at the same time.'

'You'll have to make a wish each, though,' she says.

'I know what I want,' I say. 'But it won't come true if I say it aloud.'

I want to turn the tide. I don't want to suffer from Masha's whims any more. I want to be in control. I want us both to realize that she's not always right. She's tough, but I'm wise. We can work together to be happy together. Happier than we've ever been. I deserve a life too.

'I've got a million wishes – I don't know where to start,' laughs Masha.

'We haven't got time for all of those! Give us one. A toast to your wish.' Joolka raises her glass.

'To the next fifty years!' says Masha, raising hers. I roll my eyes and we all laugh again.

When we've finally finished and everyone's leaving, Joolka turns at the door.

'Ooh, I almost forgot, I've got something here. I keep meaning to give it to you, but I haven't seen you in ages.'

It's been two months since she last came because she's getting ready to move back to England. The day she told us she was leaving Russia, she came with all three of the children. Anya went straight to our dressing table, took my lipstick out of the drawer and started painting her face. Sasha, who's twelve now, asked if we had any cheese balls (which she loves as much as Masha does) and sat with a can of them in front of the computer playing games with Masha. Both of them were popping them into their mouths one by one and shrieking at the video. Two children. And Bobik, who's six, crawled into my lap and said he didn't want to go to

England because they didn't have the Noddy cartoons in Russian there. I don't know who Noddy is, but it made me sad. Because I didn't want him to go to England either. I didn't want any of them to leave. It was like they were family and they were leaving me.

That's OK, though. I'm used to loss. Life goes on.

'It's just that things are getting so dangerous here,' Joolka had said, folding her legs up on the armchair and taking Bobik back. 'I sent Sasha out a month ago, after she got back from school, for some sweets from the local *bootka* kiosk up the road, and while she was out this big black jeep pulled up into our courtyard and gunned down two of our neighbours who were walking across our courtyard. By the time Sasha came back with her gummy bears it had been cordoned off by the militia and she couldn't get into the flat. She was just, you know, wandering up and down the street in the dark, not knowing what to do, until I went out and found her. And there are all these car bombings and the shootings in restaurants … it's, it's like you never know in Moscow, nowadays, when you're going to get caught up in the crossfire. So with these three' – she gestured round at the children – 'we need to go.'

I didn't say anything. Neither did Masha. We just kissed all the children on the tops of their heads.

She's standing at the door now, rummaging in her bag.

'Yes,' she goes on, 'sorry I haven't been able to visit for so long, but here we are, I've got something. You know the *Sunday Times Magazine* want me to do another feature on you – a where-are-they-now type thing? Well I was going through my old documents folder, and I found this envelope that Anna Yefimovna, the doctor from the Paediatric Institute, had given to me. I didn't take much notice at the time, it's only a photo of people in white coats, but then I looked on the back and it says that it's a photo of your two researchers, you know, the scientists who carried out all the experiments. Not a very cheery birthday present, I know, but I thought you'd like to have it since I'm leaving soon.' She puts the photo down on the table. 'Here we are, T. T. Alexeyeva and A. P. Kryuchkova. 'I've got some other stuff you might like too …' She goes back to rifling through her bag.

'*Foo!*' spits Masha, not looking at it. 'May they both rot in hell.'

I pick up the photo and look at it. They're standing side by side, shoulder to shoulder in their white lab coats and caps, smiling out at the camera. Two colleagues, two friends. Doctor Alexeyeva on the right, and on the left …

Anna Petrovna Kryuchkova.

Mummy.

**'Mummy'**

I feel cold as I walk back to our room holding the photo. The photo of the two scientists who 'observed' conjoined twins in a laboratory fifty years ago. I didn't say anything when I picked it up. Nothing at all. I didn't tell Joolka, or Masha.

I put it down on the bedside table and we go to clean our teeth and wash our nappy. Masha's chattering on as we get into bed, saying that Aunty Nadya should go to a doctor with that limp of hers, then she tucks the *Guinness Book of Records* under her pillow. We lie in silence in the dark for a while.

'What's wrong?' she says, after a bit.

'It's that photo.'

'What about that photo?'

'The one of those two scientists, the two scientists who studied us.'

'Yes?'

'One of them was Mummy.'

'Mummy?'

'Yes. Mummy.'

She doesn't say anything. She's thinking.

'No, it wasn't. Mummy wouldn't have done that to us.'

'It was. It said A. P. Kryuchkova. Anna Petrovna. Mummy. It said so on the back. And it's her in the photo.'

I'm waiting for her to jump up and start swearing, but she doesn't. She just lies quiet at the other end of the bed, in the darkness.

Then she says in a whisper, 'Mummy?'

'Yes,' I say, and I can feel this slow pain coming across to me from her, so I add quickly, 'But she was only doing her job. I think she loved us, Masha. I do think she loved us. How could we have loved her so much if she didn't love us back?'

There's still a dark silence.

'She sang us *bye-oo bye-ooshki bye-oo*, remember? Every night,' I go on. 'She kissed us. She kissed us, Masha. No one else in there did that.'

We lie there in the darkness of our room, in our big bed. I know she wants to cry. I move over a bit and reach for her hand. Like we did in the cot when I was scared of the cockroaches.

And then she does.

## Age 53
## 2 April 2003

### Proving we're still Together for the Medical Commission

I reach for one of the lipsticks in the drawer of our dresser and lean forward towards the mirror, pouting.

'Who're you hoping to meet down there – Prince William of England?'

'Just taking a bit of pride in my appearance, Masha, nothing wrong with that.'

'Here, I'll do it, you're getting it all over the place.' She takes the lipstick from me and frowns, sticking her tongue out as she applies it carefully. 'Might as well do me too. Don't want to look like the ugly sister, and a bit of war paint never hurt anyone.'

I paint her lips, then she picks up the comb and runs it through my hair. When she's finished I comb her hair for her and we walk over to the sofa to put our boots on.

We never talked about Mummy again. What's the point? She's still Mummy to us. I don't regret that we found out. Knowledge is power, and I don't blame her either. She was doing her job.

'Why do we have to go down now, Dasha? The Medical Commission's not even starting for half an hour …' whines Masha.

'You know that the later we leave it, the longer we'll have to stand in line.'

'Can't believe we have to go through this every year to prove we're still Together so we can get our pension – as if we're going to magically drift apart or something …'

'Chance would be a fine thing. Right, got everything? Passports?'

'Yes, yes, *gospodi*, it's like having God Almighty and the Holy Trinity at my side nowadays … *lya lya topolya* …' She flaps her thumb and forefingers at me like a quacking beak.

'God Almighty is *part* of the Holy Trinity,' I say, picking up my crutch. She rolls her eyes to the ceiling. 'Come on,' I say. '*Davai, davai*.'

'*Da-oosh*,' says Masha with a little salute. 'When the Komsomol says You Must, the People say We Will.' I laugh. Masha's funny.

We tap down the empty corridor with its shiny dark green walls and brown linoleum floor, turn the corner, down another empty corridor, two more corners and then take the lift.

The queue's already halfway across the entrance hall. I don't know why reception halls are so big in these Homes, they're like aquariums, lined with big plants and mirrors. We used to have the Politburo up on the wall and now we've got Putin, a framed portrait in pride of place with two half-furled Russian flags on either side, like wings. There's a curved text above his head, a bit like a halo now I come to look at it, one of his inspiring quotes probably, but I've never read it. We saw his latest one, in a headline in *Izvestia – Russia needs a strong state power, and Russia will have a strong state power.* Our avenging angel. Masha's starting to like him now. She says he's becoming more like Stalin day by day. As if that's a good thing … Everyone else is starting to like him more too. He's someone tough. Someone for us to be proud of. Well, apart from Olessya, that is. Not after the Kursk submarine tragedy when all those young sailors died and Putin did what every Russian leader does – Olessya says – he lied. Because an explosion on board a submarine was another flaw. And it seems Putin doesn't like flaws either. None of them do. I look around for her, but she's not here yet.

'We'll be standing in this line for an hour at least,' says an elderly lady with two sticks who's just joined the queue behind us. She sighs. 'You'd think since they're assessing invalids they'd give us appointments, wouldn't you? Or at least give us chairs, not make us stand like this.'

'Why should they, *babulya*?' says Masha. 'They've got nice comfy chairs behind that desk in the assessment room, haven't they?'

'We should get up a petition or something.'

'Our friend Olessya tried that,' says Masha cheerfully. 'It was put in the trash bin. The Administration don't listen to the ignorant masses. Never have. Never will.'

'Well, well, no use poisoning the mind by dwelling on injustice, is there,' she goes on. 'There's enough people out there trying to poison our lives without us making it worse for ourselves. Better just to accept.'

I nod at her and smile. Joolka used to say that what she loved most about Russia was how we didn't have trite, English conversations. She said you couldn't take a ten-minute taxi ride without the driver giving you a treatise on politics, love and religion.

The low hum of chatter in the hall falls suddenly silent as Zlata Igorovna sweeps through to her office. After Timur stole our money, we decided to keep all our dollars in the safe in the Administration offices. We weren't going to keep it in a bank. Not after the rouble collapsed a few years ago under Yeltsin and wiped out everyone's savings like a tsunami. Now all our money's tucked away in a dark safe. Joolka wanted us to make a will leaving Aunty Nadya all our money if we died, because otherwise it might go to our brothers, but instead Zlata persuaded us to sign a document saying it would go to the Sixth. Zlata is very persuasive … and me and Masha thought she might be nicer to us. Some hope.

'*Da, da*,' says the babushka behind us. 'No use torturing yourself with regrets, is there … for wasted years …'

'*Gospodi*, that's all we need right now, *babulya*,' says Masha, laughing. 'Good old Ostrovsky's "Man's Dearest Possession is Life" – give us a break!' I laugh too, remembering the essay she refused to write in school. Masha knew how to stand up for herself, all right. Like the time she started giving the Sanity Commission in the Twentieth a lecture about how clever I was. Or when she stood up to the crowds in the zoo while I was cowering behind her.

'All my life, all my strength …' Masha proclaims, holding one arm out like an actor, 'has been given to the finest cause in the world …'

'The liberation of Mankind!' we all chime together and laugh. We're allowed to make fun of the Soviets now.

'Well, well, we mustn't mock,' says the old lady, smiling but shaking her head. 'It was a fine idea. A grand idea. We were happy back then. We all need to believe in something.'

'I believe in Masha,' says Masha, then glances across at me. 'And Dasha.'

'Ah yes, it must be nice to be you two,' the woman goes on.

'Nice?' says Masha.

'Yes, I was orphaned in the War and then there weren't enough men to go round so I've been on my own all my life. And do you know what I miss most?'

'Don't tell us, *babulya*, I'll blush,' laughs Masha, clapping her hands over my ears.

The babushka laughs too. 'No, no, not that, you never miss what you've never had. No, I miss human contact. Just a hand on my shoulder, a little kiss on my cheek. Tenderness … You two are sweet together. You always have your arms around each other.'

'*Ei*, I'd fall tit over arse if I didn't hold on to her! But I'll give you a hug any day, *babulya* – if you'll give me a dollar.'

'*Aaakh*, I've no dollars, *meelinkaya*. I've a few kopecks and I wouldn't buy hugs with them.' She shifts painfully on her sticks.

'Why don't you go over and sit on that chair,' says Masha. 'It's stupid you have to stand up, we'll keep your place.'

'No, you fucking won't!' A man with one leg standing behind her pushes into our conversation. 'We'd all go and fucking sit down if we wanted! Then we'd all lose our fucking places, wouldn't we?' He glares at the old woman.

'That's all right, *meelinki*,' she says soothingly to him. 'I'm fine standing. We're all fine.'

But Masha's *chortik* rises up dark and flashing behind her eyes and she pushes angrily towards him. 'Well, you're a great example of *yobinny* Mankind, aren't you? Wonderful member of the human race, you are. When you need us to hold your place because you need a pee, I'll make sure not to.' He's twice our size.

'No, Mashinka!' I grab the back of her collar and pull her away sharply. She looks round at me, seething. 'Stop!' I say. 'You don't need to get into a brawl with some bullying idiot like him.' The old lady moves between him and us, making hushing sounds.

'Come on,' I say, 'this queue's going faster than I thought. We'll be in soon.'

The last time I saw Masha's *chortik* was soon after that article in *Moskovskii Novostii*. She'd wanted vodka. We'd been sitting in our room, staring at the walls. Both of us horribly, desperately, wanting vodka.

'I'm going downstairs,' she'd said finally with a crack in her voice. 'I'm going to find someone to get us a bottle.'

She went to stand but I refused.

'Get up.' She looked at me and I saw it, I saw it there, her *chortik*, dancing mockingly behind her eyes, the *chortik* that needs to be fed fear in order to exist. 'Get the fuck *up*,' she said.

'*Nyet*.' I didn't move.

'Get the fuck *up!*' She'd pulled me then, with all her body, but I wouldn't follow her. She hauled me right off the bed and I fell, flopping on to the floor, still refusing to move with her. And then she leant over me and grabbed my hair, trying to haul me up into an upright position. 'Oh yes you will fucking get up, you will, you will!' I shoved her away then, with all the strength I had, and pulled myself back on to the bed. Then I leaned over and before she knew what was happening, I put my hands around her throat and looked into her eyes. I looked right at her stupid damn *chortik*, dancing around back there, stabbing me with its evil little electric shocks and I said, '*Nyet*.' I closed my fingers around her neck, I'm stronger than her, we both know I'm stronger, and I started choking the life out of her. And then I saw the fear in her own eyes, a silver sphere which popped, and I swear I heard it burst as her *chortik* just shrivelled and shrank. It was at the moment we both knew I'd won. Finally.

And from then on, we found our balance. We found each other. I think I found the Masha who'd always been there, waiting to be told what to do. The Masha who never wanted to be a cruel, psychopathic bully but who wanted to be held in check by a strict 'parent'. And to be loved.

And as for me, I've fought day by day, month by month over the last three years to be strong, not weak. I've fought for her, because I know it's best for her, for both of us. I'd realized that, like a mother, I'd spoilt her, I'd loved her too much, and I'd created an out-of-control monster who I feared.

Until now.

'So anyway, what I meant,' goes on the old lady as if nothing has happened, 'is that you two must never get lonely.'

Lonely? I consider that for a moment. No, she's wrong. I've been lonely with Masha. I think back to the time when she wouldn't let Slava come and visit us in the Twentieth. And I was lonely after he died. I feel that, despite being Together with Masha, I've sometimes been the loneliest person in the world.

'Although I suppose we all need solitude?' she goes on. 'I've had enough solitude for ten lifetimes, but perhaps, yes, we all need solitude?'

'She gets solitude, all right,' says Masha, grinning. 'She puts those new cushioned earphones on and she's off into her world of lovey dovey *lya lya*. She might as well be Lenin in Exile for all she cares about me.'

We all laugh.

When it's finally our turn to go into the Medical Commission room, the doctor glances up at us. She's the same one we've had for the past twelve years in the Sixth.

'Still together are we, girls?' she says cheerily.

'Still together,' we both say at the same time, smiling.

'Off you go then.'

And she ticks her box.

## 13 April 2003

### We meet Father Alexander and Masha gets a pain in her side

'She needs banana skins,' says Masha, cocking her head on one side and looking at the little lemon tree she's just placed carefully out on the balcony. 'That's what Baba Iskra said. She said banana skins have potassium.'

'Who's going to get us bananas in April?'

'They must sell them somewhere. In one of those *superskii* supermarkets.' She takes out a handkerchief and starts wiping the leaves, one by one, making them gleam in the spring sunlight.

'Why's it got to be outside? Can't we have it inside? It looks pretty on our table with those little white flowers.'

'She needs direct sunlight. Baba Iskra says that sunlight through a window hasn't got all the healing properties. She's not getting her vitamin D.'

I laugh. 'Do you remember when you got us all to play truant in school because we weren't getting our vitamin D? And everyone followed you out like a flock of sheep! Do you?'

'Course I do. Valentina Alexandrovna sat right down there on that log, didn't she, and we had our lesson in the sunshine.'

'You were throwing pears at us. Or was it peaches?'

'Pears. Juicy *nyelzya* pears.'

'So, wait, you're not leaving your Lyuba out all night, are you?'

'Of course not.' She digs her fingers into the earth of the pot and gently stirs it about. 'She needs to be acclimatized, bit by bit. I'll bring her in every night. Plants need nurturing, you have to really care for them. These things take time.' She strokes the leaves again tenderly.

I've never been into plants. Or sewing machines … Masha's funny. She lights up a cigarette and backs up against the wall so she's as far from Lyuba as possible. 'Cigarette smoke kills,' she says softly and puffs carefully into the wind away from the little tree.

'You've never cared about killing *me* with your cigarette smoke,' I say.

She sniffs. 'You don't need nurturing.'

When we go back inside, Nina's trundling in with our supper of fish soup.

'Remember fish soup in the Ped?' I say, once she's gone. 'They brought it in the same bucket as they do here. Except there they slammed the bucket on the floor with that great clanging sound, and here it's on a trolley. And you always wanted the eyes. Remember?'

'Don't know why you're getting all starry-eyed about that place,' says Masha, wincing a bit as she takes her spoon. 'Reminiscing like an old …' She winces again and puts the spoon down.

'Mash, you OK?'

'My side hurts a bit,' she says, squirming to get comfortable.

She never complains about pain, unless it's really bad, so I rub her side for a while.

'Is it your kidney stones again?'

'No … Oof! I feel like something's sitting on me,' she groans. 'I can't breathe.'

I put my bowl down and stack some pillows behind her, but that doesn't seem to help either.

'Let's watch the six o'clock news then,' I say and pick up the remote control. She turns to the TV with a twisted, hurting expression on her face. I hate it when she's in pain. 'I'll call the duty nurse, Mash,' I say, leaning over her for the phone on her side of the bed. Yulia, the nurse picks up, says she's busy and puts the phone down.

'I'll get you painkillers then,' I say. But my mind's racing. What's wrong? Why has she got such a bad pain? Is it serious?

'I'll get them now, Masha, that'll help. Then we'll just go to sleep.' As I get up to open the drawer, she groans, but stands while I reach for them and then obediently pops two of them into her mouth.

Two hours later the pain's worse. It's moved to her back. I've called Yulia about five times but she's not picking up. Masha won't let me get up for more painkillers because it hurts too much. I don't feel her pain anywhere except in my helpless head. Like I felt her pain in the Ped. I want to help her. How can she be hurting this much? My Mashinka, who was once stabbed in the leg by one of the boys in SNIP and who drew the knife out slowly, as if she was taking a spoon out of a bowl of ice cream and said, 'So who's blood is going to mingle with mine now?' You should have seen them run. They ran so fast, they slammed straight into the walls.

'I think … I think you should call Aunty Nadya, Dashinka,' she pants. 'Don't you?'

'Yes. Of course,' I say. I lean over her and pick up the phone again.

'Aunty Nadya? Masha's got a pain in her back, it started out in her side and now it's in her back and she's feeling nauseous.'

'All right, Dasha,' she says. 'Stay calm. Good girl. Can she talk to me to tell me the symptoms?'

'No, she can't, not really, she's in too much pain.'

'That's OK, that's OK. So ask her if her arm hurts?'

'Does your arm hurt, Mashinka?'

'Yes,' she groans in a whisper.

'Right,' says Aunty Nadya. 'I think she might possibly be having a small heart attack. Don't worry, it's only the early signs. She'll be fine. Call the duty nurse immediately.'

Heart attack? I stare at the phone and my own heart contracts.

'I've been calling her,' I say. 'I've been calling her all the time, Aunty Nadya. She said she was busy, and now she's not picking up the phone.'

'Call again. Keep calling and tell her it's urgent. I'll call too.'

I put the phone back on its cradle until I hear the click and then pick it up and dial the medical room's number, closing my eyes tight and willing Yulia to pick up.

'Yes?'

Thank God!

'Yulia! You need to call the ambulance right now. I think Masha might have had a heart attack. Aunty Nadya says so.'

'Nonsense,' says Yulia shortly. 'Give her more painkillers and go back to sleep. I'm all over the place this evening. I'll get round to you later.'

'When?'

'Later. In an hour or two.'

'No! You've got to come now!'

The phone goes dead.

I wait for two hours, watching the minute hand click agonizingly slowly round the clock. Masha keeps moaning quietly. She's lying here in a cold sweat. She's vomited over the pillow and is still squirming in pain. When the two hours is up I call Yulia. No reply. I call Aunty Nadya again. She's the only one who can help us. The only one.

'Can you come, Aunty Nadya? Please? Yulia's not answering, and I can't get up and go to the medical room – Masha's too ill.'

'I can't, Dashinka, I can't. You know they wouldn't let me into the Sixth at night, even if my hair was on fire. Keep trying to get through to them and tell them to call an ambulance immediately. Does Olessya not have a phone? No no, of course she doesn't ... I can't call an ambulance from here, it won't come to you without permission from the Sixth Administration. Don't worry, Dasha. Don't worry. Just keep her comfortable.'

I put the phone down and look at her, she's still panting and sweating and then she vomits again. I use the sheets to wipe it up. I stroke her arm and soothe her. Why will no one come? Why? I keep fingering the cross around my neck. The only thing

I can do now is pray – just pray until Aunty Nadya gets here in the morning.

The cross feels warm in my hand. We were given our two crosses by Father Alexander. He's the Russian Orthodox priest who comes to the Sixth every week. Masha always used to despise God. 'What sort of kind Creator would put something like us down on his earth to be mocked?' But once Father Alexander approached us and started talking in his soft, reassuring voice, we were both drawn to him. And to God, I suppose … We were sitting outside with him in all his long black robes, only the other day, in the garden, on a bench in the warm spring sunshine. The snowdrops were just starting to push through the snow, nudging their pretty little heads out to show us there was life after six months of winter. One of the inmates, an old woman we didn't know, had walked up to him and bowed low while he held out the back of his hand to be kissed. Then she'd looked at us with that typical head-cocked-on-one-side look we know so well, and said, 'What's it like to be Together?'

Masha had rolled her eyes, like she does, in a good-natured way and said, 'What's it like to be separate, *babulya*?' The woman had looked confused. 'How would I know? I've always been like this.' And Masha had laughed and said, 'There's your answer then.'

She hadn't left though, she'd kept staring and staring at us, even though we were talking to Father Alexander and ignoring her, and then finally she asked it: The Question. Everyone's Question:

'How will you die?'

Father Alexander frowned at her, shook his head and waved her away until she finally drifted off. After that, we sat there on the bench for maybe ten minutes, not saying anything while the crows cawed. Then I'd looked at him. He knows about death. He's a priest.

'How *will* we die?' I'd asked. I felt Masha tense.

'Well now, *dochinka*,' he'd said. 'When one goes, the other will follow soon enough.'

'Will it be painful?' we'd both asked together.

'No no. The doctors will give the surviving sister a sleeping draught. That way you will go together.'

We'd thought for a bit and then Masha had asked, 'Where to?'

He'd smiled gently and stroked the heavy gilt cross hanging round his neck amongst his black robes. 'The Lord put you on earth to suffer the trials of hellfire and you have been through them. You have earned your place in Heaven with the ones you love.'

'But hang on, Father,' Masha had said, and pointed up at the sky. 'Are we still going to be Together up there?'

He'd paused for a moment, then said: 'No, no. You'll be separate. You have separate souls.'

Masha snorted. '*Khaa!* Well, I'm not letting her out of my sight. She'll run off like a rabbit as soon as she gets through the pearly gates, looking for her precious Slava. And then I'll be spending all of eternity charging after them.' And we'd all laughed.

But I still didn't get my answer.

## No one calls an ambulance

I look across at her. She's finally fallen asleep. She's breathing heavily, but she seems to be OK. Everything's going to be OK. Perhaps it isn't a heart attack? Perhaps it's just … bad indigestion? Yes, that's what it is, she's going to be fine. Just fine. She's tough. She won't die. Not my Mashinka. I lie back on my pillow. She's *zhivoochi*. We both are.

I asked Joolka once what sort of life expectancy conjoined twins had, and she said it was hard to say as there are so few of them – probably only six unseparated adult twins in the world. Chang and Eng, the original Siamese twins were in their sixties when they died, and that must have been hundreds of years ago. We're not going to die. Not us, no we're not going to die …

I look across at her again. She's grey and waxy. But if Masha *does*, if she *does* die … then what will happen to me? I don't mind death. I'd want to die if she'd gone, but how? How? I want to know. Why has no one ever explained to us? I'd rather she died first because she'd be lost without me.

I want to talk to her, I don't want to be alone with my thoughts, but I mustn't wake her. Let her sleep. Yes, yes, let her sleep. My heart's pounding in my chest, hard, fast and strong, but hers is fluttering back to me in weak little bursts.

I lean over towards her, I want to press my cheek against hers, to kiss her, but we're too far apart. I strain to get closer, to hear her breathing. Has she stopped breathing? Oh God! I put my fingers on her neck and can still feel the jumpy pulse. I keep my fingers on her neck and stroke her ear and her cheek with the back of my hand. She likes that. I stroke and stroke …

I open my eyes as the pink morning light is coming over the balcony and see the lemon tree, Lyuba, sitting out there all forlorn. We forgot to take her in last night. Masha will be upset. I turn to her. She's breathing heavily and slowly. I sit up and shake her arm gently.

'Mashinka? We left Lyuba out.'

She doesn't wake. I shake her again harder this time and bite my bottom lip. 'Mashinka, wake up.' I bite so hard I can taste blood. 'Mashinka … we left Lyuba out.' She still doesn't move. I know she's asleep, I can feel it, but it's a different sleep, it feels heavier. Much heavier. I shake her again, harder. 'Wake up, Mash. Wake *up*!' But she lies there like a rag doll. I have to get help. She needs to know about Lyuba. She really, really needs to know about her. 'I'm sorry, Mashinka, I'm so so sorry. She'll survive, I promise you she will.' I lean over her, pick up the phone and call the duty nurse number again. Someone answers, a man,

Viktor Yanovich I think, one of the duty doctors. Yulia must have gone off duty without even bothering to come and see us.

'Viktor Yanovich, it's Dasha Krivoshlyapova! Masha's unconscious, I can't wake her up. Quick, oh please, please, come quick! I think she's had a heart attack!'

'Calm down. I have three emergencies on the go here. I'll get there when I can.' He puts the phone down.

I dial Aunty Nadya's number.

'I can't wake her up! She won't wake up! And the duty doctor won't come!'

'Shush, shush, I'll call him myself, I'm just on my way. Keep her warm, Dasha, cover her with blankets, don't panic, I'm on my way, I'm taking a taxi.'

I lean back and stare helplessly at the ceiling. Then I reach back and start banging on the wall behind us with both my fists. 'Help! Help! Somebody *help* me!' But the thumping just reverberates with a stupid dull, clumping sound around our isolated room at the end of the corridor with no one next to us. It echoes off our big TV and our fridge and our pretty wallpapered walls. 'Help! Is anyone there? Anyone? Help!' Olessya's room is four doors down. Can't she hear me screaming in her head? Please, please, hear me. I sit back up, panting and stare at Masha's sallow face. Then I grasp her round the back of her neck, shaking her. 'Wake up! Help me, Masha! Wake up!' But she lies there, heavy and sagging, her heart flickering like a sputtering flame to me as I beat hard and fast to her. She's dying while I'm trying to get her to live. Mashinka! I remember the bolt from her when she read that letter about Slava's death. A lightning bolt straight from her heart to mine. And how many times has my heart jolted through to hers? Surely it's jolting now, jolting hers back into life? Why, why won't they come?

What seems like hours later, Aunty Nadya bursts into the room. 'Dashinka! Dashinka! Don't worry, I'm here! Where's the doctor? Where *is* he?' She runs to the phone, almost falling over the armchair. 'Viktor Yanovich, Viktor Yanovich! Get in here this instant, this is a medical emergency! Viktor?' She looks at the phone. 'He's put it down the *svoloch! Svoloch*!' She gets up. 'I'm going to the medical room, stay here!' She storms out and ten minutes later she's back.

'There's no one there. No one in Administration either, except a little bitch who says they don't have the authority to call an ambulance until Zlata Igorovna gets in. And she's not in until eleven this morning. That's not for another *hour!* This is a nightmare, a nightmare! I'm calling the hospital.'

Aunty Nadya rings hospital after hospital but no one will come without permission from the Sixth Administration. Then she goes rushing out again to look for Viktor Yanovich. I don't know how long it is until she comes back with him in tow. He doesn't even go over to Masha, who's still lying unconscious. He stands there, in the corner of the room, by the fridge, with his hands in the pockets of his white doctor's coat, looking sullen, while Aunty Nadya shrieks at him.

'I keep telling you, I can't call an ambulance until Zlata gets here,' he mutters, staring down at his scuffed shoes. He can't bring himself to look at us. I think Aunty Nadya's going to shake him. Shake some humanity into him. But instead she shrieks again and starts tearing at her hair.

'*Aaakh!* It's ten twenty, every minute counts, every second counts! Dasha – when did she first feel the pains, quick, stop crying, this is important. When?' 'S-s-six o-clock. W-e were w-watching the n-news.' 'Right. That's what … sixteen hours ago. Sixteen hours. Listen, you,' she turns to Victor Yanovich. 'If an ambulance isn't here within ten minutes they will die and then I will tell the world's press what happened here. I will get you fired. I will hold you personally responsible – not Zlata Igorovna, not the Administration, but you. You will never practise again. I will never let this rest.' He bites his lip, thinking, then picks up the phone and dials.

'I'm a duty doctor at the Sixth Home for Veterans of War and Labour. I need an ambulance. Urgently.' He puts the phone down.

'Heaven be praised!' cries Aunty Nadya. 'Come on, Dasha, get ready. What do you need, they'll be here in minutes.'

I wipe the tears off my cheeks.

'Wait, wait, Aunty Nadya, can you bring the lemon tree in? It's on the balcony. Can you just bring it in? It's cold out there.'

She stares at me as if I've gone mad. 'Dashinka, we're fighting for a life here.'

'It's Masha's lemon tree,' I explain. 'She calls it Lyuba.'

'What on earth are you talking about?'

'Please, Aunty Nadya.'

'Oh very well. Very well.' She flings open the balcony door, grabs the plant and plonks it on the bedside table next to me. Nearly all the leaves have fallen off in the harsh frost and the few remaining ones drift down on to the varnished table.

'Aunty Nadya,' I say, picking them up and putting them carefully back into the pot.

'What, Dashinka? What?' She's rushing round putting some clothes and toiletries into a bag.

'Remember to water her lemon tree. You will remember, won't you.'

She stops then for a moment and looks me in the eye.

Yes, yes, Dashinka, of course, of course I'll remember. Right, come on, there's the ambulance siren. What else do you need?'

I reach under the pillow. It seems stupid but I know they won't lock the door after us and I don't want to leave his letters. They're airmail letters, like tissue papers tucked neatly inside an envelope. I fold them into my hand. I look at them every single day. Masha laughs at me but I do.

It's almost like I'm taking him with me.

## The First City Hospital

Masha dies in the ambulance.

One minute her heart is pulsing back to mine. The next it's not.

They're rushing us through the corridors of the hospital, shouting and panting, with their white coats flapping. We're being taken to the Reanimation Unit.

I'm on my own and I'm dying. You've gone, my Masha.

Two nurses are running along with us, one on each side. They're talking, their voices muffled through their surgical masks:

*How long has she got?*

*God knows.*

*What do we tell her?*

*Nothing of course. Tell her nothing.*

The nurse bends over me and speaks loudly and slowly.

*Masha's fine, she's just sleeping, that's all.*

I start crying.

*Hush, hush, she's getting better now, the doctors said …*

They cut our clothes off us with a knife and lay us on a slab in the Unit.

*Quick … get an oxygen mask onto her … intravenous drip to counter the cadaveric toxins … decomposition starts within minutes.*

Toxins? I pull on someone's sleeve. I don't understand. Is she poisoning me? My Masha? Is that how I die?

*I want an injection, I want a sleeping draught. Father Alexander said you'd give me a …*

*Now, now, they'll bring you some soup soon … Would you like some soup? We'll give some to Masha too. She's getting better now … getting better …*

I'm so scared. I'm the one who's been left with the knowledge that I'm dying. We never knew which one it would be. But I'm glad it's not her.

I'm the stronger one.

Aunty Nadya – I want her, I look around the bare white room. Where is she? They wouldn't let her in the ambulance … please come, please come …

*Haemorrhaging into her sister … hook her up to the monitors … fascinating … observe … monitor this …*

I ache all over. Weak, dizzy, they're wiring me up to sharp, shiny instruments, freezing me, freezing, freezing … in the Spring snow … sunshine …

Now someone's stroking my arm … an old nurse … it's Mummy … *You're going now, Dashinka, you're going … go in peace … say goodbye …*

My fingers open and I let go of Masha, and the letters in my other hand fall away …

I pull back the covers and step down from the bed. Slava's side is warm, he's only just left for the meadow with the cattle. I walk across our bedroom and breathe heavily on the frosty window until I can see him down there, standing among the willow trees in the white rising mist. It's going to be a beautiful day today, I know it. The children are asleep. Let them sleep. I get up, reach for my coat, open the door and go out to meet him.

# Afterword

It took Masha seventeen hours to die following the onset of her first symptoms, and Dasha another seventeen hours to die following Masha's death. She was not given her 'sleeping draught' but died of blood poisoning. They were cremated at their own request ('We don't want scientists poking about in us even after we're dead,' as Masha put it). The funeral was attended by Aunty Nadya, a handful of staff from the Stomatological Institute – and an army of journalists. The twins are interred in the Novodevichy Cemetery in Moscow where Aunty Nadya – and, ironically, Anokhin – are also buried.

This novelization of the true life story of Masha and Dasha Krivoshlyapova is based on my close fifteen-year friendship with them. I first met Masha and Dasha in 1988 when I walked into their room in Moscow's Stomatological Institute to interview them for the *Sunday Times* Magazine, after having seen them on the Vzglyad TV show. They nicknamed me 'Joolka'. Later they asked me to ghostwrite their autobiography – heavily edited by Masha – which was published (outside Russia) three years before their death.

Almost all of the events in this book actually happened, as described to me in taped conversations and interviews with the twins, their friends, their carers and doctors. I have written *The Less You Know…* in Dasha's voice because I felt more empathy for her than Masha, and believed that as the 'silent sister' she should finally be allowed to tell her own story.

Although I knew her so well, I was frustrated at never being able to have a one-to-one honest conversation with her, because Masha, the guard dog, was always present. Her best friend was, by necessity, always going to be Masha, whether she liked it or not. There were a few occasions, when I spent the night with them, when Masha fell asleep while I was talking to Dasha, and then I was able to see glimpses of her own thoughts. But they were only glimpses. She was afraid of Masha and, therefore, like many people trapped in an abusive relationship, loyal to her. But despite this, they still had a strong sibling bond and were natural allies against the world.

Dasha was deprived of the chance to be valued in society through having a profession, but she felt that in co-authoring their memoir (even if it was filtered through the perspective of Masha) she'd been given the opportunity to do something useful with her life – to change perceptions of disability and show the Healthies that being born different was just that. Different, not Defective.

I hope that in writing this novel, I've given her the voice she never had in life.

### Slava

Masha and Dasha treated their mentally and physically disabled friends in the same way they treated the able-bodied people they knew. There was never anything in their descriptions of their friends to suggest that they had, for example, cerebral palsy, or no arms or legs. In all my conversations with the twins I was never given the impression that Slava was anything other than a fit and healthy young man. I had no idea that he was about eighteen inches high and severely deformed. Aunty Nadya also never mentioned his physical disability.

Slava was nineteen when he died. Dasha kept all his letters, which are quoted verbatim in the book. I have been unable to track down his family.

## Aunty Nadya

I kept in touch with Masha and Dasha after I returned to England in 2001, and when their death became international news in 2003 I visited Aunty Nadya, who told me the details of their final days.

I met Aunty Nadya for the last time in 2011, eight years after the death of the twins, in her one-bedroom apartment in Moscow. She told me she was dying of bowel cancer. She was completely un-self-pitying – as she always had been with the twins. In their eyes, the people who pitied them were pitiable. Aunty Nadya had no one to look after her because Little Vasya had become estranged from her in his teenage years. I offered to arrange for a carer, but she refused my help. She was admitted four weeks later to hospital where the surgeon – an old friend of hers – told her she was in remission and discharged her. She was, in fact, in the final stages of terminal cancer and died ten days later in great pain on her own in her apartment. Russian doctors do not like death statistics.

Although Aunty Nadya never told the girls she loved them, I am convinced she did. She gave them all the motherly affection she could, and, as mothers do, despite their different characters, I believe she treated them equally.

## Olessya

As far as I know, Olessya (not her real name) still lives in the Sixth, but when I went to try and visit her after the twins died, I was told I needed to apply for written permission from the Ministry of Social Protection to enter the home.

## Pyotr Anokhin

Anokhin worked closely with Doctor Ivan Pavlov, who for many years used dogs – and humans – to develop the theory of conditioned reflexes. Pavlov used electrical shocks, metronomes and a buzzer in his research – a methodology Anokhin would go on to use with the twins. After Pavlov's death in 1936, Anokhin was considered to be his successor. He was interested in human behaviour and the brain from an early age but he was also fascinated by the separate roles of the nervous system and the blood system on the body's ability to adjust to conditions such as prolonged sleep deprivation, extreme hunger and extreme temperature change. So when, in 1937, a pair of conjoined twins, Ira and Galya were born in the USSR, with identical genes, separate nervous systems and the same blood system, he removed them from their parents and took them back to his Institute of Experimental Medicine to be studied. They only survived for one year and twenty-two days. Thirteen years later, Masha and Dasha were born – a dream come true for Anokhin – who had put out an alert in all Soviet maternity hospitals following the death of Ira and Galya, asking to be informed of the birth of any more conjoined twins. He descended on Maternity Hospital no. 6 within hours. Having rid himself of their troublesome mother by telling her the girls had died, he began his studies, noting differences in behaviour from the first weeks of life. But he was treading on very dangerous ground. Not because of his abduction of the children and the ensuing experiments, but because some of his work with the genetically identical twins involved the study of their different personalities.

In June 1950, when the twins were six months old, he was denounced by Stalin's cronies at the famous Pavlovian session. Genetics was seen as a product of 'bourgeois capitalism' – convenient for a Soviet government trying to engineer the perfect social utopia. A speaker at the sessions said: 'It is an outrage that Anokhin, a disciple of Pavlov, seeks, under the guise of loyalty to his mentor, to systematically and relentlessly revise his doctrine with the rotting, idealist stance of pseudoscientific "theories" of reactionary bourgeois scholars.'

Although Anokhin defended his belief that 'we should be permitted to suggest views on embryonic evolution and mechanisms of inheritance of characteristics', his fate was sealed and he was sent into exile, leaving Alexeyeva and Kryuchkova to secretly carry on his work with the twins in the Paediatric Institute. He returned from exile a year later, after Stalin's death.

When I interviewed doctors who had worked with Anokhin on the twins, they saw no suggestion at all of medical malpractice. The experiments were considered acceptable at the time, and were published and admired not only by Soviet medics but also by American and European ones.

Anokhin's colleagues still genuinely believed that he was a hero who had defied Stalin and risked his life in the pursuit of science. They claimed he also saved the twins lives by 'rescuing' them, and they should have both been grateful.

I obtained a copy of Alexeyeva's dissertation on the twins in 1998, before Putin's clampdown, by bribing an official in the Library of the Academy of Medical Sciences (they asked for $1,000 but we ended up agreeing on $100). I also found Kryuchkova's scientific report on their differing personalities.

After the twins left SNIP for Novocherkassk, Anokhin appears to have lost interest in them. He did, however, publish an article in *Life Magazine* in 1966 when they were sixteen years old, describing how they had been taken in by doctors at birth who, he claimed untruthfully, were still caring for them in Moscow and who 'lavished affection' on them. He also mentioned that he knew who their parents were, that they had brothers, and also that they were physically able to conceive and give birth – all answers to questions that had been torturing Dasha for years. He said he envisaged that they would be in need of psychiatric help as they grew older, but of course none was ever forthcoming.

## Defectives

Dasha was, for most of the twins' lives, the victim in their relationship, but the twins were also both the victim of Stalinist science, and of the clear-cut division in Soviet society between Defectives and Healthies.

Defectology was a science adopted soon after the creation of the USSR and was concerned with the study of physically and mentally handicapped children with a view to rehabilitating them. 'Defective' children were initially categorized as being either physically, mentally or morally defective. Rehabilitation took the form of taking them away from the parents or charities who had traditionally cared for them and sending them to State organizations to be brought up by trained defectologists. However, as the myth of the Soviet Union being the 'best of all possible worlds' grew, these children were increasingly abandoned and isolated – dumped, as Olessya put it, on to the compost heap of the Soviet garden. In 1980, when the Summer Olympic Games were held in Moscow, a British journalist asked the Soviet Olympic Committee if they would also be hosting the Paralympics. He was firmly told: 'There are no invalids in the USSR.'

As the years went by, the general term 'defective' was replaced by 'invalid', a word which was broken down into other official categorizations, such as moron, imbecile and cretin, uneducable and educable, or walking and non-walking. Everyone else was just 'healthy'. Yet Soviet propaganda tarred all those who were disabled with the brush of being profoundly and incurably flawed and inadequate.

In 2006, Vladimir Putin declared his wish that all abandoned children should be placed in families rather than institutions. However, around 340,000 Russian children with disabilities are still being kept in orphanages for 'Uneducables' and isolated. If they survive, they are usually transferred to mental institutions for adults or Old People's Homes. Nearly

30 per cent of all children with disabilities in Russia still live in State care, yet 95 per cent of them have at least one living parent. The proportion of disabled children in orphanages is four times higher than in Western countries.

Services in Russia for children with disabilities very much reflect attitudes established during the Soviet era. Parents are still encouraged to leave their children to institutional care and sign forms 'rejecting' those that are most seriously handicapped. Recently, more families have ignored this advice, but mothers report facing general hostility from society when opting to take care of their children instead of placing them in a government facility. Stigma and shame concerning disability are still prevalent in Russian society and so adoption of these children among Russians is very rare within the country. In 2012, President Putin approved a bill that prohibits Russian children from being adopted by American citizens. A spokesman said that the rationale behind this was that Americans adopt children to get extra welfare benefits and 'then begin to hate this child'. Sixty thousand Russian children have been adopted by American families over the past twenty years – by far the biggest proportion of any other country – and the vast majority of them are leading happy, supported lives within loving families.

## Dissertation published in 1959 by T. T. Alexeyeva: Neurohumoral regulation of functions in the human body (research on inseparable twins)

### Introduction

For many years P. K. Anokhin and his colleagues have been carrying out experiments in the Institute of Experimental Medicine to establish the separate roles of the nervous system and the blood system on the body's ability to adjust to conditions such as prolonged sleep deprivation, extreme hunger and extreme temperature change. The research for this work was carried out on a pair of un-separated twins Masha–Dasha (ischiopagus b. 1950).

The resolution of these problems in normal experimental conditions on a single organism is an impossible task. However, un-separated twins occur in nature both among animals and among humans and are a unique object for research as their nervous system is usually completely separate and yet their blood is shared.

They can be used to establish the independent roles of the nervous system and the blood system and thus are objects of great interest as a remarkable human experiment created by nature.

From the first days of their lives the twins were kept in laboratory conditions. It was also important to study their behavioural development. It was noted that, despite living in an identical environment, developmental characteristics such as speech, movement and nervous processes were markedly different from birth.

## Blood System

To study the speed with which the blood travelled from one twin to the other we introduced various substances into the blood of one child, such as radioactive iodine, barium, glucose and sodium methane sulphonate. For example, 2,500 units of radioactive iodine were introduced into Masha after which the levels of radioactivity in the thyroid of both twins were measured with a Geiger counter ... The kidneys were observed when sodium methane sulphonate was introduced into the ulnar vein of one child. In thirty minutes a distinct change in the contours of the kidneys of both children were observed on X-rays.

## Nervous System

By the age of two months their faces began to differ. Their reaction to pain (usually introduced by a scalpel, a needle or an electric shock) differed markedly. On being given a bottle of boiling hot milk, for example, Dasha cries out, pushes her scalded hands under her pillow and refuses to touch it again, but Masha repeatedly takes the bottle and then pushes it away crying out.

At the age of six months the twins cry on seeing any instrument of pain and by nine months they cry on seeing the person who conducts the tests on pain sensitivity (T. T. Alexeyeva). Tests to establish the boundary of the nervous system in each twin were therefore carried out when they were asleep or unawares. Tests to establish discrete conditioned reflex to pain involved administering an electric shock to coincide with the ticking of a metronome. By the age of six months the ticking alone resulted in Masha crying out in fear and Dasha recoiling in anticipation of the shock.

Blood samples are taken three times a day. Dasha recoils from the needle and must be held down, but Masha no longer reacts by crying and bears the insertion quietly.

## Sleep

We assessed the depth of their sleep by waking one of them with abrupt stimuli such as a sharp pain or a loud noise in one ear. Despite the wailing of one twin, the other would continue to sleep unless awoken by flailing limbs. As part of our sleep experiments, we kept one or other of the twins awake artificially for long periods. For example, we would constantly stimulate one twin preventing it from falling asleep. Or we would feed one twin and not the other so the fasting twin stayed awake through hunger pangs. In the first year of their lives they were normally fed every three hours, but on keeping one of them fasting for up to nine hours the rhythms of sleep were successfully reversed.

At all times during experiments the heartbeats were recorded by electrocardiograms (ECG), their breathing was recorded by a penumograms (PNG), their brain activity by an electroencephalogram (EEG) and their gastric juices were analysed through tubes fed into their stomachs. Experiments were carried out concurrently.

### Thermo-regulation

Since any physical or chemical changes pass from one child to the other within two minutes, the twins represent a remarkable opportunity to examine the role of thermo-regulation through measuring the temperature of the blood. The temperature of one child was lowered for example by packing ice into six thin-walled brass cylinders and placing them on the stomach, spine and flank of one child. It took two and half minutes for the temperature of this child to fall from a normal 37 degrees down to 26 degrees. When the canisters were removed, however, it took an average of fifteen minutes for normal temperature to be restored.

### Hunger

In order to prove or disprove the theory of 'satiated' or 'hungry' blood, the twins were fed under separate regimes whereby one twin missed up to three feeds. The gastric juices of both twins were evaluated by tubes inserted directly into the stomach through the mouth. The hungry child would continue to cry until fed even if this was for a nine-hour period, disproving the theory that blood containing nutrients can satisfy the hunger of the organism. Analysis of gastric juices was undertaken when the hungry child was shown the other child being fed and also when it was isolated from its twin by a board. As babies, when the hungry twin was given an empty bottle to suck, it too produced gastric juices indicating a cortical conditioned reflex to secrete gastric juices in the expectation of food. Irritants were introduced into their stomach via a surgically inserted probe to measure the relative acidity of their gastric juices.

At two years of age they show solidarity by both crying when one of them is in pain. However, by this age Masha exhibits a clearly aggressive attitude to Dasha. Masha pinches or thumps her and takes away her spoon.

From the age of four they were subjected to more advanced tests to compare and evaluate their conditioned reflexes. On seeing or hearing a stimuli such as a metronome that signals the administration of an electric shock, Dasha reacts more rapidly and with more sensitivity. Her heart beats violently while Masha's remains relatively calm. When a spurt of cold air is squirted into the iris of their eye from a rubber tube, Dasha turns away and screws up her eyes crying while Masha just blinks rapidly and cries. We repeated this experiment sixty-two times until Dasha also just blinked instead of crying.

When left without stimuli they sometimes play 'games' together, copying adult behaviour, for example pretending to give each other injections, take blood or insert feeding tubes. When older they were moved to the window and would stare out at the cars and buses with great interest and for long periods of time.

By the age of six it is clear that Dasha is much more obedient. She listens attentively to instructions and tries conscientiously to do her best to fulfil them. Masha's behaviour is very different. She quickly loses interest or refuses to carry out the tests. For example, one game to test their reactions involved each twin holding a bladder and squeezing it on seeing a flashing light. Dasha always responded diligently but Masha turned away and threw down the bladder after eight to ten goes. When told to pick it up she sometimes refused to play altogether saying, 'Squeeze it yourself.' Masha continues to be aggressive to Dasha, who now does not fight back.

Both twins react identically to the heart/eye reflex where the heart is slowed down (and can be stopped altogether) by applying pressure to the eyeball.

In general, Dasha is far more advanced than Masha, in both speech, mobility and intellectual development. However it is evident that the tests were more difficult for Dasha's nervous system to withstand than Masha's and this points to the relative weakness of her nerve processes.

**Text of interview with Katya Krivoshlyapova**

I didn't know I was having twins. I was in labour for two nights and two days. I remember clearly, as clearly as if it was yesterday, the doctor looking down at my baby and shaking his head in disbelief: he said he'd never seen anything like it in all his life. I was frightened and started crying. Then he held the baby up to show me but I couldn't see because my eyes were filled with tears. They carried it out – I thought I could hear two cries – and after a bit, a woman in a white coat came in to see me. I didn't know if she was a nurse or a doctor but she told me that I'd had urodi, mutants. She didn't tell me why or what they looked like or even if they were still alive. She just said she was very sorry and walked away. I suppose that was their way of explaining to me that they were taking them away from me. All the other mothers in my ward had their babies brought in every four hours to feed them, but they didn't bring me my babies and they didn't tell me anything else. I suppose it was a week later and I hadn't stopped crying, day and night, dropping in and out of sleep because I was sure I could hear them, my own babies, down the corridor crying, when another doctor came in, a man. He told me to stop all this weeping and wailing because I was upsetting the other mothers. He told me I was only being kept in because I'd lost so much blood. He told me my babies weren't expected to live beyond a few weeks and to forget about them. But I couldn't, how can you just forget your children when you've longed for them so much? When you love them so much?

From then on I lay with a pillow over my head so no one could hear me weeping. I can't remember sleeping at all …

My husband was called in to look at them straight after the birth and he saw them lying on a table naked and he rejected them straight away. He told the doctors they couldn't be his and he didn't want his name on the birth certificate and he refused to see me as well. It was a terrible disgrace for him … So all I had now was my babies, my twins. I didn't know what they meant by mutants, it could have meant anything, I just wanted to see them. There was a night-cleaner there who had a young child herself and she'd sit sometimes and pat the pillow on my head while I cried. Then one night, in the early hours of the morning when there were no doctors around, the door swung open and she walked in holding this tiny, swaddled bundle with one dark head each end. They were asleep … She put them into my arms and I rocked them and sang to them and kissed the top of their little heads … my own daughters … my dochinki … they looked so perfectly beautiful.

I never saw them again. It must have been a week or so later when I was better that they asked me to sign the forms rejecting them. I asked what that meant and they said it meant they'd be looked after by the State. I asked if I could visit them if I rejected them and they said I couldn't, so then what was I to do? I couldn't sign the forms. I thought it would be better if they were looked after by the doctors than coming back to the barracks with water on the dirt floor and not a stick of firewood for the stove. But I couldn't reject them, what mother could do that? I was sent home and I was lying in bed still weak from the loss of blood and it was maybe a week after I'd left the hospital when there was a knock at the door and a woman wearing a white doctor's coat walked in, sat on the edge of the bed and told me she was a physiologist and that she was very sorry but she'd come to break the news that my babies had caught pneumonia and died ...

Aaakh, how do you think a mother would feel on being told her babies had died? How would any mother feel? I lay there for days or it might even have been weeks, staring up at the ceiling and picking over my life, piece by piece, wondering why I'd been put on earth when my one chance of joy in it had been so cruelly taken away. And Misha? I had my tears to wash away my sorrow and he had vodka to wash away the shame of having had such twins. Like every man, he had vodka ...

I went back to the doctors when I was well enough and asked to see the grave, I wanted to put flowers on it, but they told me their bodies had been preserved for science. I even went to the Kunst Kamera of Horrors in St Petersburg to see if they had been preserved in a jar there. And then all those years later when I found they were still alive, they'd been alive all these years – I felt so sorry to have not looked more for them, so sorry that I formed them like that in my womb, and then all I could do when I met them was cry. I couldn't understand why the doctors had lied to me. When I met them I thought they would have been told I was still alive. Now I think perhaps they weren't ...? I can't understand why the scientists deprived two children of a mother and let them live and grow up without me. I would have done anything for them when they were growing up, anything. And then, when they found me again it was the same, I would have done anything to make up for lost time, to make up for having formed them like that, but it wasn't to be. It was too late. They found me and then they rejected me … perhaps I deserved it. But I loved them. I always held them in my heart and loved them. I love them now.

## Characters

The majority of characters in the novel are real, as are their names. Some minor characters – such as Baba Iskra, Ivan Ivanovich, Uncle Styopa, Yemil Moseyevich, Baba Yulia and Aunty Dusya – are based on people the twins described to me, but the names are fictional. Sanya is a composite of cleaners they knew in the Twentieth and Sixth. Olessya is largely based on herself with aspects of other friends they knew throughout their lives in her character.

### Index of characters in order of appearance:

*Paediatric Institute (the Ped), Moscow; age 0–6*
'Mummy'/Dr Anna Petrovna Kruchkova – physiologist
Nastya – cleaner
Dr Tatiana Tikhonovna Alexeyeva – physiologist

*Scientific National Institute of Prosthetics (SNIP), Moscow; age 6–14*
Nadezhda Fyodorovna Gorokhova /Aunty Nadya – physiotherapist
Uncle Vasya – Aunty Nadya's husband and her former patient
Dr Lydia Mikhailovna Voroboiskaya – doctor and surgeon
Professor Boris Markovich Popov – director of SNIP
Academician Pyotr Kuzmich Anokhin – physiologist overseeing studies on the twins
Dr Golubeva – doctor in the Brain Institute working for Anokhin

Galina Petrovna – teacher at SNIP
Pasha – good-looking boy; friend in SNIP
Lucia – Masha's friend
Olessya – Dasha's friend
Stepan Yakovlich – caretaker/groundsman

*School for Invalids, Novocherkassk; age 14–18*
Konstantin Semyonovich – director of the school
Vera Stepanovna – head teacher
Irina Konstantinovna – history teacher
Little Lyuda – friend in school
Sunny Nina – friend in school
Slava – friend in school and Dasha's boyfriend
Petya – friend in school
Big Boris – Olessya's boyfriend
Icy Valya – pupil in school
Valentina Alexandrovna – form teacher
Vyacheslav Tikhonov – school cobbler

*The Twentieth Home for Veterans of War and Labour, Moscow; age 18–38*
Barkov – director of the Twentieth
Iglinka Dragomirovna – housekeeper
Sanya – cleaner
Ivan Ivanovich – guard
Uncle Styopa – inmate
Baba Yulia – inmate
Yemil Moseyevich – inmate

*The Sixth Home for Veterans of War and Labour, Moscow; age 38–53*
Zlata Ivanovna – director of the Sixth
Timur – groundsman
Baba Iskra – cloakroom attendant

## Acknowledgements

Thanks to my astoundingly talented editor Helen Garnons-Williams, for lovingly shaping the book into its final form, and for her kindness and constant encouragement throughout the whole process. To my Aunty Jenny for a legacy that allowed me the time to write this book, and of course to Dasha for opening her heart to me as much as she was able. Also thanks to Professor Jeff Craig from the Murdoch Children's Research Institute for his invaluable help and advice on research into the heritability of parental character traits in identical twins.

To read more about the twins and the writing of this book please visit julietbutler.com